SOMETHING BETTER

Joanna Monahan

D1452751

BLUE INK
PRESS

Copyright © 2023 by Joanna Monahan

All rights reserved.

No part of this book may be reproduced in any form or by any electronic or mechanical means, including information storage and retrieval systems, without written permission from the author, except for the use of brief quotations in a book review.

Something Better is a work of fiction. Any references to historical events or real people and places are used fictitiously. Other names, characters, places, and incidents are either a product of the author's imagination or are used fictitiously.

ISBN 978-1-948449-16-8

Library of Congress Control Number: 2023936778

Cover Illustrations by Laura Hollingsworth

Cover Design by Cassie Torgent

Published in the United States by Blue Ink Press, LLC

Praise for Joanna Monahan

In her captivating debut, Joanna Monahan deftly explores the temptation of the road not taken and the hazards of believing in a rosy version of the past. Middle-aged Corinne, struggling with a fading marriage and a confrontational teenage daughter, reconnects with her lost love at their high school reunion. Here, at last, is her path to something better, a rekindled relationship with the white knight she has always deserved. But is this alternative future all that she hopes for? Expertly braiding the stories of the past with the realities of the present, *Something Better* is an unforgettable story of self-discovery and redemption that tugs at the heartstrings in all the best ways. Pour a cup of hot tea and settle in for compelling characters, beautiful writing, and a wholly satisfying read.

—Rebecca Hodge, award-winning author of *Wildland*

Attending your twenty-fifth high-school reunion is a great idea. Unless it means reconnecting with a lost love, the one who got away, the man you still dream about—even as you share household chores with your husband. Corinne must choose between the fantasy of life with the man who calls her *beautiful maiden* and the reality of a loving but drab long-time marriage. In Joanna Monahan's lovely novel, *Something Better,* that choice is shown with excruciating insight. Don't miss this splendid debut, which will have you alternately cheering and cringing for Corinne.

—Charlotte Rains Dixon, author of *The Bonne Chance Bakery,* book coach, and writing teacher

For Patrick, my lobster.

July 2, 1992

Beautiful maiden,

I'm leaving.

This is the hardest thing I've ever written. Please know, no matter what you hear, no matter how you feel toward me right now, that I love you. Wildly, fiercely, singularly.

I never meant for this to happen. Kirsten didn't either; we were two lonely souls seeking temporary comfort. I was lonely, missing you. The idea that my punishment for missing you for one night is to miss you forever is a fiery blade in my breast. My heart is a broken wasteland as I contemplate tomorrow without you.

But I make this pledge to you now: We will be together again. Time cannot defeat us. Wait for me. I will come back for you, and our happily ever after can finally begin.

With everything I am,

Nick

Chapter 1

The invitation was royal blue cardstock with a white vellum overlay fastened by a small white bow. I squinted to make out the tiny print:

Cheers to 25 years!
Join your former classmates on
September 15
for the
Class of 1992 Reunion
7:00 p.m.
Clemmons High School gymnasium
RSVP
Go Warriors!

Crap.

I tipped the thick white envelope on its side to dislodge the reply card nestled inside. A plume of silver glitter spilled out. Meowsers, the family cat, padded over to investigate. I pushed him away with the toe of my shoe.

Corinne's heart hammers as she reads, then re-reads her

invitation. She imagines Nick, wherever he is, reading his own invite. Is he thinking about her too?

Stop.

I cut off the daydream, annoyed with myself. *Stay in reality, Corinne.*

I slipped the cards back into the envelope and propped it against the chipped blue china bowl on the sideboard. I drifted into the kitchen, Meowsers at my heels, tracking glitter across the floor.

Twenty-five years. Where had the time gone, and what had I done to fill it? I'd moved away from home, graduated college, married, birthed a daughter, celebrated birthdays and anniversaries and holidays. I'd buried my mother, overcome depression, rebuilt my life.

Was it enough? What had Nick done with his time?

I sighed and ran a hand over my throat, pushing the slackening skin upward, as if such a gesture might bring back the smooth, swan-necked past. My fingers drifted over my jaw and cheekbones, investigating. How would I look to him, twenty-five years later? Older? The same? Which was worse? I pulled my hair, more gray than brown, from the ponytail holder and shook it out, feeling its weight settle on my shoulders. I practiced smiling at my reflection in the toaster. "Hi, I'm Corinne. Good to see you again." The curved metal turned my expression into a grimace.

What was the point of going back? The past was over. The people who left stayed gone. A reunion wouldn't change anything for me. I would send my regrets and remain where I was—happily ever after.

Well, more or less.

The garage door rumbled to life as if the house were murmuring its agreement. I busied myself, pulling ingredients out of the refrigerator for dinner—chicken breasts, potatoes, salad in a bag.

As ever, I narrated each movement, starring in my one-woman show: *Corinne moves efficiently between the counter and the refrigerator, the swish-swish of her wide-legged pants creating the illusion of purpose as her husband and daughter walk through the door.*

First came Audra, my long-limbed woman-child, sandy-blonde curls frizzed out in a halo around her face from the late-summer humidity. Earbuds in, eyes fastened on the phone in her hand, backpack slung over her shoulder, she gave a curt nod as she strode past me, through the family room and down the hall to her bedroom, a sixteen-year-old blur with no time for her mother. Audra was of the world; I was merely an observer, the grateful recipient of any scrap of attention she deigned to grant me.

Her father, however, paused at the kitchen counter, resting his scuffed brown-leather computer bag on the package of chicken. I made a face and scooted the raw meat away. He didn't notice, instead giving me a slow once-over.

"Hey there, beautiful," he drawled in the light southern accent that used to make my pulse race.

I studied my husband's face, as familiar to me as my own: the same curly hair as Audra, close-cropped in the style he'd worn since childhood, kind blue eyes the color of his chambray button-down, the soft lines of his cheeks and chin as he cocked his head and beckoned me closer.

"Hey there." I leaned across the counter toward him.

Corinne and Sean kiss as the scene fades to black.

* * *

"Why don't you want to go to your reunion?" Sean asked later as we cleared the dinner plates. Audra had retreated to her room, claiming unfinished homework.

This part of the night was our touchstone, a habit established in our first years of dating when we couldn't afford an apartment with a dishwasher. Back then, we'd hand-washed our two place settings nightly, examining the deepest parts of our lives over a sink of hot water and a drying rack, reveling in the newfound intimacy between two people sharing one life.

When we moved into this home, with its functioning appliances, we'd condensed our routine. Sean rinsed and loaded; my job was to box leftovers and dry the big dishes while we discussed mortgages and home improvements. Our conversations shifted again once Audra was born, and I quit my job to stay home with her. Then came the years of my mother's failing health and the decision to move her closer to me, her only child. Her funeral arrangements had been made while we washed leftovers out of Tupperware containers dropped off by friends.

More and more during the last few years, I washed the dishes alone while Sean worked. He'd been promoted again, his workload tripling as a result. When he was home, he dominated the conversation, full of anecdotes and gripes about his work, the minutiae of managing accounting for a major utility company. I went through the motions of participating—listening sympathetically, laughing or groaning in the correct places. Sometimes I offered small observances about my day, spent mainly running errands or cleaning house, or the latest Parent Teacher Association drama, but the conversation always pivoted back to Sean. The upcoming reunion was the most original contribution I'd made in months.

I shrugged. "Why make a special trip back to see people I don't even know anymore? What's the point? There's no one I want to see besides Beth."

Corinne's face flushes as she turns away from her husband. The name "Nick" clogs her throat, heavy and unspoken. She coughs, swallows it down.

I glanced over at Sean to see if he'd caught my awkward lapse. He hadn't. His back was to me, and as he ran the glass baking dish under the water, suds sloshed up over the side of the chipped white enamel sink, running down to the floor. Silently cursing, I unspooled an arm's length of paper towels from the roll on the counter.

Corinne crouches, chasing dishwater around the edges of the shoe molding. The hem of her pants grazes the puddle and clings to her skin.

Sean knew I had an ex from high school. However, I'd only ever given him the annotated version: I'd dated a boy named Nick. We broke up after graduation when he moved away, and I left for college. I'd never expanded on the particulars, letting Sean assume there was nothing more to tell. He didn't need to know that Nick was my first boyfriend, first kiss, first love, first...

Corinne blushes, remembering the other "first" Nick had been.

Sean slotted the pan into the dish drainer and turned to face me as I straightened. A line of spilled water ran across the front of his shirt, underlining his still-flat stomach. He reached for me, pulling me close. I tossed the wad of towels into the trash and pressed my cheek to his shoulder, hoping to cover my reddened cheeks.

"Not that you need my permission or asked my opinion, but I think you should go." He kissed my forehead, and I could smell the ranch dressing on his breath. "We could go. You know, we haven't taken a trip since Beth's wedding. It'll be fun."

I shook my head. "It won't be fun. I haven't seen any of these people since I left for college. Not even my cheer sisters. Beth is the only person I kept up with."

"Come on. Aren't you even a little curious?" He tilted my face, now thankfully cooled, toward his and grinned. "Don't you want to see who got fat?"

Despite my misgivings, I smiled. "I hope it's Rhonda Serlow. She was such a cow to me."

Sean laughed. "Well, she's going to be super pissed when she sees that you are still one smokin' babe." He gave my breasts an appreciative squeeze with soapy hands. Water soaked into my blouse.

"Ugh, you guys are so weird." Sean and I bolted apart as Audra appeared in the living room. She rolled her eyes. "Can I go to Lana's? She wants to watch some new reality thing on Netflix."

Sean slipped back into parent mode. "I thought you had homework."

"Did it." Our daughter looked at me, one eyebrow raised, an expression inherited from her father. I crossed my arms to hide the wet handprints on my chest. "Can I?"

I flicked a glance at Sean, who lifted his shoulders noncommittally. In our house, he was the fun parent, the "yes" parent. I was the sole representative of disappointment.

"Fine. But be back by ten. It's still a school night."

"That rule is for babies." She was already moving through the kitchen toward the garage.

"Yup," I agreed, forcing a lightness into my voice. "Babies and you. Or you could not go at all and spend some time cleaning your room."

Ignoring that, Audra flipped a quick "Bye!" over her shoulder as she pulled her keys from her backpack and headed out the door, letting it slam behind her. The garage door opened, and a moment later, my geriatric minivan roared to life and backed down the driveway. The garage door rattled closed. We were alone.

Sean dried his hands on the dish towel and tossed it onto the counter. I picked it up automatically and refolded it.

His eyebrow arched, a replica of his daughter's expression moments ago. "So, we've got the house to ourselves for the next couple of hours…"

My phone blared Meredith Brooks' "Bitch" from the coffee

table in the family room. Beth's ringtone. I glanced at the clock. It was 8:00 p.m. in Charlotte, which meant it was 5:00 p.m. in San Francisco. In the telepathic manner of best friends, I knew that Beth had opened her invitation.

"Down boy." I threw the towel at Sean. He caught it and groaned, sagging at the knees as if suffering a fatal blow. I waved him off, jogging across the room to answer my phone.

"Girl!" Beth hollered, not waiting for me to speak. "Did you get it? We're totally going, right?" In the background, I could hear five-year-old Dante whooping and giggling. A crash, followed by the low, soothing mezzo tones of Beth's wife, Vi.

"No, I don't think so." I raised my voice, competing with the background noise on her end.

From the kitchen, Sean shouted, "Beth, tell her to go!"

Beth sounded genuinely shocked. "What? Of course you're going. You have to go. It's, like, a middle-aged rite of passage to attend your high school reunion. It's prom for old people. Awkward and mandatory."

I wandered down the hall to my office and closed the door, cutting off further interruptions from Sean. Sinking into my desk chair, I swiveled to put my feet up on the sagging, flowered couch wedged under the windows and stared outside. Across the cul-de-sac, two teenage boys played basketball under the glow of the streetlamp, their shouts and laughter muffled by the closed window. I recognized one of the boys as DJ Thomas, who lived next door.

I imagined Beth standing in the middle of her sunny, chaotic apartment, her pixie face blotchy with excitement. A hallmark of our thirty-year friendship was Beth's unwavering confidence in her ability to change my mind. She had a way of dwarfing me in arguments, even though I had eight inches and at least forty pounds on her.

"Come on, Rinni," Beth continued, mistaking my silence for

consideration. "We'll have a good time. I mean, think how much fun it'll be to see everyone again. Some of them will be faa-aaaat," she singsonged. "Some of them will be baa-aald. Don't you want to see that?"

I laughed. "That's what Sean said. He's all for going, by the way. Says it will be good for us to take a trip together."

"Tell Sean to back off. You're going with me. Vi's staying home with Dante, and you swore you would always be my plus-one." Beth lowered her voice, adopting a faux-serious tone. "You pinky-promised."

"That was in eighth grade. And I meant to the movies. Or a dance. A reunion is different. It's…" I faltered as I pictured walking into the gym and seeing Nick leaning against the bleachers. "A reunion is about revisiting the past."

"What are you talking about, the past?" A pause. "Are you afraid Nick will be there?" Beth never sugarcoated. I could keep his name out of my conversations with Sean, but not with her.

"No…well, maybe?" It was sort of true. I wasn't afraid, I was hoping.

"Don't worry about it. If he shows up, we'll deal with it. But do you really think Nick Elms would come back to Clemmons after all these years for his high school reunion?"

I didn't want to talk about Nick anymore. I changed tactics, voicing my other fear. "What am I supposed to say when people ask me what I do?"

"Tell them anything you want. Tell them you're a spy and you can't reveal personal details for fear of compromising national security." She snorted at her own joke. When I didn't respond, her voice became more serious. "What's wrong with the truth? You have a family you take care of. What's the problem?"

"I don't know. Aren't you supposed to have accomplished something big after twenty-five years? At least you have a cool job in a cool city."

"Oh yeah. A pharmacist's life is all glamour and glitz, baby. I could talk dosages all night. Come on. It'll be fine. Besides, everyone there will be so worried about you judging them that they won't have time to judge you."

I sighed. We were going in circles. "All right, I'll think about it." I cut her off as she started to say something. "But I won't change my mind."

"Yes, you will." From her end of the phone came a crash followed by a wail. "Whoops, that sounded serious. I better go. Call me when you've come to your senses, so we can talk plane tickets. If we both fly to Detroit, we can drive in together. Love you!"

"Love you," I parroted into the sudden silence as she ended the call.

I placed the phone down on my lap and stared out the window. The boys had gone inside.

Corinne stares, lost in thought and twisting her ponytail around her index finger. She considers the reunion and all its possibilities.

Beth was right. I didn't have to be afraid of getting hurt, opening old wounds. If Nick was there, maybe I could get some closure. If he wasn't, well, Beth would make sure I had fun.

And so what if other people had done more with their quarter century than I had? Didn't I have plenty to be proud of? Maybe this was just the thing I needed to kick myself, my life, back into gear.

It was only a reunion. What was the worst that could happen?

* * *

On nights I couldn't sleep, I wandered the house and took inventory, a grounding technique my therapist and I practiced in the months after my mother passed away. At the time, it had been the pathway out of my grief; a way of returning to the present, to the husband and daughter who needed me. A reminder of the love and security that existed within these walls.

I turned to the ritual now, seeking comfort as thoughts of Nick, the past, and the unknown raced through my mind, vying for attention. I moved around the room, marking off its familiar dimensions, a cup of peppermint tea warming my hands, scenting the air.

I loved our house. The apartment my mother and I had lived in after my father left was never more than a place to sleep, a situation thrust upon us. But the day Sean and I took the keys from our elderly realtor, I'd remembered the forgotten sanctuary of the word "home."

Over the years, as money allowed, we'd knocked down walls and converted the four original rooms into one large space that served as front hall, family room, kitchen, and dining room. Beyond the kitchen were the master suite and the garage. Another expansion added Audra's bedroom, a second bathroom, and my office, where I kept my desktop computer and old photography equipment.

I ran my hand along the built-in bookshelves lining either side of the small electric fireplace, skimming my fingers over book spines and trinkets, all familiar, all representative of a moment in our lives. I whispered each name aloud, protective talismans against the dark.

"Blue vase." Sean's gift to me for our first anniversary.

"Silver frame." A photo of Audra's first day of school.

"Ugly cat statue." A fortieth birthday gift from Beth.

I slid my bare feet along the floor until I reached the end of the area rug that demarcated the family room. The rug had been a cast-off from Sean's sister and was the only real memory I had of her. She and Sean had never been close.

"Emily's rug."

Next came the gap in the wall followed by the overflowing coat closet.

"Antique doorknobs." Sean and I had found them at a flea market in Asheville during the weekend getaway when Audra was conceived. I imagined I could see the ochre-colored glass pulsing like a heartbeat.

Turning, I passed the front door in one long slide across the cold tile, then turned right again and proceeded along the sideboard. My hand fluttered over "Mirror, mail dish, vase," all antiques inherited from my mother. A light film stuck to my fingertips. I would dust in the morning.

My hand hit something unexpected, and I heard a small *thwap* as it fell to the ground. Feeling with my toes, I located the item and bent to pick it up. It was flat and smooth.

Recognition dawned: "Invitation."

The spell broke; the illusion of protection disappeared. I was left standing alone in the dark, all my worries and doubts crowding back in.

I carried the envelope and my tea to the couch and curled up in the corner of the blue velvet sectional that was "my" spot. Meowsers jumped up on the couch and settled against my bare ankles, purring. I wiggled my toes into his fur, seeking warmth.

Cheers to 25 years! In my sleep-deprived state, I imagined the words curling up from the paper like smoke. I blinked, and they vanished.

Twenty-five years. Too much time, and yet, none at all. What would happen if I went back? Beth swore it would be fun. Sean seemed to think it was a great idea.

What was I afraid of?

Over and over, I traced the raised lettering of my name with my fingertips, as if the answer might be printed there too. The shadows of the room drew closer and my head ached from the effort of keeping my eyes open. I was exhausted but not soothed.

Corinne yawns and stretches, displacing the cat. The tea has gone cold.

Leaving the invitation on the couch, I stood and deposited my mug in the sink. I climbed into bed and listened enviously to Sean's even, untroubled breathing until I finally fell into a fitful sleep, nowhere near an answer.

Chapter 2

I began narrating my life during the early stages of my mom's chemotherapy. Audra was in kindergarten. Sean had recently moved into a new role at work, and I was left to the full-time job of caring for my mom, recently moved to an assisted-living facility ten minutes from us. The silent car rides to and from the hospital, watching as staff hooked her up to machines and poked her with needles, the appointments with doctors who never had good news, all seemed more bearable when treated as part of a story, a plot twist happening in some other heroine's life.

I began telling myself the story I wanted to hear, the one I planned on someday passing on to my daughter—the story of her grandmother's miraculous recovery from breast cancer: *Corinne watches as Marie's gurney is wheeled down the hall to the surgery ward. Corinne sits in the treatment center, watching her mother rest. The light through the window glints off the silver metal of the bed railing. Corinne reaches out a hand to push back Marie's purple headscarf, which has slipped low over her forehead where her eyebrows used to be.*

But the story didn't follow the outline I had planned.

Corinne stands in the funeral home lobby, shaking hands with those who have come to pay their respects. Corinne leans, frail and ghostly, against her husband's side, swallowed whole by grief. Ten-year-old Audra stares at her bedridden mother from the doorway. Corinne can see her daughter's luminous eyes but cannot summon the energy to respond.

As I fumbled my way through the first year after my mother's passing, I continued narrating the mundane details of my day at the encouragement of my therapist. "Focus on one moment at a time," she encouraged as I lay on her couch, gutted by the loss of the parent who'd stayed.

At first it was like a to-do list: *Corinne gets up. Corinne brushes her teeth. Corinne tries to smile.* Eventually, I found the internal chatter calming: *Corinne takes a shower. Corinne drives to the store for milk. Corinne packs up her mother's belongings.* I slowly began to take back control of my life.

During those first months, I believed I was narrating my story to myself as I came to terms with my new status as a motherless daughter. Within a year, I realized that I was telling my story to Nick.

It was as if this person I hadn't seen in years (had, in fact, forced myself to avoid searching for), had accidentally wandered into the movie theater of my mind where the highlights of my day-to-day activities played out. Distressed, I tried imagining someone else I could tell my story to, my husband, my daughter, even my therapist.

But unlike the real Nick, this Nick stayed.

And I let him. I let him take a seat and make himself comfortable while I continued to tell my story. And with each new installment, it became more apparent that he was in my thoughts by invitation. He was there because I wanted to see him.

And now, it seemed, my wish was within my grasp. All I had to do was take a chance. All I had to do was say yes, go to a silly reunion. The rest was up to fate.

What would Corinne do?

* * *

I woke in the morning, tired and preoccupied, my thoughts still consumed by the reunion and Nick. At breakfast, I burned my toast and overfilled the coffee maker so that water ran across the counter and onto the floor while the smoke detector bleated, "Fire! Fire!" I pushed the vacuum around, chasing down glitter. I caught the fringe of the hallway rug in the vacuum roller, where it wound itself tightly, giving off a scorched smell from the friction.

Later, I wandered through the aisles of the grocery store, tossing random items into the cart, trying to picture Nick, unaged, leaning against an unknown counter in an unknown kitchen in an unknown city. The background of the memory was blank, and I struggled to fill in details. Was he married? Did he have a family? Had he thrown his invitation away, or, like me, had he propped it up on his desk while deciding whether or not to attend?

My phone chirped "Harper Valley PTA" from the depths of my purse. It was Grace Phillips, PTA president and mother of Audra's best friend, Lana. I pulled my phone out and pressed *talk*.

"Hi, Grace." I brushed my free hand over a display of avocados, squeezing slightly, testing for ripeness.

"Corinne!" Grace's voice blasted through the phone. She always spoke as though she were addressing a crowd. "Where are you?"

My hand froze mid-squeeze. "At the store." My voice rose, making the answer sound like a question. Something niggled at the edge of my mind. What had I forgotten?

"You're supposed to be helping me run the fundraising table today."

"Oh God, you're right. I totally blanked it."

"How fast can you get here?"

"I'm on my way." Grabbing my purse and abandoning my cart, I fled the store. When I got to the car, I realized the avocado was still in my hand. I tossed it into the backseat.

Twenty minutes later, I raced into the cafeteria of Wildwood High School. Grace glanced up as I jogged over to her, and I saw her eyes briefly widen before she caught herself and settled her features into a gracious smile. Running my hands over my hair, I had a vision of myself through her eyes, sweaty and disheveled in my white hoodie with the coffee stain on the hem, leggings, hair scraped back in a ponytail, face devoid of makeup. I had dressed for a morning of chores, not social interaction.

As always, Grace looked flawless in a white cotton twinset and chinos, her red Converse a quirky, hip nod to the youthful environment. Her dark hair (surely a dye job?) was cut in a perfect pageboy; her razor cut bangs brushing the rims of her Vera Bradley glasses.

I skidded to a stop behind the card table and took the money belt she proffered, securing it around my waist. These were our jobs, self-assigned years ago, when we'd first started volunteering together.

"Sorry," I mumbled.

"No problem," she said, handing a student two strawberry cupcakes. "Glad you're here now." The way she emphasized "now" wasn't lost on me.

We fell into our familiar rhythm, taking money and restocking baked goods. The pungent smell of cafeteria food and the din of youthful voices reminded me again of the reunion. Time folded in on itself. I was seventeen again, wearing my blue and white cheerleader uniform and staring at Nick's flannel-clad figure across the gymnasium, unaware that my life was about to change…

"Corinne." Grace's voice cut across my memory, smearing Nick's face from my mind's eye. "I said, got any singles?"

* * *

After the final lunch period ended, Grace and I carried the folding table back to the PTA closet. It was a one-person job, but Grace had grabbed one side of the table and asked me to take the other in a tone that left no room for argument. Not that I would have disagreed; I had always been intimidated by Grace's perfect clothes, her perfect family, her perfect life. Now I was in for a grilling as we walked sideways, the table ping-ponging between our hips.

"Is everything all right?" Grace wasted no time on small talk. She was much like Beth in that way. Her sharp eyes studied me, her coral-lipsticked mouth pursed in concern. I knew she'd never let me get away without an answer.

I hoped half of the truth would be enough to satisfy her. "Oh, it's silly, really"—I conjured an apologetic smile—"I got an invitation to my high school reunion, and I can't decide whether or not I want to go."

And possibly see the ex I can't stop thinking about.

Grace laughed with relief, reaching across with her free hand to slap my shoulder playfully. "Is that all? I thought you were sick or that something had happened to Sean."

We reached the closet, and I held the table while Grace unlocked the door with the key that hung from a plastic band around her wrist. I slid the table inside, careful not to knock over a papier-mâché palm tree left over from last spring's talent show. She locked the door behind us, and we headed to the main office to turn in the money belt and sign out.

"You know, Glenn and I went to my reunion last year; it was so much fun." She leaned in. "Although I don't remember too much after the first hour. We started doing shots with the debate team, and the rest of the evening is a bit fuzzy." She threw her head back and laughed her braying laugh, proud of her audacity. "You should go. It was like being back in high school."

I snorted, amused. "You know what? That's exactly what I'm afraid of."

* * *

Snippets of conversation haunted me all the way home:

Grace: *It was so much fun.*

Sean: *I think you should go.*

Beth: *You pinky promised.*

In my imagination, Nick's voice joined in: *Come back to me.*

Chapter 3

I met my husband during my freshman year of college at North Carolina State University when he rescued me from a disastrous blind date.

I was immediately attracted to Sean's stability, his consistency, his concrete plans for our future. After the heartbreak of Nick, Sean's predictability was comforting, and I felt safe believing his promises of "forever." We married the summer after I graduated and moved to Charlotte for his job at Duke Energy. I found an entry-level position in a small advertising firm. A few years later, we moved into our house, Audra was born, and our modest version of living happily ever after began.

Now, we were still living the same story line—same characters, same roles, same setting. On the surface, nothing had changed, and yet, everything had. My mother was gone. Sean's parents had moved to Florida, his sister to Iowa. Audra was not a baby but a high school junior, her eyes trained on graduation, a caged animal awaiting release. Sean was no longer an entry-level manager and exhausted grad student; he was a middle-aged senior executive with an expense account and a golf handicap. And I was...

What was I?

I wasn't a cheerleader or a bright-eyed energetic twenty-something graphic designer anymore. I wasn't a newlywed, nor a young mother. I was no longer my mother's caregiver. Who was I, outside of "daughter, wife, mother?" What else remained of Corinne Elizabeth Murphy Fuller?

That night, I sat outside on the deck, wrapped in a blanket, an empty wine glass in my hand. Besides the office, this was my favorite place to sit. We'd built the deck with the small inheritance from my mother; it ran the length of the back of the house and had three doorways, a sliding door from the family room, and exits from both our bedroom and Audra's. As a family, we often gathered here to relax and unwind. On my own, I came out here to think. Sometimes, to hide.

As I sat, the white lights flickered on in the three crepe myrtle trees lining our back fence. The trees had soared from saplings in the years since we'd moved in. The lights had been a gift from Sean on the first anniversary of my mother's death. Large white globes, set on a timer, winked from the branches in a way that reminded me of Michigan snowstorms in the winter and fireflies in the summer. Their cheerful twinkling kept me company and reminded me to look for the light, even in dark times. Audra called them "Nana's lights."

Sean appeared at my side, wine bottle in hand. "Whatcha thinking?" he asked as he refilled my glass.

I pulled my feet off the couch cushion, making room for him to join me.

"I was thinking about how everything seems to be changing."

Sean sat, propping his feet against the stone table fire pit and took a drink straight from the bottle.

"Like what?"

I sighed. "You know, everything. Audra's a junior. She's talking about college. In California. She's driving. She has a job at the mall. She doesn't want to be around me anymore."

Sean looked at me, raising his right eyebrow. He shook his

head, disagreeing. "Of course, she does. She loves you. You're her mother."

I took a sip of wine as I tamped down a flare of frustration, beginning to regret saying anything. Lately, all our conversations ended up with me defending myself. It was as if we were living in the same house but experiencing different realities.

"Yes, I'm her mother..." I struggled to find words that would be clear enough, statements he couldn't possibly misinterpret. I needed to feel heard, not challenged. "...but she doesn't need me like she used to. It makes me sad. It makes me feel old."

He didn't respond right away. I ran my tongue across my teeth, tasting the wine. The lights twinkled merrily. Tired, I leaned my head back against the couch cushion and looked at the sky. I wished Sean would put his arm around me and tell me that I was necessary to him. That I was still someone worth coming home to.

I felt the couch shift as Sean's arm settled across my shoulders, pulling me close. I let my head fall to the side, into the spot on his chest that seemed molded to fit only me.

Corinne settles against her husband, a small smile on her lips, her eyes closed. She waits.

Tell me what I need to hear.

"It's the reunion," he murmured into my hair. "Everyone feels old when they go to their reunion." He kissed the top of my head. "You'll feel better once we get there and you see that everybody else got old too."

Wrong answer.

I turned to him. "About that..." I hesitated. "If I go"—I stressed the *if*—"Beth wants it to be just the two of us. Vi's staying home with Dante, and you've got that big client meeting coming up..." I trailed off, while I finished the sentence in my head: *And I can't talk to Nick with my husband by my side.*

Sean's expression tightened. He was still smiling, but I could see the corners of his mouth twitching, could hear the unspoken disappointment in the pause before his answer. I'd hurt him. A tiny part of me felt victorious. He'd hurt me first with the "old" comment. "Well, sure. Yeah. I get it. I don't know these people and you don't want to spend the whole night explaining to me." He stood, his knees popping, and addressed the darkness. "Look, go or don't go. Whatever you decide is fine with me." He plucked the empty bottle from the table and headed back inside. "Want to watch CSI?" he asked as he slid open the door to the family room.

"You go ahead. I'll be there in a few minutes."

Corinne sits alone, huddled under a blanket in the dark, staring at her mother's lights.

Help, Mom.

I want you to be happy, honey.

I am happy.

Are you?

Aren't I?

You have a beautiful home, a good man who loves you, and a daughter who does too, even if she's not showing it. What's not to be happy about?

Something's missing. Something…more.

Like what?

I couldn't answer. I didn't know.

* * *

I texted Beth the next morning:

Okay. I'm in.

Her reply *ping*ed back immediately:

YES!!!!!!!!!!!!!!!!!!!!!!!!!!!!

22

Before I could change my mind, I took the reply card from the bulletin board, circled *Yes* in thick black marker, and walked to the mailbox.

Corinne stands, postcard in hand, the wind ruffling her hair. She offers a small smile to the late afternoon sky as she places her reply in the mail.

Chapter 4

"Ladies and gentlemen, we have reached our cruising altitude of thirty-five thousand feet. Beverage service will begin shortly. For now, we invite you to sit back, relax, and enjoy your flight."

The fasten seatbelt sign flickered off, and my seatmate, an overweight middle-aged man with long hair and a faintly antiseptic smell, shot to his feet and hurried up the aisle to the restroom. I stayed where I was; seatbelt buckled, my forehead resting against the window. Wisps of clouds swirled past the airplane window, and I traced their shapes with my index finger.

The reunion was tomorrow night.

My heart gave a little flutter, and I exhaled, fogging the window, obscuring the view. I drew a heart in the condensation, my finger squeaking against the plexiglass on the downstroke. I leaned against the window and closed my eyes, remembering...

* * *

Nicholas Augustine Elms arrived at Clemmons High School in mid-September of our senior year. He lived with Irene and Arthur Betz, who ran the hardware store, and was rumored to be related to them, a nephew, perhaps. The complete absence of a father or a mother lent a mysterious air to Nick's arrival in a town where anyone not born within the county limits was already considered a person of intrigue.

We had one class together—Honors Lit. He sat, silent and unsmiling, slouched in the "don't care" posture that comes standard with a back-of-the-classroom seat. But his name never appeared on the blackboard list of students with missing assignments, and occasionally, Mr. Gaines would read one of Nick's brooding poems aloud. We'd started the year by reading *Wuthering Heights*, and I knew several girls who thought Nick, with his dark hair and pensive stare, was Heathcliff incarnate.

I knew who Nick was, but I never considered his existence in relation to mine until the day of the homecoming pep rally.

The whole school was in the gym, listening to the marching band perform. I sat with the rest of the varsity cheerleaders, ready to take the floor when they broke into the school fight song. In a sea of blue and white, a figure clad in all black caught my eye.

Nick sat at the top of the bleachers with the sophomores, even though we were supposed to stay with our own class. His long hair hung in his eyes and brushed his shirt collar.

He was staring at me.

My cheeks flamed. I broke eye contact and swept my gaze across the gym floor, feigning interest in the marching band's anemic version of "Louie, Louie."

Glancing back at Nick, I saw him still staring at me, leaning forward, his forearms on his knees, a slight grin on his face. Unbidden, one corner of my mouth twitched up in a smile. He sent me a wink in response, and I realized two things: One, Nick Elms was incredibly good-looking. And two, I wanted Nick Elms to ask me out.

Oh, yes, I wanted that very, very much.

* * *

Nick waited until the week before Winter Break to approach me.

The cheer team was selling candy cane grams to raise money for new uniforms, and we stood in the lunchroom in our skimpy blue cheer skirts and white turtlenecks, Santa hats and reindeer antlers affixed above our ponytails. I was so busy making change and taping notes to candy canes that I didn't see Nick until he was standing right in front of me, his dollar bill outstretched. I looked into his eyes and felt my face burn.

"One, please." His deep voice startled me. He rarely spoke in class.

I took his money with a shaky hand, almost dropping it when our fingers touched. I ignored the giggles behind me. No one else existed at that moment except for Nick and me. I managed to shove his dollar in the cash box and pushed a blank notecard and a pen shaped like a Christmas tree over to him. "Here," I mumbled. "Fill out the card. We'll attach it to a candy cane and deliver it during homeroom tomorrow."

He bent over the table, cupping his hand around the card so I couldn't read it. He was so tall; he almost had to fold in half. Kirsten Summers, my best friend on the squad, nudged me, giggling.

"Shut up," I hissed, not moving my eyes from the sight of Nick's bent head. I wanted to reach out and stroke the hairs on the back of his neck. I felt my hand start to lift as if to do that very thing. I tried to cover by reaching up and adjusting my antlers. I could tell Kirsten was still watching.

I shot her a look: *Go away.*

She widened her eyes, the very picture of innocence, and shook her head: *No.*

Finally, he straightened, pushing his hair back with one hand, and extending the pen and the folded note with the other. "Don't lose that," he said, with a teasing grin. "It's very important." He tapped a finger on the back of my hand, raised his chin a fraction of an inch in goodbye, and turned, whistling as he walked away.

I stood frozen for several seconds, until Kirsten and Jenny Byers surrounded me.

"Come on!" Kirsten begged. "Who's it for?" She peeled my fingers back.

Jenny grabbed the note. "Oh my God!" she shriek-screamed. "It's for you!"

"Give it to me!" I unfroze and lunged, grabbing the note. I raced from the table into the girl's bathroom, my friends whooping behind me. I hurtled through the door, startling two underclassmen, and locked myself into the first empty stall. With shaking fingers, I unfolded the note:

*Corinne. Proper noun. Meaning: Beautiful maiden.
Rescue me from my dragons. Yours always, Nick.*

He'd written his phone number at the bottom of the note. I turned it over, but there was nothing on the back. My heart was racing. Rescue him? Nick wanted me to rescue him? My head was spinning.

I stayed in the bathroom for the rest of lunch. I couldn't face Jenny and Kirsten. I waited until the late bell rang and then rushed straight to art, mumbling a vague excuse of "female trouble," to Mr. Hoffman as I slid into my seat.

At the end of the day, I hurried to my car, keys clutched in my hand. Normally I would wait around for Beth. We would go for a drive, stopping downtown for food, or wander the aisles of the drugstore and sample makeup. Today I wanted to go home and stare at my note.

As I neared the parking lot, the first bus pulled away from the curb, unveiling Nick Elms leaning against the passenger door of my rust-red Corolla. He waved as I approached, then held out his hand. In slow motion, I took it.

This is it, I thought, as his fingers curled around mine, claiming me. *My happily ever after.*

* * *

"Trash, ma'am?"

I woke with a start. Nick faded back into the past.

A young flight attendant was standing above me, holding out a white plastic trash bag. She rattled the bag's contents impatiently. I shook my head and she moved on. I heard her stop at the row behind me. "Trash?"

My seatmate was back, his face pale. He squeezed a stress ball in his left hand while his lips formed silent words. It might have been a prayer.

Rubbing my forehead where it'd pressed against the window, I fought the urge to ask him to pray for me too. We were about to land. This was happening. In twenty-four hours, I might see Nick again.

I wasn't ready. I wanted just a few more minutes, tucked safe inside my memories.

Corinne is trapped. Her eyes dart right and left, seeking escape.

"Ladies and gentlemen, we are now on our initial descent into Detroit Metro Airport. Please return to your seats and bring your seatbacks and tray tables to their full upright and locked positions."

Here we go.

Chapter 5

I wheeled my suitcase to the arrivals pick-up curb. A moment later, I heard a honk and a shout as Beth flung herself from a car, almost before it stopped, and threw herself into my waiting arms.

"Rinni!"

"Bethie!"

Despite her diminutive size, Beth's skinny, tattooed arms lifted me off the ground with the force of her hug.

I squeezed her back, squealing: "Put me down!"

The panic and doubt I'd felt during the last moments of the flight subsided at the sight of my best friend. Maybe Beth had been right all along. Maybe this would be fun.

"Ma'am!" A man's voice interrupted our celebration. "Ma'am, you need to move your vehicle immediately." A sour-looking security officer stood in front of Beth's idling rental, a blue Chevy Malibu. The driver's side door stood wide open, causing traffic to swerve around it.

Staring pointedly at the open door, the guard's hand hovered over his pocket as if he wanted us to believe he had a gun and might use it. His freckled face and shock of red hair hanging into his eyes made him look barely old enough to drive, let alone be assigned a weapon.

"Ma'am," he said again, starting to move toward us.

It was the repeated "ma'ams" that got Beth's attention. She lowered me to the ground and slowly walked back to the driver's side of the car, her eyes fixed on the guard.

"Sir," she said as she passed, in a tone that made it sound like cursing.

I gathered my suitcase and purse off the sidewalk and stowed them in the Malibu's backseat. I barely had my feet inside the car before Beth peeled out, cutting off an Uber driver who honked and let us know with a hand gesture what she thought of Beth's driving. Beth laughed and returned the sentiment through the open sunroof.

"Whoo-hoo!" she cackled. "Twenty-five years, baby!"

* * *

Beth drove like she lived; hard, fast, and unconcerned with other people's opinions. Ignoring honks and glares, she talked non-stop while staring straight ahead, eyes hidden behind gold-rimmed aviator glasses, one hand on the wheel, her other arm cocked out the open window, hand surfing the air. I sat back and let her talk, basking in the presence of the one person, outside of my family, with whom I felt comfortable.

"So, Vi moved into sales and spends half her week on the road traveling to client meetings…"

"The weekend shift at the pharmacy is killing me..."

"Dante started kindergarten…"

"I've got a conference coming up in Cleveland. You should fly in and meet me…"

"Vi began another IVF cycle…"

"So, the other day on the reunion Facebook page—why aren't you on there—I saw this post from Kirsten Summers—"

"Wait. What?" I interrupted. "Kirsten Summers? Is she coming this weekend?" Ice-cold dread washed over me.

Beth shot me a *get over it* look. "In fact, she isn't. She's going to a wedding." She zipped around a slow-moving semi hauling a flatbed of farm equipment. "She did private message me and ask for your email, though."

"Are you kidding? My email? Why?"

Beth shrugged. "Dunno. I deleted her message. *Poof!* Gone. The beauty of the internet." She grinned. "I figured you didn't want to hear anything she had to say."

"That's right. I have nothing to say to her, ever again." I felt the old familiar anger swell up, the bitter taste of betrayal in my throat. Kirsten had been my friend, my squad sister. I would never speak to her again after...

No. I wasn't going to think about Kirsten Summers. Especially not since I'd just decided to enjoy myself.

I turned my attention back to Beth. "So what else is happening? How are your parents? Your brothers?"

Beth rolled her head back in mock exasperation, always her first reaction when talking about her beloved, chaotic family. "Well, they're all in Florida now. My parents finally sold the Clemmons house and bought a condo in St. Pete." She shot a wry look my way. "Mom and Dad came to visit us this summer. That was an adventure."

I laughed, picturing Beth's laid-back parents living in her high-energy, high-maintenance world, trying to keep up with the precocious Dante and his everlasting energy. "I bet they were exhausted."

"They were supposed to stay a month, but they couldn't hack it after two weeks." Beth shook her head. "I know I'm a lot of work. I know Dante is. Vi is the calm one in our house, and even she was too high-strung for them. I don't think they'll be back for a while."

"Well, enjoy them while you have them. It's nice to have family around, even if they frustrate you."

Beth glanced over at me, stricken. "Oh, Rin, I'm sorry. I didn't mean…"

I waved her off. "No, no, I know you didn't. What I'm saying is that it's only such a short time that you get to have your family all around you. Like your kids." I sighed. "When they're young, the minutes feel like hours, and the hours are like years. Then, suddenly, your baby can drive and can't wait to move out. It happens fast." Beth was still looking at me with an apologetic look. "Seriously, it's fine—Watch the road!" I pointed out the front window.

Beth swerved, barely missing the bumper of the car in front of us. The driver leaned on his horn and yelled obscenities out the window.

"That's anatomically impossible!" Beth called back, accelerating around them.

My heart hammered at the near miss, but I was grateful for the distraction. I shifted in my seat, putting my feet on the dash in the way that I always warned Audra never to do, and smoothed my hair back from my face, refastening my ponytail. I reached over and turned on the radio, skimming through the presets before landing on an oldies station playing Madonna's "Crazy for You." When had Madonna become an oldie? I sang along, and after a minute, Beth joined in.

As the song faded out, we held the last note, competing to see who would break first. Beth did, years of smoking undoing all the lung capacity she'd built playing bassoon in the marching band.

"Oooooo," I kept going, leaning over the center console and getting in her face.

She flipped her black-polished middle finger at me. "You win, you win. Shut up."

Laughing, I fell back in the seat. "Thanks for making me come to this."

She raised her sunglasses and gave me a look. "Go on."

"The truth is...I'm sort of stuck right now."

Thankfully, Beth didn't immediately disagree or tell me I was imagining things like Sean would have. "Stuck how?"

"I don't know." I shrugged and pulled my feet off the dash and up onto the seat, curling myself into a tight ball with my arms around my knees. "I don't seem to quite have a handle on myself anymore. Now that Audra is older...I mean, she's counting the days until graduation, and it's still two years away. What do I do now that she doesn't need me to be her mother full time? It's like I've forgotten who I am." I didn't mention the ache in my heart, the emptiness of my days, the movie in my mind, or Nick.

"What does Sean say?"

"I haven't, you know, talked much about it with him," I admitted, staring at billboards as we zoomed by, each a memory from childhood: Lake Michigan, blueberries, a historic restaurant famous for serving mugs of bacon as an appetizer. "He doesn't see it like I do. He's excited for us to 'rediscover' ourselves." I mimed air quotes.

Beth pursed her mouth and puffed out her cheeks, considering. "Is that a bad thing?"

"I guess not." I searched for the right words. "But I don't think being a parent was ever as all-consuming for him as it was for me." I saw Beth's posture straighten, preparing to refute that. She was Team Sean. "I don't mean he wasn't a great dad. He was. Is. What I meant was"—I splayed my fingers, conciliatory —"he still had a job and outside interests while Audra was growing up. I didn't. I left my job to take care of Audra, then Mom."

"Do you wish you'd kept working? Hired someone to help out at home?"

I considered. "No. It was the right choice for everyone. But still, sometimes it feels like I left myself behind..."

"And you don't know what to do next," Beth finished for me.

"Right." I drummed my fingers on my legs in time to the keyboard line of A-ha. "I have to figure out what I'm going to do, what I'd like to do."

"Will you go back to advertising?"

"Definitely not. My portfolio would look completely antiquated next to all those bright young things and their shiny influencer campaigns."

"What about photography?"

I hesitated. "I…I don't know. Maybe." I pictured my beloved Canon, a long-ago gift from Sean, sitting on my office bookcase, gathering dust. "It's been ages."

Seven years to be exact. Since my mother died.

Beth shot me a glance. "It's never too late." She took her hand off the wheel and patted my knee, like I was Dante, winding down from a tantrum. "Look at me. I didn't get married or have a kid until almost forty. You never know what's coming around the corner, Rin. You never know when the right path is going to appear."

She pointed out the window at the billboard for Creekside Inn. "Check it out. We're almost there." She gave my knee another pat and turned on her blinker to move onto the off-ramp. "Look, don't worry about all that this weekend. This weekend is about you and me and going back to high school and showing all those punks—We. Rule." She laid the flat of her hand on the horn, giving two sharp blasts as we turned off the highway. "Clemmons High School, here we come!"

* * *

After checking in and a quick dinner at the Creekside's attached restaurant, Beth wanted to explore. We traveled the backroads from Creekside to Clemmons and wound up on Main Street, which sparkled like a Hallmark movie set.

"Whoa," breathed Beth. "It's like we're inside an Instagram filter."

I stared, mouth open in amazement. When I'd lived here, Main Street was functional but run-down, filled with everything a small town needed to survive: a bank, a drug store, the hardware store where Nick worked. There'd been one or two restaurants, including a greasy spoon breakfast place and a storefront offering take-out pizza.

Now the street glittered with upscale dining and destination shopping—an olive oil company, a kite shop, a store selling handwoven woolen items. Wrought iron dining tables lined the street under hand-lettered signs reading "Bistro" or "Boulangerie." Photogenic couples strolled hand in hand along the sidewalks, while their cherubic children licked pastel-colored ice cream, and their designer dogs strained against leashes. It was a reality-TV makeover story. Even the cars cruising the main street were upgraded. Sleek BMWs and Priuses replaced the boxy hand-me-down Fords and Datsuns of my memories. Our rental car seemed out of place, underdressed for the occasion.

Beth hung a right at the next corner, and we headed down Dartmouth, the main east/west road bisecting Clemmons. In contrast to her highway driving earlier, she went slowly, and we gawked out the window, pointing out landmarks.

"The library got a new sign…"

"That's Nancy Toler's house. She'll be there tomorrow night…"

"They tore down that old house—remember, the one with the sagging porch and the nasty couch in the yard?"

"Ugh, there's Kirsten's house."

"Want to go see if they have any rotten eggs at Shop-Rite?"

"Ha! No. Just drive a little faster, please."

Beth turned again and headed farther away from the town center, toward her old neighborhood. A moment later, we pulled up in front of the house she'd grown up in, a sprawling ranch. In the glow of the streetlight, I could see that the new owners had painted the once-white siding a dark color, either forest green or navy blue.

Beth leaned forward on the steering wheel, staring out at the house. "Weird," she said finally.

"Weird?"

"Weird that this house is still here, but some other family lives in it. Do you think they painted over the stain in the garage where Bobby's car leaked oil? Or replaced the wood paneling where Jimmy carved his name?"

I frowned. It wasn't like Beth to be sentimental. "Does it bother you?"

"Nah." Beth pulled a face, and the mood instantly lightened. "I'm just thinking out loud. It's surreal, that's all. Like, if my family doesn't live in that house, then the house shouldn't exist. Know what I mean?"

I nodded, getting it immediately. "Sure. It's one of the reasons I liked taking pictures. Capturing a moment, freezing time. Keeping the memories safe." My hands twitched instinctively as if I were holding a physical camera and pressing the shutter button.

A light came on in the house, and a silhouette appeared in the front window

"Time to go." Beth pulled away from the curb. "Don't want to get picked up for loitering." She shook her head. "Small towns…"

We wound our way back toward Main Street. My heart sped up as we crossed the street where Nick had lived.

Three blocks later, Beth hung a left and pulled over in front of a late-70s style duplex covered in white siding and red brick. The lawn was neatly mowed but sparsely landscaped, with a single birch tree gracing either side of the walkway that ran up from the curb, splitting to lead to mirrored doorways.

Our door had been the one on the left. After I left for

college, Mom found a new job in Columbus, Ohio. I hadn't been back to Clemmons since, hadn't even looked this house up on Google Maps, although I'd given Audra the address once so she could.

It seemed odd now that I'd never been back, never even considered it. At the time, it had seemed simpler to ignore my past, like it hadn't happened.

"Hey." Beth touched my arm. "Are you okay?"

"Yeah." I sat back, still looking at the apartment, remembering how the key to the front lock always stuck and how my room at the back of the house had a view of the hospital parking lot. "It's a lot of memories at once. You know how you said earlier that it's never too late? Sometimes it is. Maybe if I'd stayed longer or come back sooner, I would have gotten some answers."

Like why Nick did it, and why he left.

By never coming back, I could pretend his absence didn't hurt.

"Would answers have made a difference?" Beth asked. "Would you have felt better about…everything?" She tactfully avoided Nick's name.

I considered, looking up at the second-floor window that had been my mother's room. "No. It's in the past. Nothing I do now is going to change it."

Beth turned to look at me, silhouetted in the streetlight. "Don't beat yourself up about it. You can't change what you didn't do. You have to get used to the unanswered questions." I turned to stare at my best friend, her expression inscrutable.

I hoped she couldn't read mine either.

* * *

The next day, we sat side by side with our feet in bubbling foot spas while manicurists rubbed lotion into our hands.

"You're a genius," I murmured, my voice vibrating from the massage rollers aggressively kneading my back.

"It's true. I am." Beth leaned back, equally blissed out.

We were sitting in Très Jolie Nails, one of Clemmons' many upgraded storefronts. Back in our day, it had been a dusty antique store that gave off an ominous vibe, the mannequin in its window long reported to have eyes that followed you as you walked past.

Now it was light and airy, with ivory walls and planters of lavender displayed on every flat surface. Watching the manicurist's bowed head, I wondered how anyone could work with such precision while my hands trembled and shook from the chair's ministrations, but I quickly dismissed the thought. *You are here to relax and have fun*, I reminded myself. *Stop thinking so much.*

Corinne closes her eyes, her normally furrowed brow smooth, her lips slightly parted as she sighs with pleasure. The scented air tickles her nose and she reaches up to scratch it.

My moving hand was grasped firmly and forced back into place. Startled, I settled for scratching my nose against my shirt sleeve.

Beth continued: "I swore when Dante was born that I wouldn't be one of those parents who never took time for myself, but it got to the point where it was more stressful to find time to relax than it was worth."

"I remember those days," I said nodding as the nail technician began buffing my ragged nails into smooth arcs. "You get home tenser than you were before, out the money for a pedicure that's already smudged because you felt too guilty to sit still long enough for your polish to dry."

"Exactly. I thought I'd save the money and do it myself instead." Beth looked down apologetically at the young beautician sawing away at her heels with the dreaded callus grater. "It's never the same."

"Nothing ever is after kids."

* * *

An hour later, we left Très Jolie, our hands and feet soft and pampered. I kept staring down in fascination at my French-tipped fingers and toes, thinking they looked as though they belonged to someone else. Beth's nails sported iridescent green polish that gave the appearance of snakeskin. Her toes were blood red.

"Channeling my outer Maleficent," she said and winked.

Next, Beth announced that I had an appointment with the stylist next door. The shop had always been a hair salon but had received the same makeover treatment as the rest of Main Street and now exuded an air of small-scale luxury.

I listened in amusement as Beth described to the stylist what she envisioned for me—lowlights, cut, blowout, the works—reflecting on how insulted I'd have been to hear anyone else refer to my hair as "that mousy greige mess." But she was right. My hair had been the crowning glory of my younger years, long, shiny, and thick. But as time got shorter and the wiry gray hairs got more aggressive, I'd stopped trying to keep up. A new package of hair ties was the most attention I'd given my locks in ages.

"Okay, okay." I swatted Beth away as she sketched her vision into the air around my head. "We all agree, I'm a mess. What are you going to do while I'm here?"

"I'll be in the bookstore, looking for books that do not feature Paw Patrol." She made a face. "I am *sick to death* of cartoon dogs." She opened the salon door. "Take your time!" she called, not turning around.

* * *

I did take my time. The surrender of control, the primping, and the complimentary glass of wine were all glorious. I refused to flinch at the final bill and added a healthy tip. After years of budget-conscious trims, I deserved to splurge for once.

"Thanks again!" I pushed the door open and stepped out of the climate-controlled salon and into the haze of autumn in the Midwest. The air was warm and slightly humid, like being wrapped in a not-quite-dry towel straight from the dryer. The light had a yellow and heavy feel; shadows seemed liquid in comparison. Somewhere, someone was burning leaves. I breathed deeply, the scent evoking images of walking home from school and long nights when dusk fell before dinner. To me, it was a distinctly Midwestern smell and plucked another nostalgic chord.

Instead of heading to the bookshop, I meandered up the street in the opposite direction, taking my time as promised. I paused in front of a small clothing boutique, admiring a flowing bohemian-style top and peasant skirt that would have been my style twenty years and a couple of sizes ago.

My gaze slid from the mannequin to my reflection, and I smiled in fresh delight at the dark waves that fell past my shoulders and bounced back effortlessly when I tossed my head.

Corinne gazes in the mirror, looking as youthful as the day of her high school graduation.

I ran my fingers through my hair for the sheer pleasure of feeling the soft, ultra-frizz-controlled tresses when a movement over my shoulder caught my eye.

I watched in the window's reflection as a tall, lanky man walked out of a store on the opposite side of the street. He paused for a moment, his back to me, and hitched the paper bag he was carrying up onto his hip. Even without seeing his face, the way he moved tugged at my memory.

Nick?

Corinne stares, stricken, at the reflection of the figure across the street. She watches as he unlocks the dingy black truck parked at the curb and climbs in, his face obscured. As she watches, the shadow's profile turns slightly in her direction. Although her back is still to him, she feels the connection as they stare at one another's reflected images in the glass.

It had been twenty-five years since I'd felt the intensity of Nick's eyes on mine. My legs began to tremble. I brought my hands up, steadying myself. With ten fingers pressed against the clothing store window, I closed my eyes and thought back to 1992.

* * *

Summer was our time—mine and Nick's. We had graduated. We were in love. We spent hours talking, dreaming. Sometimes we'd go to the library and read to each other. Nick was a fan of Thoreau, Whitman, Emerson. I read him Hans Christen Anderson's *The Little Mermaid*, and we both agreed the darker, original version was more satisfying. We talked about the future and the cruel irony of fate, bringing us together now, only to rip us apart in a few short months. We avoided any direct mention of my college plans or his impending move to Alaska to work at his uncle's canning factory. Instead, we talked about our eventual, inevitable future. He'd be a writer; I'd be a photographer. We'd travel the world. Our love was bigger than one town, one state, one continent.

The day of our breakup had started normally. Nick picked me up after breakfast in his uncle's truck, and we headed straight for Clemmons Dam. "Our spot" was the picnic table under the trees down by the runoff, the only table set apart from the ones clustered around the park's community grill. Besides the privacy it afforded, it was the best place to find painted turtles. I had a whole photography series planned around extreme closeups of the patterns on their shells.

The sun was shining bright and hot, and I was already sweaty from creeping along the bank, capturing images of three small turtles sunning on a log among the reeds. My thin tank top stuck to me, and my cutoffs chafed my thighs, the denim abrasive in the humidity.

I walked slowly back to our bench, wiping my forehead with the back of my hand, feeling sweat beading along my chest and under my arms, wishing I had remembered to bring a Coke. The water fountains at the dam were notorious for running warm, sulfurous water and were often clogged with gum or plugs of tobacco.

Nick watched my approach, a strange look on his face. I straddled the bench, my hands on his knees, concerned.

"What's wrong?" I searched his face. Was he sick? He looked pale. He was dressed all in black, defiant of the climbing temperature. His shirt clung to him, and his dark jeans threw heat back onto my bare legs. His unwashed hair hung limply around his face. A few baby strands clung to the perspiration on his forehead and cheeks. For the first time, I noticed that his eyes were bloodshot and sunken like he hadn't slept. My tongue stuck to my mouth as I started to ask if he had any money for the vending machine so we could split a soda.

And that's when he said the words that blew my world apart: "I slept with Kirsten Summers."

The day went silent. I stared at Nick. I'd heard his words, but I hadn't yet comprehended them. My whole body shut down from the task of making sense of the words he'd just spoken.

I slept with Kirsten Summers.

He was forming new words now. I couldn't hear them. My heart was beating so loudly; I felt like my head would split open from the noise. I felt pressure in my throat as my vocal cords struggled to unlock, choking me.

"Kirsten Summers?" I whisper-screamed. "Kirsten-freaking-Summers?"

Nick's eyes darted left and right; his jaw clenched. He reached out and locked my hands in a death grip between us.

"You *slept* with Kirsten Summers?" I repeated, my voice cracking on her name as I wrenched my hands from his, wiping my palms on my shorts. Fresh beads of sweat formed on my upper lip, unrelated to the heat of the day. My eyesight blurred, then cleared as I stared around wildly. A young mother with two toddlers had been laying out a blanket nearby. She quickly refolded it and ushered her scrabbling brood further along the path, casting a disapproving look over her shoulder. I glared back, and she scurried away. I didn't care. Nick had betrayed me; my life was over. Everything and everyone else was unimportant.

Nick stared at the graffiti decorating the picnic table, tracing his thumb around the shapes inscribed by knives and pens and nail files. Our names were there too: Nick + Corinne. He'd carved them with his penknife during one of our first dates here.

Now I pressed my palms into my eyes, my elbows against my chest. I didn't want to see our names, side by side, evidence of love now lost. Pressure built behind my ribs; any second, the pain would come bursting out of me, exploding my eyeballs and reducing my beating heart into a million billion drops of blood. I wondered if it would be enough to cover every inch of this table, this park. I suddenly, horribly, understood why it was called a "broken" heart. Mine would never beat properly again; it was damaged beyond repair.

Beyond the darkness of my eyelids, Nick continued talking. I heard only fragments: "April...gone away...just happened...didn't mean..." His voice lowered until I could only feel the vibration of it.

I moved my hands away from my face, cupping my ears in exaggeration. "What?" I snapped. "I can't hear you. Is there more?" Each word was a dagger with glittering edges, meant to flay his cheating face to shreds.

His lips moved again, mumbling into the collar of his shirt. I leaned in.

"She's pregnant."

Without knowing how it happened, I was on my feet and running. Away from Nick. Up the path toward the concrete walkway that traversed the dam to the upper parking lot. My only thought was: *Escape.*

"Corinne!" I heard Nick behind me, trying to catch up. But I was faster, stronger from years of running bleachers. My feet pounded as I ran up the incline to the top of the dam, my flip flops making undignified smacking noises. The few people around heard me coming and moved aside, gawking at the unfolding drama. I reached my favorite lookout point and stopped abruptly, taking in long breaths of muggy, sulfurous air, and gripping the railing so hard my knuckles blanched. Bile rose in my throat, and I swallowed it. My stomach lurched. Goose-bumps rose along my arms despite the punishing heat of the day. I stared out over the churning water as Nick caught up to me, breathing heavily.

"Corinne," he gasped, "I...never meant to...hurt you. It just happened." A big wracking cough and another deep gasp. "Don't...jump."

That got me. I spun to face him, furious, grabbing at the railing to regain my balance. "Jump? You think I'm going to jump off this bridge because of you, you worthless cheater?" My dry lips cracked as I spat mirthless laughter at him.

Everyone within earshot stared at us. I didn't care. I took a step toward Nick, who instinctively backed up. My legs were rubbery from running and the heat. I shoved a finger at his chest. "I'm up here because this is my favorite spot to think, you arrogant jerk. I'm not going to hurt myself because of you. In fact," I said, a sneer curling my lip, "what I'm thinking is how I'd like to throw you off this damn dam. You *and* Kirsten Summers!" My words rose out of me on the crest of adrenaline. My mouth was gluey and tasted metallic. My body felt heavy, the hot summer air settling over my shoulders, the weight of it becoming unbearable. "I hope..." I trailed off, the words thick in my mouth. I took another step forward, stumbled. Nausea washed over me, icy-sweet in my throat. "I hope you..." My head spun as my vision tunneled and I blacked out.

* * *

"Here, sweetie. Let's help you sit up," a woman's voice said in my left ear.

"Wait!" a male voice behind me shouted. I winced. "She hit the ground pretty hard. Maybe we shouldn't move her."

Another male voice, on my right: "Paramedics are on their way. Stay still, miss."

I struggled to sit, managing to get up onto my elbows even as unknown hands fought to keep me flat. I opened one eye, then the other, struggling to focus. The sky was brilliant blue and painful. A circle of concerned faces stared down at me, three men, two women. I could hear an ambulance wailing in the distance.

Nick was gone.

* * *

"Rin? Earth to Rin!" I jumped as Beth laid her hand on my shoulder. "What are you staring at?" She looked around curiously. I did the same. The black truck and its driver were gone. "You were like a statue, standing here."

"Nothing." I lamely motioned to the mannequin in the window. My fingerprints still branded the glass, two guilty rainbows. "I was thinking about how I would have loved that outfit in high school."

Beth's look told me she didn't believe me. I held her gaze

and prayed she'd drop it. After a moment, she glanced into the shop window, and I breathed out in relief. "You always did go in hard for a broomstick skirt," she said, shaking her head. She looped her arm through mine. "Love the hair, toots. Come on, let's get something to eat. We've still got a couple of hours to go before the big night. Got to keep our strength up."

As we walked back to the car, I couldn't help taking a final look over my shoulder to where the black truck had been. A small oil stain glimmered in the empty spot, proof that I hadn't imagined it. Had it really been Nick?

Had he come back?

* * *

Corinne stands at the doorway of Clemmons High School, elegant in a floaty black dress with spaghetti straps and an ambitious neckline. Her black sandals end in flirty bows at her ankles, and her hair is styled in loose waves that brush her bare shoulders. Corinne raises her chin and—

"What are you doing?" Beth's voice cut in. She glanced up at the sign above the school doors. "Clemmons High School, Home of the Warriors," she read aloud, then looked back at me, her heavily made-up eyes sharp, questioning. "Are you having a panic attack?"

"It's nothing," I mumbled, embarrassed at having been caught mid-grand-entrance fantasy. A couple pushed past, giving me a curious glance. I clutched my purse under my arm and followed Beth through the doors and into the past.

The school smelled the same, a pungent mix of stale sweat, pizza, and industrial disinfectant. Beth and I stood, backs to the school's main entrance, in the long, wide lobby. The cafeteria and classrooms were on our right. Directly in front of us was the gymnasium, where we could already see a couple of dozen people milling around. At the same time, desultory electronica vibrated through the room, lyrics prompting one and all to "Get Ready for This."

I snuck a peek at Beth, who looked gleeful. "It's terrible," she said and grinned. "It's perfect." She bounced on the balls of her feet, obviously itching to go in.

I stepped closer to her, hoping some of her enthusiasm and confidence would rub off on me. As the afternoon had worn on and the reunion drew nearer, all the good feelings I'd had since arriving had reverted to low-grade agitation. Even the continual pleasure at my newly brown hair and perfectly groomed nails hadn't been able to distract me from the panic gnawing in my stomach. Additionally, my possible Nick sighting on Main Street had all my senses on high alert.

Corinne glances around the room. Was he here? Would she see him tonight?

Beth dug her fingernails into my arm. "You're doing it again. Stop it."

She pulled me farther into the lobby, toward the gymnasium's waiting, open maw.

"Beth! Corinne! Welcome back!" A sweet-faced woman in a peach twinset and khakis stood behind the registration table. For a moment, I thought it was Mrs. Thurber, the school librarian, somehow preserved and looking exactly as she had a quarter of a century ago. Then reality kicked in, and I recognized her daughter, Sunny.

Beth cracked a wide smile. "Sunny!" she cried and teetered around the table as fast as her tight black leather dress and high heels would allow. She threw her arms around our former class president, who hugged her back enthusiastically.

"Hi, Sunny! How are you?" I mirrored Beth's greeting and leaned across the table for an awkward one-arm hug. Sunny and I had circled each other's lives but never moved past the classmate phase into friendship. I remembered being fond of her, a quiet, smart girl whose expression matched her name, always willing to share her notes if you missed a class or nodded off during an incredibly dull lesson.

Sunny scanned the spread of name tags and deftly picked ours out. "I'm great! I took over as the school librarian a few years ago, so I get to see all sorts of familiar faces. And both my sons are here. Colin is a junior and Henry is a freshman, so I'm soaking up all the time I have left with them. It goes fast, doesn't it?" She smiled as she handed our badges over. I got the feeling she'd given that speech several times already; her words had a practiced feel to them. "I think you have a daughter about the same age as my boys, don't you, Corinne?"

I took the proffered badge and nodded. "Audra's a junior this year too. And never misses a chance to tell me how desperate she is to graduate." I laughed thinly.

Sunny smiled back in an understanding way. "Just like we were, right?"

Beth joined in. "Keep telling me how fast it's going to go," she pleaded. "Dante's still in the phase where he wants an audience for everything, and independence seems so far away. All I do is fantasize about ten full minutes of quiet time."

Sunny and I exchanged knowing smiles, and Sunny put her hand on Beth's arm. "Enjoy it while you can. Because pretty soon, he'll be locking you out of his room."

"And begging you not to come to Meet the Teacher Night," I added.

Beth clutched at her heart. "Nooo," she howled, feigning a swoon. "I won't complain. I'll read *Walter the Farting Dog* one hundred times a night! Please don't take Meet the Teacher Night away!"

Sunny laughed, and she and Beth continued catching up. My eyes roamed across the badges, searching. The names, in alphabetical order, jumped from "Wyatt Ellis" to "Mindy Frank." Nick's name wasn't there. I checked again, just to be sure. Nothing.

He wasn't coming.

The wondering was over. The fact was, I would never see Nick Elms again.

Sometimes it *was* too late.

Beth pulled on my arm, eager to check out the scene in the gym. I shifted my focus back to her, plastering a smile on my face.

"See you inside!" Beth called to Sunny, who waggled her fingers at us in return.

As we moved into the gym, I heard her greet the next couple in line: "Hi! Thanks, yes, I'm doing well! I'm the librarian..."

* * *

The decorating committee had been hard at work. I had a mental image of middle-aged women standing on ladders, duct taping silver tulle to cinder block walls and saying things like, "We want it to look *festive*." It was exactly the sort of activity I did for the PTA. I reached out and stroked the nearest panel. Through the fabric, I could see that art students were still painting their senior projects on the gym walls. Gone were the Grateful Dead bears and Spuds MacKenzies of my youth, replaced with amateur reproductions of pithy memes to "Follow Your Bliss" and celebrity headshots.

Energy buzzed through the room, a mix of nerves and excitement. A group of thick-middled men congregated under the basketball hoop. Across the gym, a cluster of stiff-haired women stood close together, screeching with laughter over something I was too far away to hear.

Beth tightened her grip, her nails digging into my bare arm. "C'mon, let's get these name badges on and join the festivities." She coaxed the safety pin out of its casing with her thumbnail and flipped her badge over, squinting at the photo. "Oh God, look what Sunny did."

I looked. Next to our names, each badge featured a black and white reproduction of our senior yearbook picture. I'd always liked Beth's picture: she'd spiked her hair and drawn a lightning bolt over her eye like David Bowie. She looked cool and edgy and much the same as she did now.

My picture, on the other hand...ugh. The grainy image obscured the acne that plagued my teen years, but the photo was cropped in such a way that the sides and top of my mile-high teased hair were cut off. It looked like my pale face was peering out of a dark cave.

Groaning, I tried to affix the safety pin through the strap of my little black dress, managing instead to pierce the skin of my chest. "Dammit," I muttered. I needed both hands free. I clenched my purse between my knees and tried again.

"Hey!" Beth nudged me with her shoulder. "There's Nancy. I'm going to say hello. Back in a sec." She tottered away, her heels quieted by the springy athletic floor, calling enthusiastic greetings to everyone she passed: "Hey, Jonesy! Tina, you look great!"

My eyes blurred as I tried to focus on the space five inches below my shoulder. Frowning, I pulled the strap away from my chest so that my eyes could adjust. The pin slid through easily this time. I clasped it and double-checked that it was on straight. Satisfied, I retrieved my clutch from my knees and opened it to check my lipstick in the little mirror sewn into the lining. I sensed Beth's return as I squinted, baring my teeth to check for leftover poppy seeds from the dressing I'd had with my salad at dinner. I hadn't eaten much; my stomach had been too jumpy. Sure enough, there was a stray seed wedged between my front two teeth. I tried to slide it out with the corner of my pinky nail but managed only to wedge it in more tightly. Frowning, I sucked my teeth and slid my tongue over them until I felt it loosen enough to try again. This time I was successful, and I flicked the offending seed from my fingertip.

"Okay, I'm ready." I sighed, turning to Beth, ready to complain about the complexities of merely preparing to enter a party at our advanced age.

But Beth wasn't standing next to me.

Nick was.

I took an involuntary step backward, and my hands fell to my sides, releasing my purse, which spilled its contents at our feet: my ID, hotel room key, cash, lipstick, and a box of orange Tic Tacs. I felt a flush of red rush up from my chest and crest over my face. Had I flashed him my boobs while fixing my name tag? Had he watched me wrestle the poppy seed? Could a sinkhole open up and swallow me, please?

Nick looked just as I remembered him: tall-boy slouch, muscular but not big, the slightly hooked nose and deep-set blue eyes, the big, rough hands that were at total odds with his graceful bearing. His clothes were different—gone were the black jeans and flannels, replaced by chinos and a well-cut dress shirt—but his dark hair was still full and worn slightly longer than fashionable so that it fell over the top of his collar. He wasn't wearing an embarrassing name badge.

It was just like Nick to crash a party he had been invited to.

As I gawked, helpless, he leaned down with the same balletic grace of his teenage self, and in a fluid motion, swept everything back into my purse, then straightened and offered it back to me. Wordlessly, I reached for it, but before I could fasten the closure, his free hand darted forward and plucked the breath mints back out, flipping the lid open and shaking several directly onto his tongue while holding my gaze. It was a gesture so intimate that I felt my face flush again, right down to the newly dyed roots of my scalp. He closed the lid with his thumb and offered it back, bowing slightly, his fingers brushing mine.

He wasn't wearing a wedding ring.

"Look who it is," he murmured, leaning in, his sugary breath filling my nostrils and mouth. "A beautiful maiden."

I snatched my hand away and held my purse up against my chest like a shield. I could feel my heart beating hard and fast against my clenched hands, pulsing through my fingertips. This was the moment I'd practiced in my head hundreds (thousands, millions) of times since I woke at the dam to find Nick gone. I had rehearsed all options of opening lines, from vengeful "How could you do that?" to dismissive "I'm sorry, do we know each other," to casual "Oh, hello Nick," to direct "Eff off."

I opened my mouth and emitted a croaking "Ah," and then... nothing. I blinked, shook my head, opened my mouth wider, and tried again. "Ah," I choked.

Nick smiled and closed the distance between us in slow motion, placing his lips against my cheek. It wasn't enough pressure to be a kiss, leaving only a faint impression of mouth on skin. He pulled back, looked me in the eyes, and winked. He took a slow step backward, still holding my gaze, then turned and sauntered out the lobby door, whistling. I heard Sunny call out a startled "Nick Elms?"

I stood, holding my purse and my breath, staring at the gymnasium door, then forced myself to move. I needed my best friend. But first, a drink.

"Um, may I ask what that little scene was all about?" Beth wore a wicked smile as I approached with a rum and Coke in each hand.

"Stop it." I frowned as I handed over her drink. "You look demonic."

She smiled wider. "I will not stop it. What was that? Nancy and I watched the whole thing from the food table. You looked like you'd seen a ghost."

I glanced over at the food table. A woman I now recognized

as an older version of Beth's chemistry partner, Nancy Toler, waved at me from beside a veggie tray.

"It felt like I'd seen a ghost. That was Nick."

"Well, no kidding, it was Nick. What did he say? Don't tell me—he came all this way to say he was sorry for dumping you and then ditching you." Beth drained her drink in one long swallow.

"At the dam?" I set up our old joke.

"The damn dam," Beth replied automatically.

"The damn dam," I parroted, raising my glass in a toast and drinking deeply.

"So, what did he say?"

I shook my head. "Honestly, nothing. He said hi, I dropped my purse, he picked it up and gave it back. Then he left."

"After kissing you."

"He didn't kiss me."

"Oh? From where I was standing, it didn't look like he was offering to do your taxes."

The spot where Nick had held his mouth burned. I felt like everyone could see it. My hand floated up and rubbed my cheek. Beth raised an eyebrow but said nothing.

How did I feel? What had been the point of that? After all this time, Nick showed up to do what exactly? Embarrass me? Check me out?

Claim me?

"Well, I need another drink," Beth said, breaking the moment and taking my arm.

Nancy joined us at the bar, and she and Beth ordered new drinks and resumed their conversation. I sipped my rum and Coke, the soda warm and flat, the rum watered-down, and looked around the room.

Corinne is not looking for Nick.

At first appearance, strangers filled the gym—middle-aged adults I'd never seen before. But as my gaze drifted around again, the veil of time fell away, and I started to recognize the kids I'd known. The man with his jacket slung casually over one shoulder was Chance Beckett, Clemmons High's former starting quarterback. The woman with the bumped bob standing too close to him and fingering his tie between her manicured fingers was Ronnie Parker, our class valedictorian. Ronnie and Chance had been a tempestuous, popular couple famous for their epic breakups and makeups during our junior and senior years. Even now, they were giving off an R-rated vibe from across the room.

I nudged Beth as we left the bar and returned to our positions near the food table. "Did you see Ronnie and Chance?"

Nancy giggled. "Just like old times, right? She's divorced; he's separated. They hooked up over Facebook after the reunion invites went out."

"Really? How do you know that?" I asked, still staring as Chance leaned forward to whisper in Ronnie's ear. She shrieked and slapped at his chest, laughing, clearly loving whatever he'd said. My mind went back to Nick. What if I'd responded like that? Would he still be here? Had I failed a test I didn't even know I was taking?

Nancy shrugged, cutting across my spiraling thoughts. "Ronnie and I are Facebook friends. She changed her status from 'Single' to 'It's Complicated' to 'In a Relationship' in the span of a week. And he posts cheesy song lyrics on her page. 'Pour Some Sugar on Me?'" Nancy made a face. "It's not too hard to figure out."

I shook my head. I was on Facebook, but mostly to keep up with school gossip and PTA events. I also periodically searched Audra's name to check that she wasn't showing up anywhere sketchy, but I never posted anything personal. What was there to say, really? Audra said I was what was known as a "lurker," always observing, never participating.

As on Facebook, so in life.

I skimmed the room again. Under the tulle-twined basketball

net, a crowd of Lilly Pulitzered blondes clustered together, their faces turned inward, their backs to us. Amid the strains of Wang Chung, I could hear cackles of laughter meant to signify that theirs was a hilarious private club to which all others were not privy. I glanced down at my shoes, toeing the faded basketball court markings. I was literally standing on the sidelines.

Oh, life.

"Want to bet they're passing around the peach schnapps?" Beth commented blithely.

Nancy smiled and shook her head. "No way. Rhonda's husband is a rep for some big drug firm down in Indy. If they're passing around anything, it's good stuff."

"Which one is Rhonda?" I pounced, eager to see the closest thing I'd had to a nemesis in high school. Nancy raised her hand as if toasting us with her drink and counted off heads with her pinky. "Six o'clock. Blue paisley shift."

My eyes swung around the circle of identical bobs and outfits, and... yes! Her blonde hair and boobs were still big, possibly fake, but her blue paisley ass was bigger.

"Ha!" I crowed in triumph. It felt good to confirm that I was now thinner than the girl who once called me a "cottage-cheese-thighed little priss" during intramural volleyball. I might have blown my big reunion with Nick, but this moment was a sweet victory.

Casually, I dug my phone from my purse and raised it in a show of taking a selfie, capturing Rhonda mid-body roll, and fired off a text to Sean:

Target acquired. Poetic justice attained.

I turned back to Beth and Nancy, who, understanding, raised their Solo cups in solidarity. Together we upended the remainder of our drinks.

"Next round is on me, ladies," I said. "We're celebrating."

I sashayed back to the bar, caught up in the excitement of the night for the first time. Who knew what other surprises were in store for this night? I was ready for anything.

Forget you, Nick.

Corinne crosses the gym, a victorious swing to her hips. Rhonda looks on in jealousy and tugs at her Spanx.

I ordered three Sex on the Beaches and was jauntily helping myself to extra maraschino cherries when I felt a presence next to me.

The hairs on the back of my neck stood on end. I knew without looking.

This time, I met Nick's eyes. *Oh, God.* Those eyes. Heavy-lidded and sexy, as if he'd woken from a deep sleep. The lazy smile, which started at the right side of his mouth, took its time traveling to the left. His eyes had more creases in the corners, and the parentheses framing his smile seemed permanently etched into his skin. His jaw wasn't as sharp as I remembered. In the half-light of the gymnasium, I could see the streaks of silver running through his dark hair.

But oh, God. Still.

The bartender, oblivious to the moment, shoved three obscenely pink drinks between us. "Fifteen dollars," he snapped. The "No Tipping Policy" sign probably had something to do with that.

Nick reached into his back pocket and pulled out a thin wallet, extracting a twenty. "Here," he said, pressing the bill across the counter. "Keep the change."

"Sorry, sir, I'm not allowed to accept tips." He put Nick's change on the counter, scowling.

Nick's eyes stayed locked on mine as he pushed the money back across. "So, have a drink on me." He tapped the counter twice with the flat of his hand as if it were a judge's gavel delivering a verdict.

I gathered two brimming cups in my hands while Nick took the third.

"I'll go deliver these," I said, my voice mercifully steady in the first words I'd spoken to him in a quarter of a century.

"Be right here," he said, indicating a vacant silver-swagged high-top table littered with glitter and abandoned novelty signs from the photo booth. "Homecoming Queen" one said in silver glitter script. A thought bubble read: "I don't remember your name either."

As fast as I could manage without spilling, I hurried over to Beth and Nancy, who had now been joined by several other classmates.

"I'll be back in a minute," I promised, pressing the cups into their hands. It sounded like the lie it was. Distracted by group conversation, they merely nodded, accepting my exit without question. I scuttled away.

As I crossed the gym to where Nick waited, I ran my tongue quickly over my teeth, praying no food (stupid sneaky poppy-seeds) or lipstick resided there. I ran my hands through my hair, hoping I looked casual and unconcerned, and sucked in my stomach, focused on staying upright on my ridiculously high heels.

Nick's look was inscrutable as I joined him, and he pushed my drink toward me.

"Where's yours?" I asked, wishing I'd been cool enough to stop by the bar and grab him a beer. The realization that I still wanted Nick to think I was cool was instantly humiliating.

"Much as I might want one, I haven't had a drink in five years."

"Oh." I fumbled for something to say, and in the silence, my mouth pounced on the first thing my brain thought of: "Why did you leave me that day on the dam?"

Oh, no no no no!

Nick's eyebrows shot up, creasing his forehead while I died inside. "So much for small talk, eh, maiden?"

"I...you..." I stammered, face aflame, struggling to regain my composure. I took a sip of my silly, fruity drink and forced myself to meet his gaze.

Corinne deserves an explanation.

"You disappeared. You disappeared and never came back."

All traces of amusement fled Nick's face. His jaw tightened. "This is not a conversation I want to have here," he said, reaching out across the table. "Let's go."

The feel of his hand, once again on mine, rendered me powerless to protest. I trailed behind him, abandoning my drink, my best friend, and our reunion. Nick led us out of the gym's side door, the one marked "Do not exit or alarm will sound," which sat propped open with a concrete block. I thought of the scene in *The Wizard of Oz* in which Dorothy and her friends arrive at the Emerald City doors only to find the sign reading: "Bell out of order. Please knock." I was leaving Kansas and entering Oz. In all my daydreams of Nick, I'd never imagined it would happen in quite this way, a confrontation and an escape all within moments.

Nick hurried across the parking lot, his hand an iron vice on mine. I struggled to keep up, a few steps behind in my impractical shoes. We passed several groups on their way to or from cars and got a couple of catcalls: "What's the hurry? You're going the wrong way!"

Nick pulled out a key fob and pointed it at a truck sitting forlornly in an unlit corner of the backlot, looking for all the world like the automotive version of Nick sitting in the back of English class. As we approached, he released my hand and went to the driver's side, pulling open the door and climbing in. After a slight pause—Sean always opened my car door for me—I rounded the truck and pulled open the passenger's side door. Papers and various drive-thru containers wafted out to freedom.

"Hang on," Nick said, leaning over to scoop the remaining papers out of the passenger's seat and into the back, where a duffel bag yawned open, spilling clothes, cords, and other unidentifiable shapes out across the floor.

I collected the papers at my feet. Maps, menus, brochures featuring various Alaskan towns. A yellow legal pad, filled with Nick's cramped, smudged handwriting. An empty Starbucks cup fell to the ground and rolled underneath the truck.

I handed the papers to Nick and climbed in, brushing stray crumbs off the seat before settling back. As the truck came to life with a labored roar, any hope of a discreet getaway disappeared. I scrunched down, not wanting to be seen. I'd wanted this moment, fantasized about this moment, but now that it was here, it seemed tawdry—the married former cheerleader sneaking off with her bad-boy ex. If Nick noticed my discomfort, he didn't say. He pulled out of the parking lot and sped down the long country road toward town. I watched as the houses grew closer together, the lights from their windows spilling out across driveways, lawns, sidewalks.

Nervous chatter bubbled out of me to fill the silence. "It's strange being back, isn't it? Can you believe how old everybody looks? I mean, I know we're older, but we don't look *old* old, do we?"

Nick grinned as the truck shuddered to stop for a red light. "No, maiden, we look fine. Everyone else got old."

I hoped he might elaborate. "Fine" was not the adjective I'd dreamt he'd used to describe seeing me. Breathtaking, ageless, gorgeous, maybe. But he didn't, and we lapsed into silence.

The light turned green. Nick gunned through the intersection, crossed the train tracks, and hung a left. I realized where we were going. The dam. The *damn* dam. Of course.

I shivered, not from the cold, but from anticipation. I was going to get answers. Finally.

Corinne sits straighter, gazing out the window. She is reso-

lute, stone. He wants her forgiveness. He wants to apologize. He raises a hand to reach across the seat and strokes her cheek. Leaning in, his eyes on hers...

Nick pulled into the parking lot at the upper picnic area. Turning off the engine, he leaned across the seat toward me. My heart raced. It was happening, just like the movie in my head! A small gasp escaped my mouth as Nick reached out...

...and pulled a canvas jacket from behind the passenger seat. He offered it to me.

Mortified, I took it. "Thanks," I mumbled.

Nick exited the truck, leaving the driver's side door standing open. He crossed in front of the headlights, casting his elongated shadow across the sandy parking lot. I waited, expecting him to appear at my side and hold the door. When he didn't, I felt for the handle, and wrestled with the reluctant latch until it finally gave way and the door flew open, pulling me with it. My foot twisted in my shoe as I stepped out hard onto the running board.

Holding the doorframe for balance, I untied the bows of my ankle straps, slid my feet out, and tossed my shoes back inside the truck. I slipped the jacket over my shoulders, fighting an urge to press it to my face and inhale, and went to join Nick.

He led me down the uneven concrete steps toward the picnic area at the water's edge. I shivered as the cold air hit my skin, and instinctively pulled the jacket tighter.

Big mistake.

Nick's scent enveloped me. It was too much, too fast. My knees buckled; I dropped onto the nearest table, leaning forward, my hands on my thighs, my chin to my chest.

Corinne is hyperventilating, choking on the past.

I willed myself to inhale and exhale steadily, counting to four, until my shaky breathing slowed, my eyesight cleared, and my heart resumed its regular rhythm.

I looked up. Nick's back was to me, and he was staring out over the water, hands in his pockets. The crickets chirped in the darkness, and the stars and the moon remained hidden behind invisible clouds. I could hear the water lapping at the edge of the sand and smell the slightly fishy scent that mingled with the musk coming from Nick's coat.

I stayed where I was, motionless, but my treacherous memory traveled back through time, recalling moments of being curled under the protective mantle of Nick's arm, my face pressed to his flannel-covered chest, inhaling this same scent. It was like he was holding me again now.

I exhaled into the silence.

"Okay." Nick's voice was soft. I looked up. He hadn't turned around. I wasn't sure if I was relieved or disappointed that he hadn't been watching me struggle and didn't seem to be having the same overwhelming reaction at our reunion. "Ask me again."

I took another breath. I was exhausted from the effort, drunk on oxygen and nostalgia.

Corinne squares her shoulders and rises to her feet. She has rehearsed this moment, knows her lines. She memorized the script years ago.

"Why did you leave? No apology, no call, no waiting to see if I was okay. Nothing. You drop a bombshell on me about"—I stumbled over Kirsten's name, bitter in my mouth—"*her* and I never heard another word from you for twenty. Five. Years." I punctuated the last three words, making each a complete sentence.

Tears pricked the back of my eyes. I pressed my tongue to the roof of my mouth, willing them away. I would not cry. He wasn't going to hurt me again.

Moonlight peered out from behind the cloud cover and illuminated small movements beneath the water's surface. Nick's reflection stretched across the water, forming a bridge to the other bank. I waited, unable to move, unwilling to join him.

Unless, Beth's voice interjected in my head, *you wanted to push him in.*

I smiled slightly. Maybe, but not yet.

"I didn't leave you," Nick said, still looking away.

I stiffened and started to protest. Sensing it, he turned, holding up his hands.

"I mean, yes, I left you. That lady went to call for help, and I went up to the parking lot to meet the ambulance. I swear," he insisted, seeing the skeptical look on my face. "I thought it was the best thing to do. You were so angry. I knew I was the last person you wanted to see. There was a whole crowd of people taking care of you. I followed the medics back to where you were, and…" He shrugged.

I remained silent. I would not help him.

"You were sitting up. You looked fine. And furious." He looked sheepish. "So I chickened out. I admit it. I got in my car and took off, hating myself. I drove for hours. I didn't know what to do. I loved you, and I'd hurt you…"

His voice broke, and he paused, recovering. "I took the coward's way out. I called my uncle and asked if I could come early, right away. Then I called Kirsten and told her she should come with me. You know, things weren't so good for her at home…" He trailed off. "But I explained all this in my letter," he said, looking at me quizzically.

Now I was the one confused. "What letter? What are you talking about?"

"I wrote you a letter before I left. I gave it to your mom." He shook his head, disbelieving. "You didn't get it?"

"No, I didn't." My resolution to stand my ground wavered, broke. I made my way to where he stood, my bare feet sinking slightly in the cool, damp ground. I remembered that day, the day after the dam. I spent the day in my room resting; my mom called in sick to work. I'd heard the doorbell, heard her answer, and never thought to ask who it was.

Nick had come. We'd been so close.

"My mom…must've thrown it out. She never said a word."

I stood, frozen, hands balled into fists. All the fury I'd pointed at Nick moments ago slid to my mother. How could she?

The betrayal was staggering.

I wanted to reach back through time and pluck Nick's letter from her hands. I wanted to rewrite history: *Corinne opens the door, her face bruised and tear stained. She sees Nick standing there, letter in hand. She opens her arms to him, and they embrace.*

All this time, I'd believed that Nick hadn't cared. That he'd left me behind without a second thought.

My mother had known the truth. She'd watched me grieve his absence and said nothing.

The realization hit me: We could have been together all this time.

Nick reached out to me and, just like that, I was in his arms. It was so much better than his jacket.

I laid my head against his chest and closed my eyes, my body registering the differences between being held by Nick and being held by Sean. Nick was taller by several inches, and my head rested flat against his chest while his arms trapped mine against my body. With Sean, who was only slightly taller than me, I rested my head in the hollow between his neck and shoulder while his arms wrapped around my waist. Sean smelled like laundry and body wash. Nick's smell was darker, its source mysterious. I felt his chin rest on top of my head, the stubble prickling my scalp. Sean was clean-shaven.

"Corinne," Nick murmured into my hair.

Goosebumps rose on my neck. My stomach dropped like we'd crested the highest hill on a roller coaster and were hanging, suspended at the top, before hurtling back toward earth. His arms tightened, and I instinctively squeezed back as best I could in my limited capacity, my lower arms capable only of an awkward T-Rex-like hug.

"I thought about you so much," he said, pressing his lips against my ear now. "Did you ever think about me?"

Only every day, I almost said. My legs shook; my body was melting chocolate. Too much more and I was going to collapse into a wobbling, boneless heap. I was going to melt to the ground, into the water, and wash away.

I couldn't trust myself. If I opened my mouth at this moment, would I tell Nick that yes, I thought about him? That I had a husband and daughter I loved, and yet I spent my days living out a private performance for him?

That if he asked me, right now, to stay with him, I might say yes?

It was that last thought, the prescience that he might ask me something like that, which finally forced me into action. I pulled away. It felt like tearing muscle from bone.

"Nick," I said, stepping a safe distance back and raising my eyes to meet his. "This is...too much to take in. I need some time. Please take me back."

He stared at me, hard. I could feel myself weakening. If he stepped forward and embraced me again, I would not be strong enough to let go.

Corinne stands barefoot in the sand. Nick watches her hair blow loose in the breeze, the lace of her dress hem swirling against her calves.

A moment passed. He dropped his shoulders and shoved his hands in his pockets, acquiescing. It was a pose so familiar that for a moment, I saw two Nicks, one younger, and the one here now, superimposed over one another. Then he moved past me, starting for his truck, and the illusion vanished. I followed him, carefully picking my way across the sand and up the stairs.

In the parking lot, his truck stood with its doors open, the interior light shining. I slid into the passenger's seat, shoes on my lap, sandy feet tucked under me to avoid contact with the truck's none-too-clean floor mats. I wrapped Nick's coat around me tighter, holding myself together.

Nick was more talkative on the drive back. He told me about life in Alaska, how he still lived in Sitka, but spent much of his time traveling, crashing on friends' couches or living out of his truck, writing. How he was back in Clemmons to fix up the old house and get it ready for sale.

Kirsten's name was absent from his monologue, as was any mention of his child.

I contributed only a few "mm-hmms," wanting to ask more, but afraid to interrupt. What other secrets might he reveal? Had I imagined how he stressed the word "alone" in his recounting of his current living situation? My mind was still spinning, grappling with the idea of Nick's missing letter. What if I'd read it? What would have happened then?

What if? What if? What if?

I pulled my phone from my purse, checking my messages, a distraction to quiet the storm in my head. There was a smiley face text from Sean in response to my earlier message. It seemed a lifetime ago. Who was that girl, the one who'd blithely celebrated being thinner than her high school rival? She had nothing in common with the woman who now sat in a messy truck with her ex-boyfriend, saddled with the knowledge that, if not for her mother's interference, they might have spent the last twenty-five years together.

I would never know which version of my life had been erased from existence by a single closing door.

As I stared at my screen, Sean texted again, asking if I was having fun. I flipped the phone face down and stared out the window, watching familiar landmarks slide by. The Miller's house, with the above-ground pool. The drive-in with thirty different flavors of handcrafted milkshakes. The empty lot where kids met to play flashlight tag on summer nights. The gas station that used to be a video rental store, the faded "two-day rentals" sign still posted in its darkened window.

When we finally pulled into the school, I was surprised to see quite a few cars still there, including Beth's. It felt like we'd been gone for hours, years. Nick pulled into the school's carpool lane and put the car in park, keeping the engine idling.

I looked at him in surprise. "Aren't you coming in?"

He shook his head. "I saw everyone I came to see." He reached across the seat, and once again, my heart leaped in anticipation. Instead, he slid the phone from my lap and swiped it with his thumb, illuminating my home screen—a silly picture of me, Sean, and Audra, sunburned and laughing at the beach. Wordlessly, Nick slid his finger across it. The picture disappeared.

His fingers hesitated above my screen. I pointed to the messaging icon in upper right corner. He typed quickly and pressed *send* before I could change my mind.

He held my phone out to me. When I reached for it, he took my hand. He turned it over and brushed his lips against my knuckles, kissing each in turn, carefully avoiding contact with my wedding ring. Then he released my hand and raised his eyes to mine.

"Goodbye, beautiful maiden."

In a daze, I clutched my phone, purse, and shoes to my chest, opened the door, and stepped down, holding his gaze the entire time.

"Bye, Nick," I whispered and closed the door.

Standing on the curb, I watched him pull away, realizing too late that I was still wearing his coat.

As his taillights faded, I looked at my phone. My hands trembled. Fear? Excitement? Both?

He had sent a text to himself from my phone. It read simply:

Call.

* * *

Re-entering the gym, I slid off Nick's jacket and draped it over a stack of chairs by the door and stepped back into my shoes. I hoped to slip into the fringes of the group, work my way over to Beth and pretend like I'd been there the whole time.

No luck.

"Rinni!" Beth shrieked over the music.

"Hey," I said, giving a half-hearted wave. She was dancing with a group of band friends, which I knew because they were now all sporting t-shirts that read "#BandGeek92." Beth had pulled hers over her dress, knotting it at the waist. While I had lived within the insular bubble of the cheer squad, Beth had found her home amongst the "band geeks and theater freaks," as they'd called themselves. I could feel a frisson of tension now as she pulled me into the center of the dance circle. Like a host body rejecting a donor cell, I was still an outsider.

I pulled back, wanting to step out of the crowd and back to the safety of the shadows, but the DJ shifted into "Eternal Flame," and Beth put her arms on my shoulders, holding me like a seventh-grade couple in their first slow dance. I was trapped.

"And where have you been?" she asked, eyes wide in mock innocence. Around us, dancers shifted, subtly expelling us from the group's nucleus.

High school, I mean, it's never over, is it?

"Nowhere." I wasn't ready to share the details with Beth yet. I needed time, space to replay every moment, every emotion of the evening before I could even begin to make sense of it all. "Nick wanted to talk, so we went outside for a minute."

"Oh, really?" Beth looked at me, suspicious. "A minute? You've been gone for at least an hour. You missed Ronnie and Chance being crowned Reunion King and Queen." She motioned with her head at the couple, now wearing plastic crowns, mashed up against the bleachers, making out. I snorted.

"More importantly," Beth continued, "you missed Jonesy puking Boone's Farm all over the bathroom."

Now I laughed out loud. "I am sorry to have missed that. Did you get pictures?" I asked, hoping to move the conversation further away from Nick.

"So, where were you?"

I couldn't fool Beth. She knew my tricks.

"Nick wanted to say he was sorry. You know, for the way he ended things at the dam."

"The damn dam?"

"The damn dam."

"Little late for sorries, isn't it? Like twenty-five years too late?"

I felt immediately defensive. "Well, actually, it turns out that he wrote me a letter explaining everything. He delivered it the next day, but Mom never gave it to me. So…" I trailed off.

Beth huffed her cheeks out and rolled her eyes. "So, he cheated on you, broke up with you, abandoned you with a possible head injury on a bridge, and then ran off with the girl he got pregnant. But he wrote a letter?" Her voice dripped with disdain. "And that's his apology?"

"He didn't know I didn't get it." It was a lame explanation, even to my ears.

"I know it was the nineties, but we still had phones back then, didn't we? Heck, we still had flowers and cards. And trying more than once. Didn't we?" Beth was pissed.

I backed off. "Anyway, it doesn't matter now. It's over. He left." There was no use in arguing. She didn't know. She hadn't been there. She hadn't heard the way he sounded tonight, so regretful, wistful. She hadn't seen the tender way he held me or felt the electricity when he touched me.

Out on the dance floor, The Bangles faded away, replaced by En Vogue. The dancers cheered.

I released Beth's waist and stepped to the side. "I'm tired," I said. "You know, like, emotionally. I'm going to call for a ride back to the hotel." I gestured to the group. "You stay; they look like they could go all night."

Beth's temper was destructive but fast-moving, like a summer hailstorm. I saw the clouds clearing as her eyes traveled back to her other friends. "Oh yeah. Ain't no party like a band geek party. You sure you don't want to stay? There's a bunch of people here you haven't talked to yet. It's been fun catching up with everyone. Did you know Jason's latest documentary made it to Sundance? And Sarah—"

I cut her off. "I'm good. Really. I'll see you back in the room." I blew a kiss, which she caught mid-air and pretended to eat before turning away and rejoining her group with whoops and hollers, the returning queen.

I exited the gym, pausing only to snatch Nick's jacket from the chairs with a guilty backward glance. Now that Nick was gone, no one was looking at me. *I saw everyone I came to see.*

In the empty lobby, I called the Creekside Inn to request shuttle pickup, then went outside to wait on the curb of the carpool loop, wrapped in Nick's jacket. The night sky had cleared, and the moon shone brightly. I waved goodnight to Sunny, who was sitting on the opposite side of the loop, passing a joint around a circle of people who looked like chaperones and couldn't possibly be our age. She smiled and waved back but didn't call me over.

The hotel had said it would take fifteen minutes for my ride. Waiting, I popped a couple of Tic Tacs (thrilling at touching something Nick's hands had held) and texted Sean back:

Had fun. I saw everyone I came to see.

I paused, then deleted the last half of the sentence, replacing it with a string of x's and o's and some heart emojis in a rainbow of colors.

I texted Audra:

> Hope you are having a good weekend.
> Love you.

She texted back a thumbs up. I put my phone away as the Creekside van pulled up to the curb.

On the drive to the hotel, I leaned back in the seat and closed my eyes. Nick's face swam into focus on the blank screen of my eyelids, the same trick as before. I saw Nick from high school and Nick from tonight superimposed over each other.

High School Nick was saying, "I slept with Kirsten."

Tonight Nick said, "Did you think about me?"

High School Nick: "I'm sorry."

Tonight Nick: "I'm sorry."

The shuttle stopped. I heard the *ding* as the automatic door slid open.

"Ma'am, wake up. We're here." The driver's voice was soft, his hand on my shoulder gentle.

I opened my eyes, momentarily lost in time. "Oh? Thank you."

As I exited, he added, "Must've been some party."

"It was quite a night," I answered truthfully before heading into the hotel.

As I fumbled through my purse looking for my key, it occurred to me that my mind had been playing tricks. Not only with visions, but with words.

At no time tonight—or ever—had Nick uttered the words "I'm sorry."

* * *

Inside the dark hotel room, I tossed Nick's coat and my purse onto the bed and kicked off my shoes, grateful to be alone. I hoped, somewhat guiltily, that Beth would be out late. I needed to think.

I turned on the shower and undressed, dropping my clothes in a pile on the slippery tiled floor of the minuscule bathroom. I stood under the stinging spray, letting scalding water run over my closed eyes and down my face, my hands rhythmically smoothing back my hair. I wanted to replay every moment of the evening, but I was so overwhelmed that I could only catch fragments. Nick's silhouette on the bank of the dam. His outstretched hand. The smell of his jacket. The scent of his shirt. The feel of his chin resting atop my head.

Oh, Corinne, you have to stop.

I stayed in the shower until my skin started to itch from the heat. I turned off the water and emerged into a steam-filled room. Water had sloshed over the shallow lip of the stall, and my beautiful black dress lay sodden in a puddle. I wrapped a child-sized bath towel around my body, holding it closed by clamping my arms to my sides, and did my best to wring the dress out over the sink before draping it over the shower rod. I scooted around the floor on the two provided washcloths, trying to soak up the remaining water. I tossed them on the counter, where they landed with a *splat*, throwing water droplets up onto the condensation-covered mirror. Little streaks cleared as they ran down the mirror and dropped back into the sink. I caught sight of myself in the stripes. I looked pale, dazed, lost.

Corinne stares at her reflection. The woman staring back is not the same. She knows the truth now.

The cold of the room was a shock after the heat of the bathroom. I hurriedly dressed in a paint-splattered NC State sweatshirt and my favorite yoga pants, so old and worn that they were indecent to wear in public, and wrapped my hair up with the damp towel. I crawled into bed and flipped through channels before landing on HGTV. I snuggled down under the thin comforter and stared at the couple picking out countertops for their kitchen, Nick's jacket pressed to my face.

"I'm sorry," I heard him say again.

But no, he hadn't said he was sorry. He had said he'd "explained." And that was different.

Corinne lies in bed, her wet hair escaping from the thin white towel, bedding pulled up to her chin, a man's jacket cradled in her arms. Her eyes are large and glassy, her face pale in the glow of the television, dark shadows under her eyes. The clock on the nightstand reads 11:57 in red glowing numbers.

I wondered if Nick was in bed, thinking of me. *Nick lies in bed in the dark. He is shirtless…*

Stop.

I wrenched my attention back to the screen with supreme effort.

I was on my third kitchen renovation show when Beth burst in the door, her key card in one hand, shoes in the other. In the screen's dim glow, I saw that her "#BandGeek92" T-shirt now sported a variety of mysterious streaks and stains. I shoved Nick's jacket under the covers.

"Hey Rinni, baby!" she crowed and took a flying leap onto the bed, narrowly missing my legs. She smelled like smoke— cigarette and otherwise—as well as the sweaty fug of alcohol. I pushed myself up to a sitting position, trying to move out of the direct path of her breath. Beth beamed at me, bleary-eyed and wild-haired, looking like a disreputable hedgehog.

I took a Kleenex from the table situated between our two beds and gently wiped at the makeup pooled under her eyes. "Looks like someone had a little fun tonight." I dropped the tissue on the comforter and smoothed her hair off her forehead. Her eyes closed at my touch.

"S'fun," she mumbled. "Travis had spray paint, tagged the big rock outside the cafeteria…" Her breathing slowed; she was already falling asleep, curling into fetal position. I climbed out of bed and gently pulled her to her feet, using my best mom voice.

"Come on, sweetie. That's right, Bethie. Good girl." I coaxed her out of the paint-smeared shirt and cleaned her face with a makeup wipe. Retrieving her toothbrush and toothpaste from the bathroom counter, I dry-brushed the teeth I could reach while she growled at me, then guided her to bed. She climbed on top of the covers, leather dress creaking in protest. I dug in my purse and found two aspirin, which she swallowed with the help of an overpriced water from the mini fridge. I had just finished pulling the blankets around her burrito-style when my phone *ping*ed on the nightstand.

It was a reply sent from the number Nick had entered earlier. This one read:

Still yours.

"Who'sh that?" Beth slurred, half-conscious. She lifted her head off the pillow and squinted at me.

I hid the phone screen against my chest. "No one," I said. "Go to sleep. It's no one." A moment later, she began to snore.

I climbed back into bed and turned off the TV. In the dark, I stared at the dim light of my screen.

Call.

Still yours.

I stared until my eyes started to close, and I felt myself drifting off, phone clutched in my hand.

My last waking thought: *Corinne is in trouble.*

Chapter 6

I awoke the next morning to the incredible sight of Beth scurrying around the room, showered, dressed, and humming cheerily as she packed. I fumbled for my phone. 8:30 a.m. One new text from Sean:

Good morning! See you soon!

He'd signed off with a line of smiling suns. I groaned.

"Good morning!" Beth chirped, looking for all the world like a smiling sunshine emoji herself. She carried an armload of products from our bathroom and dumped them on her bed. "Sunny arranged a class breakfast at Queen's, so you need to get moving. We'll head to the airport from there."

"How... how are you even awake?" I propped myself up on my elbows and watched in astonishment as she cheerfully threw everything into her toiletry bag. I never came fully awake until my second cup of coffee and was used to slow starts on weekends. Beth looked like she could run a marathon.

"Oh, I've had three cups of terrible hotel coffee already." Beth zipped up her suitcase. "Remember, I have a small child who never sleeps. I am trained to wake up at first light, no matter what time zone I'm in." She winked as she passed my bed en route to the closet. She wore faded, ripped jeans, low-top Converse, and a T-shirt reading "I can't even think straight" in large rainbow letters. Her jacket was slung over our room's only armchair, along with her crossbody bag, which belched its contents onto the floor.

"Oh, and we need to get my car," she added. "So we should leave soon." Packing done, she flopped into the armchair, on top of her jacket and bag. Rummaging under the seat cushion, she pulled out her phone and began thumbing furiously.

"Oh my God, Beth!" I sat up, chagrined that I hadn't even questioned how she'd gotten to the hotel last night. I'd been so wrapped up in myself that her safety had never occurred to me. I'd abandoned her. What kind of friend was I? "How did you get back?"

Beth laughed at something on her screen and waved her hand dismissively. "Don't even worry about it. Nancy gave me a ride."

Shamefaced, I forced myself into action, retreating to the bathroom to cover my embarrassment. This was what Nick did to me; he pushed everyone else out of my head. No wonder he and Beth had never gotten along.

I washed my face and brushed out my hair. I had gone to bed with it wet, and it had dried into the shape of my pillow. I pulled it back with one of Audra's old scrunchies, black velvet with a few cat hairs stuck to it. An extra coat of mascara to open my puffy eyes, and a dusting of powder to even out my blotchy skin, Chapstick for my lips, cracked from the hotel's recirculated air. Plain black cotton jumpsuit, chosen for comfort. I surveyed my reflection dubiously. Was I dressed too casually? Would I look washed out in the harsh light of day? Did I look old? What would Nick think if he could see me?

The thought stopped me. Nick. Oh, God. Would he be at breakfast?

"Beth," I called through the door, "I'm going to take a shower!"

* * *

While I finished the fastest shower of my life and brushed my hair back into a wet bun, Beth called the front desk to arrange for the hotel shuttle to take us to the high school. When the dark-blue SUV rolled up, I realized it was the same driver as the night before. I hurried around to the trunk, tossed my suitcase in, and took the seat directly behind the driver, hoping to remain anonymous. Beth climbed in the front seat and shot a curious look over her shoulder at me.

"Hey, it's Sleeping Beauty," the driver said, catching sight of me in his rearview mirror. He pushed his Detroit Tigers ball cap back on his forehead and pulled out of the Creekside lot, turning left to make the trip to Clemmons.

"Oh, uh, that's right. Hi again." Not wanting to invite further conversation, I busied myself replying to Sean's text:

Reunion breakfast, then airport. Miss you.

The driver looked from me to Beth. "That must have been some party. She was out like a light—snored the whole way here."

Beth laughed and began regaling him with stories from last night's activities. "She wasn't even around for most of it...Let me tell you about..."

Tuning her out, I stowed my phone and pulled out my makeup bag, wanting to get my face in order, just in case. Foundation, powder, mascara, blush. I poked myself in the eye with my liner pencil as we hit a pothole. The final product wasn't too bad. I was still dressed for traveling, but I'd added back my dangling silver earrings from last night and swapped out my threadbare cardigan for Beth's jacket.

I suddenly sat up, remembering Nick's jacket, forgotten among the rumpled bedsheets. I'd fallen asleep with it pressed to my face, my arms snaked up through the sleeves like a hug. I'd known I couldn't take the jacket home with me—how would I explain it—but the fact that I'd left it behind on accident stung, a forgotten goodbye. The sour taste of loss flooded my mouth, and I fought the urge to burst into tears, like a child who'd dropped her ice cream or let go of a balloon string.

"You okay, Rinni?" Beth threw a look over her shoulder.

I nodded, rearranging my face into a smile. "Everything's fine." Feigning nonchalance, I pulled out my lipstick and added a raspberry pink slick of gloss to my mouth while a hard knot of regret formed in my stomach. Nick's jacket was gone.

Our driver shook our hands at the school parking lot as we transferred luggage from his van to our car. He lifted his cap in farewell. "Come back and see us again soon."

"We just might do that, Jared," Beth called as we climbed into the car. She peeled out of the lot, kicking up a cloud of country road dust. I watched in my side mirror as Jared, coughing in our wake, grew smaller and smaller until he disappeared altogether.

* * *

We pulled up to the Breakfast Queen, known simply as "Queen's," shortly after ten o'clock. "Food fit for royalty since 1956," the crown-shaped sign announced from its perch atop the roof. The crushed gravel parking lot was packed with minivans and hybrids, decorated with stick families and "Proud Parent" bumper stickers. Sunny had clearly been successful in relocating most of our class for a final send off. My body hummed, nerves on high alert, as I scanned for a black truck with Alaska plates.

Beth pushed through the front door and into the crowd. I followed a few steps behind, still searching for Nick, and was assaulted by details instantly remembered. The yellow and brown interior was exactly as it had been two decades earlier, the only addition a huge flat-screen TV wedged above the jukebox on the far side of the restaurant. Sports highlights flashed, adding visual noise to the cacophony of dozens of hungover, overly caffeinated adults making the most of the last hours of their weekend hall passes before saying goodbye and heading back to lives of soccer tournaments and upstanding citizenry. The smell of coffee and frying bacon was both mouthwatering and nauseating, and I swallowed hard against a surge of bile at the back of my throat.

The diner's usual layout of tables had been rearranged into a replica of the Clemmons High School cafeteria hierarchy. The jocks sat immediately under the TV. Rhonda and her cronies sat at the next table, pretending to ignore the jocks' antics as they sipped their waters and picked at their fruit bowls. Former band and theater kids sat against the windows, where they could perform for the room as well as anyone watching from the parking lot. Beth beelined to her group among catcalls and whoops, leaving me alone, unclaimed in the crowd.

Corinne stands, frozen, her eyes raking over the room, searching...

"Corinne Murphy? Oh my God, it *is* you!"

Directly in front of me sat three members of the 1992 Clemmons varsity cheer squad. Seated at the head of the table, I saw the familiar face of Jenny Byers. How had I missed her last night? Just like this morning with Beth at the hotel, I felt another flash of remorse. I'd done what I'd always done where Nick was concerned; let him take over my thoughts, my actions. I'd handed him control of my life, and he'd taken me out of whatever experience everyone here had shared.

Always the outsider.

"Come SIT with us!" Jenny jumped up to give me a hug, which I was too startled to return. "I HEARD you were HERE!" Up close, I still couldn't tell if it was lucky genetics or good surgery that kept her looking the same age as she appeared in my memories.

"Jenny! Hi," I gasped, regaining my voice. "It's great to see you, too."

Everyone shuffled down to make room for me. Jenny retrieved an extra chair from another table, and an empty mug appeared, followed by a carafe of coffee. I poured myself a cup and drank gratefully. Jenny sat on my right. Beyond Jenny sat Heidi Graff, her infamous red hair now buzzed short and flecked with white. On my left was a girl who seemed familiar, but I couldn't place her. She caught me staring.

"Sorry," I said and extended my hand. "Corinne Murphy Fuller."

She took my hand in hers. "Brittany Huggins-Martinez. You were a base. I was a flier."

"Of course." I smacked my forehead with my hand. "I'm sorry, Brittany. I'm so bad with faces now."

Brittany laughed. "Don't worry about it," she reassured me. "I think we all look a little different without the liquid liner and crunchy perms." She ran her hand over her smooth pixie cut.

"How ARE you, Corinne?" asked Jenny. I remembered her ability to speak as if all in capital letters, which had made her a great cheer captain, but difficult to maintain a one-on-one conversation with. I smiled and shifted my eyes from her to Heidi to Brittany.

While not on par with Beth in terms of closeness, these girls had comprised most of my social life during my high school years. I'd spent hours with them: practicing, cheering at games, hanging out. Until Nick, of course.

I glanced around the room again. He still hadn't appeared.

Turning my attention back to the women at the table, we

began chatting, trading details about our lives. Jenny was a nurse, Heidi a marketing executive for a national fast-food chain.

"I'm not working right now," I hedged when my turn came. I borrowed Sunny's line: "My daughter is only a couple of years away from graduating and I want to soak up all the time I have left with her." Heads around the table nodded in agreement, and Brittany squeezed my arm in solidarity.

It turned out that Brittany had lived for several years in Raleigh before her husband's job transferred their family to upstate New York. "I wish I'd known you were so close," she wailed. "We could've gotten together." She pulled out her phone. "Are we Facebook friends? Do I follow you on Instagram? Are you part of the Clemmons 92 group?" she asked in rapid-fire succession.

"I have a Facebook account, but I hardly ever use it." Too tempting to search for Nick.

Heidi had already typed my name in. "That's okay. The point is to belong. You don't have to do anything after that if you don't want to." She handed her phone to me. "Click on your profile." I selected my profile picture, a generic photo of a gerbera daisy, from the list of Corinne Fullers and handed it back.

She beamed. "I'll add you to the Reunion Group and the Cheer Group. Of course, it would've been better if you'd been on before the reunion, but still...we're all talking about making this an annual thing for squad sisters. Right, Jenny?"

"For SURE. We've already talked about meeting up some-where for a beach weekend next summer. Especially since KIRSTEN couldn't make it..." Jenny trailed off, realizing what she'd said, and to whom. "Oh, uh, I mean..." she stammered, looking around helplessly. Heidi stared at her phone. Brittany looked entranced by whatever was in the bottom of her coffee mug.

My curiosity was too big to let the subject drop. "Don't

worry about it, Jen. It was a long time ago." I forced a smile and a small laugh. "Where is she this weekend?

Brittany looked up from her coffee cup. "She's, ah, at a wedding in Seattle. Her daughter got married yesterday."

"Oh," I said, "that's nice..." And then it hit me. Kirsten's daughter was old enough to get married. Which meant she was probably in her twenties.

Or twenty-five, to be exact.

Nick's daughter had gotten married yesterday.

I wrestled my face into a flat mask of polite interest. "Kirsten must've been so excited. No wonder she couldn't make the reunion." I sipped my coffee, stalling as my mind leapfrogged over reason and directly to wild conclusions: why was Nick here instead of Seattle? For me?

The rest of the brunch went by in a blur. I nodded and smiled and even contributed a sentence or two when necessary, all while keeping one eye trained on the door. Nick and Kirsten and his daughter and me. What was going on?

Finally, it was time to go. I made my excuses, bestowed several hugs and promises to stay in touch, and collected a reluctant-to-leave Beth.

We made our way back to the door slowly, with Beth continuing to call out to people as we passed by. "See you, Tom! Jonesy...keep in touch!" She stopped to give Sunny a hug. "Thank you for everything, Sunny. It was great!"

Sunny, looking younger this morning in jeans and a Warriors Athletics Boosters sweatshirt, hugged her back. "It was a blast! Stay in touch." Sunny released Beth and waved to me. "Bye, Corinne! It was good seeing you!"

In the lot, Beth tossed me the car keys. "Do you mind driving?" she asked. "I have a massive headache."

I gave her a wry smile. "On behalf of the entire state of Michigan, I fully support you not driving."

She stuck her tongue out at me. "Haha. I drive with purpose and intent."

I returned the face. "Is that what we're calling road rage nowadays?"

I adjusted the seat and mirrors while Beth dug in her purse and came up with a bottle of aspirin. Popping the lid with her thumb, she tossed two pills back and swallowed them dry before reclining the passenger's seat and sliding her sunglasses on. "Just need to rest for a few minutes," she said, closing her eyes and throwing her arm across her forehead.

I took the aspirin bottle from her and placed it in the Malibu's cup holder, within easy reach, smiling to myself. Even Beth had her limits now. We definitely weren't in high school any longer. It was time to go back to the real world.

I pulled out of the parking lot, heading east. The fastest way to get to the highway was to cut back through Clemmons and pick up the ramp south of town. However, I turned one street shy of Main Street and headed north. In my head, I prepared my excuses in case Beth noticed the change in direction.

Corinne drives slowly, scanning right and left, hands clenching the wheel.

There it was.

Four houses in from the corner. The two-story yellow house with a wraparound porch cluttered with wicker furniture and a refrigerator. The shutters had been repainted blue at some point, but otherwise, it was exactly as I remembered it.

Nick's house.

I eased my foot off the gas, going as slowly as I dared without coming to a full stop. I could see the alley and the separate garage behind the house, which stood open to display the front end of a dark truck with Alaska plates.

The urge to pull over and ring the doorbell was painful; my fingers twitched on the wheel, my traitorous body drawn toward the possibility of Nick. The car coasted by, almost at a crawl. I leaned forward, the seat belt cutting into my neck, and looked up at the second-floor window on the side of the house, the one that used to be Nick's bedroom. I thought I saw the curtains twitch. Was he up there, watching me? Or was it a trick of the light on the glass?

My heart raced, and I touched my foot down on the accelerator, speeding up. Small towns were always watching. I would make another loop, go around the block, drive by again. By then, Nick would have had time to come outside. I'd drive by, and he'd be on the porch, waiting. And then...

"Rin, what are you doing?" Beth's voice made me jump. She wasn't sitting up, but she'd turned her head and was looking at me, her glasses pulled low on the bridge of her nose.

"Uh..." Startled, I jammed my foot down on the gas, pushing us both against the seatbacks as the car lurched forward. "Nothing. I'm taking a last drive around town. You know, saying goodbye." My cheeks flamed. Beth pushed her glasses up with her index finger and turned away, shaking her head, but said nothing.

As I reached the corner, I turned right and headed into town and toward the highway. I could see the yellow house fading away in the rearview mirror, a figure standing in the yard, one hand raised, as if in farewell.

* * *

Beth perked up again on the way to the airport. Still reclined, she peppered me with questions that she answered herself. "And did you see Louis? Can you believe that was the same kid who used to get shoved into lockers? I mean, I'm no expert on the male form, but he looked incredible..."

I hadn't noticed Louis. I hadn't swapped life stories with Katrina, now a doctor and living in Chicago. I hadn't seen Chance propose to Ronnie in the parking lot. I hadn't seen that Martina Drake had shown up in a leather jumpsuit, looking like she was "made of plastic." Nick and I had always been the only two people in the room when we were together.

I made appropriate "mm-hmmm" noises while I turned the knowledge that Nick had skipped his daughter's wedding (for me?) around and around in my mind.

What did it mean? Was I flattered? Was I disgusted?

I couldn't help but think that if Sean skipped Audra's wedding for any reason, no price would be too high for the hitman I would hire to take him down. On the other hand, I couldn't deny the flutter of excitement that Nick had come specifically to see me. It had been a long time since Sean had made any sort of big romantic gesture on my behalf. Yes, he bought me flowers and gifts on the correct holidays and even surprised me with a date night now and again. But driving three thousand miles for one night, that was, well, it was… romantic. It was grand. Whatever Nick's motivation, it had worked. I was intrigued.

Corinne drums her fingers along the steering wheel, lost in thought. What are you up to, Nick Elms? What do you want? She thinks of Nick's texts, buried safely in her purse, and flushes a deep red.

* * *

Beth and I parted ways at the concourse. I teared up as we hugged goodbye, realizing that it could be years before we had this kind of time together again, guilty that I hadn't spent every second with her. Beth looked uncharacteristically weepy-eyed as she released me from a final rib-crushing hug.

"Think about Cleveland next month. I don't want the next time I see you to be Dante's high school graduation."

"I will," I promised, "I will." My phone buzzed in my purse, and I automatically pulled it out to check the screen:

Bye.

Nick. Another roller coaster drop of the stomach. I shoved my phone in my back pocket.

"Who was that?" Beth asked.

"Oh." I shrugged, hugging her again to hide the smile that threatened to overtake my face. "Nobody."

Chapter 7

Being gone for a weekend had put me behind in laundry, groceries, and housework. It seemed that in my absence Sean and Audra had used every dish in the house and left them all in the sink, where they morphed into a single stinking, food-caked mess. The laundry basket had mounted an aggressive takeover of the hallway, and there was nothing to eat besides cereal.

In celebration of my homecoming, Sean ordered dinner in: a crusty loaf of bread, caprese salad, marinated olives, risotto with peas and scallops. He served everything with a flourish on paper plates.

"Ta-da! No dishes!"

Audra was uncharacteristically talkative, asking about the reunion, Beth, how it felt to go back to high school after "all these years." The irony didn't escape me that this was the most interest she'd shown in me in months, and it was the first time I didn't feel like talking.

"It was weird," I hedged, helping myself to another slice of mozzarella. Sean, unasked, refilled my plastic cup with wine. "Until this weekend, everyone was still eighteen in my memory. But now, they're all old."

Sean laughed. "Which is why we didn't go to my reunion,

remember? I like my memories the way they are. It would be inconvenient to have to update them."

"Just you wait," I told Audra, pointing my fork at her. "Someday, you'll go back, and you'll wonder where all the time went. It'll feel like yesterday..."

"And a million years ago at the same time," Sean finished.

"Exactly." I nodded and popped an olive into my mouth.

Corinne remembers seeing Nick only a few hours ago, standing in his yard, watching her as she drives away.

Already, it felt like a million years ago.

That night, after Sean fell asleep in the tangled sheets of our welcome-home-sex, I climbed out of bed and took my phone into the family room. I sat in the dark watching Season 1 of *Northern Exposure* with the volume on low, hoping, praying for another message from Nick. When nothing came by 3:00 a.m., I snuck back into bed, only to wake two hours later and start checking my screen all over again.

* * *

While I outwardly chastised Sean and Audra for the house's state, I was secretly glad for the easy distraction of housework. It kept me away from my new obsession, checking my phone for more texts from Nick. I was afraid of what would happen if he reached out again, yet bitterly disappointed when he didn't.

What did *bye* mean? *Bye* for now? *Bye* forever? If he was saying goodbye forever, why did he even bother coming to the reunion? We'd already been at that stage until Saturday. And why wouldn't he reach out to me? Didn't he know that I couldn't call him? I had a husband, a child. Calling him first would be too much. However, if he called me, I could rationalize that I was simply continuing a relationship with an old friend who'd reached out after the reunion.

Perfectly natural. Harmless. Move along; nothing to see.

But he didn't call. He didn't text. He didn't anything. And so, I cleaned. I organized the linen cupboard and purged our bookshelves. I wiped down walls and patched paint on baseboards. Meowsers got his first bath in months and spent the rest of the day hiding under Audra's bed. I rented a steam cleaner and attacked the bedroom carpets.

And as I cleaned, I imagined Nick watching. *Corinne washes the dishes. Corinne makes the bed. Corinne lives her life.* Nick, whom I could now picture in present-day terms. The deep lines in his face. The strands of silver in his hair. The solidity of his middle-aged frame. All cataloged and updated.

And, as always, compared to Sean. Sean, who was older, thinner, grayer than Nick. Sean, who was home every evening and in my bed every night. Nick, who lounged in unseen chairs and slept in anonymous rooms. Sean, who sent me logistics-laden texts:

Stopping at Walmart. Need anything?

Brakes squealing. Can u make appt?

Nick, who texted in monosyllabic declarations:

Call.

Still yours.

Bye.

I roamed the house at night, visiting memories of the life I'd built with Sean, wondering what my life would look like if I shared this house with Nick. Would his poetry books line our shelves instead of Harry Potter and John Grisham? Would our framed photos be of world travels and adventures instead of recitals and family vacations? Would he have agreed to a blue velvet couch or the jewel-toned rug that I'd lugged back from an estate sale? Would it be too cold to hang lights from the trees in Alaska? Would we even have a house, or would we live in temporary spaces between adventures, sparsely furnished rented rooms bereft of memories?

I lived in my head, distracted and disjointed. Even Audra commented.

"God, Mom," she said one morning as she appeared for breakfast and saw me staring at my phone, a cold cup of coffee on the table. I was grateful she didn't know I'd been in that spot all night, unable to sleep, searching online for Nick. "You're so flaky lately."

She threw something on the table on her way to the refrigerator. "Here," she said. "There's a design class I want to take. I already checked with work. They said they'd move me from Thursdays to Tuesdays. It starts next week."

I picked up the brochure. Audra had already completed the attached registration form in small, neat block letters, including, I noticed, my credit card information. I scanned the page she'd marked with a paper clip. It was a ten-week course in interior design. Despite the credit card information (clearly an issue to be addressed), I started to get excited. I looked up, saw Audra watching me, body coiled, ready to protest, waiting for mean old mom to say no.

I smiled, genuinely pleased. "Honey, I think this is great!"

Her eyes widened in surprise. Not the response she was expecting, but I, too, could play the good cop sometimes.

"As long as you've cleared this with work and your grades stay up, I can't think of any reason not to do this." I kept smiling at her and was amused to see her physically fight the smile that threatened to spread across her face.

I took my chance. I stood, crossed to her, and hugged her.

After a momentary flinch, she hugged me back. "Thanks!" She dropped her arms much too quickly; I could've stood there all day. She reached around me and snatched the registration form from the table. "I'll drop it off today after school." Folding the paper, she slid it into her overstuffed book bag. I bit back a reprimand and hoped a rumpled registration form wouldn't count against her. Backpack slung over her shoulder, she backed out of the room, granting me another rare smile. "Bye."

My heart pounded, threatening to explode with happiness. I sat back down at the table, beaming, basking in the momentary victory.

Corinne sits in her kitchen, smiling contentedly. Her hands drift over the table, landing on the colorful brochure of courses. Still smiling, she flips through the pages, stopping at a class on photography.

* * *

My father gave me my first camera when I was ten, the first Christmas after leaving my mother and me. It came in a box with a letter addressed to me from his new home in Utah.

"You have a photographer's eye, just like your old man," he wrote.

I was conflicted about the camera, a Nikon FA. Even at my young age, I realized that it was too adult and expensive for a kid. It was the most beautiful thing I'd ever seen, and I wanted so badly to pick it up and start taking pictures. But I worried that to do so would be a betrayal to my mother. I put my beautiful gift on the high shelf in my closet alongside my out-of-season clothes and left it untouched.

One night at bedtime, my mother came into my room, took the camera down, and handed it to me, along with a paper bag containing three rolls of film.

"It's okay, honey," she said, sitting on my bed and pulling me close, camera in my lap. "You can like a gift he gave you." She tapped my chest over my heart.

"Not everyone is as black and white as the characters in your fairy tales," she continued. "Or in photos, if you prefer. Your father isn't a wholly terrible man. He's a mostly good man who did a terrible thing to us. But you can love the good and forgive the bad. We all have some hero and some villain in us." She smoothed my hair back and took my face in her hands, looking into my eyes, our noses almost touching. "It's our choices that determine which part people see."

* * *

I woke, still seated at the kitchen table, my head resting on my arms, the brochure still held lightly between the fingers of my right hand.

Corinne wakes, disoriented, in a shaft of sunlight falling across the kitchen table.

I wiped a line of drool from the corner of my mouth. I caught the last moment of my dream; my mother, the camera, hero or villain. I shook my head and pushed back from the table, taking my coffee cup to the sink.

Later, as I loaded the last of the laundry into the wash, I realized I was officially caught up on housework. I cast about for what I could do next, how I would distract myself. I rechecked my phone, nothing from Nick.

Throwing myself down onto the couch, I buried my hands in my hair, tugging at the roots until my scalp burned. I thought about Nick, where he might be, what he might be doing. Was he thinking about me like I was thinking about him? He couldn't be, or he would have reached out again. Why would he torture me like this? Surely, if he was, as he said, still mine, he would care enough to do something to prove it.

Whatever, the little Beth voice in my head scoffed. *He's doing what he's always done, Rinni. He's playing with you.*

No, he's not. You don't understand. It's complicated.

91

Whatever, Beth repeated and disappeared.

I groaned and stretched out on the couch, clutching a throw pillow to my chest. I closed my eyes and envisioned Nick as he'd been at the dam, standing at the water's edge, reaching for me, so vulnerable. He hadn't been faking then, had he? He'd been raw, exposed, desperate for the chance to put things right. To explain why he'd gone, how he'd had no other choice.

My thoughts slid sideways to the letter my mother had intercepted. Anger and regret churned in my stomach. How could she do that to me? How could she sabotage her own daughter's happiness? I wished, more than anything, that I could read that letter, know what it said. That I could, even for an instant, see what my life might have been like if she hadn't interfered.

I sat up, realization hitting me—the boxes in the garage. When we'd moved Mom here, I'd gone out to Ohio to pack her things. At the time, she was living in a small one-bedroom apartment in Columbus. Minimally furnished, it had only taken two days to pack up. Her clothes and books had moved with her into the nursing home. Her papers and memorabilia had come back with me. They were still in the garage collecting dust, waiting for the day I could face going through them.

If she had kept the letter, it would be in there.

Excited, I jumped off the couch and glanced at the clock. It was noon. I had six hours until Audra and Sean were home.

I cleared the family room floor, pushed the coffee table against the wall shelves, and moved the couches off the area rug. Next, I headed out the kitchen door to the storage shelves in the garage and pulled down four heavy dust-covered plastic bins, marked "Mom" in faded black marker. I retrieved the ratty old comforter we used for picnics and beach trips from the minivan. I made individual trips between the garage and the family room, placing the dusty containers on top of the comforter. By the time I finished, I was covered in dirt, dust, and cobwebs. I changed out of my disgusting shirt, dropping it on the bathroom floor, and rinsed off my hands and arms in Sean's sink, leaving dark streaks on the pale blue hand towel.

Back in the family room, I approached the waiting bins. My heart was racing; my palms were sweaty as if I was doing something wrong. But I wasn't, really. I was simply completing a long-overdue task. My therapist would be proud. I popped the top off the first bin, a knot of anxiety forming in my stomach.

Inside was a hodgepodge of paper, trinkets, and other items whose significance had faded like colors in the wash. It looked like I'd simply taken my arm and swept things off shelves and dumped drawers into boxes. Because, I remembered with a sigh, I had. I hadn't taken time to sort through anything; my focus had been entirely on getting my failing mother moved closer to me so I could handle her medical care. The present had been so overwhelming; I'd not given the past a second thought.

I began sorting into piles: papers, pictures, and miscellaneous, keeping an eye out for anything that looked like Nick's handwriting, or an envelope with my name on it. By the time I'd emptied all four bins, I'd filled a trash bag with dried-up pens, crumpled receipts, single buttons, discarded food wrappers, and bits and pieces of indeterminate ephemera.

I started in the opposite order of importance, with the "miscellaneous stuff" pile: a few figurines, some costume jewelry, junk drawer odds and ends. I shrieked when I moved a piece of paper and uncovered a black spider until I realized it was the plastic spider ring I'd won in a seventh-grade geography bee. I slid it onto my ring finger, where it perched over my diamond.

I continued to purge. The figurines went into an empty box for donation, and I set the jewelry aside for Audra. Swinging by the kitchen, I made myself some tea and grabbed a package of the overly processed mini muffins that Audra favored, which I secretly ate and replaced weekly.

Next up was the paper pile. I spent an hour combing through bills, lists, and correspondence. By the time I finished, my trash bag overflowed with old papers. I also had a small stack of letters, some from unfamiliar return addresses, and a few unsent letters in my mother's increasingly shaky but still-elegant cursive. I glanced through her written notes first, searching for a confession: *Dear Corinne, I am so sorry, but I have kept this secret from you for too long.* But nothing was addressed to me, and each letter's content was similarly bland. I remembered her generic letters to me in college:

All is well here. Work is good. I hope the nice weather holds.

I peered inside the envelopes addressed to my mother, my heart hammering. Maybe she'd hidden Nick's letter here, knowing her correspondence would hold no interest to young adult me. I pulled out each letter, examining every page. There was nothing in Nick's handwriting; it wasn't here. I tossed the papers aside angrily, feeling cheated once again.

I glanced at the clock; it was five o'clock in the afternoon, and I hadn't even thought about dinner. Reluctantly, I eased myself back to standing, my knees popping in protest. I stretched my back, groaning. The floor was a disaster, papers and trash everywhere, the rumpled comforter scattered with letters, dust bunnies, and muffin crumbs. I did my best to sweep up the dust and crumbs and dumped them into my teacup, which I carried to the sink, adding it to the pile of dishes left from breakfast. The trash went straight to the bin in the garage; then I headed to the refrigerator to review the food situation. It was bleak. I messaged Sean that I was ordering a pizza and he could pick it up on his way home. He sent back a thumbs up.

Relieved of dinner duty, I turned my attention to the slim stack of photos that remained. The top image was of a group picnic, dating back to the early 1970s, judging by the hairstyles and outfits. I scanned the faces, expecting to see my mother seated at one of the picnic tables, her face half-turned away. She'd hated having her photo taken. My mother was not in any of the pictures, but I glimpsed a familiar arm at the edge of one, the rest of the body cut off by an incorrectly framed shot. A man's arm furred with thick dark hair, a crudely drawn eagle tattooing his forearm. My father's arm.

I scanned through the other photos of various holiday memories, but there were no more shots of my father. I wondered what the significance was, why my mother had kept this particular image. I gathered the photos and stacked them on the bookshelf next to the photo albums. I would slot these in later.

My phone buzzed in my back pocket. It was Sean:

OMW.

I blinked when I saw the time stamp. 5:30 p.m. I hadn't ordered the pizza yet:

Oops! Forgot. Ordering now.

He sent back another thumbs up. He didn't ask what I was doing.

I pulled up the pizza place's phone number and ordered our usual, a large half-cheese, half-green pepper and sausage deep dish, garlic bread, and a Caesar salad. Then I set the table and transferred the breakfast dishes from the sink to the dishwasher.

Going back to the family room, I stacked the empty bins inside each other by the back door. The picnic blanket, now dust-covered and grimy, went into the washing machine. I shoved the furniture back into place, then went into the bathroom where I stripped off everything and stepped into the shower. As I stood under the spray, eyes closed, hands smoothing my hair back, I let out a single, choked sob as all the unanswered questions of my life seemed to rise around me like steam: Why had my mother taken Nick's letter? Where was it? Why did Nick come back? What did he want from me? What did I want from him? Was my whole life based on a mistake? What if? What if? What if?

I stood there, arms wrapped around myself, rocking until I heard the garage door go up and voices call out a minute later:

"Corinne?"

"Mom! Dinner!"

Guiltily, I swiped at my face. My tears joined the water from the showerhead, mixing and swirling around my feet before disappearing down the drain. I turned off the water and, wrapping my robe around me, went to greet my family.

* * *

I sat on the back deck and stared out at the tree lights. The air was cold, lightly scented with the tang of damp earth and leaf mold. I held a cup of tea on my lap; my legs curled up under me. On my left, the television screen's soft glow flashed through the slats of the bedroom window. Sean was in bed, working on his laptop, a football game on for company. To my right, multicolored LED lights blinked around the edges of Audra's closed blinds. I could hear the low *thump-thump* of music. Once in a while, voices rose above the music; she was talking to someone. I briefly wondered who.

The wind rustled through the trees, lifting my hair against my cheek. Steam rose from my mug, bringing the smell of peppermint, my mother's favorite tea, to my nose.

Corinne leans her head back against the chair and uncurls her legs. Her slippered feet rest upon the teak fire table, and she rocks herself gently, closing her eyes against the lights and stars.

* * *

I woke, disoriented. I was still on the back patio, my head lolled back in the chair, my feet still on the table. Someone had taken my tea and covered me with a blanket. The rear deck light was still on, but both bedroom windows were dark.

Across the yard, the lights flickered as if laughing at a private joke.

I stood and stretched, immediately becoming light-headed. My feet tingled from being elevated for so long, and my eyesight tunneled. I waited, watched as the black margins cleared, and the feeling returned to my toes. I gathered my blanket and headed back inside.

The clock on the microwave read 11:28 p.m. I'd slept outside for nearly two hours. I felt stiff from the unusual position but wide awake and, on further introspection, hungry. I'd pecked at my dinner, too amped from the day's activities to eat. Now I was ravenous.

I microwaved some leftover pizza and carried my plate to the family room to watch HGTV. Meowsers, lured by the smell of warm sausage, jumped up on the cushion beside me, meowing and headbutting my leg.

"Here, pest," I said, holding out a piece of meat. He nipped it delicately from my fingers and retreated with his prize.

I was halfway through a show about beach house renovations when my phone buzzed. I glanced at the screen. At this hour, it would be Beth.

But it was from a number, not a name:

Hello.

It was Nick.

Sitting alone in her family room, Corinne stares at her screen. She lowers the unfinished slice of pizza to her plate and wipes her hands carefully on her napkin before picking up her phone, cradling it delicately like a soap bubble in her hands. She glances over her shoulder at the closed bedroom door and makes her decision:

Hello

I began to count, "One Mississippi, two Mississippi…" I got to twelve before a new message popped up:

> What are you doing?

I bristled. No *how have you been* or *sorry I didn't reach out sooner* or *I need to explain.* I decided to play it cool. He could ask questions. I would choose whether or not I answered them:

> Watching home renovation porn. You?

> Watching regular porn.

He followed this message with a winky face. I assumed that meant he was kidding.

A noise from the kitchen made me jump. I whipped around to see the cat chasing a fly.

Heart pounding, I turned back to my screen:

> Ha ha. Very funny.

> Deepest apologies to the beautiful maiden. So what else are you doing?

> Nothing. Watching TV. Eating pizza.

> Do you still take photos?

> No… too busy with school and life stuff.

> Too bad. You were really talented.

> LOL, were?

> Are.

A moment later, a picture came through. It was a picture of a framed photo, one I'd taken on one of our early morning walks, the fog rolling in across the dam, three crows huddled off-center of the bridge guardrail, overlooking our spot.

I gasped, my hand flying to my mouth. That photo had been my graduation gift to Nick. He'd kept it.

Another text:

> I may not know much, but I know what I like.

I gulped and shot another glance over my shoulder at the bedroom. If Sean came out right now, he'd see the guilt all over my face. Nick's subtext was anything but subtle.

I moved to safer ground:

> Where are you now?

> In bed, wink wink

> Haha, I mean, are you still in Clemmons?

> For now, yes. I'll go home next month. Renting a place outside Sitka. Easier because I travel for work, writing for different websites, blah blah.

I paused, unsure how far to push but unable to resist temptation:

> I'd love to read your work sometime.

A pause, then:

> Gotta go, talk again soon.

I reread the thread several times, my stomach lurching each time I got to the line about him knowing what he liked. How could a few lines of text get me so flustered? I shifted on the couch, displacing the cat who had come back to investigate my abandoned dinner. Carrying my plate to the sink on shaky legs, I poured myself a glass of water and drank it, thoughts whirling.

I wasn't imagining it. Nick was flirting with me. His messages were too personal for casual conversation. But why? What did it mean? Was it harmless fun for him, proof that he was still desirable? Or was it more serious than that? After all, I reasoned, emptying my glass and refilling it from a half-empty bottle of merlot that I should have thrown out days ago, he'd admitted that I was the reason he came to the reunion. *Me.* My stomach fluttered as I slugged back the bitter wine. Was it shallow to be flattered? Probably. But I was flattered. And flustered. And at a complete loss as to what to do next.

Chapter 8

I lay awake in bed, muscles stiff and mind conflicted, listening to my husband's quiet snores and thinking of Nick.

Logically, I knew it was a ridiculous position to find myself in. My life was here with my family. I loved my husband and daughter. There was no question of the right thing to do. I should delete Nick's messages, block his number, and go back to my real life. My life of chores and PTA meetings and coffee dates and volunteer bake sales and late-night texts with Beth. My life with a husband who worked hard, provided for his family, stayed late at the office, and sometimes took me for granted. My life with an increasingly distant daughter who couldn't wait to move away from me. My life without a plan, my life of living a day-to-day existence, a life that had stalled out, like a computer screen waiting to load.

And yet…

In my heart, the choice was less obvious. Doubts niggled at me. What if I'd gotten Nick's letter all those years ago? What if I'd been destined for a life with him? It was the "what ifs" I couldn't let go of, couldn't ignore. As Beth said, you can't change what you didn't do. But she also said it was never too late. What if I was getting a second chance? What if the reunion and Nick's sudden reappearance in my life were all signs pointing me in a new direction? To the path I should've taken? Maybe the reason I was having so much trouble deciding what to do next with my life was that I had been waiting for Nick. Audra was almost grown. She'd made it clear she didn't need me anymore. And Sean. He loved me, but was he still in love with me? Maybe in his own way, he felt as lost as I did. We had routines and memories, but did we have a future? Only a month ago, I would have said yes, that we were simply going through a rough patch. But now? I didn't know. I couldn't ask, couldn't talk about it without telling him about Nick.

Nick. It all came down to Nick.

Sean snored on. I rolled away from him, yanking the blanket up over my shoulder with a huff, waking Meowsers. In the dark, I could see his luminous eyes regarding me.

"This is ridiculous," I told him and threw the comforter off in frustration. Sean made a sleepy protest, then rolled away, taking the blankets with him.

My nerves were violin strings plucking out dissonant chords. I pulled my robe off the hook in the bathroom and stalked out to the kitchen to make tea. The cat trotted along at my side, hoping for a midnight treat. "Go away." I shooed him off with my foot.

While I waited for the water to boil, I leaned over the counter and laid my forehead on the granite. "What am I doing?" I moaned.

"Mom?" The kitchen light snapped on. Audra stood, staring at me, a worried expression on her face. Her hair was a wild halo of blonde curls, her wrists and ankles bare in the too-short Hogwarts pajamas she refused to give up.

I straightened, embarrassed. "Hi, honey. I couldn't sleep." I pulled my robe tighter, feeling the sash cut into the flesh of my waist. "What are you doing up?"

Audra shrugged and joined me at the counter. "Couldn't

sleep either. Too much going on in here." She rapped the side of her head with her knuckles, her father's gesture.

I smiled, a rush of love for my sweet girl making my eyes well up. To cover, I turned away and busied myself by pulling out ingredients for hot chocolate, her favorite nighttime snack since childhood. I poured the water for tea down the drain and refilled the pan with milk.

"So, tell me more about design class," I said as we moved to our usual positions; me at the stove, she perched at the kitchen counter, feet twisted around the legs of the metal barstool.

"Oh, Mom, it's awesome!" She launched into a long and winding narrative. The instructor had worked for a major life-style company ("The brochure doesn't say who, but I bet it's Martha."). Audra went on to describe some of the course assignments, such as drafting exercises and creating mood boards.

She was still talking as I poured the cocoa and settled onto the stool beside her. How many nights had we spent like this? How many more nights like this did we have left? Time was moving too fast. My little girl had grown up and was growing away from me. It was impossible to accept—not only because I didn't want to face the day that she left for good, but also because it still seemed surreal. Hadn't I just been the teenager leaving my own mother? Hadn't I just been the one with my whole life waiting to unfold? When had I stepped aside, out of the excitement of life? During the lost years of my depression?

Or was it when I married Sean?

If I'd stayed with Nick, would I be the one with stories to tell, news to share?

Stop it! Beth chimed in. *Pay attention to your daughter!*

I pulled myself back to the conversation.

"...and then we have to create a board based on a childhood memory. Isn't that cool?"

"That's incredibly cool," I said, smiling at her.

If you'd stayed with Nick, you wouldn't have Audra, Beth's voice reminded me.

I know.

We finished our cocoa, and I watched Audra's eyelids start to flutter as they always did when she was getting sleepy. "Here," I said, plucking the empty cup from her hands. "You go back to bed. I'll clean up."

She yawned. "Thanks, Mom." She stood, leaned forward, and hugged me.

Surprised, I hugged her back, mugs still in my hands. "Love you, sweetie."

She pulled back. "Mom?"

My eyes were closed; I didn't want to let go. "Yeah?"

"You have crumbs on your forehead."

I opened my eyes to see her smiling in amusement at me. She raised her arm and gently swiped my forehead with her pajama sleeve. Pizza crust crumbs fell to the floor.

"Love you too, Mom. G' night."

* * *

It was almost three o'clock in the morning before I snuck back into the bedroom. Circling the bed, I cracked my toe against the footboard.

"Ow!"

Sean sat up. "What? Who?"

Hopping on one foot, I rubbed my throbbing toe. "Don't get up. It's only me."

He laid down, burrowing under the covers, already falling back to sleep. "Everything okay?" he asked dreamily.

I slid into bed and wrestled half of the covers back. "Everything's fine. Good night."

I reached for my phone and pulled the sheets over my head. Turning the screen light to low, I pulled up Nick's messages and read the thread through, again and again, memorizing and repeating the words until I fell into a fragmented, fitful sleep.

Call. Still yours. I know what I like. You were so talented. Are.

* * *

The next morning, I was back in my office with the door closed and locked before Sean finished reversing down the driveway. I listened as the garage door rattled shut, peering out between shutter slats to watch his Prius glide away.

Freedom.

I'd woken that morning with the idea of going through my old boxes of pictures, inspired by Nick's comment about my photography. It had been ages since I'd gone through them, and over the years, the photo bins had been pushed farther and farther back in the closet, hidden behind Girl Scout projects, school planning kits, cast-off clothing from Audra's closet.

Now I pulled items from the office closet, almost crazed in my urgency. I knew there were photos of Nick in there. I had the idea that if I could see the past, revisit some of the moments I'd lost over time, then maybe I could understand what was happening to me now. Perhaps seeing how Nick and I were then would provide clues to the life I'd missed.

The photo boxes were back in the corner of the closet, each decorated in different designs. I eased the oldest one, covered with Precious Moments angels, from the bottom of the stack, buttressing the others against the wall with my shoulder. Releasing them, they came to the floor with a clatter, scattering dust bunnies and cat hair tumbleweeds. I sneezed and wiped my face with my sleeve, eyes burning. From the hall, Meowsers pawed at the door. I let him in.

I settled on the couch, legs crossed under me, the box in my lap. The cat curled up next to my leg, purring. I hesitated, thinking of the myth of Pandora and the misfortune she'd unleashed because of her curiosity.

But this was different. I only wanted to reclaim what was rightfully mine.

I opened the lid. Envelopes of developed photos filled the box, filed vertically. Starting at the front, I pulled each envelope out and thumbed through the pictures. The first few sets were the work of a novice, out-of-focus, out-of-frame shots of feet, half of a group, a blurry image of the front of the Clemmons apartment.

The pictures improved as I moved on, becoming sharper, more centered, less over- or underexposed. Beth dressed for Halloween as the Wicked Witch of the West, snarling for the camera. A picture of the two of us, the witch and a princess, posing on Beth's front porch. I smiled, setting that one aside for her.

I moved on to the second storage box, this one decorated in music notes. I had taken photography electives in high school, and these photos were more sophisticated both in quality and subject matter. First up was a series of architectural details: images of cornices, brass doorknobs, stained-glass windows from long-forgotten locations. Another series featured close-ups of gravestones, carved angels, ornate markers, flowers against granite.

I grew more anxious, less careful. Where were the pictures of Nick? I remembered taking plenty of photos during our months together, including a series of artsy shots at the cemetery. In my mind's eye, I saw Nick, all in black, posing poetically against a mausoleum, staring across the mist-covered grounds.

After the dam (the damn dam), Beth and I had burned all of Nick's letters in a fiery ceremony on her dad's grill with the help of her pyromaniac brothers. Had we burned the pictures then too? The memories of those first devastating days had lost their shape, condensed into a confusion of impressions. Lying in bed, staring at the ceiling, my mother's worried face in the doorway.

Long calls to Beth, the frenzied mess of my room as I purged all the things that reminded me of Nick. The heat of flames on my face as I fed Nick's empty promises to the fire…

My mind wandered over another possibility. Had my mother thrown the photos out without my knowing? Just as she'd destroyed his apology letter?

I continued pulling out pictures, abandoning any pretense of organization.

And then…a punch to the solar plexus.

A photo of Nick and me, kissing, wedged between candid photos from cheer camp and a long-forgotten pool party. The picture was slightly off-center, the back half of my head cut off in the way of all early-stage selfies, and blurry as if I'd moved my arm just as I took the photo.

I remembered this night, the moments leading up to the picture. We were at a party—in Kirsten Summers' basement, I realized with a start.

It was the start of spring break. The cheer squad and our boyfriends had descended on Kirsten's house. Her parents had divorced the previous year, and her dad was hardly ever home, making her house the favorite choice for get-togethers. Beers were smuggled out of garage fridges, bottles in bar cabinets half-emptied and topped off with water. Kirsten's hot-pink boom box blasted Boyz II Men, while a stack of cassette tapes leaned precariously next to it. Scarves had been hung over lamps to project spots of color onto the blonde wood paneling. A TV played a horror movie with the sound turned off.

Nick and I arrived late. He'd worked the closing shift at the hardware store, stocking shelves and breaking down boxes. He picked me up straight after work, sweaty and disheveled. I didn't care. I found him unbearably sexy, all smudged and rumpled. I was dressed in my casual best, spending hours to make it look like I hadn't tried to dress up at all. A black mock turtleneck with a long black cardigan. My best jeans. Black flats. My hair was freshly washed and straightened, caught back with a black velvet Alice band. My makeup was painstakingly understated. Nick liked me neat and elegant, like a storybook princess.

We claimed an overstuffed armchair patterned in brown swirls and sporting several suspicious stains. Undeterred, Nick pulled me onto his lap, and for the next half an hour, we were oblivious to the party going on around us.

When we finally came up for air, we were alone in the room. The movie had ended, and the TV screen snowed in silence. The tape in the boom box had switched off. Above us, I could hear footsteps, voices, a microwave beeping.

Nick and I looked at each other and grinned. "I guess we scared them away," he said, nuzzling my neck.

"They're jealous," I agreed. The smell of popcorn wafted down the stairs. Nick's stomach growled. "Should we join them?"

"In a minute." Nick pulled me back down and pinned me with a gaze so intense I felt goosebumps rise on my arms.

"I love you, Corinne Elizabeth Murphy," he said, pressing his hands to the sides of my face. He looked me straight in the eyes, earnest, urgent. "I'll never hurt you."

"I know," I said, kissing him. "I know you won't."

Nick moved his hands from my face, and we stood together. "Wait." I pressed my hand to his chest as he started to move toward the stairs. I rummaged in my Esprit bag, which I'd dropped by the armchair when we'd first arrived, and pulled out my camera. I held it up with a teasing smile and pulled him close. "For posterity."

"I love you," he repeated and kissed me again as I pressed the shutter button.

* * *

The sound of "Harper Valley PTA" pulled me out of 1992 and Nick's arms. Guiltily, I shoved the picture under my leg.

Corinne sits in her office, her face flushed, her pulse racing. She smooths back her hair and takes a breath, trying to keep her voice steady.

"Hi, Grace."

"Corinne!" Grace yelled. I heard children's laughter and voices in the background, street noise. Grace was on a playground. "So glad I caught you! Listen, I'm in a bind, and I need a tiny favor, so say yes, okay?"

As if Grace would accept any answer other than the one she wanted. "Sure, yeah, I guess," I said, still pulling myself together. "What am I doing?"

"I need you to photograph the PTA awards luncheon." Besides running our school's activities, Grace spearheaded the regional council and its many events. "Our regular photographer is in Atlanta. Her father's having surgery. Anyway, it's the Tuesday after next."

Her words caught me off guard. Photography again. I fingered the edge of the photo tucked under my thigh. Had I somehow summoned this? I felt a squeeze of panic, an impulse to hang up and hide. "Oh no, Grace, I can't."

"Why not?" Grace did not accept rejection. She claimed it was part of her charm.

"Well, because..." I hesitated, not knowing how to explain why taking a few pictures made me panicky. I wasn't sure if I even understood it. "You don't need a photographer. Can't you take a few shots with your phone?"

"No, Charlie! That's not your cookie!" Grace shouted. "Sorry. One—I said put it down—one of the big muckety-mucks from the state council is giving a presentation, so we need to be on our best and most professional behavior, which means a dedicated photographer with a real camera taking actual photos. Please, Corinne, you could do this with your eyes closed."

I switched tactics. "I haven't used my camera in years. It might not even work."

"Psssh," she scoffed, dismissing this. "Of course, it will. There's nothing to it: a few talking heads, a few grip-and-grins. You used to take such good pictures. Remember? You even talked about opening a studio one day. Surely you can handle a few grown-ups holding a big fake check."

I opened my mouth to protest again, then thought better of it. It was easier to do whatever Grace asked rather than argue further. Plus, it would be a distraction from thinking about Nick all day. "Yeah, okay. I guess I could do it. Why not?"

"See? I knew I could count on you. I'll even buy you a coffee after, and we can catch up. I haven't seen you in ages and I want to hear all about your reunion. Anyway, I'll text you the address. Charlie! Get off that right—" The call ended abruptly. I realized I was sweating. I wiped my damp palms on my pants.

Grace's call had broken the spell, the mania I'd felt looking for pictures of the past. I set the phone down and looked around me. Discarded photos, envelopes, and boxes littered the floor. Perhaps the universe was trying to tell me something else, bring my attention back to the present.

I sighed and began to pick up, returning the photos to their spot in the closet. I felt exhausted, defeated, done.

The picture of Nick and me lay on the couch. I picked it up, a guilty flush inching up my cheeks as I stared at a younger version of myself kissing another man. I felt like I was cheating on Sean just by looking at it.

Corinne raises her head, closes her eyes. She imagines Nick, as he is now, pressing his hands against her cheeks, leaning forward, bringing his mouth to hers.

My phone chimed, a text notification. Heart pounding in embarrassment, like I'd been caught doing something sinful, I checked my messages:

Thinking about me, maiden?

Oh, God. I looked around the room as if expecting to see Nick standing there, watching me. How did he know?

My palms were sweaty again as I held the phone and tried to come up with an answer.

Another text came in:

I'm thinking about you.

I slammed the phone down and hurried from the room. I couldn't do this. Somehow, I'd signaled Nick when I found this picture, and now the only thing I could think of was that I needed to hide it away in a safe place. But where? Not in the office where anyone could find it. Not in the photo albums in the family room. Unsure of what else to do, I took it into the bedroom and tucked it in the back of my nightstand drawer, under a stack of treasured cards and childhood artwork from Audra.

I slowly crossed the house, peeking into my office at the phone lying face down on the couch as if it were a snake, coiled and ready to strike. Gingerly, I reached out and picked it up. One new message:

Talk again soon.

I wasn't sure if I was disappointed or relieved. Leaving the photo boxes and sleeping cat, I fled my office. I had to get out, get away, clear my head.

Corinne promises not to think about Nick Elms anymore today.

Chapter 9

An hour later, I was back in the office, pulling up Facebook.

"Don't judge me," I told the cat.

In the wake of the reunion, I'd received friend requests from Sunny, Heidi, Brittany, Jenny, and amazingly, Rhonda Serlow-Green. I accepted them all, spending hours working my way back through years of posts, piecing together individual histories, a compendium of Clemmons High School Class of 1992.

And always, under all of it, my brain was on high alert for any mention of Nick. My eyes scanned photo backgrounds for his face, his profile, a scrap of his jacket. Post-reunion, there'd been an onslaught of selfies and group shots posted from the gym, Queen's, various spots around Clemmons. My stomach lurched each time someone posted a new photo. But Nick remained uncaptured, untagged.

I'd also Googled every combination of Nick's name:

Nick Elms.

Nicholas Elms.

Nicholas A. Elms.

N. Elms.

N.A. Elms, and so on. The closest I'd gotten were genealogy reports with deceased relatives sporting partial matches to my search, and claims of "We found Nicholas Elms," which all ended in a request for my credit card number.

I'd tried to find him through his writing, but I didn't know what he wrote about or who he worked for. I'd gotten excited when I'd found a hit for a journalist named N. Elms, but when I clicked on a link, the photo was of a young blonde woman named Natalie.

I felt a flash of resentment. Why would someone disappear so entirely only to reappear, like a figure in the mist, a quarter of a century later?

I had one more option: Kirsten. She had access to Nick and might mention him in her comments or post a picture that included him. Within minutes, I was staring at the profile for Kirsten Summers Baxter. Oh, thank you, internet algorithm gods.

Kirsten looked much as she had in school, tall, leggy, broad-shouldered, with long blonde hair worn swept away from her face. She had a few wrinkles (didn't we all), but they were around her eyes and mouth, the smile lines of a happy woman. In her profile picture, she stood next to a bride, presumably the daughter who'd just gotten married.

I zoomed in, then sat back, open-mouthed. The bride was Natalie Elms, the journalist I'd found while searching for Nick. His daughter. I pulled up her journalism profile again, wondering how I'd missed the similarities before; she had Nick's dark eyebrows and the same jawline. I could also see Kirsten in her smiling mouth, the wide-set eyes, and blonde hair. According to Natalie's profile, she was "one to watch" for her environmental science reporting and her role in climate change education. I wondered if she knew how many holes her mother had punched in the ozone with Aqua Net. Another line leaped out at me: "Natalie lives with her mother and father and two sisters in Seattle. She is engaged to Matthew Simmons, also of Seattle..."

So Natalie had Nick's name but didn't consider him her father. My heart went out to Nick. It was sad, but not unheard of, for younger children to align with one parent during acrimonious separations. Even without divorce, distance could spring up at any time between parent and child—wasn't I proof of that?

I went back to Kirsten's page and scrolled through the wedding pictures half-heartedly since I knew I wouldn't find Nick in any of them. After the wedding pictures ran out, most of Kirsten's posts were forwards of recipes or school fundraiser announcements. Her page resembled mine, in fact, and I felt a moment of remembered affection for her. She'd been my squad mate and compatriot before she'd stolen Nick from me.

By five o'clock, my head was pounding, and my stomach was growling. Meowsers had abandoned me. I scrolled through Kirsten's past updates, looking for any mention of the man she and I had shared. Nothing. I closed out of my account and deleted my search history as I heard the front door slam. Audra was home. I went to greet her as she kicked off her shoes into the hall closet and slung her jacket over a hanger.

"Hey," I said, startling her.

She pulled an earbud out of her ear. "Hi."

"You're home early."

She shifted from one foot to the other, clearly itching to escape to her room. "I didn't have to work today. Remember? I told you last week."

I didn't remember, but I nodded anyway. "Right." I cast about for another question, anything to keep her talking. "Are you hungry? Want me to make you something?"

She shook her head. "Nah, we stopped at Dunkin' after school."

I swallowed my protest that a doughnut didn't count as a meal; who was I to judge? My lunch had consisted of leftover popcorn while reading Kirsten's profile. "How's Lana?"

Audra started to say something, then stopped. "Fine."

"I talked to her mom today. She asked me to take some pictures for the PTA luncheon."

"Cool." Audra acknowledged this with a raised eyebrow. "I have homework."

"Okay, go," I said, smiling at her.

With Audra safely shut in her room, I pulled my phone out of my back pocket and checked for messages. My heart lifted when I saw a new text notification, but it was only Sean saying that he was working late, something about quarterly budgets blah blah blah, and not to wait for him for dinner. I was alone with my thoughts for a little longer.

My eyes traversed the room, following the same route as my nighttime walks. This was my house, the container for the life we'd built. I had picked out every wall color, every picture, every piece of furniture. I'd built a haven for us to live in, a place to come home to. But at this moment, it seemed like a prison. I'd made my choices long ago, and there was no way of walking them back now. Too many people's lives were involved.

I thought again of the picture of Nick and me, kissing, never imagining that in a few short months, we'd be torn apart.

What if...?

I froze, suddenly hearing familiar lyrics and piano chords coming from Audra's room, a male voice singing.

It was our song. Nick's and mine. "Somebody" from Depeche Mode's *Some Great Reward*. Nick had given me the cassette tape for my eighteenth birthday. Had Audra found it? If so, how? Where? What else had she seen?

I crossed the hall and stood outside my daughter's room, listening, mouthing the words.

The door opened. Audra peered out, looking annoyed, then alarmed as she took in my stricken expression. "Mom? What's wrong?"

I jumped. "N-nothing," I stammered. "Th-that song. Where did you find that?"

Audra looked at me, her boundary-invading, hallway-lurking

115

mother. I could only imagine the scathing text she would send Lana about this: *My mom has lost her mind.*

"Dan…" she said and hesitated. "A friend sent it to me." She shrugged. "I like it. It's good."

I tried to rearrange my features into a smile. "You're right. It's really good. It just...surprised me." I took a step back. "Sorry for interrupting. I came to ask what you wanted for dinner. Dad's working late, so we're on our own."

She gave me one last quizzical look, eyebrow arched. "I already told you, I'm not hungry." She shut the door, leaving me in the hallway with my memories.

* * *

I was born on February 15th. Having a birthday around a holiday was frustrating, to say the least. Yes, the kids with December and January birthdays had it worse, but at least their birthdays came with the assumption of gifts and a day off for festivities. The day after Valentine's Day was a celebratory no man's land. You didn't get the day off from work or school, and everyone was either too over-sugared and tapped out from the night before or, alternately, too bitter and resentful to get in the mood for another party. My mother always did her best to make February 15th special; however, frugality meant that my party decorations, favors, and gift wrappings were always heart-themed, purchased the morning of my birthday when all seasonal decorations went on clearance.

Nick was the first person outside my family to treat my birthday as its own unique occasion. The night of my eighteenth birthday, he'd packed a picnic of crackers and cheese, which we ate under the stars in the back of his uncle's flatbed truck. It was our first visit to what would become "our spot" at Clemmons Dam. I wore long underwear under my best Guess jeans and my heaviest sweater. Bundled in coats, hats, gloves, and boots, we cuddled under his uncle's camouflage sleeping bag, which he used in deer hunting season. Nick produced a bottle of Boone's Farm Strawberry Hill, which we drank straight from the bottle, passing it back and forth. The wine was chilled and made me shiver. We kissed between sips, and Nick chafed my gloved hands in his. When he tried to put a hand up my sweater, I'd yelped at the frigid air hitting my skin. He pulled back in surprise and started to laugh.

"This is hopeless. Let's get in the truck."

The truck cab smelled like cigarettes and sawdust and something metallic that might have been animal blood. But it was warm, and I was with Nick. He removed two small packages from the glove compartment, wrapped in plain butcher paper. I was so touched that he hadn't used Valentine-themed paper that my eyes filled instantly.

"Hey now," he said, chucking me gently on the chin. "None of that. Here." He handed one of the packages to me. "This one first."

I unwrapped a cassette tape. "*Some Great Reward*," I read aloud before opening the case. "It's empty." I looked up at Nick, confused.

"I had to open it," he apologized, "to forward to the right song." He reached behind his seat and pulled out a small cassette player. He pressed *play*, and the cab filled with music. We sat silently, listening. By the time the music faded, my tears were falling freely, running down my face and into my scarf. I burrowed my head, trying to wipe them away.

"That was beautiful," I managed. "Thank you."

"You're beautiful," he insisted, tracing the tracks of my tears with his thumb. "Open your other present."

Inside the second box sat a black leather tie bracelet with a single blue ceramic bead. "Oh, Nick... I love it." He tied it onto my wrist and kissed my hand. "Thank you."

"Happy birthday, my beautiful maiden."

After presents, we finished the wine and listened to the song —"Our song," Nick called it—over and over. The windows of the cab fogged up, and I was perspiring inside my coat and sweater. Nick had a fine line of sweat above his upper lip. His kisses were salty.

A light in the passenger window and a knock on the door caused us to bolt apart. I rolled down my window with a shaky hand, my adrenaline racing.

A uniformed police officer shone his flashlight into my face. "What's going on here?"

I shielded my eyes, squinting against the brightness. My heart hammered in my chest. I had never been in trouble with the police.

"N-nothing," I stammered, trying to look innocent. I smiled uncertainly at where I thought his face would be.

"Miss, are you okay?" he asked, clicking off his light. I was blind again in the sudden darkness.

"Yes, I'm fine." My voice wavered with nerves. I heard, rather than saw, him move around the truck to the driver's side. The flashlight came on again.

"Please exit the vehicle, sir."

I glanced sideways at Nick. His face was stone. I reached out to squeeze his arm but felt only empty air as Nick climbed out of the truck. I kept my head down, peering through a curtain of hair as Nick joined the officer in the glare of the truck's headlights. Their voices were low, and I strained to hear what they were saying. The cassette tape ended with a *snap* and I jumped, knocking the player to the floor, where it hit the empty wine bottle. Trying to keep my upper body still, an eye on the two silhouettes outside the truck, I felt with my foot for the bottle and slid it with the toe of my boot under the passenger seat. I scooted my purse in front of it and crossed my feet at the ankles, hoping that the officer wouldn't ask to search the car.

"Miss?" The officer knocked on my door again. I could see

now that he was young, maybe early twenties. He had pale skin with freckles across his cheeks and dark curly hair. He looked more like a Boy Scout than a policeman. I relaxed marginally and managed a more confident smile. "Yes, sir?"

"Are you here by your own consent, miss?"

I blinked, the meaning of his words sinking in. Was I there by my own free will with Nick? I almost laughed. "Yes, I am. It's my birthday, and my boyfriend brought me here for a picnic and to give me my present." I held up my wrist with the bracelet on it. "I'm fine, but thank you for stopping to check on us."

The young officer paused momentarily before he nodded, satisfied. "All right, you two head on home. The park is closed to visitors after dusk. If I find you out here again after hours, I'll have to give you a ticket and call your parents." He touched a finger to his temple in a small salute. "And happy birthday."

"Thank you," I called as he walked back to his squad car. Nick climbed into the car, and we sat, mute and unmoving, as headlights flooded the cab, receding as the officer backed away and finally turned and exited the parking lot.

All the way home, Nick railed against the injustices of small-town life while I wordlessly spun my bracelet and looked out the window. "That's why we've got to get out of here, Rin," he said, emphasizing "get out" with the flat of his hand against the steering wheel. "People are always going to be watching us here. We need to go somewhere we can be together without all eyes on us."

I stopped spinning my bracelet and turned to look at him. He was staring intently out the windshield at the dark roads, but he reached over and took my hand. "My uncle owns a cannery in Alaska," he said, glancing sideways at me. "He's offered me a job there this summer. It's hard work, but good money, and a free place to live. He's got cabins on his land."

"Alaska?" I was stunned. I'd received my acceptance letter from NC State the previous week. Nick was the first person I'd told, and he'd been happy for me at the time, calling me his "beautiful, brilliant girl." I knew Nick had no plans for college. He'd already had interest from a few local publications in some of his short stories, which he took as proof that he didn't need a college degree. He'd even made a couple of references to the fact that he could write anywhere in the world, which I'd optimistically interpreted to mean North Carolina.

Apparently, we had different definitions of "anywhere."

"I can't stay here, Rin," he said, glancing at me. "You know what it's like. Never any privacy, everyone knowing your business. I want to live in a city where I'm not being watched by half of the town."

"But…. Alaska?" I asked again, holding his hand tightly in both of mine. "I'll be in North Carolina. Couldn't you…we could…" I faltered, not wanting to jump too far, too fast, "…be together." I heard the begging tone in my voice and was ashamed. *Don't leave me,* it cried.

He pulled his hand from mine to make the left turn onto my street, pulling into a pool of light from the streetlamp and putting the car in park, but leaving the engine running. "Rin," he said, facing me, "we are always going to be together. Always. I love you. I don't want to leave you." He cupped my gloved hands in his, bringing them to his lips, kissing them. "But we're bigger than this place, you and me. We have to get out, start our lives somewhere else." He released my hands and pulled me to him. The seatbelt strained against my chest, and I fumbled to unlatch it. I slid across the seat into his arms. "Taking this job means I can save enough money for us to start a life together, anywhere you want."

"I'll miss you so much," I said, starting to cry against his shirt. "I don't know how I'll make it."

"Shhhhh…" he soothed, rocking me, sliding his hands over my hair. "It won't be so bad. We can write and call, and you can come to see me on your breaks."

"I love you," I said, looking up into his face. "I'll never love anyone the way I love you."

"I love you too," he said, smiling down at me, kissing my tears. "It'll all work out, you'll see."

We sat, holding each other, the truck engine idling until my mother's silhouette appeared in the door frame, and the porch light flickered on and off, her signal to come inside.

I sighed and pulled away, reluctantly gathering my things: my purse and camera, the box the bracelet had come in, the wrapping paper, the cassette tape and its case. I leaned over for another kiss. "Thank you for a wonderful night," I said, suddenly shy.

"Happy birthday, Corinne Elizabeth."

I stood on the porch steps as he drove away, his blinker at the end of the street like a knowing wink to me. Nobody else could ever understand.

We were in love, and it was forever.

Chapter 10

Somehow I made it through the weekend, keeping myself occupied with small chores: laundry, baking brownies, pulling the last of the summer weeds from the mulch beds. Audra worked at the mall and spent her free time with friends. Sean sat on the couch with his laptop and worked on a presentation, a never-ending stream of football games playing in the background. I was on edge, wishing I could be alone.

Nick hadn't texted since Friday.

I got out my camera on Sunday afternoon, replacing the batteries and checking the memory card in preparation for my "tiny favor" for Grace. I took a few uninspired practice shots of the floor, the ceiling, Meowsers, deleting each. It would take more than a few tries to get my old rhythm back.

I called Beth, needing to talk. "Bethie?"

"Rinni!" I could hear Dante's shrieks and giggles in the background, as well as splashing.

"Is this a bad time?"

Beth laughed. "Is there ever a good time?" A gleeful crow from Dante. "It's perfect timing. D just threw a cup of water at me, so it's Mommy Vi's turn to take over bath duty while I change."

"Hi, Corinne!" I heard Vi's deep mezzo voice in the background, followed by Dante's "Hi Aunt Rinni!" I chuckled, hearing Dante's high-pitched machine-gun giggles fade as Beth moved away from the bathroom.

"Okay, hang on a sec while I change my shirt." Muffled sounds, a cry, and an expletive, followed by undefined scrabbling noises before Beth came back on the line. "Okay, sorry," she said, out of breath and still swearing. "Sorry, I got the...*gosh darn* shirt zipper caught in my hair." She heaved a sigh. "I'm trying to watch my mouth. Dante's in a copycat phase." She sighed again. "I'm getting a gosh darn drink." Footsteps echoed as she walked down the hall, followed by the sound of cupboards opening and shutting. I waited, listening to bottles clinking, ice hitting the bottom of the glass. "So, what's up?"

"You know what? I need a gosh darn drink too." I hoisted myself off the barstool to fill a coffee cup with the last of our wine. I took myself outside, settling into the chaise lounge. The sky had darkened, and thunder rumbled in the distance. I pulled my sweater tighter around me. "So, I want to ask you a question, but you have to promise not to read too much into it."

"I will promise no such thing but ask away."

I hesitated, careful with my phrasing. "Do you remember the night we burned all of Nick's stuff?"

Beth snorted. "A bunch of bad poetry, some letters, that ugly bracelet you wore all the time."

My chest tightened. I'd forgotten burning the bracelet. "Right, um, so..."

Beth continued. "We torched some cassette tapes too, remember? Stunk to high heaven. Dad was pissed because the plastic melted onto the grill racks, and he had to throw them out."

"Did we burn all my photos of him?"

Silence. I rushed to fill it.

"I was looking through old pictures the other day, and I

thought it was strange that I don't have any of him. It seems like I would unless—"

Beth interrupted. "What are you doing? Is this some teenage-nostalgia-reunion sh…shenanigans?"

"No!"

"Really? You're not sitting there, all starry-eyed and daydreamy? Looking through pictures, wanting to relive the good old days?"

"Of course not," I countered, cheeks burning, thinking of the photo hidden in my bedside table drawer, the texts on my phone.

Liar, liar, Corinne.

"Are you wishing for another chance with Nick?" Beth scoffed over the phone. "Because honey, I was there the first time." Her words sharpened. "Yeah, we burned his pictures. I used extra lighter fluid to make sure they went up in flames." She slowed down. "Look, I'm sorry things have been tough for you and Sean lately. But this is not something you want to do. You—"

She broke off, as Dante called, "Beth Mommy? You fussin'?" I heard his little boy breaths come closer, and I pictured him climbing into Beth's lap, laying his head against her shoulder, hair still wet from his bath, snuggling close.

Beth's voice turned soothing. "No, baby, of course not. Beth Mommy's only talking."

"Mmmm hmmm," he said, his voice drowsy. I closed my eyes too, grateful that, for the moment, we'd avoided an argument.

"I should go." I struggled to keep my voice low and unemotional. "I'll talk to you another time."

"Okay." Her voice matched mine in calm, measured words. "You know I love you."

"I know. And I love you back. That's why I keep calling even when you're mean to me."

Beth chuckled, and Dante whimpered in protest. "Honey, I'll always be here to keep you right whether you like it or not."

"Bye, Bethie. Bye, Dante."

"Bye."

I held my phone, looking out across the trees until a light rain began, forcing me back inside.

* * *

I snapped at Sean when he asked what was for dinner.

"Why do I always have to know what's for dinner? Why can't you ever come up with an idea?" I slapped the towel I'd been using to clean the bathroom against the vanity. The smell of disinfectant made my head pound.

Sean looked at me, bewildered. "Whoa, uh…right. Dinner. Idea. Um…okay, how about Chinese?"

"Whatever," I snapped, stalking out of the bathroom. I whipped the dirty towel into the laundry room on the way to my office and slammed the door. I sank into my desk chair, covering my eyes with my hands and shaking. What was wrong with me? Why was I picking fights?

Because I hadn't heard from Nick, that's why. Because I hadn't found any more pictures of him or tracked him down online. Because I was feeling more and more untethered each day, uncertain about my life and what it was supposed to all mean.

Sean knocked lightly on the door and called out, "I ordered dinner. It'll be here in about twenty minutes."

I pulled myself together and went to open the door. Sean stood there, looking worried. "I know you shouldn't be the only one responsible for dinner," he said. "I'm sorry for upsetting you."

I leaned against him, felt his familiar arms encircle me, smelled his clean scent, the smell of security, of home. So different from Nick. "No, I'm sorry. I didn't mean to get angry. I don't know what's wrong."

Sean rested his cheek to mine. I could feel his eyelashes flutter. "What's going on? You've been so distant lately. Did I do something? Is there something you want to talk about?"

Here was the opening I needed, the chance to tell him everything.

I couldn't do it.

Instead, I hugged him tightly. "Of course not. I'm just a little jumpy about this photography thing Grace asked me to do."

"What photography thing?"

I stiffened. "The PTA luncheon next week. I told you about it." Friday night. We'd been at the sink, washing up. I'd told him about Grace's call, how it had set off a minor panic, how it had been so long I wasn't sure I could even take a decent group shot anymore. I thought he'd been listening.

"Oh right." I could tell by his vague tone of voice that he didn't remember. "But you used to like taking pictures. What's the big deal?"

I sighed. "Probably nothing. But it's been such a long time since I picked up a camera. What if I'm no good anymore?"

Sean smoothed the hair back from my forehead. "Sure, you are. And it's not like these are going in a museum, right? Relax." His words, meant to reassure, rankled.

Corinne stands in her husband's arms, but her mind drifts away. The corners of her mouth tighten.

"You're right. It'll be fine. Everything's fine."

* * *

Everything's fine.

The lie repeated through my head as I walked the house that night. Moonlight spilled in through the sliding glass doors, casting shadows, forming patterns across the floor. I made a game of following the shadow outlines instead of the room's perimeters. Around the elongated silhouette of the basket chair, a long step to the right to follow the floor lamp. My arm brushed against the bookshelf, and the stack of family photos toppled to the ground, sliding to a stop in a staggered line, like cards laid out before a dealer.

I knelt, knees creaking, and gathered them up. I carried them to the kitchen table and retrieved my mother's photo album from the bookcase's bottom shelf. It was an old 1970s-style album with a slippery blue vinyl cover and yellowed self-adhesive pages covered in plastic. In the front and the back of the book were folder pockets for storing loose photos. The word "MEMO-RIES" was stamped across the cover in swirly gold foil letters. I'd slot these pictures into her album, a nice mindless task, a diversion. *Everything's fine.*

I sorted through the photos, guessing at a timeline. The picture of the barbeque and my father's arm, I slotted in behind a picture of my father and some of his Marine buddies holding Budweiser cans up in a toast toward the camera. I slid a picture of me, four years old and missing a front tooth after a roller-skating accident, among a page of pictures of me riding a horse, a carousel, feeding ducks at a county fair.

A picture of my mother at Christmas went into a space toward the back of the book. I'd caught her standing in front of the small tabletop tree in our apartment, a halo of lights around her, her face half-turned away, laughing at something off camera. She was young, hopeful, unaware of the cancer that would one day consume her, one bite at a time, until it swallowed her whole. Me in pink footie pajamas, sitting in my father's chair, holding *Andersen's Fairy Tales.* I was eight or nine years old. I'd loved listening to my father read those stories, and I'd often tried to imitate him, holding the book, moving my eyes diligently across the pages as though I understood every word. My favorite story was "The Snow Queen." I'd loved the adventures of Gerda as she searched for her dear friend Kay, whose heart and eyes had been pierced by pieces of an enchanted mirror, distorting all the good in the world.

I sighed, my enthusiasm for the task fading. I took the rest of the photos and slid them into the pocket at the back of the album, promising myself I'd finish the job another time. I needed to go to bed.

Tomorrow, I promised myself. *Tomorrow, I will get my mind right. I will stop obsessing about the past. I will delete Nick's texts and block his number. I'll stop looking for his name online. I'll stop comparing everything Sean does with what I think Nick would do. I'll be happy with everything I have.*

The photos refused to slide into the folder, scattering to the floor when I picked the album up. Something was wedged into the pocket. I could feel a slight bulge, hear the crinkle of paper. My nails were too short to pry whatever it was out, and I went and got a butter knife from the silverware drawer. Wiggling the knife back and forth, I slipped the point down under the item and loosened it, slowly drawing it and the knife blade back up and out. Setting the knife aside, I reached in and coaxed the object free. It was a plain white envelope; its corners crumpled from years of confinement. The flap was tucked in but unsealed. Curious, I slid my finger under it and felt the edge of the envelope slice into my skin.

Annoyed, I stuck my finger in my mouth, hoping to ward off the sting of the papercut, wincing when it came a moment later. My left hand fumbled to extract the letter I could see inside. I unfolded the page of plain white notebook paper.

I gasped as I recognized Nick's cramped, block lettering.

She'd kept it.

July 2, 1992
Beautiful Maiden,
I'm leaving.
This is the hardest thing I've ever written. Please
know, no matter what you hear, not matter how you
feel toward me right now, that I love you...

I read the rest of Nick's letter, heart pounding. Here was the proof I'd been seeking. Nick hadn't left me after all. He'd always meant to come back.

I'd found it.

Chapter 11

I was ten years old the day my father announced that he was leaving. He had another family and he was going to live with them full time. My mother hadn't seemed surprised. She'd simply retrieved his suitcase from the basement and helped him pack.

I, on the other hand, had been stunned. How could my father possibly live outside of my existence? Didn't parents cease to exist when their children were not around to call them by name? I cried. I begged for him to stay. I followed him out to the family station wagon as he loaded his things into it. Years of reading fairy tales had convinced me that I could reverse the spell my father was under if only I could find the right combination of words.

But nothing I said had stopped him. Not "No," not "Why?" not "Please."

I ran into the street, watching him drive away, tears running down my face, listening to the rattle of the dragging tailpipe that was as familiar as my father's voice. The sound faded, taking my father with it. I stayed there, motionless, until my mother came out and led me into the house. She tucked me into bed, and I'd slept for the next three days because I hadn't known what else to do.

The aftermath of discovering Nick's letter reminded me of those days. Once again, I didn't know what to do. Everything I thought I knew was wrong. I was Alice, hitting the bottom of the rabbit hole. I was Dorothy opening the door to Oz. Nick had said the magic words to undo the damage he'd wrought; I just hadn't heard him in time.

I'd spent years grieving Nick, believing myself to be the injured party, when, in fact, I had left him. Nick never meant for our separation to be permanent. I tortured myself, imagining the look on his face when he realized that I hadn't waited for him. Had his uncle or one of his cousins told him about my engagement announcement or sent him my wedding photo? My mom had insisted on putting it in the local paper. "People in Clemmons watched you grow up, Corinne. They'll want to know." At the time, I'd wondered if Nick would be one of the people who wanted to know. I'd imagined him reading the notice with Kirsten, casually noting that I'd moved on, pleased that my life was fine without him in it.

Now I saw a new scene: Nick, unfolding the paper, seeing Sean and I smiling on the church steps. His heart breaks, realizing that the second chance he'd hoped for would never come. Instead of proving that he hadn't hurt me, I'd hurt him by moving on. I imagined him running his finger over the newsprint, tracing my face, perhaps tearing out the picture and stowing it in his shirt pocket, close to his heart. Nick, forging ahead, brave and alone.

What was I supposed to do now that I knew the truth? How could life ever be the same? Were there words I was supposed to speak, to undo the damage? How could I live the same old life now that I knew that everything could have been different?

* * *

Sean and I stood at the sink, washing dishes in silence. Phrases from Nick's letter whirled around in my head, broken by flashes of what I imagined to be. *I'm leaving.* Nick, writing the letter, eyes bright with unshed tears, handing the letter over, driving away with Kirsten. *Wait for me.* Nick hoping for a phone call, a message, a sign that I was still there, waiting for him. *We will be together again.* Nick, staring at my marriage announcement. *My heart is a broken wasteland.* Nick, moving on with his life, mourning what could have been. Courageously attending the reunion, hoping for a chance to explain, make things right, recover what we'd lost. *Time cannot defeat us.*

A wet plate, one of my favorites, slipped through my hands and shattered. Tears filled my eyes.

"Don't move," Sean said as he motioned to my bare feet. "I'll get the broom."

He tiptoed carefully across the floor to the mudroom. I stood, useless, towel in hand, while he swept shards of china into the dustpan and ran a wet paper towel around the floor to pick up any stray pieces. He dumped everything into the trash and tied the bag closed.

"You go. I'll finish up here." He patted my cheek on his way out to the garage, not noticing that, like the plate, I was falling to pieces.

* * *

I couldn't stay in the house another minute. On impulse, I reached for my camera and camera bag. The weight of the camera in my hands was soothing; the pull of the strap across my shoulder comforting.

I hurried up the street, hoping not to hear the noise of Sean's feet behind me, asking where I was going, offering to join me. I needed to be alone.

I turned left at the corner and headed toward the community

center, toward the picnic tables and tennis courts. It was dusk but not yet dark, and the evening was chilly; I'd forgotten a jacket in my haste. I walked, crossing pools of light as the streetlamps switched on.

The tennis courts were empty. I entered the security gate code and turned on the floodlights. Dropping my bag at the entrance, I stood, camera in hand, and wondered where to start. It felt like a test, my first real photo in years. I should choose something important, something profoundly symbolic and metaphorical.

I stood, indecisive, then raised the camera to eye level and took a series of quick shots; the shadows of the wire fence against the clay flooring, the white court lines dissecting the dark. Amateurish, uninspired, but I relaxed. The first pictures were out of the way. I rolled my shoulders, my neck.

Loosen up, Corinne. It's like riding a bike. Take it slow. Find the shot.

I moved further onto the court and turned, pointing my camera to the lights, making some adjustments, taking a shot of the halo around the court lights, finding my rhythm.

Corinne moves silently across the deserted court, her whole body absorbed in the choreography of photography, crouching, leaning in, camera raised.

I stayed out until my arms, unconditioned to holding a camera up for such a length of time, screamed in protest. I walked home, camera bag slung over my shoulders, massaging my sore biceps, a smile on my face. I felt different, had felt the shift the moment I picked up my camera again. Something inside me had taken root and sprouted, like a seed cracking open, a fresh green bud reaching up to the sun.

"Thank you, Nick, for reminding me," I said into the sky.

* * *

The last time I took pictures with my camera rather than my phone was a sunny spring day in 2010, a few weeks before my mother died. Audra had been nine. It was a teacher workday at school, so we made a picnic lunch and took it to my mother. At that point, she had moved into an extended care facility. Audra, with the resilience of the young, was accustomed to seeing Nana sporting various tubes and needles and made her way confidently around the community center, making friends with other residents and readily accepting their compliments of "pretty girl" and "so sweet."

We bundled Mom into her wheelchair. She wore her heavy purple wool coat and a pink chenille blanket over her legs, though the day was warm and Audra and I were both in light clothing. We wheeled outside to a spot near the man-made pond filled with overweight koi who floated lazily near the shore, hoping for scraps. Audra and I ate peanut butter sandwiches, which she'd cut into butterflies and flower shapes with her cookie cutters, and I spoon-fed my mom the smoothie I'd made from pureed mangos and strawberries. She'd been lucid and talkative, more than she had been in the weeks since finishing her final round of treatments. The warmth of the day and the light playing across the new green leaves had made me optimistic, and I'd thrown my camera in the car at the last minute, just in case. After lunch, I retrieved it and spent twenty minutes posing my mother and Audra until my mother said she was tired and wanted to go inside.

I'd meant to develop the prints right away, planning to frame the best shots and hang them in my mother's room, but that night Audra woke up with a fever and a stomachache. For the next few days, I ran myself ragged as my child had the most virulent, toxic stomach flu I'd ever seen. My days and nights ran together, differentiated only by glimpses of light or dark sky outside as I trudged across the house with yet another load of soiled laundry. Sean had been out of town for work, and instead of returning home, he'd gone to his co-worker John's house for a couple of days while I disinfected the house. If there was anything worse than a sick child, I knew it was a sick child *plus* a sick husband.

By the time Audra was on the mend, it was a week later, and she and I were both pale, thin, and weakened. Every surface, every floor, every light switch, doorknob, and drawer pull in the house had been cleaned. It smelled like a hospital, even though I opened the windows every chance I could, airing out the germs and the bleach fumes equally. Sean came home and took over Audra's care while I lapsed into a nasty cold born out of exhaustion and stress. I did my best at keeping up with my mother by phone, but I was afraid to visit, fearful of infecting her. Our calls were frustrating and jumbled; my mother often forgetting who she was speaking to and lapsing into bewildered silence. I would wait, clutching the phone, listening to her labored breathing, until a nurse came by and brought the call to an end. I managed one final visit, sitting across the table from her in the dining hall, watching as the shell of what was once Marie Murphy sat hunched and diminished over her tray of untouched food, while outside, rain fell in sheets against the windows.

She died two weeks later, and my need for creative expression was replaced by grief and the logistics of loss. I was too preoccupied tying up the loose ends of another person's life, as well as answering the questions of a child who didn't understand where her Nana had gone.

* * *

I stared now at the picture that had languished on my memory card, hiding in plain sight next to the photos I'd taken at the tennis court. Audra stood behind her grandmother; their hands intertwined on my mother's shoulders, in a hugging gesture. In the right of the frame was my mother's rolling IV; I could see the tube snaking out of her coat. Audra's blonde ringlets fell forward, resting on top of my mother's colorful scarf, wisps of my mother's thin hair escaping around her temples.

I pressed *print*, and the photo printer whirred arthritically to life. Tomorrow I would buy a beautiful frame and place it on the mantle, a reclaimed piece of family history.

Was it fate that Nick was the one to bring this moment back to me?

Once or twice, I'd attempted to rekindle my love for photography, taking pictures, as Grace reminded me, of Audra's Brownie troop, school plays, birthdays, Christmases. Sean had tried to be supportive, dutifully purchasing tickets to photography exhibits, giving me beautifully bound books on the works of Ansel Adams, John Fielder, Dorothea Lange. But somehow, his efforts, though thoughtful and well-meant, felt more like a judgment on me, a reminder of the profession I was not pursuing. He eventually noticed my lack of enthusiasm, and the photography-themed gifts stopped. Once again, I put my camera away on a high shelf, where it remained untouched, a relic from another time. I'd never really picked up my camera again, never wanted to.

Until now.

Until Nick.

To Sean or Grace, the idea of taking a few simple pictures seemed like no big deal, but they didn't understand that it was like opening the door to a room I'd blocked off years ago inside myself. I expected the space to be dust-covered and sepia-toned and had instead found it sunshine-filled and clean, everything waiting just as I'd left it for my eventual return. It felt inevitable, like my reunion with Nick. It had merely been invisible until this moment. Until I had eyes with which to see. Somehow Nick had restored my vision in a way my husband had failed to.

With Nick, I was different. Nick saw only me. He didn't see my daily lists, my chores. His version of me skipped over all the years where I'd lost the outlines of myself. Instead, he'd walked back into my life at the moment when I needed him most, and *seen* me. The encouragement he gave was based on the potential he remembered. He knew the girl I had been and believed that the woman I was descended directly from her.

Sean was too close to me to see me that way. He'd seen me through the years of college, the cheap apartments and cheaper beer, followed by the endless nights of toggling between a crying baby and crushing work deadlines. He'd been there for the later years, the demands of an inquisitive toddler and a terminally ill mother. He'd seen me lying in bed for days on end in my pajamas, grieving and sleeping. He'd watched as I'd pulled myself together, joined the PTA, and become a super volunteer in an effort to stay busy, relevant. Sean knew me too well to see me differently. As he'd said about his reunion: "I like my memories the way they are. It would be inconvenient to have to update them." He would find it inconvenient to change his perception of me.

But Nick...Nick was ready to believe in me. The Corinne of texts, the Corinne I used to be, the Corinne I could be again. The idea of starting over, the chance to be this new-old Corinne... Well, it was sexy as hell. I couldn't let it go.

Chapter 12

Nick began texting more and more. It was as if he was testing me, making sure I was still out there, waiting for him.

It was working; I was.

I carried my phone everywhere and checked it frequently: in line at the store, at stoplights, every few seconds in the privacy of home. One afternoon, I walked down the driveway to retrieve a package left in the mailbox. I brought my phone with me, staring at the screen, willing a new message to appear.

"Hey, Corinne."

I looked up, startled. It was our neighbor, Sheila Thomas. Sheila and her son, Daniel Junior (DJ to us), moved in two years ago after Daniel Senior had died unexpectedly from a heart attack. DJ and Audra were the same age, but DJ still attended his old school, so we rarely crossed paths except in the way neighbors do—at the mailbox, on the greenway, over platters of hors d'oeuvres at block parties. Sheila was a real estate agent, her picture smiled at me from For Sale signs along my regular errand routes.

The same smile faced me now. "Oh, hey," I said, trying to keep the irritation out of my voice. I knew, I just knew, if I concentrated hard enough, I could make Nick text me. I opened the mailbox and slid the contents out—the padded Amazon envelope addressed to Sean, a letter from the property management association, Audra's latest home decorating magazine, a donation request from the local cat shelter. I closed the mailbox and reluctantly slid my phone into my back pocket, resigned to making the required small talk: the weather, the HOA, the latest antics of Mr. Perkins, the neighborhood eccentric who shot squirrels with a BB gun from his porch.

But Sheila stopped me cold with: "Isn't it wonderful about Audra and DJ?"

I gaped at her.

Corinne stands, dumbfounded, staring at her neighbor, the forgotten mail falling from her grasp.

Sheila leaned over and picked up the scattered letters while I remained frozen. She handed the stack back to me, looking concerned. "Corinne, are you all right?"

I took the mail, holding it to my chest like a shield. "I'm sorry, Sheila. You just…you surprised me." I shook my head. "I'm trying to…what about Audra and DJ?"

Sheila's expression morphed from concerned to puzzled. "Well, they've started dating. In my day, we called it going together." She looked at me, quizzically. "Did you not know?"

I shook my head, embarrassed. *Corinne is a bad mother.* "Audra doesn't confide much of anything to me these days." I shrugged, hoping to convey an offhand what-can-you-do? vibe. "But you're right. It's wonderful. DJ is a sweet kid." I was babbling.

Sheila looked at me strangely. "Well, Audra's been spending a lot of time over at our house. She and DJ do their homework together in the kitchen. And he's been driving her home from her Thursday night class. He works over by the school. I'm so sorry to surprise you like this. I never dreamed you didn't know."

"No, no. Don't worry about it. It's wonderful," I repeated, wanting to escape this conversation. "It's great. Thank you for telling me. I have to get back inside now. I...uh...left a pot on the stove." I fled up the walkway and into the house, slamming the door and leaning against it as if Sheila might try to break down the door behind me.

* * *

"Did you know about Audra and DJ?" I asked Sean that night.

Dinner had been a quiet affair. Lost in thought, I'd picked at the food, preferring my wine. Audra had offered monosyllabic answers to Sean's questions about her day: "Good," "Fine," "No." ("How was your day," "How's design class going," "Do you have homework," respectively). I'd studied her over the top of my cup, gauging the right moment to ask her about DJ. She'd shot me several suspicious glances, had even asked her own question: "What's wrong?" to which my answer of "nothing" had earned an eye roll of gargantuan proportions.

Sean watched this exchange and gave up trying to engage either of us in conversation. We ate the rest of our baked ravioli in silence, punctuated only by the clicking of silverware on plates and Meowser's wheezing snores from the family room. Audra retreated the moment her plate was empty, snagging a piece of garlic bread on her way out, claiming that she was helping Lana with math over FaceTime. Alone, Sean and I looked at each other across the table and sighed in unison.

"She'll grow out of it, right?" Sean stood and began to clear the table.

"God, I hope so." I drained my wine in one large swallow. I stood, feeling a little woozy.

It'd taken most of the washing and drying for me to approach the subject of DJ. I wasn't worried that Sean would object. Audra had gone on dates before. I was nervous about giving myself away—that I'd been too preoccupied with my one-sided fantasies to notice the reality around me.

Now I set the dried casserole dish down and turned to face my husband, who was elbow-deep in suds. "So," I repeated, "did you?"

He turned the faucet on and sprayed out the pasta pot, handing it to me before answering, "Sure, I knew."

"Did she tell you?" This was the other question I didn't want answered. Since my depression, Sean was Audra's go-to parent, the recipient of her confidences. It was a sore spot between us, a bruise that we avoided prodding as much as possible.

Sean dried his hands on the towel draped over the stove handle. "Not outright. They went out with a group for pizza once, and then a couple of weeks later, I saw them talking by the mailbox. I asked, and she answered. Plus, she's been texting him constantly and doing her homework over there." Sean cocked his head, looking at me in much the same way Sheila had earlier. "What is up with you?"

"Nothing's up with me." The wine was making my words thick, my gestures big. "I just find it hard to believe that our daughter has been dating the *literal* boy next door, and no one thought to say anything to me, her mother, about it." I flung down my towel and stormed through the kitchen to our bedroom, slamming the door behind me.

Shaking, I sank back onto the bed and covered my eyes with a faux fur throw pillow. The room spun in lazy circles. It wasn't fair. Audra was getting her chance at high school romance just as I was trying to get over mine. I knew it was wrong, so wrong, to be jealous of my daughter's happiness, but I lay there in the dark, wallowing in it and thinking small, mean thoughts.

I wanted to feel that way again.

A knock at the door and Sean's voice: "Can I come in?"

He didn't wait for my answer but opened the door slowly and approached the bed, like an explosives technician approaching a ticking bomb. He lowered himself beside me and held his arms out. I snuggled up under his chin automatically, draping my leg over his, while his hand went to my hair, smoothing it back. Would spooning with Nick feel different, I wondered. Would we fit together like this? I tried to remember how we used to be, frustrated when the memory eluded me.

A *ping* from Sean's phone broke the moment.

"Sorry," he said, leaning to the side to fish it from his pocket. "I need to make sure this isn't work." He checked his messages, and satisfied, laid the phone face down on the nightstand. He turned my face up to his, holding my chin gently with his thumb and index finger. "I'm worried about you. No, let me talk," he said as I opened my mouth to protest. "You've been checked out and moody for the past few weeks. What's got you so upset? Our daughter has a boyfriend, that's all." He opened his eyes wider, eyebrows reaching for his hairline. "Is something else going on? Is there anything we need to talk about?"

I pushed myself up on my elbow, my arm buzzing as the blood began circulating again, my head heavy. "No," I said, mirroring his expression, eyes wide and earnest. "There's nothing to talk about." I held his gaze, trying not to blink. The room tilted on its axis; I swallowed down a rising wave of nausea.

Sean looked away first. "Have it your way." He stood and left the room, closing the door quietly behind him.

Alone in the swirling dark, I tried to organize my thoughts, to pinpoint the sense of foreboding that permeated the room. Audra. A boyfriend. My husband's worried face. Is there anything we need to talk about?

Nick.

* * *

I was at the breakfast table the next morning, waiting for Audra to appear. Despite last night's argument and wine, I'd slept well and woken up brimming with energy. I'd even showered and done my hair and makeup, preparing with care for this conversation.

Corinne sits in the quiet of the morning hours, looking poised in wide-legged tan linen trousers and a long sleeve black cotton shirt.

I sipped my coffee, mentally running potential opening lines as Audra entered the room:

"I spoke to Mrs. Thomas yesterday."

"How is DJ?"

"Got any plans this weekend?"

Audra set the cooking time for her pancakes and turned to face me. "So, you heard about Daniel?"

I blinked in surprise. She'd veered off script. "Um, well, yes. I spoke with Mrs. Thomas yesterday, and she told me. I think it's wonderful. DJ's a sweet boy," I said, echoing what I'd told his mother. It was true; DJ was a sweet boy. He was polite and never parked his car in front of our garbage cans on trash day. When he mowed, he did the shared strip of grass between our homes. "I don't understand why you didn't tell me. Did you think I'd, *we'd,* say no?" I wanted to make this point clear. I wasn't going to be the bad guy. I was siding with Sean, and we were on her side.

The microwave beeped, and Audra took her pancakes out, juggling them between her hands as they steamed, and joined me at the table. "He goes by Daniel now, not DJ."

"Okay, I'll try to remember."

"And it's not like I thought you guys would mind, or say no or anything, it's just"—her face reddened, and she rolled her eyes, looking embarrassed—"it's new. And it's private. It's mine, and I didn't want to share it yet, you know?"

Oh, I knew. I glanced at my phone, sitting to the right of my coffee cup. A thought struck me. "Your father knew."

She shrugged. "Dad's different. He doesn't get all *parent-y* on me."

My mouth tightened. Of course.

Audra went on. "And it wasn't, like, something we planned. Our football team played theirs, and we got to talking at the game. Afterward, we went for pizza."

I leaned forward. "See, that's the part that bothers me. Where did you say you were going that night? Did you lie to us about where you were going or who you were with?"

She shook her head, affronted, curls bouncing. "No, I told Dad where I was going. You weren't even home that weekend. You were at your reunion," she said with a shrug.

Corinne is not the only one with secrets.

"Besides," she continued, tearing pieces off her breakfast, "I didn't think you'd care. You've been so spacey lately." Audra pushed back from the table, crumpling her napkin. "Look, I'm sorry I didn't say anything sooner. I should have. And I'm glad you know now. I...really like Daniel." She blushed, and my heart went out to her. Who better than I to sympathize with the flush of first romance? She gave a quick half laugh, embarrassed, not meeting my eyes but skimming past my face as she shouldered her backpack. "So we're going to the movies tonight. I'll be home after school, and then he's going to pick me up." She glanced backward at me as she headed for the foyer to wait for Lana. "You'll be cool, right? I mean, he doesn't have to come inside and *talk* to you?"

I gave her my most understanding smile. "No, we know Dee...Daniel. He doesn't have to come in. But I do expect him to walk you to the door. And," I continued, even as Audra's hand rested on the doorknob, "no more secrets. Got it? In this family, we are honest with each other."

* * *

The doorbell rang at precisely six o'clock. Sean and I had stationed ourselves as casually as we could in the family room. He was stretched out on the couch with his laptop, spreadsheets strewn across his legs; I was curled in the hanging basket chair, staring at a magazine I wasn't reading. One foot was tucked under me while the other grazed the floor, giving a gentle push whenever the rocking slowed. Even the cat stood sentry, grooming himself on the entryway bench.

"I've got it!" Audra called, racing to the door. Sean and I looked at each other as we heard the door open. First, Audra's voice, whispered and urgent, followed by DJ's even baritone response. A moment later, he stepped into the room, smiling. Beside him, Audra glowered, daring us to say a word.

"Hi, Mr. and Mrs. Fuller," he said, raising his hand in a waist-high wave.

I found myself doing some swift updates to my mental picture of my daughter's beau. *DJ* was a scrawny boy with feet and hands too big for his body, wearing athletic shorts and a school sweatshirt regardless of the weather. *DJ* wore braces, sported adolescent acne, and didn't speak above a mumble. *Daniel* was a tall, broad-shouldered young man, with smooth skin and perfect teeth, wearing a button-down blue oxford and chinos. DJ had morphed into Daniel, and Daniel was the one dating our daughter, herself a changeling from a child with wild curls and grubby knees into this cool, sophisticated woman in a black maxi dress and cropped denim jacket. They were young, and they were beautiful. I couldn't tear my eyes away, the photographer in me longing to capture the chiaroscuro of their intertwined fingers.

I stared too long; the moment teetered into an uncomfortable silence.

Sean, ever the diplomat, stood and crossed the room. "Hey

Daniel," he said, shaking Daniel's hand. "Good to see you." The awkward moment passed.

"Have a great time," he added, laying a fatherly hand on Audra's arm. "Home by eleven, please."

"Bye, Mr. Fuller, Mrs. Fuller," Daniel nodded in my direction.

I smiled, gave a small wave. "Bye. Have fun."

Audra mouthed "Thank you" behind Daniel's retreating back, and then they were gone. Off into the night to enjoy their youth, their beauty, their freedom. It hurt to watch them go, to be excluded, to stay behind.

Returning to the couch, Sean turned to me, eyebrow raised suggestively. "Alone at last, Mrs. Fuller. What should we do to pass the time?" He powered off his computer, moved the papers to the floor, and patted the seat beside him.

My phone vibrated against my hip. I knew it was Nick. I felt a jab of irritation with Sean for being in the room, for looking at me expectantly. If he wasn't here, I could answer Nick's message.

I must've scowled because Sean's expression changed. "Are you okay? You're making a weird face."

"I'm fine." I pushed myself out of the chair, reluctantly leaving my phone where it was. I sat a safe distance away from where Sean had indicated and picked up the remote. "Want to watch TV?" I kept my eyes on the list of new series releases, ignoring, but still feeling, the hurt look on my husband's face.

His unasked question loomed between us: *Is there something I should know?*

We binge-watched a show I couldn't recall later and ate popcorn I didn't taste. My eyes kept stealing over to the chair, where Nick's message waited. Always the optimist, Sean draped his arm behind me on the couch and inched closed until our knees touched. We talked in vague observations about the actors: "Is that the same guy from that British thing we watched last month?" and "Wait, what did she say?" Passing the time until curfew.

It was ten thirty when the finale's credits rolled. I stretched, my knees and hips protesting from being in one position for so long. I flicked the channel to a decorating show and began picking up escaped popcorn kernels.

Sean put a hand on my knee to stop me. "Wait," he said, taking the popcorn bowl from me and turning off the television. He took my hands in his.

"Look," he started, then paused and cleared his throat before continuing, "I don't know what's been going on with you lately, but I wanted to say that, whatever it is, you can talk to me."

My heart hammered; my cheeks flushed. I worked to keep my eyes on his. Looking away was a sure sign of a guilty conscience. What did he know? My mind ran over the last couple of weeks. Had he seen my texts? I'd been so careful to keep my phone screen hidden. Had he found the photo in the nightstand drawer? No, he never looked in that drawer.

"I know you're going through some stuff with Audra right now. I know she's tough on you." Audra? Was he worried about my relationship with Audra? My shoulders relaxed a fraction. Sean noticed, taking it as a sign to continue. "I've been working on this project, and we haven't had much time to ourselves..." He stopped, took a deep breath.

"So I thought that it might be good for us to talk to someone. To see someone. Together." Sean looked over my shoulder. "Not the same doctor you saw after your mom...I got the name of a couple's therapist from John. He said she specializes in this kind of thing—empty nesters, he called it. John and Kelly saw her after Emma left for college. I called and she can see us a week from Tuesday." He met my gaze, more confident now that he was back to his specialty, problem-solving.

I felt violated, annoyed, defensive. "What are you doing

telling people at work about our problems? If you think we have problems, you should talk to me! I'm your wife!"

"I have tried talking to you! You're never here!"

"What do you mean? I'm here all the time! I don't have anywhere else to go!"

"Sure, you're in the house, but you're not *here*, Corinne. You haven't been for weeks. You're always checking your phone or locked in your office doing God-knows-what on the computer!"

I thought I'd been so smart, so sneaky. Now I was trapped. If I said no to this suggestion, to therapy, he'd want to know why.

"Fine." I rose from the couch, collecting the dishes. "I'll do it. I'll go."

Sean stood and put his hand on my arm to stop me. We locked eyes, and I knew, felt in my bones, the new question he wanted to ask: is there some*one* I should know about?

Audra came in the front door, calling, "I'm home!"

"Hey, honey." Sean gave me a final look and went to greet our daughter. I moved to the kitchen, putting some space between us. I glanced toward my phone, still lying abandoned on the chair cushion, on my way.

I washed dishes and wiped down counters, killing time. Sean crossed through the kitchen on his way to bed, stopping for a glass of water and giving me a peck on the cheek. "Love you," he said. He looked tired.

"You too," I answered automatically, eyes drifting back to my chair. Nick was still waiting.

I waited through the interminable noises of Sean's bedtime routine—emptying his pockets, throwing clothes in the hamper, brushing his teeth, relieving himself, washing his hands. Finally, the light turned off under the bedroom door, and I was free. Sean was probably reading, but he wouldn't get up again. Even if he did, I'd hear him open the door.

Not that I was doing anything wrong. I was just checking my

phone. I could be talking to Beth. I'd sat up late at night, texting or talking with my best friend lots of times.

A single message from Nick greeted me. A photo of the Clemmons dam, of blue sky over a stone bridge. The water was foamy, caught in motion. In the foreground, his hand held up the local paper, today's date visible:

Wish you were here

I replied without hesitation:

Me too.

Chapter 13

Everything changed after that. Nick and I had crossed the watershed by finally acknowledging our growing desire to be together.

Before, Nick's one-word texts were infrequent and unexpected. Now we texted constantly, multi-text missives starting with: *Remember the time...* and covering everything between our first date to prom. In unspoken agreement, we did not talk about my husband or daughter. Nick did not mention any girlfriends, current or past. We didn't discuss Kirsten or our breakup. Our texts inhabited two specific topics—highlights from our six-month courtship in 1992 and present-day discovery.

It was maddening, but I limited my "Nick time," as I thought of it, to the hours when Audra and Sean were out of the house. I sat outside on the deck with a cup of coffee, phone cradled in my lap, and a portable charger nearby, reliving long-forgotten memories with Nick until it was time to return to the present.

I couldn't get over how intimate our text sessions felt. When Sean and I texted, we spoke in the shortest amount of words, conveying only facts, logistics.

But with Nick, texting was exciting. I held his words in my hands, each message like a whisper meant only for me. Even the language was suggestive—swipes, strokes, sending, receiving…I craved the buzz of my phone, those three little dots. I lost hours waiting for a reply to some comment I made, a story I'd shared. I was hooked on the foreplay of waiting for Nick.

I also texted with Beth, mining her for new high school stories until she got suspicious:

Why so many questions? What's up?

Just more teenage-nostalgia-reunion shenanigans.

I don't believe that for a second. Whatever you're doing, knock it off.

I spent more time on Facebook, creeping around the comments on Kirsten's page, hoping for a slip, an offhand remark about her "ex" to a friend. However, she remained annoyingly upbeat and generic in her public comments, all thumbs up and LOLs. I zoomed in on one of her old profile pictures, a throwback shot of her in her twenties, blonde toddler Natalie on her lap. Leaning in to see if I recognized Nick among the background figures, I accidentally clicked the "like" button.

Corinne Fuller likes this, the caption below the photo declared.

"Noooooo!" I screamed, stabbing the keyboard until the blue thumbs-up icon disappeared. Heart pounding, I logged out of Facebook and turned off the computer completely, as if somehow that would erase all evidence of my mistake. Mortified, I stayed out of the office and the house for the rest of the day, driving to a park to lose myself in photographing the explosion of fall colors. By dinner, I'd almost managed to convince myself that it was no big deal. What were the odds that Kirsten had been looking at her account right at that moment?

No, I'd been fast; she would never know.

I would be more careful in the future.

Because I couldn't stop.

* * *

Now that her secret was out, Audra was more forthcoming in sharing her plans. She bubbled over with excitement about school, design class, and Daniel, talking more during dinner than I'd heard from her in months. On nights when Sean was home, they could be found chatting comfortably together, his work and her homework spread between them at the table. Her face shone with happiness and the blush of first love.

She was also spending more time next door. Through my remembrances of hormone-addled adolescence (some more recent than others), I worried that the appeal of Daniel's house was that they often had the place to themselves. I needed to have a mother-daughter talk with Audra. We'd had "the talk" years ago, involving basic terms and hypotheticals. But circumstances had changed; nothing felt hypothetical anymore.

I vividly remembered my own mother's single failed attempt to broach this very subject. It was March, a few weeks after my birthday. I came downstairs on a snowy Saturday morning after a late night out with Nick. Mom was waiting for me at the kitchen table, staring into the tea mug clasped between her hands like a fortune teller communing with her crystal ball. The image was seared into my mind: her long graying hair, hanging straight, parted down the middle and tucked behind her ears. Her over-sized glasses sliding down her nose, her face free of makeup, eyes watchful and worried as I poured a bowl of cereal and joined her at the table.

"Are you having sex with that boy, Corinne?"

"Oh my God, Mom!" I'd shouted and fled back to my room, slamming the door. I'd stayed there for the rest of the day, eating potato chip crumbs scavenged from the bottom of my bookbag, thinking I would rather starve than eat a meal with her. How dare she? It was none of her business.

The next morning, a package of condoms appeared outside my door, alongside an appointment card for an ob-gyn. I'd canceled the appointment, kept the condoms, and the subject had never come up again, although I could see the question, awkward and unanswered, on her face every time I left to meet Nick.

Well, that wouldn't happen to me. I would be supportive and nonjudgmental. Audra would instantly be at ease, inspired to share confidences. It would be like talking to a knowledgeable older sister. I had this.

I knocked on Audra's door.

"Yeah?"

Corinne squares her shoulders and opens the door. She exudes confidence, patience, and loving understanding.

Audra was sprawled across her bed typing on her laptop, the universal "doing homework" pose. Her phone was propped against her screen, facing away from me. Ambient electronica floated from her computer speakers.

She lifted her eyes in acknowledgment. "Yeah?"

All of my careful opening phrases flew from my head. "Are you having sex with Daniel?" I blurted.

"Oh my God, Mom!" Audra cried.

Oh my God, Corinne.

We looked at each other, simultaneously stricken with horror. A moment passed, then a light cough broke the silence. "I'll uh, call you back."

"Yeah." Audra's eyes stayed fixed on mine. "Bye, Daniel," she said pointedly.

"Bye." Daniel's disembodied voice floated across the room. "Um... Bye, Mrs. Fuller."

I wanted the floor to swallow me whole. This was a disaster.

"Goodbye, Daniel." I paused, waiting until I was sure he had hung up. "Oh, honey...I didn't mean to...I'm so sorry."

"That was...not great." Audra closed her laptop and pushed back onto her knees, glaring at me. "And not that it's any of your business, but no. We are not having sex."

Her frank admission was more startling than if she'd said yes. "Oh, well...that's good. I thought—you spend so much time at his house..."

Audra rolled her eyes. "Because it's quiet there. Because it's comfortable. Because she buys the good popcorn from Costco. Geez, Mom."

"Right. Popcorn," I babbled. I'd gotten an honest, frank discussion, but it was all down to my daughter's maturity, not mine. I tried to salvage a shred of parental authority. "What I really came in here to say was if you ever need to talk, I'm always here. You can talk to me about anything, honey. Okay?"

Her posture did not relax. "I'm not going to do anything stupid."

"We don't keep secrets in this family." My face flamed as I said this.

"Yeah, yeah, I know." she heaved a sigh and flopped back against her pillows.

"Sweetie, I am so sorry. Please apologize to Daniel for me." I closed the door and leaned my forehead against the wall.

Get it together, Corinne.

Chapter 14

On Tuesday morning, I was sitting on the couch, flipping through a magazine, waiting for Sean to leave for work. Audra had left with Lana ages ago. The minutes ticked by, and still, he didn't appear. I grew more and more agitated. Under my leg, my phone buzzed with an incoming message. I knew it was Nick's usual *Good morning, maiden* prompt that started a new day of texting.

Finally, I couldn't stand it any longer. I threw down my magazine and marched through the kitchen to our bedroom, throwing the door open with force.

Sean looked up at me, startled. He was sitting on the bed, his laptop on his legs, dressed in casual weekend clothes: jeans and a long-sleeved button-up chambray shirt. The television was on but muted, turned to the local news.

"What are you doing?" I barked. "You were supposed to leave half an hour ago!"

Sean looked confused. "I'm working from home today, remember? We have our counseling appointment this afternoon. I thought it would be easier."

I'd pushed the appointment out of my mind, hadn't given it a thought since he'd initially brought it up. "You didn't tell me you'd be home today."

"I did. I texted you yesterday." Sean picked up his phone and scrolled until he found the message. He held up his screen as proof.

I thought back. I had been teasing Nick, asking why I couldn't find any of his articles online:

> I like my privacy, maiden. I use a pseudonym.

I'd spent the rest of the afternoon making guesses, much to Nick's amusement. I must've dismissed Sean's text without reading it.

I backtracked. "Right. I forgot."

"I thought we could go out to lunch beforehand, make a date out of it." He smiled hopefully.

"I can't. I have Grace's PTA luncheon today."

Now it was his turn to pause, look surprised. I felt a gloating sense of victory at his confused face; the tables now turned. "I told you weeks ago. Grace needs a photographer for the presentation. I'll have to meet you at…there." I couldn't bring myself to say "counseling" or "therapy."

I turned, tossing my hair triumphantly over my shoulder, and stalked into the bathroom to get ready.

* * *

Corinne steps out of the house and pauses on the top step, face to the autumn sky. Her hair falls in loose waves around her face, her highlights winking in the morning sun. She takes a deep breath, inhaling her freedom, then runs lightly down the flagstone path to her car. She stows her camera in the front seat, a confident photographer ready for her first assignment.

I sat in the driveway, minivan idling, and checked my messages. Two from Nick already.

An hour ago:

> Good morning, beautiful.

Five minutes ago:

> Did you forget about me?

I responded:

> Of course not. Busy morning.

> Not too busy for me, I hope.

> Never.

Smiling, I reversed down the driveway, pausing to wave at Sheila as she pulled out into the street ahead of me. She waved back before driving off.

* * *

The PTA luncheon went smoothly, just as Grace promised. I worked quickly, my confidence building, snapping photos of the council president speaking, shaking hands with our local representatives, smiling, posing in group shots for the quarterly newsletter.

By a quarter of one the room was empty except for banquet staff bussing plates and cups through the swinging double doors to the hotel kitchen. Grace was on the stage, closing down her laptop. I joined her, collecting the foam core PTA signs that flanked the podium and stacking them in her rolling cart.

"Thanks for coming today. For taking pictures. The superintendent was pleased with the whole event."

"You were right. It was easy," I said. "And fun. So thank *you*."

"I'm glad," Grace said, packing her cords away. She turned the projector light off, waiting for the machine to power down completely before turning her attention back to me. "We needed a good picture for the newsletter. Last time I let Louise take the photos, she managed to cut off the top of everyone's heads."

"I've been thinking about getting back into photography, so this was good practice," I said casually, trying the words out loud for the first time.

Grace smiled. "That's great, Corinne. I always thought you could do more than take pictures of troop outings." Her phone buzzed, and she looked down, frowning. "It's the babysitter. Charlie's home with a fever. I know I promised you a coffee, but do you mind if we reschedule?" Without waiting for my answer, she turned away, already pressing the phone to her ear. I stacked her laptop in the wagon with the signs and added the projector. Grace turned back from the side of the stage, still talking on the phone. She motioned for me to leave the rest of the packing to her. I gave her a wave, grabbed my camera and tripod, and left.

In the lobby, I checked messages. A text from Sean, reminding me to be at our appointment early to fill out paperwork. I didn't reply. I also had a missed call notice from an unknown number and a new voice mail. I hit *play* and pressed the phone to my ear.

"Hi Corinne, It's Sheila. I hope it's okay, but I got your number through Daniel from Audra. Audra mentioned last night that you were photographing an event today and well...I could use your help. I'm with a client right now. We're supposed to do her listing photos, and my photographer just canceled on me. Would you be willing to do it? The stager is already here; everything's ready to go. Call me when you get this, please."

The message was timestamped ten minutes ago. I found Sheila's number in my call log. She answered before the phone rang on my side. "Hi! Corinne! Thank you so much for calling me back. Did you get my message? I know it's a huge favor to ask, and you probably have a hundred things to do this afternoon, but these are important clients, and they expect better than crappy pictures with my phone..."

"I'll do it!" The answer flew unbidden from my mouth, an involuntary response. What was this magic? I mentioned to Grace that I wanted to get back into photography, and now this? It was a sign—a gift. The universe was showing me the way. "What's the address?" She read it slowly as I typed it into my navigation system. "I'm about forty minutes away."

"That's perfect. I'm just finishing up with the stager. I'll send my clients out for a late lunch while you and I work out the shots."

I called Sean, got his voicemail. Good, that was easier.

"It's me. Look, I am so sorry to do this, but I have to miss our appointment. I got a call from Sheila. She's in a bind and needs someone to take some pictures for a listing this afternoon. I'm headed there right now. I should be home before dinner. I hope it's not too much trouble to reschedule. I'll call when I'm on my way home, okay? I'm sorry. Bye."

Then I sent a quick text to Nick:

On my way to a PHOTOGRAPHY ASSIGNMENT!

He replied immediately:

Told you you were talented.

Corinne races across the parking lot, her face flushed with excitement.

159

Thank you, Nick. Thank you for bringing magic back into my life.

* * *

I couldn't stop smiling as I drove home, despite the stop and go annoyances of rush hour traffic. I sang along with the radio as mentally I reframed and cropped shots from the photo session.

Sheila's clients' house was a beautifully restored Georgian in an upscale neighborhood. I took three dozen photos of the beautiful red brick exterior alone, each picture like stretching a muscle. By the time we moved inside, my blood was pumping, and I was invigorated, on an adrenaline high.

The next few hours flew by. Sheila, as promised, had sent her clients off to enjoy a leisurely lunch on her tab, while she and I moved room to room, discussing shot angles and lighting options to bring out the home's best features. Sheila acted as both my director and assistant, making suggestions on which angles to shoot from, and the details to focus on.

"You're a natural, Corinne," she said as we worked the guest bedroom, a small but light-filled room. I'd glowed with pleasure at her praise. Real estate photography was something I'd never considered before, but I'd thoroughly enjoyed the day. I couldn't wait to review my work at home on my desktop screen.

Sheila had offered to pay me, but I'd refused. "You're doing me a favor," I said. "I haven't had this much fun in…ages." I was shocked to realize it was true. When was the last time I'd had fun? First, the luncheon, now this.

I pulled into the driveway, humming as I parked and gathered my things. A light rain, barely more than a mist, had started. I hurried to the front door. The porch lights were off, and the door was locked. Puzzled, I juggled my phone to the other hand, unlocked the door, and stepped into the foyer. "Hello?" I called. No answer.

I peered down the hallway toward Audra's room. The door stood open, and I could see clothes scattered across the floor, threatening to seep into the hallway. "Audra?" I called. No reply.

I dropped my keys and purse onto the sideboard and moved into the family room. Empty.

In the bedroom, I found Sean's leftover coffee cup and a still-unmade bed. Annoyed, I yanked the sheets flat and made the bed, punching the pillows up. I carried the dirty cup to the sink, where it joined the rest of the breakfast dishes. I sighed at the sight of dried cereal crusted in a milky ring around the drain. Blasting the sink with dish soap, I left the mess to soak.

My phone buzzed from the foyer, and I went to retrieve it, noticing that the mail was in its customary place. So, Audra had been home and had gone back out. I glanced through the glass pane of the front door toward the Thomas' house.

I had three unread texts from Sean, and one missed phone call from his work number:

Where are you?

What do you mean reschedule?

Call me.

The last text had come through at three o'clock. The phone call was newer; I'd missed it during the drive home. Sean's voice, flat, giving no clue to his emotional state, told me that he was heading to the office for a budget meeting and not to hold dinner. I deleted the message as well as his texts. We'd talk when he got home.

I felt a stab of the guilt I'd been suppressing since leaving the message from Sean canceling on him. He'll understand, I told myself; it's Sean. He gets annoyed, but he doesn't get angry.

There was also a text from Audra:

At Daniel's. Did homework. Home by 10.

No word from Nick, which was disappointing. I grinned, thinking of how much I had to tell him now. How much one afternoon had changed things.

Humming to myself, I went to upload my photos and get to work.

* * *

It was after nine o'clock when I heard the garage door open and Sean's footsteps a few moments later.

I leaned back in my chair, stretching. I'd been absorbed in my work the entire evening, pausing only to eat some popcorn and refill my wine glass. I'd sent the edited photos to Sheila only twenty minutes ago and was now playing around with some layout ideas for a listing brochure.

I waited in the office, wanting to tell Sean all about my day, listening for clues about his mood. I heard him moving around, but no slammed doors or frustrated noises. When he still hadn't appeared fifteen minutes later, I went in search of him. I would be the bigger adult.

He was in the bathroom, already changed into pajama pants and the Life is Good T-shirt Audra had given him last Father's Day. He was brushing his teeth with short, aggressive strokes. When he spat into the sink, the foam was flecked with red.

"Hi," I said, positioning myself in the doorway so he could see me in the mirror.

He dried his face with the hand towel. "Hi," he said, speaking to my reflection.

"How was work?"

"Work," he said, overemphasizing the word, "was fine. The rest of my day sucked."

"I'm sorry about the appointment today. I am. But Sheila was in a bind and needed my help. There was nothing I could do..." I trailed off, waiting for him to forgive me. That was the way of our arguments: I apologized, he absolved.

Sean turned to me, his face thunderous. I took a surprised step back. "Of course, there was something you could do. You could have said no. You could have met Sheila later or another time. You had choices, and you made the wrong one." He stepped past me into the bedroom and pulled back the sheets on his side. A throw pillow fell to the ground, and he kicked at it angrily, sending it into the corner where it collided with a floor lamp. For a moment, we both watched the light teeter before righting itself back onto its wide brass base. Sean sat on the bed with a defeated *whump*.

"Look, I know you didn't want to go today. I know you said you never wanted to see another therapist. But what I don't understand is why couldn't you go simply because I asked you to?" He looked at me. "What made you decide it was more important to help out Sheila—an almost total stranger—than to keep your promise to your husband?"

I started to answer, but he cut me off and held up his hand, his go-to gesture for ending a conversation. "You know what? I'm done. It's been a long day. I'm going to bed."

I bristled. "Wait a second. How about all the times you cancel on me? How many times a week do you call to say you won't be home for dinner or you're running late? How come you're allowed to do it, and I'm not?" My voice rose, my fists balled at my sides. "I am sorry I canceled, but you should under-stand how much today meant to me!"

"I have no idea how much it meant to you. You never talk to me anymore! That's what today was supposed to be about!" He climbed under the covers and reached for his Kindle before turning back to me. I closed my mouth. "If you don't want to talk to a counselor, that's fine, Corinne. But I'd like to think you would talk to me." He turned off his light. In the glow of his screen, his face looked tired and lined. He stared straight ahead as I walked around the bed and out of the room, closing the door behind me.

Back in the family room, my phone buzzed. It was a new text from Nick:

Tell me everything.

A smile stretched across my face. I settled back on the couch, pulled a blanket over my legs, and began to type.

Chapter 15

"Corinne."

I woke to Sean standing over me. I'd fallen asleep on the couch. I jerked awake, hands scrabbling for my phone, praying it wasn't spilling all my secrets. Nick and I had texted for hours last night.

My phone was on my lap, faceup, with a blank screen and a dead battery.

Phew.

"What time is it?" I rubbed at my eyes, which were gritty with last night's mascara.

"Early. Six." Sean was already dressed, moving past me and back into the kitchen. "I have a breakfast meeting." He popped a Keurig pod into the machine and set his battered NC State travel mug under the spout. His laptop and wallet lay on the counter. He rejoined me in the family room, perching on the coffee table in front of me, legs wide, hands clasped, leaning forward like he was about to deliver tough news to an employee. I sat up straighter; body tensed for another confrontation. Behind me, the coffee maker hissed and spat.

"Look," he said, "I was hurt that you skipped out on our

counseling session yesterday. I feel as though I ask for very little, and I was disappointed that you chose to break your promise to me." He jutted out his chin, assuming a pose of resolve, of renewed strength. "I would like to talk more about this, about what comes next, but I have a busy couple of days coming up, and I don't want things to be tense. So," he reached over and took my hand, "I suggest we put this whole situation aside for now and come back to it at a better time. Does that seem like a fair compromise to you?"

I wanted to point out that we couldn't have a compromise because I hadn't asked for anything, but at that moment, I heard Audra's door open and the bathroom door close. I wanted to change and clean up before she left for school. So I nodded. "Yes, that's fair." I squeezed Sean's hand, resisting the urge to shake it instead.

Sean's face relaxed, became familiar again. "Good," he said and leaned over to kiss the top of my disheveled hair like I was an obedient child. "I'll be home late again. Don't wait up."

After he left, I tossed the turquoise throw blanket back over the couch's arm and straightened the pillows. In the bedroom, I plugged my phone into its charger and changed out of yesterday's wrinkled clothes, kicking them into the corner of the closet. I threw on leggings, a blue T-shirt, and a black cotton duster. I swiped away the makeup pooled under my eyes with a tissue, redrew my eyeliner, and brushed my teeth. I pulled my hair into a ponytail, tugging at the elastic band as I headed back to the kitchen to start my coffee, replaying last night's conversation with Audra.

She had come home shortly after my fight with Sean. I was still on the couch, texting in the dark with Nick, immersed in detailing every second of my first foray into real estate photography.

She'd entered on tiptoe, sliding out of her shoes, latching the door softly.

"Hi," I said, switching on the lamp.

"Gah!" she shrieked. "I mean, hi. I didn't think you were still up." She flipped on the overhead light. Even from a distance, I could see that her chin was red and rough-looking, and her shirt was buttoned wrong. I bit back a remark.

Corinne is the cool mom.

"Your dad's asleep, and I didn't want to bother him. You want something to eat before bed?" I put down my phone and swung my feet to the ground.

Cool mom, ready to be deployed.

She shook her head. "Thanks, no. Mrs. Thomas brought home sushi." To my surprise, instead of retreating to her room, Audra moved closer and leaned over the side chair farthest from the couch. I had a momentary flashback of her when she was little, doing flips over the back of those overstuffed cushions, shrieking as her feet flew over her head. "She said you did some work for her today. Shooting pictures for a listing."

I nodded, pleased she'd brought it up. "I did. She needed someone, and it was an emergency." I tried not to sound too effusive. Nothing scared off a teenager like being overeager. "I want to thank you for telling her that I was a photographer. She wouldn't have called me otherwise." I beamed at my daughter, proud of her, proud of me, and treasuring this small creative connection between us. "So thank you. It was fun."

"She raved about you over dinner."

I flushed, pleased by the compliment and the fact that Audra had not only heard it, but repeated it. "It was a good way to spend the day."

Audra smiled and motioned down the hall with her head. "I'm going to bed. G'night."

I smiled back, happy. "Good night, honey."

She turned to go and then turned back. "Who are you texting? Aunt Beth?"

"Yes," I said, without hesitation. "Aunt Beth."

"Tell her hi for me."

"I will."

Now I greeted Audra with another smile, hoping for an encore of last night's connection, but she only grunted in response and tossed her backpack on the kitchen island, making various keychains and embellishments clatter. I winced, thinking of how many germs she'd deposited on my clean(ish) counter. From outside, a horn honked.

"Oh, shoot, I'm late," Audra muttered and grabbed a package of mini muffins from the pantry. She shouldered her backpack and hurried to the door. She paused, halfway out, and called back, "I forgot to tell you. Mrs. Thomas said she'll be contacting you about some more listings if you're interested. Bye!"

I smiled into the empty house. Sheila had liked my work enough to ask me to do more. My daughter thought I'd done something cool. Despite the misery of the situation with Sean, things were looking decidedly up.

I couldn't wait to tell Nick.

* * *

The next two days were a dance of formality. I was frosty but pleasant when Sean came home, asking about his meetings and if he was hungry. In response, he was polite but impersonal, like I was an estranged cousin seated with the wrong family at a wedding.

On Thursday night, Sean and I ate dinner together while Audra was at her design class. It was the first time since our fight that we'd been alone. I couldn't help comparing his formal efforts at small talk to Nick's supportive texts. When I'd told Nick about the additional jobs, he'd responded with an all caps "WAY TO GO!" and applause emojis. Sean, on the other hand, managed a clipped "I'm happy for you," before taking his half-finished dinner plate to the sink and retreating to the bedroom to work. One more sign pointing me in Nick's direction.

Alone at the table, I sighed; my appetite was gone. I stood and began clearing the table and loading the dishwasher. I skipped rinsing the dishes; that was Sean's job. I slammed the dishwasher closed with more force than necessary—take that, Sean—and stalked to the office. I dropped onto the couch and ran my hands over my hair.

What was Sean's problem? Why wasn't he happy for me?

For the first time in years, I had the promise of my own work, a reason other than my family to get up in the morning. It was exhilarating to have something that was solely mine again. It was as if someone had taken a Sharpie to me and outlined edges that had faded over the years. I felt defined, solid, promoted from the background to the foreground once again.

And beside me was Nick. His was the voice in my ear, offering ideas, encouragement, validation. He had gone from being a passive audience member of the movie in my mind to an active collaborator and confidante, sharing my life with me in real time. I felt closer to him than ever.

* * *

The next morning, I came out of the bedroom, freshly showered, ready to send everyone on their merry way. Instead, I was flabbergasted to find Sean still in his pajama pants and a shirt, making pancakes, *SportsCenter* on TV in the background. Audra was seated at the kitchen counter, her pancakes side by side on a plate, decorated with sliced banana noses and chocolate chip smiles, Sean's specialty.

They were laughing but cut off quickly when they saw me. Whatever magical spell existed had been broken by my appearance. Audra wiped her mouth on her napkin, then scooped the rest of her breakfast onto it, bananas and chocolate chips tumbling, and headed to the door. "Bye, Mom!" she called without turning. "Bye, Dad. Thanks for making breakfast."

As if I hadn't made her breakfast every morning of her life.

"Coffee?" Sean appeared at my side, a full mug already in his hand.

"Oh," I said, startled. "Thanks." I took a sip. He'd made it exactly the way I liked, half bitterly strong coffee, half skim milk, with a sprinkle of cinnamon on top. It occurred to me that there was luxury in having someone in your life who knew how you took your coffee. That thought was replaced almost immediately with another: Why was he here?

"I'm taking the day off," he announced, reading my mind. "I've been working long hours, and I need a break."

He saw the disbelief on my face and laughed. A real, honest laugh. At that moment, he sounded like Sean. Not Sean, my husband, but Sean, the boy I'd met in the NC State student union all those years ago. I felt a stab of nostalgia. I hadn't seen that boy in years.

And I hadn't been the girl he'd courted in longer than that.

He continued, "I know it's been rough going for us lately, but I want to move past it. I want to slow down, start spending more time with you and Audra." His eyes crinkled as he smiled, that slow, good ol' boy smile that I'd first fallen for. "I'm sorry, honey. I know you didn't want to go to counseling, and I apologize if you felt forced into it."

An apology. Another unexpected moment in this unexpected morning. Surprise made me effusive. "And I'm sorry for canceling on you. I should have tried to find a different solution." I was even more surprised to realize I meant it.

"And I'm sorry," he said, laying his hand on my arm, his fingers radiating warmth through the thin material of my shirt, "that I wasn't more understanding about the opportunity Sheila was offering. I know how much photography means to you. I'm thrilled you're getting back into it."

Sean held out his arms. I set down my mug and stepped into his embrace. "Thank you," I said as I wrapped my arms around his waist.

We stayed that way, our breath synchronizing, our bodies making little adjustments to find all the familiar nooks and crannies. I relaxed into the moment. This was nice. More than nice. Familiar. Soothing. Comforting. Certain.

After a while, I shifted, intending to break free. Instead, Sean grinned and, still holding me, began walking us backward toward the bedroom.

"Oh no," I said. I recognized that look, the way his eyes wandered down my body, followed by his hands. I pushed against his chest, resisting. "Sean, I've got a hundred things to do this morning."

His roaming hands found mine, entwining our fingers behind my back, one of his slicker moves. "Name one."

"I have to go to the store." I braced my foot in the doorway.

He kissed my forehead and took another step backward. "Write a list. I'll do it later."

"I have laundry to start."

He kissed my neck. We were now in the bedroom. "We'll wear the same clothes twice."

"I have to check my email."

He dipped me for a kiss. "Email can wait an hour."

Laughing, I wound my arms around his neck as we moved further into the room. The backs of my legs hit the footboard. Sean's hands found their way under my shirt, his touch familiar and insistent.

"Sean, I—"

He kissed me hard, cutting off more excuses.

"You're very convincing," I said, smiling against his mouth as we fell back onto the bed.

* * *

Later, we drove uptown for lunch, and it was like old times. We sat on the restaurant patio and played People Poker. A combination of Cow Poker and people watching, it was a game we'd started playing in college when we were too broke to go out, with a complicated point system that we'd revised and perfected over the years. We ordered wine with lunch and dessert, including a piece of Death by Chocolate cheesecake to bring home to Audra.

"Man bun, five points," I said as a young hipster biked by.

Sean took a sip of his wine, swirling it in mock seriousness. "I'll see your man bun and raise you ten points for the woman who looks like her dog." He cocked his head to the side, indicating the middle-aged woman with the silvery pouf of hair and the Pomeranian trotting beside her.

"Fold," I said, toasting him. "You win this round. But I'm still ahead by sixty points."

"Enjoy it now," he said, raising his glass, "because when ugly sweater season comes, I'm taking back my crown." We were laughing when the waiter brought the check and a to-go box.

"This is nice," I said, dizzy on wine and food and the novelty of feeling, for once, like myself, beyond the definitions of "wife" or "parent."

Sean shrugged in mock resignation. "We may as well start practicing. We're going to have a lot more time alone together after Audra graduates."

I let his comment drift away on the breeze. I didn't want to talk about that. Instead, I looked out across the plaza, at the trees turning gold and red, wishing I'd brought my camera. "I'm glad you convinced me to take a break today."

Sean chuckled. "I enjoyed convincing you. Twice." Under the table, his foot tapped mine.

I threw my napkin at him. He caught it midair with a flourish, making me laugh. Like old times.

Nick swam to the surface of my consciousness, wanting attention. I willed him away.

We wound our way back to the car after lunch, taking our time. The bag with Audra's dessert hung lazily from my right hand. My left was tucked under Sean's arm. We walked in rhythm, and I leaned in, letting my body collide lightly with his. I took a deep breath, smelling his Sean smell, and felt a surge of love. This was my husband. The man I loved. Why was I texting another man? I didn't want to hurt Sean. I didn't want to hurt our daughter or endanger our life together. I had to stop. Before this thing, this obsession, went any further, I had to stop.

I would stop.

Today.

"I was thinking," Sean said. "We haven't been on a real vacation in ages. What if we plan a trip—something big—after Audra leaves for school?" He glanced at me. "What about Greece? Or Rome? Someplace with lots of old stuff for you to photograph."

I considered this. We'd taken family trips to the beach and tagged along with other families for long weekends in the mountains, but apart from Beth's wedding and two trips to Disneyworld, we hadn't gone on vacation together for more than a few days since our honeymoon.

We stopped at the crosswalk, and I squeezed Sean's arm. He looked at me, the midday sun illuminating his face, as familiar to me as my own. "I'd love that," I said, kissing him as the light turned green.

He kissed me back. "I love you."

In the car, I stared at Sean's profile, my heart swelling. I had a husband who loved me, and a daughter with whom I'd finally found a way to connect. I couldn't risk losing that.

I would end things with Nick today.

* * *

I sat in my office, listening to Sean, Audra, and Daniel's laughter. They were watching a movie in the family room, one of the superhero epics that I couldn't get into, no matter how hard I tried.

I felt like a superhero myself—resolved, strong. I hadn't texted Nick all day, though he'd texted me three times:

> Good morning

> Was thinking about that time at the park.
> Remember the geese?

And finally:

> You there?

I had erased each message without responding. I was strong. I could do this. I sat in the office and rehearsed what I would write: *Nick, we have to stop. Nick, I can't do this. Nick, I love my family.*

Cheers exploded from the other side of the door. The hero had saved the day.

I typed:

> We need to talk.

Three dots appeared. A minute later, his reply came through:

> I agree.

I sighed, relief flooding my body like warm bathwater. Oh, thank goodness. He wanted to end it too. We'd had some fun, rehashed some good memories, but it was time to go back to our real lives. I was giddy, limp-limbed.

My thumbs hovered over the keyboard, twitching, working out my goodbye when another message came in:

I think we should meet.

I dropped the phone in horror as if it had suddenly turned into a tarantula.

At the same time, Audra's head appeared in the doorway. "Mom?" she said, still wearing the remnants of laughter on her face. "Dad wanted to know if you wanted some popcorn." She looked at me and her brow creased. "Are you okay?"

Sean's face appeared next to Audra's. He waggled his eyebrows. "Would milady like some popped corn?" he asked, teasing. His expression changed. "Hey, are you okay?"

"I'm fine," I said quickly, rearranging my face. "I, uh, there was a spider…" I pointed vaguely at the floor. "I'd love some popcorn. I'll be right out."

They disappeared, leaving the door open. I kicked it closed, then hunched under the desk to find my phone. With my head hitting the underside of my keyboard tray, I reread the exchange.

We need to talk.

I agree.

I think we should meet.

As I sat there, squished under the desk, breathing hard, head spinning, a new message popped up:

What do you say?

"Mom!" Audra called from the kitchen, "your popcorn is ready."

What do you say?

"Coming!" I called.

What do you say?

Chapter 16

The weekend was a blur. I skimmed along, present in body only, while my mind was lost in a loop.

Whatdoyousaywhatdoyousaywhatdoyousay?

What happened to Friday afternoon, when everything seemed so right, so sure? I had chosen my life here, confident in my decision. Then Nick swooped in and shattered that certainty.

What do you say?

I couldn't meet Sean's eyes, so I took the coward's way out and avoided him. I grocery shopped, I cleaned. I took Audra on a long overdue shopping trip for new shoes. Afterward, we sat in the coffee shop, matching vanilla lattes and blueberry scones on the table between us, and scrolled through our phones. For once, I was grateful for the silence.

What do you say?

I needed to talk to someone. I needed a sounding board, a voice of reason.

I texted Beth:

> Need to talk. Call when you can.

It was late afternoon before she called. I leaped up from my chair on the deck, where I'd been pretending to read the latest Oprah recommendation. Sean sat across from me, laptop open, muttering to himself as he hunted and pecked out a report.

"I'll go inside, so I don't distract you," I said, giving his arm a quick squeeze. He nodded, not looking up from his screen, lips mouthing along as he wrote.

I shut myself in the office and dropped onto the couch; phone pressed hard to my face. I could hear a TV in the background, cartoony music and canned laughter, punctuated by Dante's occasional giggles.

"What is it?" she asked, sounding worried. "Is everything okay? Are Sean and Audra okay?"

"They're fine." I took a deep breath. "Look, Beth, it's about Nick—"

"Aha!" she crowed. "I knew it!"

"Don't," I begged. "Please don't make this worse. Just listen."

"Fine. But for the record, I knew something was up when you kept asking all those questions about our senior year. You've never been interested in nostalgia before."

"I know. You're right. You're a genius."

I told her everything, starting with the reunion, his apology at the dam—"Not an apology," Beth broke in—finding his letter, and our subsequent text relationship culminating in his final message: *What do you say?*

It was a relief to confide in someone, to say Nick's name out loud. To make my case.

"So…" She sighed forcefully into the phone and my ear. I could picture her, a patented Beth look on her face—cheeks puffed out in thought, eyes up to the heavens, preparing to deliver brutal honesty.

I braced myself; I'd asked for this.

"What I hear you saying," she said slowly, her words

measured, "is that you are considering putting your marriage of two-plus decades at risk for a guy you dated for six months a quarter of a century ago? Do I have that math right? And don't even get me started on how you'd be torching your relationship with Audra..."

Beth's honesty was like childbirth. I always forgot how painful it was.

"I know what it sounds like," I said, choosing my words just as carefully. "But you don't understand. I'm at this place with my family, with my whole life, where I wake up in the morning, not knowing who I am anymore. With Nick, I know. He doesn't need me to be more than who I am. He wants me just for me. I think the universe is telling me something. Everyone keeps talking about this next phase of my life that's coming. Maybe Nick is part of it."

"I'm going to stop you there," Beth cut in. "You know I love you. But you are in real danger of doing something stupid. I mean, come on. Do you seriously think Nick is worth ruining your life for? He's not. He's not worth it, Rin. Believe me. I have heard some things about him lately, and he is not good news. For instance, did you know that he missed his daughter's wedding to come to the reunion?"

I sprang to Nick's defense. "Yes, but he came to the reunion to see me, to set things right with me."

"Who skips their own kid's wedding to travel thousands of miles to see someone they haven't talked to in years?" She sneered, not pausing for an answer. "Stalkers, that's who. It's not romantic, or grand, or whatever you think it is. It's creepy and gross."

"But what if we were always meant to be together?" I argued back. "We were so good together in high school. If things hadn't gotten so messed up; if my mother had given me his letter, we might—"

"If he hadn't slept with your friend and knocked her up, you mean?" Beth said sharply. "I don't know why you're glossing over the facts, but let me break it down for you. One, he cheated on you. Two, with your friend. Three, whom he knocked up. Four, and then he ran away."

I started to protest, and she cut me off with a scolding noise like I was Dante asking for a cookie before bedtime. "Uh-buh-buh. He ran away. And then. THEN," she emphasized, "he ghosted you for years before coming back in some bizarre attempt to rewrite the past. Are. You. Serious. Corinne."

"But I'm still in love with him." My voice was small, as I heard myself say the words I'd been afraid of since I'd looked into Nick's eyes over a box of Tic Tacs. "Beth, I love him."

"No, you don't."

"I do. I think I do."

"You love the idea of him."

"I love the way he makes me feel. The way he encourages me. The way he sees me and hears me for who I am in a way that Sean and Audra don't. Or can't, I don't know. It's like they have some interpretation of me, and that's who they see, no matter what I do. But Nick...he listens. He *sees*. I'm someone to him. Someone I like."

"You can't..." Beth faltered for the first time in the conversation. I forged ahead.

"I know he made mistakes. But didn't we all make mistakes back then? Don't we all have things we wish we could go back and change?" I was pleading, begging her to see it my way. To understand how I felt, how I needed to be relevant, seen, appreciated. Loved. "He made a huge mistake and spent years regretting it. That's why he came back. To make things right. What if this is my chance to find out how it could have been with us?"

Beth sighed again into the phone. "Then I don't know why you called me. You don't seem too interested in the truth. You're only seeing what you want to see." Bitterness tinged her words.

"You're an adult. You're thousands of miles away. I can't stop you. Instead, I'll say this. Nick knows you're married, right?"

"Yes."

"He knows you have a daughter."

"Yes."

"So, you need to think about what kind of guy asks you to leave your family. Does a good guy do that? Does someone who cares about you ask you to do that?"

"Nick only wants what's best for me."

"Nick only wants what's best for Nick. Always has. Do you think your relationship in high school was a romantic fairy tale? I was there, remember? I saw you. I watched you follow him around and do everything he asked. You stopped hanging out with me. You stopped thinking for yourself. You let him direct every little thing you did."

"That's not true! You're jealous—"

"Whoa, girl. I am not jealous. I'm worried." Beth paused, and when she spoke again, it sounded like she'd made a decision. "Do you know when Nick and Kirsten got together?"

The abrupt change in the conversation startled me. "What? When?" I asked, all other thoughts flying from my head.

"It was the weekend you went to North Carolina. Do you remember? You had a big fight about it. He didn't want you to go, kept talking about moving to Alaska or some nonsense? Do you seriously not remember this?" I could practically hear her shaking her head in disbelief. "But Marie insisted that you go to the freshman preview. She had taken off work, was driving you to Raleigh herself. You called me in hysterics. I had to talk you down for an hour. Convince you that your mom was right, that you'd survive one weekend away from Mr. Wonderful. Anyway, so you finally left, and what did your boyfriend do? He went to Kirsten's house, to one of her lame parties, and hooked up with her."

I was floored. "How do you know that? You didn't go to those parties."

"Nancy told me," she said, simply. "After the reunion, a bunch of us started a group chat, and last week someone mentioned something about Kirsten's famous squad parties." I imagined Beth making sarcastic finger quotes. "And Nancy said her younger brother—he was dating that girl on JV—anyway, he told a story about that night, how he saw Kirsten and Nick sneak off, and later heard Nick boasting how they'd had sex in her basement," she scoffed. "Sounded super romantic."

"You're lying," I spat. "You were always jealous of my feelings for Nick."

A deafening pause. "Wow." Beth's words were ice. "Okay. I think we're done here."

She hung up. I hurled my phone across the room, where it clattered against the closed door.

Tears of rage and betrayal stung my eyes. How dare she say those things about Nick? About me? She didn't understand. Only Nick and I understood how things had been between us.

"Everything okay in there?" Sean shouted.

I swiped at my face. "Everything's fine," I called back.

I knee-walked across the floor to where my phone had landed in the corner. A crack ran diagonally across the screen. Fabulous.

I palmed my phone, broken screen facing in, and opened the office door. Sean had relocated to the family room sometime during my talk with Beth. He looked up as I walked through. Was he looking at me strangely? Had he overheard my part of the conversation? I didn't think I'd been loud; Beth had done most of the talking, but had he overheard any of it? Had he heard the word "Nick?" Did he suspect anything?

"I heard a noise. Did you fall?" he asked.

"Everything's fine," I repeated, not stopping on my way to the bedroom. His eyes were already sliding back to his laptop.

Everything's fine. Nothing to see here. Just the flaming dumpster fire Corinne's life has become.

I passed through the bedroom and into the bathroom and closed the door. I slid down the wall to the cold white tile and rested my forehead on my knees, hugging my legs, holding myself together.

What do you say?

Rationally, I knew I should listen to Beth. I'd called her, seeking advice, and for better or worse, had gotten an earful of it. Beth had no reason to lie. She knew all the players in my life's story. She knew the stakes.

But Beth never liked Nick. She was like my mother, who thought he would hold me back from my true potential, and I could never convince her otherwise. Being Nick's girlfriend was everything I'd wanted in high school. Everything I never knew I was missing, a gateway to an exciting life full of adventures. When he left, I thought that door was closed forever. But now… maybe…She didn't understand what I'd lost, what I was being offered.

He cheated on you with your friend. He knocked her up then ran away. Beth's heated words came back to me.

I'd never asked, not in all this time. I hadn't wanted to know. But I needed to know now before I made my decision.

I opened my phone and texted Nick:

> Tell me about Kirsten.

His reply came immediately:

> Why do you want to know?

> Why did you do it?

> It was a mistake.

> But why?

I don't want to talk about it.

> I need to know.

No answer.

Sean knocked on the bathroom door. "Corinne? Are you okay?"

"I'm fine," I called from the floor. "I have a headache. I'm going to take a nap."

"Okay," he said, sounding concerned. "Let me know if you need anything."

His footsteps receded, and I heard him settle back into the family room and turn the TV volume up. I dragged myself off the tile and into the bedroom, hiding my phone in the sleeve of my cardigan. I closed the door and pressed the lock with a soft *click*. I climbed into bed, fully dressed, and fell asleep waiting for Nick's reply.

* * *

I woke to Sean knocking on the door. The sun had set, and the bedroom was dark, with only the faint glow of the kitchen lights seeping in under the door. "Hon? You okay in there? Why's the door locked?"

Groggy, disoriented, I fought my way out of the nest of covers and pillows. I must have thrashed around in my sleep. "Oh, sorry, I didn't realize…I'm fine."

"Okay." Sean sounded unconvinced but didn't press for details. "I'm going out to pick up dinner. Want anything?"

"No," I called back, feeling up my sleeve for my phone. "Thanks, though."

"Okay," his voice floated through the door. "I won't be gone long. Feel better."

I had seven new texts from Nick. "Take your time."

"Love you."

"You too."

Moments later, the back door shut, and the garage door rose. I was alone. I pushed myself up to sitting, resting my phone on my bent knees, and began to read:

> First, I want to say that it was a mistake. I was upset. You were leaving. Things were changing.

> Kirsten was having one of her parties. I didn't have anything else going on, was missing you, so I went.

> Everyone paired off except us. We started talking about how we couldn't wait to graduate. She told me about her mom leaving and how she was basically on her own.

I paused. I remembered that. Kirsten's folks had split the previous summer, and her mother had bolted town. Rumors started soon after that Kirsten's dad spent most nights in the downtown bar, drinking until close, never going home alone. Kirsten joked about it at practice, saying how she could do anything she wanted, that her dad wouldn't notice if she burned the house down. At the time, we'd been envious of her freedom. In hindsight, it made me sad. I knew how abandonment felt.

Poor Kirsten. She'd only been a little older than Audra was now.

> We split a bottle of Jack. Somehow, we ended up kissing. And then more.

> We agreed it was a one-time thing. I didn't tell you because it didn't mean anything.

> After graduation, she came to see me. We went for a drive. She told me she was pregnant. Said she was keeping it, and what did I want to do?

> You know the rest. I called my uncle. Asked if I could start my job early, bring her along. Figured it was as good a place as any to raise a family.

That was it. The messages had come in while I slept, spaced out over twenty minutes, a few minutes between each text. I imagined Nick carefully choosing his words, trying to explain without hurting me. But in hindsight, I could see how it happened. Raging hormones and emotions made for poor choices. In the end, didn't it say something that Nick had made the right decision in choosing the mother of his child? Shouldn't he be commended for his choice, not vilified? I'd been the wronged party, but his child had been the innocent one.

I was more confused than ever. I visualized myself standing in a blank space, half black, half white. One side of me was Nick and the question "What if?" while on the other side stood Sean and Audra and the question "What next?"

I texted Nick:

> Need some time to think. I'll get back to you.

He didn't respond. For the first time in weeks, I put my phone away. I had no one to call. Beth was mad. Nick was waiting. Sean, for obvious reasons, was not an option.

I got back into bed and pulled the covers up over my head.

* * *

I feigned sleep when Sean finally came to bed. I kept my eyes closed and evened out my breathing, not responding to his questioning hand on my hip. He held it there for a moment before rolling over. I continued counting in and out, marking time until Sean began to snore. Then I slid out of bed, palmed my phone from the nightstand, and crept out of the room.

I sat in the office, phone in my hand, typing and retyping a reply to Nick:

Yes.

No.

Yes.

I can't.

It was too hard. I gave up and instead texted Beth:

I'm sorry.

Her reply came quickly:

Make good choices.

That was one thing off my mind. I cast about for something else to do, a distraction from the decision hanging over my head. Sheila had sent information on another client, so I spent some time cruising real estate listings, noting what did and did not work in other agents' photos. She'd also suggested I make up some business cards; she had friends in her agency who could use my services. I played around with font and color before landing on a final design, a simple but elegant card in black, white, and turquoise. I placed my order, at the last moment springing for the embossed lettering, and sat back, mind sufficiently quieted enough to consider sleep.

I moved to the couch and laid down, folding my hands across

my stomach and closing my eyes, listening to the soothing hum of the computer.

I loved my husband. I loved my child. I had a good life. Was I seriously considering throwing everything away? So what if we were a little…stuck right now? Our daughter was growing up; our lives were changing. Things would be different soon.

That left the most important question: What did I want? If I was no longer "mother," then who was I? I would be "wife" to Sean, but could I still be his wife and remain "Corinne?" Could I pursue my interests while remaining part of our team? I'd had a glimpse of hope on Friday. We'd talked about our lives and what might come next. But would he be willing to expand his definition of me? Sean liked things the way they'd always been. Change was not what he did well. He lived in the same city he grew up in, his closest friends were people he'd known since high school or college, he'd never once suggested we move from the first home we purchased. How would he react to having a wife who suddenly wanted more? Something different? I feared it would be more arguments in the mirror, more silent Thursday dinners. What if we were too used to each other to do the work of getting to know one other again?

And was I willing to do the same? I knew Sean, knew all of his mannerisms, his pet peeves, his reactions. I could predict, with 99 percent accuracy, what he would say before he said it. I knew him like I knew myself. And try as I might, I wasn't sure that I could see a future for the old him and the new me.

I was wavering. I had to decide what I wanted and make a choice.

Corinne closes her eyes. She could be asleep, except for her mouth, which moves ever so slightly as she chants, "What do you say? What do you say? What do you say?" into the night.

* * *

I woke to the sounds of Meowsers pawing at the office door. I glanced at the time on my phone, 4:37 a.m. Too early to get up, too late to go back to sleep. I staggered to the door and let the cat in to keep him from waking Audra. He stalked in, perplexed at finding me in an unaccustomed place, and jumped lightly onto the desk and paced back and forth. I sat at the desk and petted him obligingly until he'd had enough and jumped down to groom himself. I brushed the cat hair from my hands and pulled the keyboard to me, bold in the early morning hours.

I typed in "How to have an affair," my finger hesitating over the search button. Then I pressed *enter.*

It was done. I had put a name to the possibility in front of me: affair. It was a strange word since there was nothing fair about it at all. I thought about the French phrase, *à faire*, which meant "to do." An imperative. A calling to action. I was being called to decide, to make a move. I skimmed the list of choices my search had returned, selected one, and started reading. When I finished, I deleted my search history and stared at the words I'd scratched onto a Post-it:

alibi, vague, no paper trail, pay cash.

Breathing hard, as if I'd already been caught, I tore the words into tiny pieces and dropped them in the trashcan.

The time had come. I had to choose.

* * *

I waited until midmorning before texting Nick:

Where do you want to meet?

His reply came immediately:

Roller coaster.

I knew exactly what he was referring to.

The Clemmons Senior Class always took a trip to Mayfair Amusement Park the day before graduation. But our original trip had been postponed due to a summer storm, and by the time the rescheduled date came around, Nick was gone. I'd stayed home, too ashamed to face my friends, insisting to Beth and my cheer sisters that I wasn't going because I didn't like heights.

Now Nick was offering an on-ramp to resume where we'd left off. We'd revisited the dam. Now it was time to pick up the first significant piece of "might have been" and see where it led us. It was perfect.

I texted back:

Yes.

* * *

Coming up with a cover story was disarmingly easy. Beth had unknowingly provided the perfect alibi when she mentioned her upcoming work trip to Cleveland. Mayfair was only sixty miles away. I told Sean that Beth had a conference in Ohio (true) and had asked me to come along (true). That we were also taking advantage of the proximity to Clemmons (true) and meeting up with some people (sort of true).

The hardest part of my plan was asking Beth to be my cover. The few texts we'd exchanged since our fight had been strained. I spent an hour writing and rewriting my text before pressing *send:*

Coming to Cleveland like you suggested. Looking forward to reconnecting with friends from the reunion. I'll call you with details.

A moment later, my phone rang.

"Hi."

"What are you doing?" Beth sounded unhappy.

"I have to." Heavy, disapproving silence. I pressed on. "I have to know. You know I do. I need to know if this is real."

"More real than your family?" Beth's voice was sharp, her words biting. I flinched as if struck. "Are you prepared for this? Are you ready for the fallout? You can't take this back. You're putting your whole life on the line for someone who broke your heart and left without a second thought."

"I know." I slumped over the kitchen island, laying my cheek on the cold granite countertop, the phone trapped under my ear. "I know that he did all that. I remember everything. But I still can't..." A tear slid down my cheek. "I can't forget how he makes me feel."

After a long moment, Beth sighed, and I knew I had won. I waited, drawing circles with my finger on the counter. One, two, three...I made it to fifteen before she spoke again. "Okay. You're coming with me to my conference in Cleveland for a...reunion." She said the word with disgust.

"Thank y—"

"But I don't like this. Sean's a good man. Audra's great. Nick isn't worth it. He's selfish and arrogant for trying to put himself back in your life. If he cared about you, he'd respect you enough to keep his distance."

I stayed silent, still circling my finger. Sixteen, seventeen, eighteen.

"I'm sorry you're unhappy. I know how hard you struggled after Marie died. I know that parenting feels like death by a thousand papercuts." She gave a half laugh. "I'm devastated every time Dante tells me to go away, and he's only five. You don't have much time with Audra left. Are you going to throw that away? There's no coming back from this."

She'd made her case and rested it. Part of me longed to

accept it, to take back everything I'd said, to tell her she was right and that I was calling the whole thing off. But I couldn't live without knowing. Despite the consequences, I had to know. I'd made my choice. I closed my eyes, lay still. My cheek was getting numb.

Beth sighed again. "I've got to go."

She clicked off before I could say "goodbye," or "thank you," or "love you," or "help."

Later that night, I texted her the details of my flight.

Her reply came back immediately:

Don't do it.

Chapter 17

The plane taxied into the Cleveland airport. I'd stared out the window the entire flight, Depeche Mode playing through my headphones, my heart pounding. I'd always thought that all the tropes about nerves were literary inventions, but my heart was actually racing in my chest. My mouth was dry; my palms were sweaty. I was grateful I'd declined Nick's offer to meet my plane, insisting instead on getting a car and getting situated into my hotel first. I'd had to put the car and hotel on my credit card but was paying cash for everything else, avoiding a paper trail. If anyone cared to investigate, I was staying at a hotel near Beth's conference and needed my own transportation while she was working. From there, where I went and who I saw would remain untraceable.

Nick and I had plans to meet later this afternoon. We'd chosen to meet at the Iron Dragon, "The Ride of a Lifetime," as the ads proclaimed. I needed a shower and a few moments to collect my scattered thoughts and prepare myself.

I texted Beth first, letting her know I'd landed. She didn't answer.

I texted Sean from the rental car line:

> Arrived safely.

He replied as I turned out of the rental car lot in my Chevy Malibu:

> Have fun. Hi Beth. Love you.

A second later:

> You, Corinne, not you, Beth.

Again:

> I mean, you're great, Beth, but I don't think it would work between us.

I turned off my phone. I couldn't bear Sean being sweet right now. Not when I was about to...I couldn't even finish the thought.

It's not too late, Beth's voice pleaded in my head.

But it was. It had been too late since the moment I'd responded to Nick's message suggesting that we meet. It'd been too late since the moment he pressed the Tic Tacs box into my hand, and my skin remembered his touch. I'd come too far not to see this through, no matter what the ending held. I couldn't bear another minute of standing outside my life, wondering "what if?" Even as I wiped a tear from my cheek, guilty excitement bubbled up, popping and fizzing in my brain, and my body felt glittery. I was doing it. I was going to see Nick again. Finally, I would know. Had I made the right choice?

Was there something better out there for me?

I fiddled with the car radio and found a decent station among the presets. "Playing the hits of yesterday, today, and tomorrow," the deejay proclaimed over the opening strains of "Tainted Love." I turned the volume up and sang along, enjoying the freedom of being able to sing to my heart's content without Audra rolling her eyes and pointedly putting in her earbuds.

The car ride sped by, aided by the radio—songs about love, loss, and the one that got away all felt poignant and profound. I was one with the universe and the universe approved. Nick and I were meant to be together.

I pulled into the hotel parking lot and gathered my bags. It was time. I was here. I'd been called to action, *à faire*.

I flipped down the makeup mirror and did a final check. I'd washed my hair, then dried and straightened it before pulling it back into a ponytail (not too high, but tight enough that I imagined some facelift benefits). I'd kept my makeup simple, but thanks to the high-end primers and plumpers scrounged from Audra's enviable makeup samples stash, my skin looked dewy and flawless. Plain gray shirt for hiding any dirt picked up from the rides, faded jeans, white slip-on sneakers. I left my jacket in the car; the day was unusually warm for mid-October. My only jewelry was my wedding ring. I'd debated taking it off, but its absence seemed more incriminating than the ring itself. Plus, I rationalized, why should I take it off? I wasn't doing anything inappropriate. I was meeting an old friend in a public place. I could be married and do that. It wasn't like I was cheating on Sean by riding a roller coaster with Nick.

Beth's voice broke in: *If you weren't doing anything wrong, you wouldn't have lied about where you were and who you were seeing.*

I slid from the car and locked the doors, sliding the keys into my black crossbody purse. I hesitated even to bring a bag, feeling it made me look too "mom-ish," but in the end, practicality won out. I needed my phone, license, and money—all items that could easily fall out of my pockets during a high-speed ride. The worst thing that could happen is that I could lose my ID or my cash and have to call home for help.

I paid the admissions fee in cash and declined to pose for a commemorative keychain photo. As I fastened the paper bracelet that served as my entry pass around my wrist, I caught sight of a familiar slouching figure leaning against the stone wall of a fountain beside a souvenir shirt kiosk.

Forcing myself to walk at a casual pace, I approached Nick. It was my first time seeing him in daylight, and I drank him in, noting every detail. He watched me with sleepy eyes, an amused grin tugging at the right side of his mouth, looking for all the world like the Big Bad Wolf from the fairy tale. He was dressed similarly to me, black shirt, khaki pants in some sort of high-tech fabric, brown work boots. I felt a stab of relief that I'd chosen my outfit correctly; couples dressed for different dates were worth twenty points in People Poker. I noticed his wallet was on a chain, a look I'd always hated—like his wallet was a small animal that might run away if left unleashed—but I skimmed past it, chalking it up to necessity, like my purse.

My eyes traveled up again. Nick's hair was in the same style as it had been last month, pushed back, finger-combed, the ends curling against his shirt collar. A line of sweat beaded his hairline. He looked as though he'd been working in the sun before meeting me. Sean always looked cool and crisp, like he'd just stepped out of an air-conditioned room, even on summer days when it was one hundred degrees plus humidity. Nick gave the impression of feverishness, intensity. I resisted the urge to blot the perspiration from his forehead and felt my temperature rise. My clothes felt too tight. When he finally smiled, wrinkles appeared in the corners of his eyes and mouth. In the unfair way of aging men, the wrinkles didn't make him look older.

He raised a finger and ran it down the bridge of my nose. "Hey," he said softly. Even his fingertip exuded heat.

"Hey," I whispered back. My legs were shaking; I was nervous. "Are you ready to go on the ride of a lifetime?" I asked, quoting the park's tagline.

Nick's shoulders shook with laughter as my face flamed at

the double entendre. I covered my burning cheeks with my hands. He reached out and pulled them away, taking my hand in his. There was a moment of confusion as we tried and failed to align our grips. When Sean held my hand, my little finger was on the outside. But Nick held my whole hand, my fingers squashed together, my thumb sticking out. It was like wearing a mitten.

"I was born ready, maiden," he said, pulling me closer. There was no mistaking his meaning. His thumb swept over the back of my hand. His fingers were rough, calloused, different. My body swelled at his touch, ready to lift off. The reality of his hand on mine was all that held me to the earth. I was a balloon; he was my string. At that moment, I would follow him anywhere.

* * *

We strolled through the park, not speaking. My world shrank to the space inside our hands. My fingers buzzed with the electricity coming off his skin. My arm was hypersensitive to the occasional brushes of his arm hair or shirt sleeve against my skin. I caught a few curious glances from people as we walked by, and I stared brazenly back from behind my sunglasses. I wondered if onlookers were jealous of, or repulsed by, the sight of two middle-aged people holding hands. Could they feel the chemistry we were emitting? Did they notice the wedding ring on my hand and the absence of one on his?

I snuck glances at Nick as we walked, memorizing his silhouette against the late afternoon sun. I wished I'd brought my camera, but I couldn't take pictures of this. Maybe we'd have years ahead of us to take photos, to illustrate our story. But today was private, existing only for us to remember. The people around us had no idea what they were witnessing. I almost felt sorry for them, to be so blind.

I was once like you, I telegraphed to the grim-faced couples herding children from ride to ride. *You don't have to be unhappy. You can change your life.*

Arriving at the Iron Dragon, we took our place in line, standing close together. "The wait from this point is 30 minutes," a sign warned. I regarded it in awkward silence. All those weeks of texting and flirting and "remember when," and I didn't know what to say now. I didn't know enough about Nick's real life to pick up a thread of conversation. This, the physical closeness, was all I had thought about. What would we talk about now, here, face-to-face? Sean and I had dozens of conversations that we could pick up and continue at any point without preamble. I realized with a start that I'd been imagining speaking to High School Nick in all of our text exchanges. This Nick, the one in front of me, was somebody else, a stranger.

A moment of panic snuck in. *Had Nick been talking to High School Corinne or to me?*

The line shuffled forward. As we settled into our new spaces, Nick took the opportunity to move closer. We were now standing inches apart. He unclasped his hand from mine and rested his fingers at my waist. I tensed, waiting. Slowly, he slid one finger under my shirt and stroked the bare skin above the waistband of my jeans.

My eyes flew open, and I exhaled a strangled, "Oh!"

Nick's expression was cunning, a fox cornering his prey. I gripped the metal guardrail for balance, not trusting my legs to hold me up. The moment stretched on. I broke away, needing the space.

"Um..." I struggled for words. "Did I tell you about my latest listing? We get up to the master bedroom, and there's a huge, I mean massive, portrait of the homeowner wearing nothing but a leopard skin tie." I laughed weakly. "I had to get pretty creative with photo angles."

He looked bemused but offered no comment. I tried again.

"I've been reading about aerial photography. You know, using drones to get video footage? I think it could be exciting…"

"Mmm-hmmm," Nick murmured, his attention fully absorbed by the inch of skin his finger was caressing.

The line moved forward. Nick turned me so that my back was against his chest, his hands moving to my arms, holding them to my sides, taking control. My heart beat crazily in my chest. My whole body felt like fireworks exploding. I was the grand finale, a hundred explosions, one after another.

We kept moving forward, and each time Nick found a new way to stake his claim on me. A finger twisting through my ponytail, his hands on my hips, his breath on my neck. He smelled different than Sean. Sean's scent was a clean smell of freshly mown grass and laundry soap with an undercurrent of mint toothpaste. Nick's clothes smelled smoky, like a wood-burning fireplace, with a film of sweat and cologne over it. After several exploratory sniffs, I recognized the scent as Polo, which all the boys in our high school had worn, including Nick. He'd either never changed brands or had bought it especially for today.

I tried again to draw him out, to replicate that easy back and forth that we'd had in our texts. "So, mysterious man," I said as I placed a daring hand on his forearm, felt the matted hair covering it. "Are you ever going to tell me your pen name?"

Nick's chest rumbled as he laughed, the vibrations traveling through my back, making my fingers tingle. He spun me to face him, then put his lips to my ear. "You'll have to torture me first."

Now his hands were in my back pockets. I felt a small alarm go off in my head. This was a lot of PDA. What if we attracted attention? What if that group of teens ahead of us decided to post a picture, or worse, a video, and it somehow got back home? "Middle-Aged Horndogs!" the headline would scream above a grainy photo of Nick and me. "Accountant's Wife Named in Steamy Amusement Park Scandal."

My heart rate climbed; my breath came shallow and fast. I pulled away, fanning my face with my hand.

We shuffled forward again. I could see the end of the line where excited thrillseekers lined up in chutes, waiting their turn for the ride of a lifetime. I suddenly remembered that I hadn't entirely been lying when I'd canceled on the senior trip. I didn't like heights. Sean always rode the bigger rides with Audra while I waited at the bottom, holding jackets and sunglasses. I watched a car climb up, up, up the coaster's first hill. I heard the screams ripped from riders' mouths as they plunged down, down, down. I swallowed nervously.

Nick's hands shifted again, snaking up under my shirt and stroking the skin of my lower back. It tickled, and I flinched away. I'd always had a thing about my lower back. Sean knew that. Nick's hands moved away then returned to the same spot, rubbing more insistently this time. I stepped further back, out of his reach, and shot a glance at the group of teens. Were they staring at us? What was that girl typing on her phone?

My anxiety skyrocketed as we neared the front of the line. I felt overloaded, unsure of what was triggering me. Fear of the ride? Fear of getting caught? The scent of Polo caught in my throat, and I gagged. I felt an icy sheen of sweat break out across my back and arms and realized I was going to faint.

"I'm sorry." I broke away from Nick, who had hooked his thumbs through my belt loops. "I can't do this." I pushed my way past the kids in front of us, and awkwardly climbed over the observation area's railing. I heard whistles and catcalls of "Chicken!" as I fled. I didn't care; I had to get out.

I leaned over the railing and dryheaved, my hands clutching the warm metal. My heart raced; my vision tunneled to pinpricks; my skin was clammy. My legs gave out, and I slumped to the ground, consciousness flickering.

I heard voices asking: "Is she okay? Do you need us to call

an ambulance?" I heard Nick murmur something as I concentrated on making the world come back into focus.

This can't be happening again.

Darkness.

* * *

"Welcome back, maiden."

Nick's voice sounded far away. My head pounded. My heart skittered. I was sweat-drenched. My body felt like an elephant was sitting on it.

"Water," I managed through gluey lips that stuck to my too-dry teeth. My tongue felt twice its normal size. I opened my eyes. Nick was kneeling beside me, a worried look creasing his face. He held one of my hands in his, rubbing the back of it with his palm.

A crowd surrounded us, but I only had eyes for Nick. I looked woozily up at him, my chapped lips cracking.

"You stayed."

* * *

After cautiously helping me stand up, Nick took my arm and steered me to the nearest concession stand, waving off offers of assistance from the crowd. I didn't resist. There was nothing romantic about us now that I was a feeble old woman who fainted in roller coaster queues.

He bought two bottles of water and a cup of ice and led me to a bench in the relative shade of a sickly ash tree. I drank my water in small sips, careful not to chug it and risk everything coming right back up. I felt the water trickling down my throat and imagined it spreading through my body, reconstituting me. The fuzziness in my head receded by degrees, leaving a dull ache in its place. My heart gave a few more jumps, then settled back into its regular rhythm.

Nick held an ice cube to my wrist. "Put ice on your pulse points, here and here." He pointed to the insides of his wrists.

I nodded, remembering Sean using a similar trick at Audra's soccer games, his big capable hands encircling her skinny wrists as she sat, red and sweaty on the sidelines, grinning at him. Had Nick ever done the same for his daughter?

"I don't know what happened," I mumbled. My vision clicked another step closer to clear.

Nick slid an arm around me, his too-warm body uncomfortable against my skin. "You overheated. Have you eaten today?"

I thought back and realized that I hadn't. I'd had a granola bar on the way to the airport and a latte at the terminal, but that had been hours ago. I shook my head, feeling foolish. "No, I guess not." I didn't mention that fluttering in my stomach now had nothing to do with physical hunger and everything to do with an appetite for a man who was not my husband.

Corinne stares at Nick. You stayed.

We sat on the bench as I drank my water and held melting ice to my skin. We watched braver souls climb aboard the rides, all show and pretense; the guys posturing and preening for each other and their dates, the girls giggling and hanging off each other in mock fear. A couple wearing matching airbrushed T-shirts boarded the front car.

I nudged Nick's knee. "Matching couples' outfit, fifteen points."

He looked at me, confused. "Huh?"

I blushed. "Never mind."

My phone buzzed against my hip. I unzipped my purse and glanced at the screen.

Sean.

I swiped *decline* and flipped the phone over quickly as if he could see me, tucking it back into my bag. I'd call him back later when it didn't require me to acknowledge his existence while looking at another man.

Nick jogged me with his elbow. "Ready to try again?"

I wasn't. "Would you mind terribly if we left?" I was achy and hot. The casual-chic outfit I'd chosen so carefully felt glued to my thighs and back. I'd perspired through the armpits of my shirt and was careful to keep my arms to my sides as we rose to go, ignoring Nick's outstretched hand.

We walked back to my car, not touching, not talking. I was disappointed. Humiliated. The day hadn't gone at all as I'd hoped. One simple roller coaster ride, a symbol for our whole relationship, and I couldn't even follow through. I glanced at Nick, his expression inscrutable. He seemed content in the silence, even relishing it.

At least he'd stayed. This time I hadn't woken up alone. It was a small comfort. Maybe tonight would be different. Would there be a "tonight?"

We leaned against the door frame of my rental car, shoulder to shoulder, wreathed in the golden light of early evening. I played with the zipper of my purse. The unspoken next step waited. Who would bring it up first?

"Where are you staying?" I finally asked, skirting the real question.

Nick shrugged. "I didn't make a reservation anywhere. I thought"—he paused meaningfully—"that my plans depended on you."

It depended on me. Nick wasn't assuming that he was staying with me. I would have to say it. Ask him to stay. And saying it would mean another real step toward him, another step away from Sean.

As if on cue, my phone buzzed again. I peered into my purse. Audra. I slid my finger across *decline*.

"I'm, uh, at the Mayfair Inn," I said, stalling.

Nick nodded. "I've stayed there." *When?* I wondered. *Have you done this before*? "They have a decent lounge area. Do you want to go back and rest, and I'll meet you there in an hour?"

My phone buzzed again. This time, a notification *ping*ed, indicating a voicemail.

Distracted, I nodded. "Yeah, that would be fine. I need to check in with my…" I stumbled over my word choice: Husband? Family? Both were acknowledgments of everything that Nick was not. "…voicemail."

Nick smiled his crooked half-smile, the one that used to melt my heart from across the room. I felt a small skip in my chest. Anticipation? Guilt?

"I'll see you in an hour, my beautiful maiden," he said and leaned down, touching his mouth to mine.

It was such a shock to feel someone else's kiss that, for a moment, I didn't react. I hadn't kissed a man other than Sean in more than twenty years. But at the same time, Nick's kiss was familiar. Like a favorite song you hadn't heard in ages but still knew all the words to. I registered all of this in an instant as his mouth molded itself to mine, finding purchase. My treacherous arms snaked around his neck. He pulled me closer, so roughly that I gasped, momentarily breaking contact.

The rational part of my brain was horrified as I did the thing I once vowed I'd never do: *Corinne is unfaithful. Corinne is cheating on her husband.*

The rest of me existed only in the physical space of Nick's arms: *Corinne is kissing Nick Elms. Nick Elms wants Corinne.*

My fingers slid up and buried themselves in his hair, twisting in the damp strands at the base of his neck. He groaned, his breath hot in my mouth. Our teeth scraped together. I was used to Sean's kisses, which grew in intensity, increasing the anticipation of what was to come. Nick's kisses were uniformly demanding, insistent. His hands pulled at my clothes. It was the fear that he might strip my shirt off right there in Lot J that finally forced me to stop.

I pulled away, feeling like I was physically being ripped apart, and leaned back against the doorframe of the car. The loss of Nick's body against mine was a shock, and I shivered even as my skin burned where he'd touched me.

Nick looked as dazed as I felt. His heavy eyelids were half-closed, and his mouth hung slack. His hands hovered between us, long fingers searching, trying to pull me back in.

"I have to go." My voice was ragged; my lips were swollen. I reached into my purse, fumbling for my key fob. My shaking fingers missed the unlock button. The sudden shriek of the car alarm pierced the air.

"Sorry!" I gasped, pressing blindly at buttons until the alarm fell silent. I heard the *click* of the door as it unlocked and groped behind me for the handle. I opened the door and collapsed into the driver's seat.

"Maiden," Nick's voice was hoarse. His frame pressed into view and held the door open. He started to say something, then stopped and shook his head. "See you soon."

He stepped back and carefully closed the car door. Turning, he made his way lazily through the sea of parked cars. I watched until he disappeared before starting the car and driving away, my hands shaking on the wheel.

Chapter 18

Back in my hotel room, I leaned against the door. My jellied legs buckled, and I slid down to the scratchy commercial-grade carpeting, my hands on my knees, thankful for the impersonal solitude of the room, its unassuming beige decor a welcome counterpoint to the noise and adrenaline of the afternoon.

The ghosts of Nick's hands were on my arms, on my back, in my hair. I closed my eyes and remembered his face closing in. I ran my tongue over my lips and tasted his mouth on mine. I rubbed my hands together, feeling the oil from his hair on my fingers. I sniffed my shirt which carried our combined scents.

What was I feeling? Lust? Longing? Regret? In the heat of the moment, the novelty of surprise, I'd responded with force, kissing Nick hard, feeling pleasure at being wanted, reveling in doing something so forbidden. But if I was honest with myself, it was all a little disappointing. I hadn't felt the internal "Yes!" I was seeking; an instinctive gut reaction that would tell me once and for all if I was making the right decision.

It was good to feel wanted, but was it real?

I ran my hands over the prickly carpet fibers, tracing the raised beige swirls until my palms itched, mind racing over the possibilities still to come. I had an hour to clean up and present myself to Nick. We would sit in the bar, without noise, without witnesses, without childish games, and we would, what? Talk? Text? I imagined us sitting at a table in the dimly lit bar, messaging each other in carefully plotted sentences. Was that the only way we could communicate? Or would we skip talking altogether and return immediately to this room?

That was it, I realized. Talking. That was what had been missing.

There had been hardly any real conversation today, no organic connection other than the physical moments. Nick had barely reacted when I mentioned photography. He'd evaded my questions about his writing, choosing to touch me, manipulate me, rather than talk to me. He'd seemed so supportive, so invested in listening to me before. What had changed?

A thought struck me, and it was so obvious that I was embarrassed by my surprise: was everything up until now an act? Was it really, as Beth predicted, only about Nick's ego? Sex with the ex as a way to recapture his youth? Combat the reality of growing older? Growing up?

I looked around the room, taking in the double bed with its cheap quilted comforter and two skimpy pillows, the small bathroom with the chipped tile floor. Was this the way I'd envisioned my relationship with Nick beginning again? Was this where I wanted my marriage to end? My thoughts circled round and round again, chasing each other.

Was this the end? Was this a new beginning?

My whole body vibrated. No, wait, that was my phone. I pulled it from my bag and stared at the notifications filling my screen. I had missed calls from Sean, Audra, and Beth. Even Sean's parents' Florida number appeared in my call log. I had texts and voicemails, several from unknown numbers. As I called my voicemail, my phone buzzed again, and Beth's number flashed on the screen. I answered, a feeling of dread building.

"Bethie? What's going on?"

"Corinne! Where have you been? I've been trying to reach you for an hour!" Beth, unflappable and steady, sounded near hysterics, her voice shrill and accusatory. She rushed on, not waiting for me to answer. "Look, I don't know where you are, and I don't want to, but you need to go home. Sean's been in a car accident—"

"What?" The word ripped out of my mouth like a scream, but my voice was no more than a whisper. I licked my bone dry lips with a sandpaper tongue and tried again. "Beth, is he...?" It was the most I could manage. It occurred to me that I was lucky that I was already sitting down. People always ask you to sit down for bad news. Had I known somehow that my coming here would end like this? With bad news on the floor of an anonymous room?

My mouth filled with a sickening mixture of saliva and stomach acid, the taste of guilt. I swallowed hard, forcing it down.

"Some idiot sideswiped him on the highway—sent him into the barrier on the median. He's in the hospital."

"Oh God," I moaned, rocking, my forehead pressed to my knees.

Corinne chose wrong. Corinne is being punished.

Beth kept talking. "He's got a broken arm, some broken ribs, and they're keeping him under observation for a possible concussion." She paused, letting the information sink in.

Tears fell, hot and thick on my cheeks. My nose began to run. I sniffed, wiping at it with the back of my hand like a child. I pushed myself to my feet, needing to move, to do something. "I can be at the airport in an hour. I'll fly standby. I'll drive back if I have to. Oh God, Beth, I have to get out of here..."

I grabbed my duffle bag and threw it on the bed, denting the smooth covers. I ran to the bathroom and gathered my toiletries to my chest with a sweep of my arm. A bottle of perfume slipped from my grasp, fell to the floor, and shattered. I left it.

Beth didn't ask if I was okay. "The medics tried to call you. When you didn't answer, they called Audra, who called me." She laughed bitterly. "I told her we weren't together this afternoon, which at least, was the truth."

I forced the zipper closed on my bag. I looked around the room, spied my purse by the door.

"Audra's at the hospital now. You need to call her. You need to go back to them."

"Thank you." I was still crying, and my words came out in gasps. "Thank you for calling me. Thank you for everything." I knew that she hadn't forgiven me—not by a long shot—but she hadn't abandoned me either.

Beth sniffed. For the first time, it occurred to me that Beth might be crying too. "I hope whatever you did today was worth it. Now get your head out of your ass and go home." She ended the call.

I flew into action. I collected my purse and keys, slung my bag over my shoulder, and raced out into the hallway to the elevator.

"Come on, come on," I pleaded, jabbing the *down* arrow.

Everything felt sped up and jumpy, like a film with missing frames. I left my room key with the same clerk with whom I'd checked in only a few hours ago and paid for the room I wouldn't use. I raced to my car, threw my bag in the trunk.

Idling in the hotel parking lot, I dialed Audra's number with shaking hands.

Audra answered on the first ring. "Mommy? Where are you?"

"Sweetie, I'm in my car on the way to the airport." I was sobbing. *Mommy.* "How is he, honey?"

"Unconscious. He broke his arm and a couple of ribs on impact." Audra's voice trembled, as it had when she was a little girl and overtired, toppling into tears. "The doctors are worried about a concussion and internal bleeding."

Unconscious. Broken. Concussion. Bleeding. Words my daughter shouldn't have to say. Words she shouldn't have had to hear alone. I should have been there. Oh God, please let him be okay, let us be okay, let everything be okay. I'll do anything, anything, anything...

"Honey, I'll be there as soon as I can." I looked around the car for something to wipe my face with, but the rental car was devoid of practical amenities, so I settled for the hem of my shirt. I put the car in drive and turned toward the hotel exit.

"Where were you?" Audra's voice, thin and reedy, slapped at me through the speaker. "I needed you, and I couldn't reach you."

"Oh," I paused, scrambling to remember what Beth had told Audra. "I didn't have service—"

Audra cut me off, and she didn't sound like a little girl anymore. "You declined my calls. You never do that. Where were you?"

"Honey, I'll be there soon," I dodged. "I promise."

"Good." She hung up without saying goodbye. I'd been hung up on twice in a row.

* * *

My return to the airport was a blur; I had only vague recollections of returning my car and standing in line to rebook my flight. I finally snapped back into reality when I heard my flight called. I looked at the boarding pass clutched in my hand. My knuckles were white and bloodless, and I was aware of a throbbing in my shoulders. My mouth tasted metallic. I flexed my fingers, feeling the tingle as blood rushed back in, and lowered my shoulders, rolling my head side to side. There was no difference, no relief. I was hollowed out; tension was the only thing holding my shell up.

The announcement crackled again over the loudspeaker: "Flight 927 to Charlotte will begin boarding shortly."

I glanced at the clock behind the boarding gate. I had gotten lucky with my flight; if we took off on time, I would be back in Charlotte by 11:00 p.m. My clandestine weekend adventure had lasted less than twelve hours.

"Please let everything be all right," I prayed.

I gathered my purse and my bag and made my way to the women's restroom. In the stall, I checked my messages. I'd called Audra again after leaving the ticket counter and got the recording that she was unavailable. I tried Sean's number on the off chance that Audra had his phone, also with no luck. Now I sent messages to Sean, Audra, and Beth with my updated flight information, letting them know I was about to board and that I would text when I landed.

I also had several unread texts from Nick:

7:01 p.m.:

At the hotel.

7:26 p.m.:

Still here.

7:45 p.m.:

Where are you?

I also had a missed call and a voicemail from his number. We'd never crossed the line between words written and words spoken. I pressed *play* on the message, despite a knock on the stall door.

"Somebody's in here," I snapped, pressing the phone to one

ear and my hand against the other to drown out the sounds of toilets flushing and water running.

"Hey, I'm here. Did you forget about me? Where are you? Call me back." His voice was tense, angry.

I erased the message. Nick wasn't my priority right now. I took the coward's way out and messaged him:

Had to go. Emergency.

I turned off my phone and tossed it in my purse, flushed, and exited the stall, ignoring the glares from the women waiting in line. Washing my hands, I studied myself in the fluorescent lighting. My hair, which I'd so painstakingly styled this afternoon, was frizzy, while my eyes, huge, red-rimmed, and scared, dominated my face. My natural-looking makeup had worn off, leaving only natural me behind. My shirt was wrinkled and sweat-stained, sporting a black streak of mascara across the hem. I looked old, tired, scared, and alone. I dried my wet hands on my jeans and went to take my place in line to board the plane that would bear me home.

* * *

Soon after the seat belt sign flashed off, beverage service began. I handed the flight attendant a twenty and asked for two glasses of wine. "Please," I begged. "My husband was in a car accident today. I'm trying to get home to him. Please."

The flight attendant, "Gil," his name badge read, looked at me skeptically, as if weighing what kind of scene I'd cause if he refused. "Are you sure, Ma'am? This is only an hour flight." My seatmate also looked uncomfortable, keeping her eyes glued to her lap where she was filling out the airline crossword puzzle in pen.

"Please," I said again.

Gil looked left and right, then passed me a napkin, a plastic cup, and two miniature bottles of chardonnay. I waved away his offering of pretzels.

"Thank you." I opened the first bottle and tossed it back. From the corner of my eye, I saw my seatmate make a face.

The back of my throat was still tender, and the wine hurt. I gasped in pain, choked, coughing into my napkin. I turned and stared out the small window, wiping my mouth with my hand. Below, I imagined Nick, sitting at the hotel bar, a glass of water in front of him, his long fingers tracing shapes in the condensation of the glass, waiting for the beautiful maiden who would never appear. Was he angry? Sad?

The thought that I might never see Nick again would have terrified me yesterday. Now my only objective was getting home to my family. I'd skirted dangerously close to disaster, and the universe had pulled me back from the edge in the most dramatic way possible. *Go home*, it was saying. *Your family needs you.*

I needed to see Sean and tell him I love him. To tell him and Audra that they meant more to me than anything or anyone else. That losing them would be the end of my world, and that I'd do whatever I could to make everything go back to the way it was before. I'd learned my lesson. I was going home, where I belonged.

Oh, so now it's Sean, you want, Beth's voice chimed in. *A few days ago, you thought Nick was the one you couldn't live without. Why should anyone believe you?*

Because it's true, I argued, railing against Imaginary Beth. It occurred to me that I might be a little drunk, that the wine I'd pounded had shot straight from my empty stomach up to my head.

We'll see about that, Beth snorted and disappeared, leaving me alone to stare out the window and into the black expanse.

"Please, please," I whispered to the star-filled sky and the powers beyond it. "Please don't let it be too late."

Chapter 19

It was summer. The sky was blue and cloudless; the sun felt warm on my skin. I stood at the dam, overlooking the churning water, the peaks of waves sparkling in the sunshine. Nick's hands held my waist, and I leaned back, resting my head against his chest. My eyes closed; I was at peace. The lights behind my eyelids extinguished as the sun disappeared. A scream ripped apart the silence, and my eyes flew open. A roller coaster car raced down through the sky, which was now dark and filled with angry red clouds. It was heading right for us. I saw Sean in the front car, hands above his head, mouth open and screaming, eyes wide and staring. Was his face a frozen mask of fear or joy? Nick and I sprang apart, diving in opposite directions as the car crashed into the bridge. Flames erupted all around me, and I could hear Sean and Nick both calling my name. Shielding my eyes against the smoke, I edged toward the wreckage, one arm outstretched, blindly reaching for survivors. The heat was unbearable. I could feel the hair burning on my arms, tiny wicks against my skin. A hand wrapped itself around my waist and began pulling me backward, away from danger. At the same time, another hand grabbed my wrist and started pulling me deeper into the blaze.

I opened my mouth to scream, but smoke filled my throat, choking me. I was blinded, struck dumb, pulled in two directions while the world burned down around me.

* * *

I woke with a start, cracking my head against the airplane window. Rubbing my temples, I glanced furtively at my seat-mate, who was thankfully also snoozing, the abandoned cross-word resting in her lap.

I checked the time—10:40 p.m. We would be descending soon. I dug into the seatback pocket and retrieved the second bottle of wine. The last image of my nightmare replayed in my head, even as other details faded: I had been caught in flames, unable to move, equally drawn toward danger and safety. I opened the bottle.

"Ladies and gentlemen, we are now beginning our initial descent," the pilot's announcement crackled overhead. Around me, passengers began to stir, and the cabin lights came up. I drained my wine and handed the empty bottle to Gil as he came by collecting trash. I met his judgmental stare head-on.

"Honestly, Gil, if you'd had my day, you'd be drinking too."

I rolled my head and felt the *pop-pop-pop* up the side of my neck. My whole body ached from two flights in one day, not to mention the adrenaline rush of seeing Nick and the fear spike of Beth's call. Oh, and don't forget that little fainting spell. Or the nightmare. And the not eating.

"Flight attendants, please prepare for landing."
Corinne, please prepare for landing.

* * *

215

The cab ride passed in a blur of phone calls and texts. I called Sean and Audra's phones, which both went unanswered. I sent messages saying that I'd landed and was on my way.

A text from Nick arrived as the cab pulled up at the hospital entrance:

Need to talk to you.

I deleted it, paid the driver, and grabbed my bag.

The smell hit me as the automatic doors whooshed open— that sterile ammonia-laced stench. Unprepared, I reeled backward, gagging, chardonnay-flavored spit flooding my mouth.

"Honey, are you all right?" a woman's concerned voice said somewhere above my head.

I looked up. The hospital's bright lights made me squint, and the face belonging to the voice appeared blurred. "Yes," I said and staggered to my feet, declining the hand she held out in assistance. "Thank you, I…don't like hospitals very much."

"Do you need me to get a nurse?" the woman asked, seemingly reluctant to abandon the disheveled mess keeled over in the hospital breezeway. Now that we were eye-to-eye, I could see that she was an older woman, around the same age my mother would have been. She had buzzed white hair and brilliant blue eyes, which peered at me, taking stock. Oversized purple glasses hung around her neck on a beaded chain along with a hospital name badge, which identified her as "Julia, Volunteer."

"I'm fine," I gasped, still leaning against the wall for support and waving her away. "Thank you anyway." I tried not to breathe on her; the alcohol would have alarmed her further.

"Okay, if you're sure," she said, casting another dubious look over her shoulder as she entered the hospital. I put my hands back on my knees and did a round of breathing to slow my racing heart. Breathing through my nose was slightly less panicking, I decided. At least I didn't feel like I was suffocating on recirculated air and other people's illness. I clamped my mouth shut, squared my shoulders, hoisted my bag, and entered the hospital.

As the smell washed over me again, I was instantly transported back to the days of wheeling my mother up and down hospital halls, her shrunken figure hunched over in the wheelchair, a pink blanket over her legs, her claw-like hands gripping the arms of the chair. I would stare down at the brightly colored scarf tied around her head and chatter on about inconsequential things: the weather, that day's menu in the cafeteria, the latest contestant to be voted off *Dancing with the Stars*. I talked about anything except the effects of the latest round of chemo or how we were running out of treatment options. I'd nod to doctors, nurses, patients, and their families as we made our rounds, a community formed around worst-case scenarios.

Now I walked up to the information desk, willing my voice to stay calm, my hands to stop shaking. "Can you direct me to the room for Sean Fuller?" I asked.

"Mom!" Audra's voice was the sweetest sound I'd ever heard. I turned and opened my arms as my daughter charged into them. I embraced her and lifted my face upward in gratitude as she shook against me.

"He's going to be okay," she said between sobs, and now I was crying too. "The doctor says he's going to be okay!"

I will never leave again. I promise. Everything I need is here.

"You're squishing my ribs," Audra protested, sniffing.

I laughed and held her face in my hands, her beautiful face, and kissed her once on each cheek. "Precious girl. Let's go see your father."

* * *

We sat by Sean's bed, one on either side, each holding a hand while he slept. Around us, a nurse bustled about, checking machines, updating her clipboard, and clicking her tongue, letting us know that we were in her way. I stroked Sean's hand, running my finger over the pale line where his wedding ring usually was. "He'll be out for a few hours," the nurse told us as we took up our vigil. "He's had a lot of painkillers."

"I'm not leaving," I told her brusquely. She didn't understand how far I'd come to be here. If she thought a little nap was going to scare me off, she was sorely mistaken. Defiant, I scooted my chair closer to Sean's bedside.

The on-call physician appeared just after one o'clock in the morning looking harried and tired and every bit like the sleep-deprived resident he probably was. The good news was that there were no signs of a concussion or internal bleeding. The bad news was that the recovery time for his other injuries was four to eight weeks. He'd need to remain in the hospital for another day for observation. The cast on his arm would come off in two months. He'd need full-time assistance until he mended. Was there someone available at home to care for him during his recovery? I assured him that I was equal to the task. Audra also promised to do everything she could to help.

An hour passed, then two. Audra's head started to bob as she struggled to stay awake.

"Why don't you go home? I can stay. Go get some rest."

She protested, but her body language told another story. I offered to arrange an Uber, but she deferred. "Daniel said he'd come get me," she said, gathering her things. "I called him while I was waiting for you to get here."

"Honey, it's three in the morning," I reminded her. "Daniel's asleep."

"He said I could call him anytime." She texted him as she spoke, showing me his immediate response:

OMW.

"That's sweet of him," I said, smoothing back her hair and kissing her forehead. We sat together on the small plastic-covered couch under the window. I put my arm around her. "Are you okay staying home overnight by yourself, or do you want me to get someone to come stay with you?"

"Mrs. Thomas made up the guest room for me tonight," she said, her hands holding mine. "And then I'll stay with Lana." Her fingers played over the back of my hands and caught on the paper bracelet around my wrist. "What's this?" she asked, turning my wrist to read the writing. "Mayfair Amusement Park?"

Oh no.

"Part of Beth's conference," I lied, guilt making my stomach churn. "They always plan outings for the attendees." Inspiration struck. "That's why I didn't answer your calls. I was in a huge crowd, and it was noisy." That part, at least, was true.

"But when I called Aunt Beth, she was at her hotel." Audra mused sleepily, running her finger around the bracelet. "She wasn't in a big crowd." She let go of my wrist.

I pivoted back to the truth. "We weren't together when you called. I'm so sorry I didn't answer, sweetheart. If I even thought for a second that it was an emergency..." But Audra was asleep. I squeezed her shoulder and let her doze until her phone buzzed to say Daniel was waiting outside.

I bundled Audra into Daniel's car and elicited a sleepy promise to text when they arrived home. I waved as the taillights vanished around the corner. I pulled at the Mayfair bracelet until it snapped and dropped it into the trash bin next to the hospital entryway.

Despite the late (early?) hour, I pulled up Nick's number and pressed "Call." He picked up on the third ring but didn't say anything.

The message was clear: *I'm waiting.*

"Nick," I started, "I'm back in Charlotte. I had to come home. There was an accident. My husband is in the hospital."

Nick remained silent. I waited, anxious for his reply. Would he ask how Sean was? Would he offer sympathy? Forgiveness? Did he even know my husband's name was Sean?

"Nick? Are you there?"

"I'm here." His emphasis on the word "here" made his meaning clear: *I'm here, you're not.*

I realized I remembered this side of Nick. This was Nick at his most disagreeable—churlish and sulky when he didn't get his way. I flashed back to my conversation with Beth: "Remember that big argument about going away to school?"

The argument had been wiped from my memory at the time in favor of more rose-colored moments. Now I recalled it in one giant rush, like a camera flash illuminating the dark, turning shadows into objects.

We'd stood outside my locker; it was last period on a Thursday. I was leaving the next morning with Mom to drive to Raleigh for my prospective freshman weekend. My arms groaned under a load of books. I'd collected homework from all my teachers and would be doing it in the car while my mother drove.

Nick's face was deep red, his handsome features twisted in anger. His voice was low, but his words were hard-edged and bruising. "Why do you even want to go to that school?"

My chin wobbled. "Nick," I begged, hating the whiny tone in my voice, "you knew I was going. I told you weeks ago. NC State has an excellent design school. Mr. Mack says I've got a great chance at one of the photography scholarships—"

Nick huffed derisively. "You don't need a college degree to take pictures."

I was shocked at this new side of my boyfriend. My arms protested as my books grew heavier. I shifted them slightly, trying to rest them between my hip and my locker, but instead, they tumbled out of my arms and onto the floor. World History, the heaviest, landed on Nick's foot. He howled with surprise, then slammed his palm against the bay of lockers. The hollow *thud* echoed down the hallway.

"Fine. Do what you want," he said, limping past me. "But don't expect me to be happy about it."

I remembered watching him leave, throwing the double doors at the end of the hallway open, never once looking back at me. I remembered gathering my books and trudging to my car, head down, sniffing, willing myself to hold it together. I'd driven directly home and called Beth in a flood of tears. Just like she'd said. I'd forgotten until this moment.

"Just don't expect me to be happy about it." Nick's voice echoed out of the past. It was a threat. And cast a completely different light on his presence at Kirsten's party the next night. Very different from the carefully worded story he'd told me about a lonely soul seeking solace after his heartless girlfriend abandoned him.

All this flashed through my head in a moment, then retreated to the background, awaiting further examination. I was back in the present, standing outside in the dark, shivering in my thin shirt, searching for an explanation that would satisfy the angry voice at the end of the phone.

"Nick, what was I supposed to do? My daughter called. She needed me. I mean, what would you have done if it'd been your—"

He cut me off. Family, mine or his, was not a subject we discussed. "So, I guess you made your choice, then, huh?"

"Nick." I pleaded, unable to reconcile the cold voice on the other end of the call with the warmth of the mouth that had kissed me hours earlier. How could they be the same? "He's my husband."

He's my husband.

I heard myself say it. And for the first time in months, I

meant it. Sean was my husband. He wasn't some fling, some guy that I'd just met. He was the man I'd spent the past quarter-century building a life with. My husband. My family. My constant. My choice.

Sean was my choice.

"Nick," I said, firmer now, "I have to go." Taking a page from his playbook, I didn't say "I'm sorry." I wasn't. I ended the call without saying goodbye and stood for a moment, hugging myself in relief. It was over. I was home. I'd made my choice. I could go back to my old life.

Sean never needed to know.

* * *

Back in Sean's room, I unfolded the sleepaway bed and made it up with linens left by the efficient nurse. The sheets were thin from repeated washings and smelled like disinfectant. It was the same smell as years before, of hospital rooms all over the oncology department and later, hospice. It was the smell of inevitability. You only slept in rooms like these if you knew what would happen next, and you knew you had to be there for it. You slept in a hospital room when you had a baby. Or when someone had surgery or an accident. Or when the doctors had done everything they could, and all that was left was to pray and wait. That's when you took up vigil. Because you wanted to squeeze every last second from the time you have left. And you couldn't bear the possibility that the final moment might come when you'd turned your head or left the room, even for an instant. The last moment was your final chance to make things right or start a lifetime of regret.

I was here now to make things right. With Sean, with Audra, with myself. I'd come close to ruining everything, but I'd woken up in time. Things were going to be okay. Sean would come home from the hospital, and we'd be a family again. We'd all be present in our home together. I would block Nick's number and throw out the photo and letter. I'd stop trying to relive my past. I would focus on the future. I would never talk to Nick...

"Corinne?" Sean's voice was husky, dry, parched earth. I sprang up and rushed to his side. I clasped his hand too forcefully, and he winced, his good hand holding his side. "Ouch. Careful."

"I'm sorry." I leaned down and kissed his forehead before pulling away to study him. He had a split lip and a nasty bruise down the left side of his face. His eye was red from a broken blood vessel. He looked ghoulish as if he'd dressed up for a Halloween party. I wanted to laugh and cry but was afraid if I started to do either, I'd never stop. I settled for a watery smile. "How are you feeling?"

"Like someone hit me with their car," he said wincing.

"What a weird coincidence. You look like someone hit you with their car. You're worth at least forty points now." I smoothed his hair off his forehead, careful to avoid the angry purple welt. "The doctor said they'd keep you here for another day, and then you can come home."

There was an awkward moment.

"Sean."

"Corinne," he said at the same time.

We both halted, waiting for the other to speak.

"Go ahead," I finally said. "You first."

He licked his lips, and the sound of his tongue scratching across the chapped skin made my toes curl. Audra's half-melted cup of ice sat on the rolling bed tray. I scooped up an ice chip with my fingers and held it against his lips, wetting them.

He tried again. "I know things haven't been—"

The nurse bustled in, interrupting him. I wanted to scream. After months of secrecy, all I wanted to do was get everything out in the open. Well, maybe not everything. But I wanted to make things right with Sean, put them back the way they used to be. A hospital bedside seemed the perfect place to make a fresh start, renew our vows, to make promises. It was suitably dramatic and even slightly, if morbidly, romantic.

But Nurse Ratched wasn't having any of that. "You need to come to the desk," she announced, leaving no room for argument. "There's quite a bit of paperwork to fill out."

I looked at Sean helplessly. "I'm sorry," I told him, rising, "I'll be back as soon as I can."

"I'll be here."

"I love you."

"I love you too," he said, closing his eyes.

* * *

As I plowed through the mountain of admittance papers and medical history forms and emergency contacts, I remembered I had never called Beth back. Sliding my phone from my purse, I typed in a quick text to let her know that Sean was beaten up but stable.

Her reply came quickly:

> Thx.

No *XOXO,* no sent love.
There was another text from Nick:

> We need to talk.

It'd come in an hour ago, immediately following our phone call. I deleted it. As far as I was concerned, we didn't need to talk. I'd said what I had to say. I blocked his number. Done.

There was also a message from Audra, reporting that she was at Daniel's, and a quick note from Grace:

Don't hesitate to call if we can do anything for
you. We love you! Xoxo.

I texted her back a short *thank you*, mentally making a note
that I owed her a more extensive thanks later. The same for
Sheila, who had sent a message confirming Audra had arrived
and telling me not to worry about any of our appointments, that
there would be plenty of work for me when I was ready. She
ended with:

Let me know if you need anything.

I was surprised at how much these offers meant to me. I had
always considered Beth my only close girlfriend, but it dawned
on me now that I had friends here. How had I not noticed?

Back in the room, Sean slept. Too wired to sleep, I went to
the bathroom and cleaned myself up as best I could. The mirror
showed a stranger; the hollow eyes and sunken cheeks belonged
to someone else. Not my mother, whose thinness had been a
symptom of her illness, but more like my father, I realized. The
expression on my face was one I'd seen countless times on my
father's face—haunted, tired, eyes that looked through me, not at
me. I washed my face with scratchy brown paper towels and
liquid hand soap from the dispenser, wanting to erase the
disturbing image of my father staring out at me.

You're my daughter, it seemed he was saying.

No, I'm not. I'm nothing like you. I came back.

Really. For how long?

Forever.

*We'll see about that. This ain't no fairy tale, kiddo. Ain't no
happily ever after in real life.*

I ground the heels of my hands against my temples. I was
exhausted, hallucinating.

"You're gone," I told my father, wherever he was. "You're

gone and out of my life. You don't know me, and I will never be like you."

Ignoring the just-made bed, I curled up in the uncomfortable armchair wrapped in an astringent-smelling blanket. I held my sleeping husband's hand and stared out the window until light crept across the sky, and it was morning again.

Chapter 20

Two days later, we returned home. I drove while Sean sat in the backseat with Audra. Her hands hovered midair, steadying him every time I hit a variance in the road. It reminded me of driving home from the hospital with Audra as a newborn, Sean at the wheel, driving ten miles below the limit, while I sat in the back staring at the tiny figure asleep in her car seat, so delicate and fragile it seemed as if the slightest bump could harm her.

I pulled in at the house, veering as close as possible to the front door, which had fewer steps and obstacles for Sean to maneuver. Audra helped as he struggled up the steps and through the propped open door. I brought up the rear, lugging our bags. The irony was not lost on me that I'd packed for a romantic getaway and had ended up sitting a hospital vigil.

Don't think about Nick.

Several times in the hospital, my phone had received calls from unknown numbers. I ignored them all. Once, a call had come in, and Audra had picked up.

"Hello? Corinne Fuller's phone." She paused a moment, then put the phone down, shrugging.

"Hang up," she said and continued whatever she was doing, not noticing that I had stopped cold. Was it a wrong number? Or was it Nick? The adrenaline of not knowing made my stomach flip.

Don't think about Nick.

But still, I wondered. Was Nick trying to contact me to win me back? I told him it was over, and I meant it. But the idea that he might still be fighting for me, that he wanted me so badly that he would risk defying me, was undeniably thrilling.

The maiden Corinne returns to her kingdom, but the brave knight continues to slay dragons in her name—

Stop it.

Don't think about Nick.

I would stop this ridiculous obsession; I would stop envisioning myself starring in a movie just for him. I was past such absurd fantasies. I was back with my family now, and that was all that mattered. I was home, my husband was home, our daughter was home, and we were going to use this time to heal. Sean's broken arm and ribs weren't the only casualties suffered in the Fuller household.

I had a lot of work to do.

* * *

Sean's initial recovery kept me in constant motion. He needed help managing his pain medication, as well as standing, sitting, adjusting his pillows, getting dressed, or eating on the rare occasions he felt hungry. I waded through follow-up phone calls about the accident report and lost hours on hold with the insurance company.

Sean's mother called each day to check in, and for once I was grateful for the emotionally detached relationship between Sean and his family. They were not the type to fly up to help. I couldn't have handled one more person in our house, one more responsibility. I was exhausted, running on empty, reminded of the first days of motherhood when every moment was filled with irrational fear and never-ending chores. I was so tired that I fell asleep in the grocery store parking lot while reviewing my shopping list. I woke half an hour later to Audra's panicked phone call. "Where are you? Dad needs help in the bathroom, and he won't let me do it." I raced home to do what needed to be done, telling myself that it was no less than I deserved. I'd brought this on us, and would pay my full penance to make everything right again.

I left Beth an apology voicemail and sent her an over-the-top floral arrangement full of daisies dyed garish colors that came with a vase and a teddy bear. For five dollars more, I'd added a mylar balloon reading, "I'm sorry," with a sad emoji face. It was so tacky; I knew she'd love it.

"I'm not your freaking girlfriend, save your flowers," she said when she called the next day. "And Dante took the bear and the balloon."

"You'll always be my girlfriend," I teased before turning serious. "I'm sorry."

"You should be. Is it over?"

"It's over. I came to my senses. You were right."

"Music to my ears, girl. Say it again."

"You were right."

"I always am."

Audra went back to school midweek, but when she was home, she was Sean's bodyguard. She sat near him on the couch or in our bed, arranging the complicated system of pillows we'd devised to prop him up, or sprawled across the floor doing homework while he napped. Meowsers also played nursemaid and could be found sleeping on Sean's feet.

Under normal circumstances, I would have been jealous. But these were hardly normal circumstances, and all I could do was smile gratefully at my daughter and kiss the top of her head as I passed, another load of laundry in my hands. For the first time, I could see her devotion to her father for what it was, rare and special. Unwavering. She was better to him than I was. She deserved to be by his side.

My days and nights were an endless cycle of errands, meals, medicine, and lending an extra hand whenever needed. I was glad for the extra work; it distracted me from thinking too hard or too long about the disaster I'd almost created.

What if, I wondered as I made meals, swept floors, or measured out the next round of medicines, what if Sean hadn't been in an accident? What if I'd met Nick for that drink? What would have happened next?

I played it over and over in my mind, the final frame going blank before I could see how the scene ended. One moment, I would remember Nick's lips on mine, his hands at my waist, his fingers on my bare skin, and feel a flutter of desire. The next moment, I'd remember pulling away, the sense that something was wrong, my irritation at his overt seductions even as I'd been fighting nausea. It shamed me to have to wonder if I would have left on my own.

Don't think about Nick.

Inevitably, these thoughts were interrupted as Sean or Audra called for me, sending fresh waves of guilt through my body. I would hurry to check on Sean to see what I could do to help. And he would squeeze my arm with his good hand and thank me.

"What did I do to deserve you?" he said, over and over. "I love you."

"I love you too," I'd say, kissing him gently, while inside, I died a little more.

Corinne promises to be better. To be worthy of Sean's trust.

Are you watching this, Nick?

Don't think about Nick.

* * *

It was Friday afternoon. Sean had been home for five days. He was awake for more extended periods, and I'd gotten so used to the sound of the television that the house now seemed louder when it was off.

I was sitting in the office, enjoying a moment alone. Sean and Audra were watching a movie before she left for her date with Daniel. I debated taking a short nap while she was still home but knew that I'd only wake up groggy and resentful, unable to fall asleep later. I powered on the computer instead.

My phone was full of texts and voicemails from all sorts of well-wishers and offers of help. Grace had called no less than six times since the accident, offering to start a meal train or do a grocery run. I'd sent her a couple of texts thanking her and promising we'd get together soon, that I missed her too, that it was good of her to offer help, but I had things under control. I'd sent similar thanks to others from the PTA and Sean's mother, as well as to his work. Myra, the office manager, had sent an enormous bouquet of lilies and a get-well-soon card on behalf of the accounting department. Sean had smiled when I brought the lilies in, staggering under the sheer size of the arrangement.

"Heavens," he said, his eyebrow raised in amusement. "Did I die?"

Audra looked up from the floor where she was using colored pencils to sketch out a multifunctional living space. "In China, lilies are used for weddings. They represent one hundred years of love. They're good luck."

"They're gorgeous," I said, setting them on the kitchen counter. "But they're also dangerous to cats." As if on cue, Meowsers appeared from the bedroom, looking curiously at the big new plaything on the counter. I pursed my lips, considering. "Why don't we take these next door to Sheila? They're too beautiful not to be appreciated by someone." I plucked the card from the arrangement and snapped a picture. I had to use a landscape view to get the entire bouquet in the frame.

I typed an appreciative email and sent it to Myra with a photo of the flowers attached. That completed, I pulled up Facebook, needing a break from my life for a few minutes.

News of Sean's accident traveled fast. People posted notes of encouragement, offers of help, and promises of prayers sent. Grace had spread the word at school, and there were half a dozen private messages from PTA volunteers, wanting to know how I was doing and how they could help. There were also notes from Brittany and Jenny, saying how sorry they were to hear about my husband's accident and wishing him a speedy recovery. Each message ended in hearts and a string of x's and o's.

The final private message was the oldest, dated October 19, the day before I'd left for Cleveland. It was from Kirsten Summers-Baxter.

My vision zoomed in as if I were looking through a lens on my camera. Kirsten's message took up my entire field of vision; her name seemed to fill the computer screen. I vaguely realized I was grinding my teeth. I relaxed my jaw and leaned in to read.

"Dear Corinne, I hope you are…" the preview read. I would have to click on the message to read what she hoped I was.

I bit my lip and opened the message.

Dear Corinne, I hope you are well. I need to talk to you. I understand you may not want to talk to me, but it's important. Here is my cell. Please call. Kirsten.

Under the brief message, a second bubble displayed her phone number. I Googled the area code. It was a Seattle number.

I sat with my elbows on the keyboard tray, my hands over my mouth, staring at the screen. What else could it be but Nick? What else could we possibly have to talk about?

Don't think about Nick.

I fervently wished that I could call Beth and ask her. But I couldn't call her with more Nick-related drama. I was on my own.

"Mom?" Audra called from the family room. "Dad's asleep, and it's time for me to meet Daniel."

I pushed my chair away and started for the door before remembering to close Facebook. I stared at Kirsten's message a moment longer and then reached out and tapped "delete."

* * *

On Saturday morning, I stood in the kitchen scrambling eggs for Sean's breakfast, thinking about Kirsten's message and if I'd made the right choice by not calling.

Audra wandered in and lifted herself to the kitchen counter in a single fluid motion. She wore running shorts and a voluminous yellow sweatshirt that I didn't recognize, possibly Daniel's.

"So, not that it's any big deal," she said, her bare legs swinging too casually, betraying her words, "but my birthday is Monday."

I was scraping eggs onto a plate as she said this. The last bit of egg missed the plate and landed on the floor as I swung around.

"Oh, honey, I completely forgot."

Audra waved her hand, dismissing my distress. "No, seriously, I get it. You're super busy with Dad. I just"—she shrugged —"you know, wanted to remind you. We don't have to do anything. Daniel and Mrs. Thomas said they'd take me out for dinner."

I felt doubly worse. "Of course, we can do something. It has to be something your father can do." Inspiration struck. "Why don't we invite Daniel and Sheila here? Maybe Lana too? We could order pizza."

"Can we get cupcakes from that bakery uptown?"

"I'll call them today."

Audra smiled as she pushed off the counter. "I'll text Lana and ask Daniel and Mrs. Thomas this afternoon."

I moved toward my daughter, catching her arm before she disappeared. "I really am sorry, honey. Things are so busy." I squeezed her arm, transmitting the offer of a hug.

She patted my hand for a moment, then gently shrugged me off. "I know. It's fine. Really. I'll see you later. Tell Dad I'll pick up a movie for us to watch tonight."

* * *

Later that day, while Sean was napping, I went into the office and began digging through the closet. I was back in the photo boxes again, this time searching for family photos to use as decorations for Audra's party.

I sifted through photos, each picture a smile, a memory, a moment of internal "Yes." Audra, hours old, in her hospital knit hat and armband reading: "Baby Fuller." With my pinkie, I traced her mottled raisin face with its fringe of black baby hair that would fall out a few weeks later, to be replaced by blonde curls. In the next picture, she was sitting on a blanket in our front yard, her first picnic. Here was four-year-old Audra holding Meowsers as a kitten. A family photo of the three of us in front of a Christmas tree at a Duke Energy holiday party. A slew of pictures of Sean and Audra holding hands, playing at the beach, executing various daring poses on the neighborhood playground.

It struck me how few photos there were of me in our family's history. In the past, I had accepted my role as the family historian. It was Sean and Audra's job to make the memories and my job to record them. Now I wondered how different things would have been if I had put down my camera and participated.

You can't change the things you didn't do, Beth had said.

But I could change what I did next. I could be more present, get involved, speak up, be grateful for everything I had. I could be in the pictures and take part in the memories. We had only so much time left together; I had to make the most of every moment.

I realized I was gripping the holiday party photo too tightly, causing it to crease through the middle. I set it aside and put an old dictionary on top of it, hoping to iron out the damage.

Next in the pile, as if the pictures were tarot cards chosen by my subconscious, was a copy of our wedding photo. The original was in our wedding scrapbook on the shelf in the family room. The extra had been tossed in here, relegated to the past.

A black and white photo, Sean and me in silhouette against the stained-glass windows of the Victorian house where we'd held our ceremony and reception. In the foreground, the wedding cake, three-tiered, traditional. We stood behind it, kissing, a life-size replica of the little plastic figures on top of the cake. Sean in his black suit and black tie, me in the tea-length white taffeta dress that I'd found at a church basement sale, my hair pulled back into a high ponytail. We took my breath away. We were so young, so hopeful, so ignorant about what would come next. All our promises made in perfect faith, positive that nothing could ever come between us. That every day would be our best. That together, we were better, stronger than life's challenges.

I envied that couple.

My phone buzzed, and a message popped up. It was Sean:

Help.

Which meant anything from *help* getting dressed to *help* reaching something on a high shelf to *help* with anything in between. I put aside the photos and went to see what he needed.

The nice thing about history was that it waited for you to visit. The present didn't have the same patience.

* * *

"Mom," Audra's voice called from the doorway. "You got a letter."

It was later that same day, and I was in the kitchen, staring into the depleted fridge, searching in vain for something to eat.

"Here," she said, laying the mail on the counter. "Who do you know in Seattle?"

"Whom," I corrected. I selected a strawberry yogurt and closed the fridge. I turned the envelope over to check the return address.

The handwriting grabbed my memory first, and then the name: Summers-Baxter.

"Mom?" Audra was still waiting for an answer.

I struggled to keep my tone casual. Put the letter down, went to the silverware drawer to get a spoon. "Oh, it's no one you know. A friend from high school."

Audra raised an eyebrow. "And she wrote you a letter? How vintage." Mystery solved, she left, her mind already occupied with more interesting topics.

Slowly, cautiously, I approached the letter as if it might explode at any moment. I could almost hear it ticking. I was torn between reading every word or tearing the letter up and burning the pieces immediately. I wanted to know what it said, but I didn't want to read it.

Yogurt and spoon in hand, I picked the envelope up by its corner and took it outside before opening it. Six folded pages of lined paper, the kind from a spiral-bound notebook, fell out. A few still had their rough edges attached, and I pulled at them absently, dropping them onto the cushion next to me. I pulled the lid back on my yogurt carton, took a deep breath, and started reading:

Dear Corinne,

I got your address from Sunny. I hope it's okay that I'm writing to you after all these years. I waited all weekend for your call, and when I didn't hear from you, I decided to write. You don't have to respond, but I hope you will.

First of all, I am so sorry about what happened with Nick. I betrayed your trust and our friendship, and for that, I genuinely apologize. I was in a bad place after my parents split up and couldn't see beyond my own circumstances to appreciate the consequences of my actions. I say this, not as an excuse, but to provide context for why I thought, at the moment, that my behavior was justified. (Can you hear the years of therapy behind that sentence, haha).

To say that my indiscretion with Nick meant nothing would be untrue, because, out of that terrible situation came the most wonderful miracle, my daughter Natalie. In that way, Nick, and by extension, you, gave me the greatest gift imaginable, so, in addition to my apologies, I must also offer my gratitude.

I know that it must have looked like I was maliciously running away with Nick, but he was simply in the right place at the right time. My life in Clemmons was a shambles, and the offer of a new start (including a job and a place to live) was too good to pass up. Nick and I attempted to make things work, to be an actual couple, for the first years of Natalie's life, but it was no good. We were never anything more than vague acquaintances who happened to have a child together.

So, Natalie and I became a unit of two, and Nick went back to what he does best, being charming and alone.

I never tried to keep Natalie from him; I encouraged him to keep up a relationship with her. By the time she was in school, it was clear that he would never be a proper father to her. There are only so many times you can watch your child's disappointment over an ignored invitation before you have to step in. Sunny told me you have a daughter too, so I am sure you understand.

Natalie and I moved to Seattle when she was in first grade, and I met Keith a few years later. I worked at Starbucks (so cliché, I know, haha), and he would come in each morning for his triple shot espresso. He had two young daughters from a previous marriage, and they immediately treated Natalie like a sister. Keith and I have been married for fourteen years and are very happy. I am blessed.

Let me pause to say again that I am so very sorry for any unhappiness I caused you. I wish I could take it back. I hope we can be (at least) Facebook friends going forward. I would love to see you at the squad reunion next summer. Go Warriors!

Now, for the real reason I am writing to you. I heard through the Clemmons grapevine that Nick came to our class reunion. I also heard that he spirited you away for most of the night and that while you returned to the festivities, he disappeared in typical dramatic Nick fashion.

BE CAREFUL, CORINNE. That is what I want to

say. Nick is charming, good-looking, and attentive. But he is also narcissistic and incapable of long-term commitments. He likes his playthings shiny and new. And he wants them on his terms, collecting and discarding as he sees fit. I tried to make things work with him, for Natalie's sake. He was not interested. He started writing more after we made it to Alaska, and he would abandon his day job, not to mention us, for weeks on end, living out of his car or camping on some stranger's sofa while he worked. To him, this was the epitome of romantic and daring, all those things he imagined himself to be. He was Heathcliff roaming the wuthering moors; he was Shackleton exploring the Antarctic. But in reality, he was a deadbeat dad, avoiding responsibility and his family. I worked multiple jobs those first years in Alaska, on the canning floor, or doing weekend office work while Nick's aunt looked after Natalie. I also worked evening shifts in a local diner while Nick's cousins babysat. His family spent more time with his biological daughter than he did. Of course, he was drinking at that time too, which he has managed to stop, but one good decision has not made him a better person.

I have been there and have fallen for his charms. So have you. I am afraid he will try to get you back, Corinne. He always referred to you as the love of his life, even to me. The picture you took of the Clemmons Dam was the first thing he hung in our apartment. I have to admit, I hated that picture. I was jealous. I thought his inability to commit to me was because of you. Finally, I realized that Nick was unable to commit to anyone but himself. He only has his own interests at heart.

Against my advice, Natalie sent him a wedding invitation. I KNEW he wouldn't come, and it broke my heart to watch my daughter pretend she didn't care that he never responded to her. I called him, begged him to come to the wedding. He wasn't interested in her happiness. He has only ever been interested in the things that serve him. He skipped Natalie's wedding to come to a reunion at a school in a town that he swore he had nothing but contempt for to find you. I don't know what his plans are, what he thinks the future might hold for you both, but I am warning you as a mother, as a wife, and as a fellow casualty of his ego, please be careful. He is not worth whatever you are thinking of risking. He will charm you, lead you on, and leave you. He will be dangerous to you and your family if you let him in.

Take care, Corinne, and I hope to see you next summer. I'd like to give my squad sister a long-overdue hug.

With love,
Kirsten

* * *

They say that bad things come in threes.

Sean's accident was first. Kirsten's letter, while not exactly bad, felt ominous. I read and reread it, attempting to uncover any hidden agenda in it, but her letter seemed honest, her apologies sincere. It was hard for me to think of Kirsten in favorable terms after years of casting her in the worst light possible, but my gut reaction was that she was telling the truth. At least the truth as she saw it. Was my Nick the same as Kirsten's Nick? Was he reckless and self-centered or romantic and focused? Pursuing what you wanted could be considered selfish, I guessed. It depended on the goal.

I put Kirsten's letter in my side table drawer, and I wondered, what would be the third thing, and when would it come?

It came two days later, on the night of Audra's birthday.

Chapter 21

We gathered in the family room, waiting for the party guests to arrive. Sean settled against his pillows in a new button-up shirt and clean sweatpants, his hair damp from being washed over the sink in the laundry room. Audra was wearing the purple T-shirt I'd express-ordered with the phrase "Mischief Managed" printed across the chest and a black and white striped long-sleeved shirt underneath. She looked like a gleeful witch.

I pointed at her jeans, torn at the knees and hem. "Don't forget to change your jeans before everyone gets here."

She looked at me, incredulous. "I did. This is my best pair." She shook her head and went to check on the pizza.

I looked around the house. Everything was ready. Two large pizzas were cooking in the oven, and a tower of cupcakes adorned the counter. From the pot rack hung the happy birthday banner that we trotted out for every celebration. A bouquet of yellow roses decorated the kitchen table, along with the photo collage and birthday cards from us, Sean's mother, and Beth, Vi, and Dante.

The doorbell rang, and Audra ran to open it, welcoming Daniel, Sheila, and Lana in a group.

"Happy birthday!" they chorused. Lana blew a noisemaker that sent the cat running for cover. The party had begun.

* * *

We sat in the family room, the adults on chairs and the kids on the floor, talking over one another. Audra sat with her legs stretched across Daniel's, her head on his shoulder, laughing along with Lana at whatever story she was telling. Sheila was talking to Sean about which energy-efficient upgrades were best for resale values. I sat in the chair closest to Sean, content.

Everything Corinne needs to be happy is here.

"Mrs. Fuller, how did you and Mr. Fuller meet?"

I started at the sound of my name. "I'm sorry, what?"

Lana waggled her perfectly French-tipped fingernail between Sean and me. "We're talking about how Daniel and Audra met because they were neighbors. And Daniel's parents were high school sweethearts. And my parents met when my mother demanded to speak to a manager at the store where my dad worked." Lana shrugged. "But my neighbors are all old people, everyone in my school sucks—present company excluded—and customer complaints are filed online now, so how am I ever going to meet anyone?" She sighed.

"Sean and I met in college," I said, smiling. I looked over at my husband, quizzically. "You want to tell it?"

"You start, and I'll take over when you start telling it wrong," he said, his typical response.

Audra put her head in her hands and groaned. "Oh God, not this story again."

"Oh, that does it," I said, nudging her foot with mine. "Now I'm telling the long version…"

* * *

243

By rights, our paths should never have crossed. I was firmly entrenched in the romanticism of being away from home for the first time and swept off my feet by the ideas and artists surrounding me. I was staying up late, drinking too much coffee, arguing deep artistic nonsense. Meanwhile, Sean spent his time studying in the library or goofing around with his fraternity brothers, playing beer pong on weekends, and football between classes.

But fate placed us both in Talley, the student union, late one February afternoon, where I was enduring a horrible blind date. My roommate Millie had fixed me up with one of her musician friends, assuring me that he was "super cute, in a Seattle grunge kind of way."

When I arrived, I took in the vast crowds of people and cursed myself for not getting more details on who to look for. I stood, wavering on the steps, insecurity taking over. It was my first date since starting college, and I began to wonder if I should cut and run.

"Corinne?" A voice cut into my thoughts. I swiveled. And gawked. Kurt Cobain was standing in front of me.

Okay. Not Kurt Cobain. But the guy in front of me looked enough like him to warrant the double take. Even as I stood staring, I noticed several girls (and guys) turn their heads as they passed to get a better look. Messy but attractive, he looked exactly like the photo on his T-shirt, bleached blonde hair with dark roots framing a pouting mouth and heavy-lidded, soulful eyes.

"Corinne?" he asked again, and hypnotized, I nodded.

"I'm Curt," he said, offering his hand.

No way. "Really?" I asked unbelievingly.

He shrugged and motioned to a nearby table. We sat. Well, I sat. He sort of... wilted into a chair. "Well, if you ask my mother, it's actually William, but I'm changing it to Curt. Curt Kobain."

"I think the name Kurt Cobain is taken," I said, smiling, waiting for the punchline.

"No. Curt Kobain. Curt with a C. Kobain with a K."

"Ohh," I replied like it made a difference. I was going to throttle Millie for this.

Curt went on, not realizing that I was looking at him like he was deranged. "It's a tribute. To what his music means to me. To the world. What Nirvana is doing is changing the world of music as we know it…"

And he was off. For the next half an hour, I sat, trapped, listening to a full dissertation on the genius of Nirvana and how he was going to spend next summer living in his van, playing every coffee shop in Seattle until he was discovered. Every time I thought the conversation was winding down, or at least approaching a natural lull in which I could suggest that I go order us some coffees and flee, he would branch off onto another subject.

I was slumped over, staring at the table, all pretense of active conversation gone, when a light southern drawl suddenly interrupted, "There you are!"

I looked up, startled, to see the owner of the voice: male, medium build, sandy blonde hair, crinkly blue eyes, and a big friendly smile, staring expectantly at me.

* * *

"Ta-dah!" Sean interjected from the couch. "The hero enters to save the fair damsel."

Sheila, Lana, and Daniel all shushed him. I continued.

* * *

The stranger smiled at me, then turned to Curt. "Hey man, sorry to interrupt, but her brother sent me to find her. It's

245

family dinner night, you know." He smiled apologetically and, turning back to me, offered his arm. "I'm here to walk you home."

Curt unfolded himself out of his seat. "Yeah, sure," he said, seemingly out of words at last. "Okay, well, it was nice to meet you. See ya around." Curt shoved his hands in his pockets and slouched away.

"See ya," I repeated in a daze and allowed myself to be led away from the table by the fictional best friend of my imaginary brother, not meeting his eyes until we were safely around the corner and he pronounced the coast clear.

"I'm sorry. I never do things like that. But I've been watching you from my table over there for the past twenty minutes, and you were so clearly miserable, I thought I should help...." He trailed off.

"I'm Sean," he said, reaching out and taking my hand.

"Corinne," I answered, not letting go.

* * *

"He took me out to dinner that night, and by dessert, we were dating," I finished.

Everyone applauded, laughing. Even Audra gave a grudging golf clap. I flushed with pride. It was a great story.

I looked over at Sean. His skin was sallow, and his arms curled protectively around a pillow pressed against his chest. This was the most time he'd spent sitting up since the accident and he was clearly flagging. He caught my eye and gave a weak smile.

Sheila also noticed. "Okay," she said, shooting to her feet. "I think we better be on our way." She turned to Audra, who was scrambling to her feet. "Happy birthday, sweetie." They hugged.

Lana stood and began clearing plates. I took them from her, hugged her. "Thank you for everything you've done to help our girl this week. Tell your mom I'll give her a call. I'm sorry she couldn't make it tonight."

Lana rolled her eyes. "Don't be too sorry. Charlie had some kind of stomach bug and gave it to her. It's pretty gross."

I laughed as we walked *en masse* to the door, Sean calling his goodbyes from the couch. I caught Sheila and gave her a spontaneous hug, surprising her. "Thank you for letting Audra spend time at your house. You've been a lifesaver."

Released, she squeezed my arm. "Anything I can do to help. I mean it." She started to move, then stopped. "And whenever you want to start working again, let me know. No pressure. Just know it's there for you." She smiled and waved her fingers in Sean's direction.

"Mom." Audra was pulling her coat from the closet. "Daniel and I are going to go for a drive." She leaned forward and gave me a peck on the cheek. "Thank you for having everyone over tonight. It was nice." She walked backward out the door. "Don't wait up. Bye, Dad!"

"Bye, Mrs. Fuller. Mr. Fuller," Daniel called, following Audra out the door.

I waved as everyone filed down the sidewalk, Lana climbing into her car at the curb, Daniel and Audra walking Sheila home. I hugged myself in the night air, marveling at the simple miracle of time.

My baby was seventeen. And Sean and I were here to celebrate with her.

Had I really thought I could give all this up? It was as though I'd lost myself for a few weeks, and only now could I look back and see how irrationally I'd been acting. What would have been worth giving up this night? I shook my head. Nothing. Nothing would have ever been worth it. I had everything I ever needed right here.

"Corinne?" Sean called. "I need help, please."

"Coming," I called, shutting the door.

I helped Sean to bed. He was slower than usual, exhausted by the evening's activities, the unaccustomed amount of socializing. His eyes were already dropping closed by the time I placed a glass of water on the nightstand.

"It was a good party," he mumbled. "S'was fun."

I dropped a kiss on his forehead. "I can't believe our little girl is seventeen."

"M'neither."

"Good night. I love you."

"Mm-hmm."

* * *

I was cleaning up party debris and waiting for Audra to return when my phone vibrated on the counter. A glance showed an unknown number.

"Ugh, telemarketers." I tapped *decline*.

A moment later, the phone buzzed again—the same unknown number. The back of my neck tingled as if a ghost were breathing across it. A telemarketer wouldn't call this late.

Bad things come in threes.

It was Nick. I knew it. I tapped *decline* and waited. Two calls. A third would come. I headed for my office; the phone clutched in my hand. A moment later, the phone buzzed again.

"Nick?" I kept my voice low.

"Corinne," Nick's voice oozed out of the phone. Despite my resolve to never think about him, let alone *speak* to him again, I shivered, remembering the feel of his mouth against my ear.

Instead of hanging up the phone, Corinne waits to hear what Nick has to say.

"Come outside."

My head snapped up so hard my neck popped. I pushed up one of the slats on the plantation shutters and peered out into the darkness. Sure enough, there was a truck parked five houses away, on the wrong side of the street, headlights low. The interior cab light was on, and I could see a solitary silhouette in the driver's seat. As I looked on, the truck lights flashed, signaling me.

This couldn't be happening.

"What are you doing here?"

"You wouldn't talk to me. I had to see you." He sounded calm, rational as if this were the most logical situation in the world.

"You have to go," I whispered fervently. This wasn't how the story went. "I told you I wasn't going to do this. I have a family. I am married. I do not want to—"

"Come outside," he said. I could hear the smile lifting the corner of his mouth, the pull of his words. Nick the snake charmer, the Pied Piper, the Big Bad Wolf. I was helpless to do anything but follow. "Just for a minute. If you come outside and tell me to leave, then I will. I want to see you."

Corinne is the snake. Corinne is the rat. Corinne is Little Red.

He was playing with me. He didn't think I could resist him face-to-face because I'd never been able to before. Well, this time, he was wrong. I could do this. I was seeing him clearly for the first time.

"Okay," I said through gritted teeth, "I'll come out for a minute. But only to tell you to leave. And then," I lowered my voice again in warning, "you have to go. My husband is in the house, my daughter will be home any minute, and if you don't leave, I'm going to call the cops."

"I'm waiting."

I hung up the phone, stabbing the *end* button furiously, wishing I had a receiver to slam down. I shoved my hands into my hair and pulled, screaming into my closed mouth. This was bad.

Calm down. Go outside and tell him to leave. Tell him it's over; you've made your choice, and he has to go.

I looked down at myself. I'd changed into my pajamas after the party, an old pair of leggings and Sean's Panthers sweatshirt. A few weeks ago, I would have been horrified to think of seeing Nick without full makeup and the perfect outfit, but now I needed him gone. I pulled my hair back with a hair tie filched from Audra's bathroom counter and ran my fingers under my eyes to erase any escaped mascara. I felt like screaming. How was this my life?

In the front hall, I eased the closet door open and jabbed my feet into Audra's yellow Crocs. I unlocked the door with a soft *click* and slid out and crossed the lawn to where Nick stood waiting.

"What are you doing?" I snapped. "Get in the truck before Neighborhood Watch sees you." I yanked furiously on the passenger's side door.

Nick looked amused at my fury. "It's locked, maiden. Let go of the handle."

"Argh!" I threw my hands up in disgust. The door unlocked and I wrenched it open with such force that it bounced back and caught me in the legs, knocking me against the leather seat. I cursed as I climbed in, pulling the door almost all the way closed, but not entirely, in case I needed to make a quick escape.

Nick climbed behind the wheel and closed his door. He turned, left arm propped in the open driver's side window, the other on the back of his seat, head resting in his hand, watching me. He looked tired but serene as if his being here were entirely natural—a quick chat between friends. I wanted to throat punch him.

"What are you doing here?" I said through clenched teeth. I stayed as far back in my seat as I could without toppling out of the truck. If he went to reach for me, I would sprint back to the house. I was beginning to regret the Crocs.

"I had to see you," he said, hands opening upwards in an "isn't it obvious" gesture. "First you disappear on our date, then you hang up on me, now you're blocking my calls. This was the only way for me to get you to talk to me."

Be careful, Corinne, Kirsten's warning sounded.

I stared at Nick, and suddenly, I understood. His expression was a picture-perfect description of "lovelorn," but now I could see it for what it actually was, resentment at being denied what he wanted. It was a child's ploy, a trick to guilt the other person into giving in, giving him what he wanted.

And Nick didn't want me. Nick wanted to feel young again, to be reassured that someone still wanted him. Beth had warned me, and she'd been frustratingly, unwaveringly right. I'd denied Nick what he wanted, and so he wanted me more. If I'd given in before, he wouldn't be sitting here now.

The thought struck me hard: This is the reality, the answer to "what if."

The truth was, I would have been miserable. Played with, guilted, ghosted, and discarded while he went on to something newer and shinier. Kirsten had lived it for me.

This was the alternative I'd been pining after? The grand romance on which I'd gambled my life? It was cotton candy. A fantasy. It was a fairytale—a lie.

I had to get out of here.

I glanced out the windshield and over my shoulder out the back window. At any moment, a porch light could come on, Audra and Daniel could drive by, a neighbor could be out walking their dog. We were too public; there were too many ways to get caught.

"I don't want to talk to you. I love my family, and I don't want to hurt them anymore. You need to go. This is over."

Nick blinked, once, twice. His face hardened. The feeble interior light cast shadows that made his thin face look positively haggard. I felt an anger rise in the air between us in the car and briefly worried that he might strike me. He hit the steering wheel instead. "I thought you wanted a second chance! I drove twelve hours to get you." He glared at me, shaking his head. "We can do things right this time. We can finally be together like we were supposed to be all those years ago. I'll be a full-time writer; you'll finally be a real photographer—"

"I am a real photographer." I was pissed now. "And you haven't heard a word I'm saying. I have a family that I love. A husband. A daughter. I am not leaving them. My life is here."

"You said…" Nick fumbled for his phone, scrolling through his phone, thrusting the screen in my face. "Right here, you said, *'It's so nice to talk to someone who understands the need for artistic expression.'* You said it! He doesn't know you. I know you." Nick jabbed a thumb at his chest. "You and me, together. We're what's good. This is how it should be."

I felt like tearing my hair out. How could he not hear me? How could he not understand? "No. It was twenty-five years ago. Get a grip." In a flash, everything that Beth had been saying for months fell into place. "You skipped your daughter's wedding. You drove across the country to do what, exactly? Rewrite history? Prove that you're not a screw up who abandoned his daughter? So you came after me? Tried to get me to abandon my family so you could try again? Kirsten was right." I scoffed. "You only want the toy the other kid has."

He did a double take. Under other circumstances, it would have been funny. "Kirsten? When did you talk to her?"

"Surprise, Nick. Once from a small town, always from a small town. She wrote to me and warned me. She told me how you abandoned her and Natalie, how you've wasted all these years holding onto the sham of being young, reckless, and free. The romantic artist, the freewheeling writer, going wherever the wind blows. But guess what? You haven't been eighteen for a long time. You had responsibilities. Being irresponsible isn't the same thing as being free. You had a chance to prove yourself more than what people in Clemmons pegged you for, and you blew it."

I reached out and pushed the truck door open. "We're done. Whatever we might have been was over years ago. It shouldn't have started again now. I made a mistake, and it almost cost me everything. You need to go. Move on. This is over. This is the end."

Making sure the street was still deserted, I stepped out of the cab onto the running board. At the last minute, I turned. Nick was staring straight ahead, hands gripping the steering wheel. "I should say thank you, though, for one thing. Thank you for forcing me to wake up. I've been living my life halfway for years. You helped me see that I need to change. If I don't, I'll be left behind, no longer part of my family's story." I stepped down to the curb and paused. "Take care. I hope you find what you need." I swung the door shut with a final *thud* and started for home

"Corinne!" he called out his window.

I swiveled, looking around nervously. Had anyone heard?

"If you leave now, that's it. We're over. I'm gone for good. Is that really what you want?"

I looked at him, the terrain of his face. I remembered those eyes, that mouth, the hair. I remembered the feel of his hands and his body next to mine.

But those were memories. In real life, he was a stranger.

"Goodbye, Nick."

I turned and walked away, Crocs squeaking with each step. Behind me, the truck engine rumbled to life, the headlights illuminating the street. I listened, not looking back, as Nick cranked the truck into a U-turn, tires squealing, and roared around the corner, blowing through the four-way stop. I listened as the sound grew fainter until I couldn't distinguish it from all the other late-night noises.

I'd spent twenty-five years fantasizing about Nick Elms, and it was a relief to think that I'd never see him again.

The curtains come down as Corinne returns home.

I was reaching for the door handle when the porch light switched on.

Chapter 22

I blinked in the sudden light, shielding my eyes with my hand. Sean stood in the doorway in sweatpants, bare from the waist up other than his cast and bandages. His hair came to a point above his left ear, his face still wore the imprint of pillowcases. His eyes, however, were wide awake, sharp and flinty.

And I knew. I just knew.

"Who was that?"

"Sean, I—"

He pointed, wincing with pain. "Not here. Inside."

I followed him inside and shut the door as he hobbled to the couch, grimacing with every step. He had to stop halfway to catch his breath, holding a chair back for support.

My stomach clenched. I felt like someone had poured cold water inside my skull; ice curled down my arms, into my fingers, and the backs of my legs. The irony of being caught now, when I'd finally done the right thing…There would be no more hiding; it was all going to come out.

Sean stood by the couch, panting in pain, staring at me. He needed my help to sit, I realized, and rushed to his side. He flinched as I put my hands under his arms and lowered him down, arranging the cushions behind and around him. I sat on the coffee table next to a forgotten plate. It hardly seemed possible it was still the same night.

"Who...was...that?" Sean repeated between pain spasms. He radiated anger that struck me like fists.

"No one," I said quietly.

"Who was that?" Sean's voice remained solid steel.

"No—" He stopped me with a look of pure fury. The lie caught in my throat, and I choked out the truth. "An old friend. I swear, I didn't invite him here."

"Stop lying to me."

"I swear—"

"Stop LYING!" he shouted, kicking out at the coffee table. I threw my arms out to keep from falling back. The basket of remotes clattered to the floor, startling Meowsers who streaked from the room. Sean groaned, clutching his arms to his ribs, sweat breaking out across his forehead. His face was contorted with pain, his breathing fast and shallow. He shrugged off the hand I put out to steady him.

"I can explain." My voice came out thin, the phrase lifting at the end like a question.

"Can you?"

I heard footsteps, followed by the front door opening. Audra appeared in the hallway, engrossed in pulling off her coat. "What are you guys still doing up? I'm not that late. You wouldn't believe what we—" She looked up, saw our faces, our body language, absorbed the tableau, and all its tension. "Is everything okay?"

"We're fine," Sean and I chorused.

"You don't look—"

"Go to bed." Sean's tone left no room for argument. She stood motionless a moment longer before retreating and slamming her door.

I cocked my head at Sean, indicating that we should go into our room before continuing. He held up his hand.

"I need a minute," he said, his face still mottled from overexertion.

"Of course. I'll, uh, finish cleaning up."

It took ten minutes for Sean to feel well enough to stand; I watched the microwave clock as I waited by the sink, my thoughts racing in time with my pulse. I didn't know what was going to happen, or what Sean was going to say. All I knew was that I had brought this on myself. I had no one's actions to point to but my own.

My choices, my actions, my fault, I thought as I scrubbed the plate.

By the time Sean signaled that he was ready, I'd loaded and started the dishwasher, gathered and tossed all the paper plates and wrapping paper, and swept the floor of cake crumbs. The "happy birthday" banner still hung from the kitchen light, the lone reminder of the night's festivities.

After helping Sean to the bathroom and then back into bed, I stood at the foot of the bed, a prisoner awaiting a verdict.

"I didn't." I looked my husband in the eye, seeing only disbelief, shattered trust. "I didn't do what you're thinking," I repeated. "But I thought about it." I swallowed, forced the words out. "I thought I wanted to."

I thought of Nick, the way his fingers had brushed the small of my back, and how my body had instinctively flinched away, rejecting him. How had I convinced myself that was what I wanted? How had I gambled everything on someone I didn't even know? On empty words? How had I built up the fantasy so much that I thought this, the reality in front of me now, was a fair price? I hadn't only gambled with my life, but with Sean and Audra's too. I was pathetic, ashamed, in my silence. All I could do now was wait for what came next.

I watched Sean struggle, warring emotions racing across his face. The tic of his jaw as he clenched his teeth—anger. The way his eyes closed for a moment, a deliberate blink—sadness. The way his features suddenly sagged, as though gravity gave a sharp yank—belief. Watching anger slip away while betrayal moved in was the worst thing I'd ever seen. Anger could be matched with anger; both parties felt justified in their viewpoints. There was no equality in betrayal. One person was hurt, and the other one was responsible.

"You thought about it," he repeated. A moment passed. "With who?"

"Whom," I corrected automatically.

He looked at me in disbelief. "Really?"

"Sorry, I…Nick."

"Your ex?" He stopped, surprised. "When did you..." He halted, backtracked, and fit the pieces together. "The reunion."

I nodded. "He showed up. We talked, exchanged numbers. Some texts." I paused, uncertain how much to say, how much truth to inflict. I looked around the room, avoiding eye-contact. Beyond the sliding glass door, the lights flickered in the trees.

Help me, Mom.

Sean picked up my hesitation. "Is that all you did?"

There it was—the point-blank question. I could lie, say that was as far as it'd gone, and maybe we could move past it. That I'd simply done some thoughtless texting, caught up in a nostalgic fantasy. But the lie would fester, and our relationship would warp and twist. What came next would forever change us, good or bad.

I swallowed again. The time for lies and half-truths was over. I had to tell the entire truth if I was going to be bold enough to ask for forgiveness. I sat down on the bed.

"No." It was the hardest word to say. "I went to meet him." Sean recoiled as if I slapped him. "But nothing happened, I swear." I pleaded, starting to reach across the distance to touch Sean's arm, console him. He crossed his right arm over his cast, shielding himself. I pulled my hand back, picking at a loose thread in the comforter instead. "When I told you I was going to see Beth, I...met Nick instead. We spent the afternoon together. *In public*," I stressed. "Then I got the news about your accident, and I came right home. That was it. I didn't know he was going to come here tonight. I told him it was over. That I love you and Audra, and I wouldn't risk losing you over some silly fantasy."

"You were with...*him*...when I got hurt?" Sean's voice was a stranger's; his eyes were empty, unfamiliar. "Audra said the first few times she called, you didn't answer. You were with him then?"

I nodded. A trembling started in my stomach, spreading outward. I wrapped my arms around myself, trying to hold still. I was suddenly freezing.

"Did you ignore her calls to be with him?"

I hesitated a fraction of a second before whispering, "Yes."

Sean stared, his blue eyes wide, taking in every inch of me, seeing every moment of betrayal. I saw the love I'd taken for granted fade, leaving a stranger's gaze behind.

* * *

I slept in my office that night, waking early enough to put my blanket and pillow away before Audra's alarm went off. By the time she appeared, I was waiting at the kitchen table with a plate of avocado toast and a bowl of strawberries.

"What is all this?" she asked.

"Oh, I thought I'd try something new," I said, sliding onto the stool next to her, coffee mug between my hands. "You know, they say that breakfast is the most important meal of the day. And those cardboard circles you eat don't count."

Keep things light. Keep talking about nothing; don't talk about last night.

"Okay, weirdo," she said, eyeing me. But she ate her breakfast with enthusiasm. Why hadn't I done this before, I wondered.

Why did it take almost losing someone to make you appreciate them? I tried not to think about Sean, how it might already be too late for us. I vowed to make everything up to Audra, even though she'd never know what I was doing.

Or why.

"That's a lovely bracelet Daniel gave you," I said, reaching out and running a finger over the silver bangle shining on her left wrist.

She smiled. "Yeah, I like it." She slid the bracelet off her wrist, held it up. "He had it engraved."

I squinted; the morning light too weak for reading such tiny print. "What does it say?"

She blushed. "It says, 'I love you.'" She slid the bracelet back onto her wrist and pulled her sweater sleeve down as if embarrassed at having shared so much.

My heart went out to her. To them both. If anyone could appreciate the intensity of first love…I put my hand out and covered hers. "I'm happy for you both."

She looked me in the eye, ready with a sarcastic comeback before changing her mind. "Thanks, Mom. Me too." She patted my hand as Lana honked her car horn outside. "Got to go. Don't forget to pick up candy for tonight."

"I won't." I swiped at my eyes with my sleeve. "Reese's cups and Kit Kats, right? How about a couple of pumpkins? You and Daniel could carve them before the trick-or-treaters start showing up."

She gave me a quick thumbs-up before slamming the door behind her.

Silence descended. I put two more pieces of bread in the toaster and mashed the rest of the avocado—a peace offering. I knocked tentatively on the bedroom door and peered in. Sean was awake, propped against the pillows, looking at his phone. He did not look up when I entered.

"Happy Halloween," I said, smiling tentatively, laying the plate in his lap. "Trick or treat."

No response.

"Do you want some coffee?" I asked, trying again.

He shook his head no, continuing to stare at his phone.

"I'm going out to pick up candy. Want me to see if they have those disgusting black and orange peanut butter candies that you like?" I teased.

Silence.

"Well, do you need help in the shower or getting dressed before I go?" He was starting to need me less as his strength returned, and he acclimated to his reduced mobility, but there were still things best done as a team. Needing me could be the bridge to forgiving me.

"Get out," he said, still looking down.

"Sean, I know you're angry, and you have every right—"

He looked at me then. "I don't need your permission."

"If we could talk..."

He put down his phone, folded his arm over his cast, judging me. I stayed as I was, hands palm up, supplicating.

"There's nothing left to say. You cheated on me. You cheated on our daughter. You..." he paused, weighing his next words. "You had an affair." His eyes blazed, and he gave a short, mirthless laugh. "Do you know what's funny? I used to be grateful that your first boyfriend was a schmuck because I knew I'd always come out on top when you compared us." He snorted, looked toward the window to the back deck. "Turns out, I still came in second."

"No!" I protested, putting my hand on his leg. He jerked away at my touch, flinching with pain. "You were never second! I was..." I stopped, searching for the words to explain, to mitigate the damage. "I was unhappy. I've been unhappy for a long time, and Nick was a distraction. A *temporary* distraction." I emphasized. "I know better. I knew better. Beth tried to tell me, but I was too caught up in the fantasy to listen." Sean didn't turn back toward me, but he also didn't stop me.

I kept going, taking his silence as permission, a good sign. "The reality is that Audra is growing up. Away. She doesn't need me anymore. And you…" I wanted to be careful and picked my way slowly through the minefield of explaining the impossible. "You were busy with work—providing for our family, I know— but I felt lonely. Unnecessary. Like I was written out of the story." I paused, hoping for a reaction. I didn't deserve one, but I hoped. None came.

I continued. "I should have talked to you about it. I should have gone to counseling when you asked. I should have done anything except what I did." A possibility struck me. "I can call the counselor today," I offered, pulling my phone from my pocket. "We can try again. I'll do anything to prove that I love you, that I don't want anyone else." I sniffed. I could feel the tears starting to form. I held the heels of my hands to my eyes, forcing the moisture back. "Please?" I asked, blind.

"The counselor," Sean said, a mocking tone to his voice. "You've been so caught up in your little fairytale that you haven't paid attention to anyone but yourself."

I took my hands from my eyes and looked at him, questioning.

"That first session, the one you bailed on," he said, blinking rapidly, his eyes wet. "I didn't cancel. I kept it. I've had three appointments." He gave another half laugh and held up his cast. "I was coming from a session when I had the accident."

I stared in disbelief. I'd been dealing in secrets for so long, caught up, as Sean said, in my drama, that I hadn't stopped to consider that Sean's story had been unfolding at the same time.

"Did you…" I didn't know what I wanted to ask. "What did you talk about?"

"Does it matter?" he shot back, then softened. "I talked about you. Us. That we were in trouble and I was worried. I wanted to fix it."

I sat immobile. I had no defense. I'd been so busy building my case against him that I'd never considered that he was trying to build a bridge between us. It was a horrible, painful miscommunication: two people, two sides, one marriage.

"Sean, I'm so sorry," I said. I struggled, trying to think of more persuasive words. "Sorry" wasn't enough. It was a fragment, an incomplete sentence.

Sean picked up his phone again. "You're sorry because you got caught and because things didn't turn out the way you thought they would. The time to be sorry or ask for help was months ago. Years ago." He looked straight at me. "We should have been doing this together. Instead, you wrote Audra and me out of your life and brought this other character in to save you. And now, too bad for you, you don't get the happily ever after. None of us do." He reached over and held out the plate of food. "You can have this. I don't want it."

I took it and left the room, closing the door quietly behind me. Like a sleepwalker, I walked through the family room and out on the back porch. I stood still for a moment, then screamed and threw the plate to the ground, sending egg and broken china flying across the flagstone. Then I curled up into a ball on a lounge chair, rocking back and forth.

I'd thought that Sean, and then Nick, was the villain in my story, but it was me.

It was me all along.

Chapter 23

It was midnight, and I couldn't sleep. It had been another lousy day in a week of lousy days since Nick had shown up at my house, and my world had fallen apart.

Each morning, I woke early and moved from the office, where I'd been sleeping, to the kitchen to start breakfast, still trying to keep up the appearance of normalcy for Audra's sake. After she left for school, I would check in on Sean, shower, and leave the house, unable to stand the purgatory of silence. Some days I drove aimlessly, filling the hours with meaningless errands or long nature walks with only my camera for company. At night, I made dinner, and we ate together, acting as naturally as possible, talking to our daughter and through her. I caught Audra watching us covertly with worried eyes.

I did the dishes alone.

The hardest moments of my day were those spent with Sean. He was getting stronger and could now stand and sit independently. However, he still couldn't lift anything heavy or reach for anything above or below waist level. It was a specific type of torture, I realized, to be physically next to someone who had mentally cut you out of his life. To be trapped in a house with someone who only tolerated your presence out of necessity.

Sean made it clear that he no longer wanted anything to do with me. Instead, he spent hours on his phone getting updates from work, as well as group texting with friends who were still checking in on him. He'd started asking people to come around, and I'd often hear a knock at the door to find a college or work friend bearing food or a sixpack. He held court in the family room while I retreated to the office or the back deck.

I accepted this new arrangement as a necessary cover-up for Audra's sake. As long as Sean talked to others, Audra might not notice that he was no longer speaking to me.

I'm sorry, Sean. I'm sorry, Audra.

Corinne is so very sorry.

Now I lay on the couch with the moonlight through the shutters cutting stripes across my legs, wallowing in self-recrimination. I was sorry, not only in an apologetic way but in the state of things. I was a sorry, soggy mess. I was disgusted with myself. I was angry at Nick. I was furious with Sunny for organizing the whole stupid reunion in the first place and with Beth for talking me into going.

Beth.

I sat up and reached for my phone. She'd be up. I could talk to her. I took my phone and my blanket and tiptoed through the darkened family room, letting myself out onto the back deck.

"Hey, hey, Jezebel."

It was so good to hear Beth's voice. "Hi." I sighed.

"Uh, oh. That sounded ominous. Are you okay?"

"I've been better."

As always, Beth could read my mind. "Sean knows?"

"Everything."

"And?"

"And he's furious. And not talking to me."

"Yeah, there's been some of that going around." I heard the gentle teasing in her voice. "How about Audra?"

"She knows something's wrong, but she's staying out of it. I think she's hoping it'll blow over."

"And Nick?"

"Gone."

"Good." She paused. "How's Sean doing, physically?"

"Much better. He still needs my help with some things, which is a blessing. Otherwise, I think he would have kicked me out."

"Do you think..." she hesitated, "do you think you guys will make it?"

I spent most of my sleepless nights wandering the house, wondering the same thing. "I don't know. He still needs me right now, but needing me and wanting me are two separate things. I'm just grateful he hasn't said anything to Audra. I don't think she would ever—" I broke off, as Audra came out on the deck.

I covered the phone with my hand. "It's after midnight! What are you still doing up?"

"Working on a project for design." She pointed at my room, indicating she needed something in there. "I'll be quick. And quiet." She cut me off as I started to object. She waved and mouthed, "Hi Aunt Beth," as she crossed the deck and disappeared inside.

"Hello?" Beth said. "You still there?"

"Sorry, I got distracted." I glanced at the bedroom window, wondering what Audra needed from our room, especially this late at night. I prayed she wouldn't wake Sean. "Anyway, what I was saying is that I don't think she would forgive me. She would never understand. At least Sean might."

Beth sniffed. "Maybe. I guess it depends on what his definition of cheating is."

"But that's the thing," I protested. "Nothing happened. I mean, yes, it did, but we didn't do...that."

"Sex isn't the only way to cheat, my dear," Beth countered. "There's physical affairs and emotional ones." I could hear noises from Beth's side of the phone, the clink of a bottle, the hollow *whump* of a cork being pulled. "Have you thought about it at all from Sean's side? I mean, you were talking to another man for weeks, not your husband. You, my dear, were deeply involved in an emotional affair with Nick. From Sean's perspective, that's a major thing to forgive. I don't know if I could do it."

"You aren't making me feel much better," I said, playing with my toes, chipping off the remains of my elderly pedicure.

"Not my job to fix things for you, sweets," she said. "But for the record, I forgive you. You made a dumb choice, and I wish you hadn't, but you never held my dumb choices against me, so…"

I smiled a little. "Well, I tried to warn you that your face shape would not support bangs."

Beth laughed her sharp "Ha!" making my heart lift. "See? We're both idiots."

"I'm glad you're still my idiot," I said, wishing I could reach through the phone and hug her. My arms ached for human contact.

"I'll always be your idiot," she said. "And you'll always be mine."

"You bet."

"Go win your prince back. Bye, babe."

"Bye."

I ended the call and sat, looking out over the lawn, at the lights, daring to hope that everything might still work out. My best friend had forgiven me. My husband was angry but hadn't kicked me out. And my daughter, thankfully, blessedly, had been shielded from the worst of it.

Thank goodness she'd never know how close I came to making a massive disaster of our lives.

"What is this?" Audra materialized in front of me, holding out a stack of papers.

I blinked in surprise and took them. "Hey, sweetie, what's what?" I asked and glanced at the papers in my hand. The blood drained from my face.

Kirsten's letter, out of its envelope. Nick's letter. The photo of Nick and me. "Where did you get those?"

She stared at me as if this was the dumbest, most inconsequential question I could ask. Which, of course, it was. "I'm working on my project, you know the design based on a childhood memory, so I wanted to look through some of my old artwork in your nightstand. And instead, I found this." She pointed accusingly. "Who is Nick? And why is this Kirsten woman warning you that he's trying to win you back?" She pointed at the picture. "Who is that?"

"That's Nick."

"The Nick from this letter?" she asked. She was getting dangerously close to asking the question I didn't want to answer.

I nodded.

"And did he?" she demanded. "Did he win you back?"

"No." My voice rose.

Please stop asking questions.

"Where were you really when Dad got hurt?"

I said nothing, but I could tell by how she looked at me that she could see the answer anyway.

If I told her the truth, I'd lose her. If I lied, I'd lose her.

So, under a deep black velvet sky, with the lights from the trees flickering, I confessed everything to my daughter.

She never sat down. She stood over me, stoically, in her too-short pajama pants and her boyfriend's sweatshirt, while I admitted that I'd betrayed our family. She remained motionless as I repeated how deeply, truly, cosmically sorry I was.

I finished, cotton-mouthed from talking and shivering in a way that had nothing to do with temperature. I sat, looking up at my daughter, who looked back at me as though I were a stranger.

"Does Dad know?"

"Yes."

"Does he forgive you?"

"Not yet."

She dropped the letters and photo in my lap and slowly walked back to her room. Pausing in the doorway, she turned. "Don't ever make me breakfast again."

Chapter 24

I drove to meet Grace and two other PTA moms on a dreary and overcast Thursday morning. It was mid-November, and the holidays were bearing down on us. Multicolored lights glittered from rain-soaked storefronts, and displays for pumpkin spice everything filled shop windows. I didn't have any holiday spirit, and I was downright dreading the coffee date. I wouldn't have gone at all if it weren't for the fear that I might be discussed more in my absence than in my presence.

I hadn't told anyone about my situation at home. As far as I knew, neither had Sean. It was Audra I couldn't read. I was pretty sure Daniel knew, but I couldn't be certain of what she shared with Lana or any of her other school friends.

Grace texted when I'd finally responded *"yes"* to the group invite:

> Is everything okay?

> We thought you might have run off on us.

I tried to convince myself that her question was casual, a

mild joke. However, I was still unsettled. It was a known fact that Grace didn't joke.

I texted back:

> Everything's okay. Busy with Sean and work.

It wasn't a lie. I was busy avoiding Sean and working to avoid Sean. My days were an endless series of near misses and listening at doors for a clear coast in which to show my face.

Speaking of faces, I checked my reflection while sitting at a stoplight. I sighed at the bruise-colored half-moons glowing under my eyes despite my concealer's promise of "revolutionary results!" My forehead also seemed impervious to the purported "twelve hours of lifting power!" of my new moisturizer. I looked like a ghost. Moreover, I felt like one. I wafted through the house, performing my daily duties, such as grocery shopping and cleaning, but no one spoke to or acknowledged me. I left individual meals in the fridge. There were no more family dinners. I washed dishes by myself at the sink, staring out the window. Evenings were silent, tortuous. Doors closed when I crossed over the invisible thresholds of personal space. I was a specter haunting my own home.

It had been four weeks since Sean's accident, and he was stronger, more mobile, and self-sufficient. His desire to stay away from me proved to be a powerful motivator. Most days, he didn't need any help, or at least he could manage on his own until Audra came home. Sometimes I would see him struggling and move in to help, only to have him back away and snap, "I don't need *you*." He was also working again. John would pick him up and drive him to and from team meetings, or Myra would come by to deliver reports that he would review in bed.

Outside of school or work, Audra was spending most of her time with Daniel or Lana, coming home only to shower, sleep, or help her father. She wore sunglasses in the house, and her earbuds stayed firmly implanted in her ears. These were her armor against my attempts at reconciliation, and they felt impenetrable.

To stay busy, distracted, I'd begun taking on new projects with Sheila. In addition to the novelty of a paycheck, work offered bite-size respites from the icy silence of my house. If no deadline loomed, I would grab my camera and head out to a park or simply walk around the neighborhood, reacquainting myself with all the different ways to communicate through photos. I practiced taking pictures of a home's exterior, experimenting with different ways to capture what I thought of as a house's soul, the thing that would shine through the photo to clients and say *choose me.* I also photographed trees, flowers, and clouds in the sky, delighting in capturing nature's quiet details. I found the brochure from Audra's design course and pored over the photography course offerings.

I spent hours touching up listing photos, long past the point of necessity simply to avoid the moment when I had to give up and eat another dinner alone. I only thought I'd been invisible before. I was learning now what it was actually like. I had been cropped out—the headless figure in a photograph, my father's phantom arm.

Corinne is a ghost. She leaves no imprint, casts no shadow. She is the uninvited guest, haunting those who would be happiest to see her disappear.

I rubbed at my forehead and tried to order my thoughts. I needed to take control of my life. That much was clear. But how? What could I do to make things better? Sean still hadn't broached the topic of me leaving, and I clung to this small shred of hope like a life preserver. As long as I was still in the house, invisible or not, I would believe there was a way through. I had to. It wasn't much to go on, but it was enough.

A horn honked behind me. I jerked my foot from the brake to

the gas in surprise, and the van lurched through the intersection. I was surprised to realize that I'd reached my destination. I didn't remember the drive. My grief was a bandit, stealing moments from my day only to add them to the endless landscapes of my sleepless nights.

I pulled into a space in the shopping center lot and sat in the car for a moment, gathering courage, the engine still idling. Grace pulled in directly across from me. She tapped the horn lightly as she slid out of the car and hop-skipped to my door, as if physically unable to restrain her delight at seeing me.

"Hello stranger," she said, catching me in a one-arm hug as I stepped out of the minivan. The bracelets on her wrist jangled behind my back.

I closed my eyes to savor the moment of human contact.

She stepped back and gave me an appraising look. "Bless your heart, you're so skinny. You look like you were the one in the accident."

I gave a grim smile and fell in step with her as we crossed the street. "You have no idea."

Inside, the air was thick with the heft of freshly ground coffee and scalded milk. Two more PTA members waved to us from a table near the milk and sugar station.

"Go ahead," Grace insisted. "I'll get your coffee." She gave me another once-over. "And a croissant." She waved off my protestations, and I went to greet Tammy and Louise and bask in more hugs.

"How's Sean?" Tammy asked as we settled back into our chairs. Grace hovered near the pick-up shelf, too far away to join in the conversation. It didn't matter; she probably knew enough via Lana. Maybe too much.

"Better," I said, placing my purse under my seat and hooking my ankle through the shoulder strap as my mother taught me. "He's cut way back on the painkillers, and he's a lot more mobile." I didn't add that the reason for his marked improvement was an urgent desire to get away from me. "He should be able to start driving again once his cast comes off and we replace his car. We see the doctor in December."

"Well, bless you all," Louise said, reaching over and patting my hand. Louise had big curly hair, teased high and wide, and wore masses of black mascara and pearly pink lipstick. I imagined that she looked exactly like her high school senior photo. Her heart was as big as her hair, and her chin quivered a little as she regarded me over the top of her lipstick-smeared cup. "I hope you'll call if there is anything we can do. You know, I feel just awful. We should have started a meal chain for you. I can't believe I'm only thinking of that now!" She gave a little wail, punctuating her distress.

I almost laughed. To think of all those family-style meals waiting in the freezer for a family that would never eat them. "No, no," I assured her, patting her hand in return as Grace joined us, placing two vanilla lattes and a plate with a croissant down in front of me with some ceremony. "I told Grace not to worry about it. Audra and I have everything covered." I looked around the table at these three women and felt an acute stab of loneliness.

They were so kind, so willing to help. My eyes welled up as I realized that I was the reason for the distance between us. I was the one who had backed away, treated them as though they were secondary characters in my story, ceasing to exist once I exited the scene. Like Sean had said, I had been so wrapped up in my drama, not just with Nick, but for years now, that I had stopped considering that other people were starring in their own life stories.

It was a lonely realization.

Grace saw my eyes fill and leaned over to give me another one-arm hug. "Oh, sweetie. You must be exhausted." She pressed my head to her shoulder with her hand, patting my cheek. "Remember, we're here for you. Anything you need." Tammy and Louise murmured in support.

"Thanks, you guys," I said, sitting up and wiping my eyes with the backs of my hands. My knuckles came away mascara streaked. "I mean that. Thank you. It's been a rough couple of months..." I trailed off. I'd said "months" when Sean's accident was only one month ago. I saw Tammy shift in her seat, turn toward me. I evaded eye contact by sipping my latte and looking out the window at the rain that had started falling. Louise's hand fell to mine and squeezed, consoling me.

I held my breath, coffee cup still at my lips, until Tammy looked away. The moment passed, and the conversation moved on to other topics; how long it had been since we'd all gotten together, how this semester was the busiest yet, how the kids were doing in school and which teachers were the worst. Tammy's daughter, Maggie, hung around in the same circles as Lana and Audra. Louise's son, Will, was a senior and in full college application mode.

"His first choice is Duke," Louise was saying, as I picked at my croissant, only half listening, still on edge. "But we want him to apply to at least four more." She lowered her voice. "Honestly, I don't think he's got the grades for Duke, but how do I say that to him?" She gave a what-can-you-do shrug of the shoulders and added another packet of sugar to her coffee. She looked at me. "Where is Audra thinking of applying next year? Is she still interested in design?"

I opened my mouth to answer, then realized I didn't know. I hadn't asked her about college in weeks. I was covered in shame all over again. "Oh... you know, it seems like they change their minds every week, doesn't it?" I played the sympathy card, feeling a stab of guilt at doing so. "We haven't spent too much time talking about it since Sean's accident." I took a bite of croissant, signaling that I had said all I wanted to on the topic.

Grace spoke, saving me. "I hate even thinking about it. I

want Lana to stay close enough that she can visit anytime she needs us." She looked around the table. "That's the dream, right? They move out, but they still want to be near you. They stay close enough to stay in your lives?"

"But they do their own laundry," Tammy put in, and everyone laughed.

The conversation turned, inevitably, to gossip. Who'd said what, which members weren't pulling their weight on the fundraising committee. Then Tammy leaned forward conspiratorially. "Did you hear about Duane and Eva?"

We all leaned in, myself included. A drama that wasn't my own? Tell me more.

"She kicked him out. She found a receipt in his pants pocket for dinner at some chichi restaurant from a night he claimed he'd been working late at the office."

I started to feel nauseous. I didn't like where this conversation was heading.

Tammy continued. "So she went through their phone records and found all these calls and texts to a number she didn't recognize. And when she called, guess who answered?"

"Who?" Grace and Louise asked in unison.

"Jenna Sweeney. It turns out the two of them have been having an affair since last year." Tammy sat back, the triumphant herald of bad tidings. "Eva kicked him out on the spot. He's living with Jenna in her apartment by the airport. Can you believe it? Fifty years old and carrying on like hormone-addled teenagers."

I was stunned. I knew Duane and Eva, and their twins, Kevin and Geoff. Duane coached the boys' baseball team. I knew Jenna and her son, Carson. Jenna was a single mom and worked at Duke Energy with Sean. I saw her every year at the company holiday party. She'd always seemed sweet. And Duane had always seemed like such a committed husband to Eva. Where had their relationship gone off track? I wondered if

Duane, Eva, Jenna, and I compared notes, how alike our stories would sound.

I pretended to listen as Tammy and Louise continued talking. Grace, I noticed, also stayed quiet, sipping her coffee. She caught my eye over the top of her latte and gave a small shrug.

Oh, God. She knows. The coffee shop suddenly seemed too hot, too loud.

Louise stopped talking and stared across the table at me. "Are you okay, Corinne?" she asked. "You look pale."

Thank you, Louise.

I pushed my chair back. "You know, I feel a little sick," I said apologetically. "Excuse me, won't you?"

I grabbed my purse and headed to the counter for the bathroom key. Once inside the restroom, I locked the door and took several deep breaths, feeling like I'd narrowly escaped disaster. I checked my face and hair in the mirror. It was as bad as Louise's reaction said it was. My hair, initially smoothed back in a low ponytail, had escaped in small frizzes around my face. A bead of sweat trickled down the middle of my forehead. My lipstick had rubbed off, leaving my lips thin and bloodless. My wrap shirt bunched unflatteringly, giving me a distorted, lopsided look. Crescents of sweat peeked out from under my arms.

I had to get out, go home. I headed back to the table, weaving my way through the line of people waiting for their drinks. I saw Tammy and Louise leaning in, speaking quietly. Most of their conversation was too low to hear, but I caught in the gaps between the noise from the milk steamers and the coffee grinders, "Audra says..." and "sleeping in separate rooms."

They were talking about me.

I slowed my pace, hoping to hear more. I couldn't, thanks to the barista shouting out order names ("Venti latte for Jackson!" "Triple shot espresso for Katie!"), but the guilty faces that turned toward me as I returned to the table confirmed my suspicions.

"You'll have to excuse me, ladies," I said, picking up my

coffee. "I'm not feeling well. No, no, don't get up." I said, motioning as they all began to rise out of their seats. "It was so good to see you all. Grace, thank you for the coffee. I'll see you at the concert next week." I looked over their heads as I said goodbye, not wanting them to read the guilty expression in my eyes or see the condemnation in theirs, and fled.

Chapter 25

I wandered the perimeter of the house, a cup of tea in my hand, replaying the coffee shop scene again and again. I couldn't get over the shame of others knowing what I'd done. Somehow, it had never occurred to me that the news would ever go past my inner circle. Now the parents of my daughter's friends knew. My husband's co-workers probably knew. Who else knew?

It had seemed like such a small thing when it started; a text, a smiley face, a few carefully curated words. Now, as I circled the family room, sliding my fingers over the familiar landmarks, I realized how a few wrong actions could paint over an entire lifetime. I could never look at the things that filled our home or the photos that lined our shelves the same way again.

The teapot I admired in a shop window in Asheville, that Sean snuck back and bought for me, before the affair.

The picture of the three of us skiing at Grandfather Mountain, before the affair.

I would never again be Corinne Fuller, wife and mother. I would always be Corinne Fuller, *the one who had an affair*. I'd forever altered my description. Sean and Audra would have to endure the whispers and knowing looks too. Another piece of my heart broke.

I love you, Sean. I love you, Audra. I'm sorry.

I wiped my eyes with my sleeve. I needed to talk to someone. I was tired of my own company. I took my phone and my tea to the office and called Beth.

"Hey, sweetie." Beth's voice was barely above a whisper, her most soothing tone, as she answered the phone. I promptly burst into tears.

"I'm sorry, I know you're probably busy," I croaked. "I'm having a rough night."

"Shhh.... I know, I know. It's okay." I heard Beth mumble something and Vi's sigh in response. I listened to the rustle of covers.

Sniffling, I stared at my hands, noticing the bitten-down fingernails, the cracked skin on my thumbs. When I rubbed my thumb against my pointer finger, it made a sound like sandpaper.

"I can talk for a few minutes," Beth said, her voice still low and soothing. "Dante's been having trouble sleeping, so he's in bed with us."

From thousands of miles away, I heard Dante's sleepy voice say, "Hi Auntie Rin."

"I should let you go..." I said, not wanting to go at all.

"I'm already up. I'm just going into the other room." I heard the *swish* of sheets as she slid out of bed, the echo of footsteps, the closing of a door. "How are you, babe?"

"I had coffee with some of the moms today." I told her about the coffee shop, about Duane and Eva and Jenna Sweeney, and not knowing where Audra wanted to go to college and the real-ization that I'd been ignoring my friends. "It's so hard." I sighed. "Knowing that I messed up. Knowing that everything is a mess because of what I did."

"Mm-hmm," Beth murmured.

"And I'm so angry at Nick," I continued. "Why did he flirt with me? Why did he play those games? He didn't care about me, what I wanted. Why did I fall for it? Why was I so stupid? Why did I let him trick me like that?"

Beth coughed. "I'm going to stop you, okay? First of all, I love you, but I am not interested in having another conversation that fails the Bechdel Test, so I'm going to lay it all out for you, okay?"

I stayed silent, knowing I wouldn't like what was coming. Beth continued.

"I've been patient with you all your life while you played these little games and told your little stories—poor Princess Corinne, damaged and fragile, waiting for someone to rescue her from her tower. Never thinking for a moment that you should rescue yourself. You waited for your dad to come back, looking for your mom and me to tell you what to do. You let Nick choose you, shape you into who he wanted you to be. Then you molded yourself into who Sean and Audra and your mother needed you to be. And then you let Nick come back into your life and lead you right into danger. Where were YOU during all this? When did YOU ever stand up and fight back? When did you ever say NO?" Beth stopped, breathing heavily as if she'd been holding onto those words for a long time, and was relieved to finally let them go.

"I—"

"Now you're back on the sidelines waiting for others to make things right again. You want Sean back? Fight for your marriage. You want Audra to forgive you? Fight to win back her trust. Fight for what you want in life now, for who you want to be now. Everything up until now is already written. It's up to you to fight for the right ending.

"And I don't know if this is the right time to tell you this," she continued, "but Vi is pregnant again." She stopped, letting that sink in.

I was caught off guard, speechless for a moment before reacting. "That's great! I'm so happy—"

She broke in. "I've wanted to tell you for weeks, but I was waiting for you to ask how I was doing, how Vi was, or Dante. But you've been so wrapped up in yourself that you haven't been interested."

Her words hit home: *You haven't been interested.*

She was right. I hadn't been interested in her, in Sean, in Audra, Grace, Tammy, Louise...not in any of the people who loved me (or simply liked me enough to take time out to meet me for coffee). I'd only been interested in the one who had been telling me the things I wanted to hear. I'd tuned all other voices out, been uninterested in what they had to say, had treated them like they meant nothing to me while expecting them to treat me better.

I was ashamed of my behavior. I'd acted as if they didn't exist. What had Sean said? I'd written him out of my story without giving him a chance. And written in what I thought I wanted: Nick, the conquering hero.

But heroes weren't people who appeared out of nowhere. Heroes were the ones that were there every day. And I was fortunate enough to have a whole cast of characters that fit that description. Beth was right. It was up to me now to show up for them.

Starting right here, right now, with my best friend. Beth had seen it all; she'd been there through Nick, Sean, Audra, my mother, all of it. She'd been my friend, my sister, my surrogate mother. I might have lied to myself throughout the years, but Beth never had. She was my constant, and it was time I started listening. She was right. It was time to stand up and fight.

"You're right." I chose my words with care. "I haven't been there for you. I haven't been there for anyone for a long time. I've been too caught up in myself to see the other side of the story. I'm sorry. And I'm so happy for you. And Vi and Dante."

Beth sighed into the phone. "Thank you. And I forgive you. Again." She paused. "Do you know that Vi suggested the name

Nicholas if it's a boy?" She started laughing. "I told her over my dead body."

I began to laugh too. It felt good, like something toxic had been dispelled.

"Thank you," I said when the laughing fit passed. "Thank you for always being here for me. You're right. I know what I want, and I know who I want, and I need to tell them."

"Go get 'em, girl."

"I will. Love you. Hugs to Dante and Vi." I paused. "And baby Nicholas."

She snorted, and I relaxed. We would be okay. "Love you too. Good luck."

* * *

The next evening, I gathered my courage and knocked at the bedroom door.

After a long pause, Sean called, "Come in."

He was on the bed, typing on his laptop, files spread around him. In a few weeks, he would be fully recovered, and then what would we do? Would he want to move out? Would he ask me to leave?

I stood in the doorway, waiting for an invitation to come closer. But, no, that was the old Corinne. The room was stuffy. I crossed the room and opened the sliding glass door to let in the cold November breeze. Across the back deck, light shone from Audra's window. She had come home early from work, declined dinner, and disappeared into her room. From where I stood, I could faintly hear music.

Sean cocked an eyebrow, regarding me over the top of his screen, but made no other movement. An uncomfortable silence grew. I felt my resolve waver. I wasn't used to making the first move. I took a deep breath.

Put on your big girl pants and fight, Beth cheered in my head.

"I want to talk," I said, my voice wobbling, making it sound like a question.

"What's there to say?" he asked, shrugging, eyes back on his laptop.

Fight for him! Imaginary Beth raised her fists above her head.

"I want to talk about what comes next. How we heal from this." I sat down on my side of the bed, carefully, between paper piles.

Sean sighed and closed his laptop, reaching down to lean it against the bed. He groaned as he tried to straighten up, his balance faltering with the pain. Instinctively, I put my hand out to steady him, to pull him back up. He looked at my hand on his arm. I boldly left it where it was, around his bicep, below his shirt sleeve, above the top of his cast. Skin to skin, I could feel the warmth of his arm under my fingers. I visualized a thousand memories of our life together flowing from my fingers past his skin into his bloodstream. From there, they would spread throughout his body, swaying his feelings, making him soften toward me, and remember why he once loved me. I willed him to feel the love radiating from my touch.

After a moment, he plucked my hand from his arm and laid it on the bed.

"I don't know what you want me to say," he said sadly. "You want me to forgive you and for us to move forward. But it's not that simple. See, you did something bad, and you want forgiveness. That's the easy part. You know the part you're playing in this. But I'm the one who has to grant it. And that's hard. Because not only do I have to forgive you, but I have to forgive myself too. You betrayed our family, but I'm the one who stood by and let it happen."

He swung his feet to the side of the bed, sending papers fluttering to the floor. He stood (his strength was so much better, I noticed) and crossed to the open screen door. He fumbled with the latch a moment before sliding the screen back and stepping out to the deck, breathing deeply as if what he needed to say required more air than our bedroom contained. I followed, leaving the door open.

He stood with his back to me, looking across the lawn. "I knew you weren't happy. I saw you struggling after your mom died, and again after Audra started high school. I knew things had changed. I told myself to give you time. That you'd come to me when you wanted to talk." His voice shook a little. "Maybe you did, and maybe I missed the signals. You always seemed so busy, all those PTA meetings, volunteer events. I thought you had figured it out, that those were the things you wanted."

I had been standing by the bedroom door; now, I crossed to where he stood. Light spilled out around the edges of Audra's curtains and threw shadows across the deck.

"I convinced myself that you were happy, and we were fine. This fall, after your trip with Beth, I knew something was up. I could see the changes. You would scowl at me but light up when your phone buzzed. Or you'd find a way to leave any room I walked into. You were always in your office with the door shut. I started to worry. But still, I held off, waiting for the right moment."

How much time had I, had we, wasted waiting for the "right" time? There was no right time. There was only right now.

"Then, I started seeing Dr. Jill, and she helped me think about all the ways I should be trying to reconnect with you. I cut back my hours at work, started spending more time at home, trying to talk. But it was too little, too late. And that's on me. It's so easy to see all the times that I should have done more, how I hurt you, us, by doing nothing. And now, it's my decision about where we go from here, and I don't know what I want to do."

We were standing side by side, the fabric of my sweater

brushing his cast. I ached to put my hand out, touch him, convey how sorry I was, that he didn't need to apologize, that I forgave everything. Somewhere in the silence, a dog barked, and I realized that I couldn't hear Audra's music anymore.

Sean walked around the firepit so that we were on opposite sides, looking across the unlit surface. "I'm furious with you. I'm angry and exhausted all the time. I'm an emotional and physical wreck. I don't know if I have it in me to be better, to do the right thing. To be honest, doing something to hurt you like you hurt me sounds pretty good right now."

My eyes must have widened because he made a sound that was almost a chuckle. "What? Don't you think it's ever come up? All those late nights at work? The client dinners, the out-of-town conferences? I'm not saying there've been tons of opportunities, but there have been a few. I never did it, but sure, I thought about it."

"You thought about it?" It flew out of my mouth; I was so surprised. Jenna Sweeney's face popped into my mind. Was it her? I felt a stab of jealousy.

He looked at me, incredulous. "Our marriage isn't a fairy-tale." He held up his hands. "That's not judgment or blame. We're both in this relationship. We're both responsible. You're not the only one who has felt lonely or wondered, at some point, if we were still meant to be together. You're not the only one who's ever wondered 'what if?' And when I look at it from that perspective, I can almost see how we could move forward, past this.

"But then, I remember that you lied to me, that you traveled to meet another man, and that only an actual emergency stopped you, and I think—screw it. Screw her and her apologies. She deserves every bit of misery I can cause."

"That's the thing," I said, hoping that the words would come out right. "I wouldn't have gone through with it. Yes, I lied to you, and yes, I went to meet Nick. And, yes, it was exciting and new and different, and all the things I'd thought about. But even before I heard about your accident, I realized that he wasn't who I'd imagined in my head. The fantasy and the reality were two different things. I didn't want the reality of him."

I moved around the edge of the table until I could reach my hand out to Sean's, daring to run my thumb over his knuckle. "I only want the reality of you. And I am so sorry that I put my schoolgirl fantasy before our family," I said, leaning forward, not daring a kiss but moving close enough to feel his breath against my face. "I know that, no matter what happens, I want the reality of you. The reality of our family, good or bad. I will do everything I can to prove to you and Audra that, yes, I stumbled and lost my path for a while, but I've found my way back, and I never want to get lost like that again."

For the briefest of moments, his thumb squeezed mine. Then he shifted, taking a step back. "I don't know if things can ever go back to the way they were."

Fight, Corinne.

I shook my head, needing him to hear me, to understand. "I don't want things to be the way they were. I want them to be better. For us to be better. You said that you wished you'd talked to me sooner, done something sooner. Well, I feel the same way. I should have talked to you, should have spoken up when I needed help." I looked around as if all our past failures were there with us, on display. "I was unhappy for a long time, but if anything good has come out of this, it's that I realized that our family is worth fighting for. That you and I are worth fighting for.

"I need to figure out what is next for me, what I'm going to do next when Audra leaves. I need to explore all the 'what ifs'." I took a deep breath. "I only know for sure that I want to be a better me with you. Here. In our home. I know that we can all be better together."

I saw a shadow move from the corner of my eye, and the

curtains fall back into place. Audra. Had she been listening? A small flicker of hope ignited, warming my chest.

"I need time." Sean was speaking to me, but his eyes were on Audra's window. He'd seen her too.

"Of course." I kept my voice steady, although my hands shook. I balled them up, fingernails cutting into my palms.

"I'm going to bed." He began moving back toward the bedroom, hunched over, holding his cast across his midsection, as he had in the first weeks of his injury, all previous signs of strength gone, sapped by the intensity of the moment.

I helped him inside, sliding the glass door closed behind me. I gathered the fallen papers from the floor and stacked them on his nightstand while he slid underneath the covers.

Leaning over, I pressed a kiss to his forehead. He was too tired to move away; his eyelids were already sliding closed.

"I love you," I whispered and crept from the room, closing the door behind me.

I stood in the hallway, hands gripping the door frame, and listened to my husband weep.

Chapter 26

I was encouraged by my conversation with Sean. Asking for time to think, rather than a flat out "no" seemed like a positive sign. I did my best to grant his request; I continued to stay out of his way, keep quiet when in the house, and do everything I could to make sure he felt he had the time he needed. Whenever I started to feel a little anxious or impatient, I reminded myself of the possible alternative.

The next apology I owed was to my daughter. This was tricky as she'd grown adept at avoiding me. After four days of failed attempts, I vowed that today would be the day. It was Thursday, the night of her design class. I would wait for her outside her room all evening until she came home.

By early evening, I was getting nervous, going over and over everything I wanted to say. To pass the time, I retouched the photos from Sheila's latest listing and sent them to her.

A few minutes later, I received a text back:

Thanks! These look great!

A minute later:

I just opened a bottle of wine. Want to come over?

I texted back, hoping she couldn't sense my desperation:

Sounds terrific.

Shoving my feet into my boots, I practically ran out the door, eager to escape the silent loneliness of my house.

Over a delicious glass of malbec, I confided to Sheila that Sean and I were "having troubles," leaving out any mention of Nick. Faced with the threat of losing my husband and daughter, Nick had become the least important part of the story.

It was a relief to have someone to talk to. I was tired of my own company. Internal narrative Corinne was exhausting, over-analyzing every word of every conversation. She was keeping me up all night.

The weather had finally turned from unseasonably warm to appropriately chilly, and Sheila and I were both bundled in chunky sweaters and leggings. It was luxurious to be cozy and warm in her cluttered, companionable kitchen. I could see why Audra preferred it here. Our house felt cold all the time now.

I finished my story, parched, both physically and emotionally. I took a sip of wine.

Sheila regarded me from across the table. "Wow," she said finally.

"Yeah," I agreed. "It is sort of wow."

"Truthfully, I'm not sure what to say," she admitted. "But thank you for telling me."

"Thank you for listening," I said, leaning forward in my chair and rolling my shoulders, which were permanently tense these days. "Sean and I both appreciate that Audra has a safe place to go while we sort things out."

"Anytime. She's a lovely girl, and I enjoy having her around." Sheila winked. "As long as DJ leaves his door open."

"That reminds me..." Covering my eyes in embarrassment, I confessed the disastrous sex talk I'd had with Audra.

After laughing so hard that she cried, Sheila admitted she and Daniel had had much the same conversation. "I knocked on his door," she chuckled, pouring herself a second glass of wine, "and when he opened it and saw me standing there with a handful of pamphlets about safe sex, he said 'nope' and shut the door in my face."

Hooting with laughter, she tilted the bottle toward me and refilled my glass. I felt a shift in the air as we passed from neighbors into friends.

"How does Audra seem to you?" I finally asked once the hilarity subsided, replaced with a fresh wave of guilt. It was my fault that I had to get updates on my daughter through third parties.

I had to make things right. I couldn't lose these last years with her.

Sheila looked thoughtful, then said, "Sad." She made an apologetic face. "I'm sorry, but she does. She hasn't talked to me about any of this, of course, but I know she talks with Deej. That's a good thing, right? Better out than in?"

I nodded. "Better yes, but still painful." I hesitated, then put my hand over Sheila's. "Thank you again. I mean it. Between what you've done for me and what you're doing for my daughter, I don't know how I can ever repay you."

She smiled, patted my hand, her manicured nails covering my ragged, bitten ones. "It's not about owing anybody anything. I'm here whenever you need me."

"Audra is lucky to have both Daniel and you in her life right now."

"I feel the same way about having her in our lives." Sheila

sat back and picked up her wine glass, swirling the dark red liquid thoughtfully. "I've debated on whether to say anything, but I think you'll understand what I'm getting at when I say that I am so happy that Daniel and Audra are together, but that I hope they will still make the choices that are right for them."

She looked at me quizzically. "Do you know what I mean?" she asked. "Daniel grew up with stories about his high school sweetheart parents, and I don't want him thinking that's the way it has to be. They're so young. They may want very different things next year. Or in a few months. I'd hate for them to start limiting their choices now."

I nodded. "I completely understand." *Boy, did I ever.* "I think they both have pretty solid ideas about who they are and what they want." I ran my finger around the rim of my almost-empty glass. "I also know that we have to let them make their own decisions. We need to be there for them to talk to, and offer advice if they ask." I smiled. "Even sometimes when they don't. But we can't make their choices for them." I stood abruptly and carried my glass to the sink so that Sheila couldn't see the tears forming. "We don't want them to grow up wondering 'what if?'"

Out of Sheila's window, I could see the tops of our trees over her viburnum bushes. The lights glittered and winked.

I understand, Mom. I know you were trying to help. I know you wanted to protect me. I wish I could talk to you, tell you that you were right. I just needed to learn it by myself.

I rubbed my eyes, feigning tiredness, and turned to find Sheila watching me from the table. "I have to go," I said, winding my scarf around my neck for the short walk home. "Thank you so much for the drink and the talk."

Sheila saw me to the door, wrapping me in a huge hug. I hugged her back, thankful for the unexpected friendship and support that had been right next door all along. I clung to the moment a heartbeat longer before turning and making my way home in the chilly night.

It was time to talk to my daughter.

* * *

I waited, seated in my office chair, facing the door. I'd arranged myself in different settings for the past hour and finally settled on my office. Waiting at the front door seemed too aggressive, the kitchen too avoidable. Audra had to pass me to get to her room; I could head her off before she locked herself away.

Sean was asleep already. I hoped he wouldn't wake up. This moment, this conversation, was strictly between Audra and me.

The door slammed. She did not yell, "I'm home." She preferred keeping her location private these days.

I rubbed my clammy hands together and stood on rubbery legs, waiting. I heard the pantry open and shut, followed by the fridge, then the *clomp* of her Doc Martens in the hallway. I stepped into the doorway.

"Hi, honey."

She halted, body rigid, instantly on high alert. Her earbuds were in, and the bassline seeped out into the silence that followed. She could have darted around me but seemed frozen by my presence, as if unsure what to do with a mother who actively sought her out. I took a step into the hall and held out an arm, directing her to the sofa in my office. She eyed me, making sure I was serious, then rolled her head back in exasperation and slumped over to the couch, throwing herself down into it, not removing her backpack or her earbuds.

I put my hands to my ears, mimed taking the earpieces out. She arched an eyebrow but complied. She waited, silent. It was up to me.

I started with the most important facts. "Honey, I am so sorry I hurt you. I love you. I love Dad."

She looked past me, out the open office door, uninterested.

"I want to work things out with Dad. I want us to be a family again. But that means making things right with you too. I want you to tell me what I need to do."

Audra looked at me now, contempt darkening her hazel eyes. "Nothing. There's nothing you can do." She stood, towering over me. "Are we through here?"

"Wait!" I reached for her arm as she pushed past me and bolted for her room. I shot out of my chair and caught her backpack strap as she was halfway into her room. She stumbled, taking a step back into the hallway. I used the momentum to wrap my hand tighter around the strap, bringing us closer. She shrugged the pack off her shoulder. It fell with a thud to the floor, pulling me off balance. I groped blindly and caught her by the wrist as I righted myself. She brought her wrist up, eyes wide at finding herself trapped.

I wedged myself into the door frame, foot bracing the door open, and pulled her closer. I needed her full attention. "Honey, listen to me. I messed up. I can't change that. But nothing is more important to me than this family. You and Dad are the most important people in my life. I got confused for a while, and I forgot what matters. The truth is, I was unhappy with myself. I was unhappy, and I was selfish, and I am so, so sorry that I hurt you." I wanted her to believe me, hear the resolve behind my words.

She looked at my hand on her wrist, in a way so reminiscent of Sean that I caught my breath. "You did hurt me," she said quietly. "You betrayed me. You betrayed Dad. What can you possibly do to make it up to us?'

I released my death grip on her wrist and laid my hand on her shoulder gently as we locked eyes. I was shocked at the woman's face looking back at me. The last traces of the little girl had disappeared when I hadn't been looking. Audra's face had thinned out, acquired edges where there used to be curves. Even the tilt of her head as she stared at me seemed older.

"I can stay and spend every day proving to you that I know

what's important. My dad cheated on my mom and then left us. He never came back, never said he was sorry. I'm not him. I made a terrible choice, a terrible, awful mistake, but I will be damned if I let you think, even for a moment, that I don't regret it. That I don't know what's at risk. I will fight for you, Audra. I will fight for your father. For this family. I will fight any dragon that threatens my family. Even if—especially if—the dragons are mine."

We stood, locked together, in her doorway, my hand on her shoulder, her arms hanging stiffly at her sides. Moments ticked by. I blinked through tears, but I didn't look away.

I sent waves of love through my fingers, willing them to find their way into her consciousness, find purchase, and take root.

I love you. I'm fighting for you. I will never betray you again.

I felt a shift in her shoulder. Her hand drifted up and, for a moment, landed on mine, her fingers flexing slightly. Wordlessly, she ducked under my arm and into her room, forcing me back as she closed the door.

I stood alone in the hall. My hand pulsed, Audra's phantom fingertips still on my skin. I brought my hand up to my face and brushed it against my wet cheek, trying to transfer her touch. We'd had a connection—a moment. I'd spoken. I could only hope now that she'd listened, had felt the truth in my promises. That this moment would fan any small flame that still burned inside her, would fuel any love she felt for her flawed, human mother.

It was enough for now.

* * *

The weekend slogged by in silence, each of us staying in our appointed corners. By Sunday afternoon, I'd had enough of the oppressive silence and had taken my camera and driven to the botanic gardens where I spent a blissful afternoon, lost in the magic of capturing frost on leaves, the silhouettes of bare branches against a Carolina blue sky.

I came home to an empty house and a hastily scribbled note on the counter:

Took Dad out for dinner. Back later.

I stared at the note, tracing my finger over Audra's loopy cursive. *Took Dad out... Back later.* If anyone had been watching, they might have thought I was annoyed, upset that I'd been excluded from dinner plans. That my trembling lower lip was a sign of unhappiness. But the truth was, I was overwhelmed. It was the first small sign of hope that maybe, just maybe, my daughter might forgive me. She had taken the time to write me a note. It was enough for now, a place to start.

I hugged the note, kissed it, and reread it before carrying it to the drawer of my nightstand—a new cherished memory.

I opened the drawer, saw the mess inside. I hadn't opened this drawer since the night of my confrontation with Audra on the back deck when she'd discovered my secret while searching for childhood memorabilia.

Now the stack of cards and drawings was gone, presumably in Audra's possession. All that was left was Nick's letter, Kirsten's letter and the picture of Nick and me kissing. I removed the letters and photo and tenderly placed Audra's note in the empty drawer, nestled among the fallen glitter and dusty macaroni noodles of art projects past.

I carried everything to my office and sat in my chair, considering an idea that had been simmering at the back of my mind for days.

What if I reached out to Kirsten?

It made me nauseous and excited at the same time. For so long, I'd considered her the enemy, the bad guy. Well, I knew better now. Stomach flip-flopping, I brought up Messenger and typed a quick note with shaky hands:

Kirsten, thank you for your message and your letter. I'm ready to talk if you are.

I added my phone number and pressed *send* before I could lose my nerve.

I gathered up the letters and photo, grabbed a sweater from the back of the couch, and went out to the deck. The early evening was cool but mild; the sun vanished for another day, the stars slow to make an appearance.

Removing the lid from the fire pit, I pressed the ignition button and waited while the flames sizzled and spat their way to life. The breeze picked up, and I shuddered, pulling my sweater around me, despite the immediate warmth of the fire. I heard a car turn onto the street, followed a moment later by the rumble of our garage door opening.

I stayed where I was. I had unfinished business.

First, I tossed the photo onto the flames. For a second, it remained perfectly preserved. Then fire licked the edges, and the image began curling in on itself. I watched, fascinated, as red, then yellow, then black streaks consumed Nick and me. Our faces, pressed together, were the last to go.

Next came the first page of Kirsten's letter. I watched as her words of warning blazed and crackled. *Dear Corinne...*

The screen door slid open behind me. I continued feeding Kirsten's letter to the flames. Sean appeared at my side. I felt, rather than saw, Audra's silent presence in the doorway.

When the last page of Kirsten's letter had burned away, I handed Nick's letter to Sean.

"What's this?"

I shrugged. "Just something I've been holding onto. Something I don't need anymore."

Sean balled up the letter and tossed it in. Wordlessly, we watched it ignite and burn, the smoke drifting up in lazy swirls to the sky.

Goodbye Nick. This is the end.

Sean and I stood together, long after the flames had done their job, feeling the warmth of the fire on our faces, the evening breeze on our backs. When we turned to go back inside, Audra was gone, but she had set my place at the table with a takeout box of chicken and broccoli beside it.

It was the best meal I ever had.

* * *

I was rinsing my dish at the sink, savoring the lingering taste of soy sauce, when my phone rang. It was the default ringtone, so I had no idea who could be calling. Curious, I wiped my soapy hands on my jeans and answered.

"Hello?"

A *click*. A pause. A tentative voice. "Corinne?"

"Yes?"

"It's Kirsten." Another pause. "I hope I…is this a good time?"

"Kirsten," I repeated. I'd been prepared to wait days, weeks, forever. "Yeah, I mean, yes, this is great. Give me a minute. I, uh, want to go outside."

I left my plate on the dish towel to air-dry and went back outside to sit beside the still-burning fire. I tucked my feet up under me and wrapped my sweater around my knees. The temperature had dropped considerably in the last twenty minutes.

I counted to five, slowly, willing my voice to be there. Kirsten, to her credit, waited silently.

"Hey," I said, more as an exhale than a real word. "It's been a long time."

"You can say that again." Kirsten gave a breathy laugh like she was a little unsure of her voice as well. "I'm glad you reached out. I wasn't sure you would."

"Me either," I admitted, wedging the phone between my cheek and shoulder and holding my hands out to the fire. "But I wanted to say thank you."

"For?"

"For warning me." I pulled my hands back and cradled the phone so that my words wouldn't sound crushed or mumbled. "I went to meet him. Nick, I mean. I didn't get your message and letter until after I got back, but it still helped." I took a breath, unsure how much to share. "It helped me put him into perspective."

Silence from Kirsten's end. Maybe I wasn't explaining it right. Perhaps she thought she'd helped me choose Nick. I was about to say more, anything, when she cleared her throat.

"Thank you," she said, and I could hear the catch in her voice like she was crying but didn't want me to know. "I've felt so guilty for all these years, feeling like I stole something from you. Feeling like I ruined your life, Nick's life, and my own with one bad choice. I never meant to hurt you, Corinne. You and the squad were like my family. I was so embarrassed. I couldn't face you."

My heart went out to her. I knew what it was like to wake up every morning and dread getting up, knowing the life you were waking up to was your own doing. I knew what it was like to fall for fake promises and surface charms. I knew all too well what it was like to follow a path only to find yourself at the edge of a cliff.

Kirsten continued. "I wanted to write to you, but the longer I waited, the harder it got, until one day, it became impossible. So I let it go and thought that maybe the universe would show me how to make it up to you.

"And then, when I called Nick about Nat's wedding, he told

me he was going to Clemmons. I guessed he was going to see you. I hoped I was wrong. But I knew I had to warn you, just in case."

"You weren't wrong," I admitted.

"And are you...are things okay?"

I shook my head as if she could see me. "Not yet. But I'm hopeful. I've told my husband and daughter everything, and I'm hoping they'll be able to forgive me."

Kirsten sighed. "Oh, Corinne, I'm sorry. I was praying it wouldn't come to that."

"Don't be sorry. Things were a mess long before this. In a way, what happened with Nick brought everything out in the open."

"Well, that's good, I guess."

"I hope so. At any rate, it's what happened and where we are, so it's as good a place as any to start again."

"Mmm," she murmured. I translated it into a sound of agreement. "Well, I won't keep you any longer. It must be getting late out there."

"Thanks for calling, Kirsten, And please, don't feel guilty about anything that happened. Anyone can make a mistake. It doesn't mean you have to spend your life paying for it. At least I hope it doesn't."

Kirsten gave another breathy laugh. "Hey, has Jenny sent you the info about next summer?"

"No, but she mentioned it at Queen's."

"I'll forward you the email. We're talking about a long weekend in Hilton Head next June. I hope you'll come."

I smiled—a weekend with my high school cheer squad. I could just see it. Fruity drinks with umbrellas. Laughing too loud. Talking too much. An ill-advised attempt at some of our old cheer routines..."It sounds wonderful," I said, honestly. "Count me in."

"Yay!" Kirsten gave a cheer, and for a moment, I could

picture her as she was in high school, ponytail and poms flying, arms outstretched as the V in Victory.

"Hey Kirs," I said, the old nickname flying out of my mouth.

"Yeah, Rin?" I could hear her smile.

"Can I ask you something?"

"Anything."

I cleared my throat, embarrassed. "What's Nick's author pseudonym? I couldn't figure it out. He never told me."

Kirsten's tentative laugh became a full-throated guffaw; a belly laugh instantly remembered from a hundred different bus rides, practices, homework sessions. "He told you he was a writer? Oh, that's perfect."

I was shocked. "You mean he's not?" I thought back to her letter, now reduced to ashes in the table my feet currently rested on. "But I thought you said his writing career took off when you moved to Alaska." My mind raced. What did he do if he didn't write?

"Oh, he tried going legit for a while. Got a job writing for the events section of the newspaper. You know, five hundred words on the ice sculpture contest or which park trails are the most family friendly." I could hear the resignation in Kirsten's voice and imagined that those assignments hadn't paid too well. "But he gave that up. He's still working for his uncle. The only writing Nick does now is submitting stories to adult websites."

"What?" I screamed in shock. Clapping my hand over my mouth, I lowered my voice. "You're kidding."

"Nooooope." Kirsten drew out the word seeming to relish every syllable. "You can Google him if you want. He writes under the name Hugh Jass."

"Huge...?" I trailed off, hand still covering my mouth. It was too horrible. "No, no. You have to be kidding. You're kidding, right?"

"Not even a little." She laughed again, then sighed happily.

"Oh, Rin, I'm so happy to talk to you. Please stay in touch. Friend me, text me, whatever. I can't wait for next summer!"

We said our goodbyes, and I sat outside, holding my phone, thoughts reeling. Kirsten and I had made up. Nick wrote erotic stories under a juvenile alias. What in the world could happen next?

Chapter 27

The following Tuesday, I pulled up to the high school with all the excitement of a prisoner attending her execution. It was the annual holiday concert, featuring performances by the school band, orchestra, and choir. The PTA always staffed a snack table to raise funds, and I had signed up with Grace ages ago. I did not want to be here. But I said I'd go, and the last thing I could do at this moment was bow out of a promise.

I flipped down the mirror from my visor and did a final check. Hair washed and still air-drying, gray roots creeping in. Makeup working overtime and unsuccessful in masking the bags under my eyes. I bared my teeth, checking for food, rubbed off the lipstick smeared on my front teeth. It would have to do. I flipped the mirror closed, squared my shoulders, and exited the car.

I was counting out the cash box when Grace arrived, looking frazzled, her sweater coat flapping around her ankles as her heels *click-click*ed across the tiles. "Sorry I'm late! Lana forgot her flute, and we had to go all the way back home." She clucked her tongue and shook her head. "How anyone forgets their flute when they're going to a band concert is beyond me." She pulled off her coat, throwing it unceremoniously in a heap under the table with her keys, and began hoisting boxes of candy bars and pretzels out from the PTA closet. I finished counting and came over to help.

We finished setting up as the first concert attendees entered, shoulders hunched, heads down against the cold. We sold a few candy bars to parents who would use the treats as bribes for younger siblings to wait quietly in their seats. This would backfire the minute the sugar hit the bloodstream, but we shrugged our shoulders mentally and took their cash.

"Where's Charlie?" I asked during a lull in sales. Usually, Lana's hyperactive little brother was one of the screaming siblings forced to attend this event.

Grace shook her head. "He and Glenn are at a Cub Scout party. Is it bad that I'm totally fine with that? It's so much easier to come to these events alone."

She must've seen the look that crossed my face because she immediately apologized. "I'm sorry, I didn't mean—"

We were interrupted by a group of giggling students who seemed to regard our selection of chips and chocolate as a dinner menu, and we spent a frenzied few minutes selling snacks and counting back change. By this time, the lobby had cleared out, and we could hear Principal Taylor making her opening announcements.

"Want to go in?" I asked, closing up the lockbox.

"Corinne, wait." Grace put her hand on my arm. "Look, I wanted to say I'm sorry. Lana told me about what you and Sean are going through, and I'm here if you want to talk about it."

I felt my face flush. My sweater set felt too warm for the lobby. "I know you are. I appreciate it. And thank you for being there for Audra. I know she's been splitting her time between your house and Daniel's." I moved to go, but Grace held my arm firmly.

Instinctively, I started to pull away and then caught myself. What was I doing? This was Grace, my friend. I had to stop running away. I relaxed my body and took a step back toward Grace.

The old Corinne shut her friends out. The new Corinne needs all the friends she can get.

Grace lowered her voice and leaned in. "I don't know if you ever knew this, but Glenn and I went through something similar. It was after Charlie was born."

I looked at my friend in surprise. "Glenn had an affair?"

Grace shook her head. "No, I did." She gave a small sigh. "With one of the dads from Lana's music class. His wife was—well, probably still is—a surgeon, and he was the stay-at-home parent. We started talking during class, and pretty soon we were meeting for coffee and, well, one thing led to another..." she trailed off, holding her hands up.

I was gobsmacked. Glenn and Grace were the most stable couple I knew. They always seemed so in love, so dedicated. Glenn was jovial, easygoing, the kind of husband that ran the grill at every barbeque and helped coach every sport his kids played. Grace's favorite phrase at PTA planning meetings was, "Glenn will do that." I couldn't imagine that they'd ever had a day of disagreement, let alone gotten to a place where an affair could happen.

Grace saw my face and laughed. "I know, I know. Hard to believe, isn't it? But it was one of those things. I was home. I was lonely. Glenn, as much as he tried, couldn't help. Everything he tried to do seemed to make things worse. Charlie cried when Glenn held him. If he tried playing with Lana, she'd want me instead. If he made dinner, he left the kitchen a mess. I was done with it. With him. Then I met Cole, and he seemed like he got it, you know? The whole stay-at-home thing. And suddenly, I felt like my life with Glenn was wrong. Like I'd made the wrong choice. All I could think about was being with Cole and how much better my life would be with a man who understood me."

"So, what happened?" I asked, fascinated. Here was a whole

other side to cool, calm Grace that I would never have guessed existed.

She shrugged. "We got caught. His wife confronted him with the credit card statement showing all our lunch dates. Told him to break it off, or he'd never see his daughter again. So, he did. I don't blame him. And I came clean to Glenn. It was awful. We fought, we cried, he moved out for a few weeks." She shook her head. "We told Lana he was away for work. I still don't know if she ever figured it out. Anyway, we started going to couples' therapy, having date nights, the whole thing. We came through it, but it took a couple of years to get to the point where he trusted me again."

She smiled at me, a world of understanding in her expression. "So, believe me when I say you can talk to me. I've been on the dark side. And I found my way back. It took almost losing everything to realize I needed to step up and get involved in my own life." She gave a knowing wink. "Why do you think I'm president of everything?"

The first notes of "There's No Place Like Home for the Holidays" sounded from inside the auditorium.

"I wish the best for you and your family," she said sincerely. She leaned in and hugged me. I squeezed back, grateful. It wasn't a promise that everything would be all right in the end, but it was another moment of hope.

I released Grace, and we stood, holding each other's elbows and smiling like the old friends I'd forgotten we were.

"Come on," she said, taking my arm and leading me to the auditorium doors. "Let's go watch the show."

* * *

Driving home after the concert, I reflected on what Grace had shared. I'd always been in awe of her clothes, her confidence, her seemingly effortless marriage. It floored me to realize that we were not so different after all. She, too, had made the wrong choice borne out of a need to connect. I remembered her quiet shrug at the coffee shop while Tammy and Louise gossiped about Jenna and Duane's affair. At the time, I'd been sure she'd been judging me. But maybe she'd been thinking of her own experience and how slippery the slope was between love and loneliness.

I pulled into the driveway and killed the engine. Blue light flickered in the window; a television was on. The porch light shone through the dark, welcoming me. It was nice to know that there were people in my life who understood and supported me. And it was nicer still to think that there might be people at home who wanted me to find my way safely back to them.

Chapter 28

Audra was spending Thanksgiving Day with Daniel at Sheila's sister's house across town. It was a big family, Sheila assured me. Lots of cousins in a range of ages; Audra would have plenty of activity to distract her if she felt like joining in and enough chaos to deflect attention from her if she felt like being quiet. It reminded me of dinner with Beth's family, and I knew Audra would be happier there than eating silently at our table or alone in her room.

As for us, I didn't know what the day held. Sean and I still weren't talking; his request for time to think had been the last real sentence he'd said to me.

I drove to the store with forced optimism, fought the crowds, and bought a package of turkey breasts and two anemic-looking sweet potatoes to make a small Thanksgiving meal. I also bought a pie crust and ingredients for chocolate chess pie, Audra and Sean's favorite. On the way to check out, I splurged and grabbed two bottles of decent chardonnay. Anything to help the day along.

Back at home, I turned on the Macy's parade, made a cup of coffee, and curled up on the couch. The house had taken on a musty, lived-in smell. I couldn't entirely dismiss the idea that it was the smell of loneliness. I got up and opened the windows. Sean seemed content to stay in our bedroom. Space yawned between us, waiting for the people to fill it with noise and laughter as in holidays past.

At noon, I dialed Beth's number. She didn't answer, and I remembered that they were spending Thanksgiving with Vi's brother in Napa. I left a message, making my voice as upbeat as possible.

"Hi, Bethie, Vi, and Dante! It's Aunt Rinni calling to wish you all a Happy Thanksgiving. I hope you're well, and I miss you all so much!" I made kiss noises into the phone and ended the call. Silence descended back around me.

By midafternoon, I was jittery from caffeine and claustrophobic from isolation. Sean hadn't appeared yet, although I'd heard the shower running earlier.

I ventured into the kitchen and opened the first bottle of wine. I set the oven to preheat and began to assemble pie ingredients. The wine warmed me. I turned the TV to the holiday music channel, and Johnny Cash's "Thanksgiving Prayer" poured into the room. I scraped pie filling into the premade crust and put it into the oven, careful not to slop any over the sides.

Twenty minutes later, the pie's heavenly aroma began to permeate the air. I poured another glass of wine and sat on the couch, content for the moment. From the coffee table, my phone buzzed. I picked it up.

It was a text from Sean:

Are you making a chess pie??????

Brazen from the wine, I typed back:

See for yourself.

A minute later, Sean emerged from the bedroom, scratching

the skin above his cast. He'd changed into clean pants and a button-up shirt. His beard was patchy, and he needed a haircut, but he'd made an effort to dress up. My heart gave a little skip, and I felt almost nervous as he joined me on the couch, settling back, his feet on the coffee table next to mine.

"You made pie?" he asked, hopefully.

"I did." I took a sip of wine, then offered him my glass.

He took it and tilted it toward me, a small toast. "Thank you. I can't think of anything I'd like better."

I went back to the kitchen and retrieved a second wineglass and the bottle. I traded him the full glass for my now-empty one, which I refilled before settling back into my seat.

"Can I ask you a question?" I said hesitantly. The smell of pie and the proximity of my husband's body to mine made me impulsive, brave.

Sean raised his eyebrow. "As long as I get to decide whether or not I want to answer," he said.

I nodded. "Fair enough." I took a sip of wine, taking my time. "Did it help? Seeing the counselor?"

Sean considered the question then nodded. "It did. It was nice to have someone to put things in perspective in ways I couldn't. I told her I was worried about you, how distant and sad you'd become. How I couldn't seem to reach you, no matter what I did. We talked about how common it is for husbands and wives to get to a crisis point in their marriages, especially when their kids are getting older." He looked toward me, not at me precisely, but over my shoulder, toward the bedroom door. I shifted slightly, adjusting myself into his sightline. He looked away, back toward the window again. "We talked about how spouses can feel invisible, like everything they do is taken for granted, unappreciated. We talked about how much time I was spending out of the house and how I could start actively participating in the family again."

I shifted uncomfortably. I needed to talk about this, but it didn't mean it was easy to hear. "Do you think she could help me too? Start participating in our family again?"

Sean cocked his head, looked straight at me. "You mean if Audra and I forgive you?"

Ouch.

"No. I mean, yes, I hope you'll both forgive me. But even before all of this, before..." I took a deep breath, took responsibility, "...the affair, I was not participating in our family. A part of me has been standing on the sidelines since Mom died, waiting for other people to make me happy." I leaned forward, searching Sean's face, hoping I was getting through. "I was unhappy with me. And I need help to make things better. With you. With Audra. With myself."

I put my hand on Sean's leg. I felt his muscle tighten beneath the fabric, but he didn't pull away. I set my wine down on the floor, reached over with my other hand to cup his cheek. His beard scratched against my skin, tickling my palm.

"I would like to go to counseling with you," I said, looking straight into his eyes. I was inches away. If I wanted to, I could close the gap and kiss him. But I wanted to make my final argument, my most sincere promise. "I am so sorry for what I did, and I want to find a way to get through it. Together," I emphasized. "I want every day to be another day I get to spend with you. With our daughter. As a family." I moved my hand from his leg, framing the right side of his face. "I believe we can be a family again. I hope that you believe it too."

We sat, staring intently at each other, breathing in rhythm. Behind us, the over timer went off, its insistent *chirp-chirp* breaking the spell.

I removed my hands and picked up my wine, carrying it to the counter. Sean stayed where he was. I took the pie from the oven and set it on a cooling rack near the open kitchen window. Needing to keep busy, I removed the potatoes from the pantry, washed them, and began to peel the skins into the garbage disposal.

"Are you hungry? I can start cooking dinner." The question came out naturally, casually. Why not? I'd said everything I could. I'd rested my case. All I could do now was start proving that I'd meant what I said.

He joined me at the sink. "Can I help?"

I shook my head. "Not a lot you can do one-handed. I guess you can dry dishes for me."

He made a face. "Oh, my favorite."

I threw a towel at him. "Pipe down, lefty."

We both stopped. It was a moment that could have come from before. Before the affair. Before Nick. Before the divide opened between us. It was only a moment, but that was how a lifetime started, wasn't it? Stringing moments together until they formed a chain, a life to be looked back upon and remembered. Good moments, bad moments, and all the medium moments in between that make up a marriage.

I smiled at Sean tentatively. He smiled back, a real Sean smile, and my heart swelled with the thought that here was the moment I would point back to from a million moments down the road.

Here was the moment we started again.

"What would you say," I suggested, "if we skipped the turkey and went straight for dessert?"

"I'd say that was the best idea you've had in a long time, Mrs. Fuller."

"I love you," I whispered to my husband and moved in to kiss him as he whispered it back.

* * *

We sat on the stairs of the deck, drinks in hand, the half-eaten pie between us, watching the white lights blink in the darkness until the stillness was broken by the sound of the front door opening and shutting. A light came on in the kitchen, casting our shadows out over the steps and onto the fallow grass.

"Dad?" Audra's voice called, muffled through the sliding glass door. A pause. Then, quieter: "Mom?"

It was the sweetest word ever. My heart clenched. My eyes filled. Sean felt me react and reached over to squeeze my hand in support. He did not let go.

A moment later, the door slid open, and Audra stepped out onto the deck. She hesitated briefly before joining us, sitting on the other side of Sean. I watched her as she sat, deliberately looking straight ahead. Sean set his drink down and took her hand. We still said nothing.

I sat, one degree away from contact with my daughter, connected through the man who loved us and whom we loved in return. I yearned to reach over and brush her cheek and tell her again how sorry I was, how I'd lost sight of what was important, and that she and her father were the most treasured people in my life. How I promised always to choose them. Us. This life. Our life.

But I stayed still. For now, this moment was enough. I could wait. I wasn't going anywhere.

A family sits together under the night sky, watching white lights flicker among bare tree branches. They do not know what is coming next, how they will take their next steps, or where those steps will lead, but they are ready to find out together.

I was ready.

I am ready.

Life wasn't a fairytale, I reflected. There were no promises of happily ever after. We were a story without an ending. We could always change our course, create a new beginning.

The beginning of something better.

THE END

Acknowledgments

First, and always, to Patrick, Millie, and John– You are my world and forever my reasons why. I love you.

Mom & Dad, Aunt Annie, Aunt Sammy, John & Janet, Joe, Kathy & Damon, Maggie, Jackson, Katie– Thank you, thank you, thank you, for always believing in me.

Blue Ink Press– As both publishers and authors, you welcomed me in. I am honored to be part of the Blue Ink Press family.

The Women's Fiction Writers Association provided me with the support, education, and community I needed to turn a hopeful draft into a living, breathing manuscript. Thank you especially for matching me with Monica Frederick and Ava Teedro, whose thoughtful feedback has made me a better writer, reader, and community member.

Charlotte Rains Dixon and Rebecca Hodge– Thank you for your guidance and encouragement. I made it here because of you.

Patty Keck– Thank you for always demonstrating how to lead with kindness.

Cassandra Howland and Tom Youngdahl– You've been along for this ride since the start. Thank you for being just a call or text away.

Becca Koch of Rebecca Interiors graciously talked me through the elements of design and staging. Dr. Holly Cox shared her insights on the psychology behind emotional affairs. Heather Johnson of Heather C. Johnson Photography honed

Corinne's camera skills. I am honored to know such brilliant, talented women. Any mistakes you find are mine alone.

Page 158 Books– Thank you for celebrating and supporting books and authors of all kinds.

To the MH Literary Society– Thank you for continuing my literary education through inspiring conversations and challenging book choices. I promise to (try to) stop dog-earing pages.

The 2023 Debuts– Thank you for answering every question possible and for all the hilarious tangents. I can't imagine surviving this process without this amazing group.

To my baseball families, library friends, and Bedford moms – Thank you for the conversations, laughter, and always understanding when I disappeared into work. Also, for driving my kids around.

To the MHS Class of '91– How lucky I am to still call so many of you friends. I promise that you are not in this book. Corinne's high school experiences (good or bad) are purely products of my overactive imagination.

To the Instagram writing community– especially Jennifer Brasington-Crowley, Tracy Brown, Jodi May, Gilly Fisher, D. Allyson Howlett, Mary Rook, Elle Houston, Dara Levan, Shail Rajan, Jeannée Sacken, Delise Torres, Shari Mitchell, Kara Lacey, Beth Weg, Lindsey Wood, and Saffron Amatti. You accepted me without question. It's said that writing can be a lonely occupation; thank you for keeping me company.

Finally, to you, my reader– It is a dream come true to have you hold my book in your hands. Thank you for reading to the very, very end. You are amazing.

About the Author

Joanna Monahan lives in North Carolina with her husband, their two children, and one hangry cat.

Before she began writing Women's Fiction, Joanna worked in marketing and special events. She spent several years as a professional organizer and wrote articles on organizing for various websites and print publications.

When she isn't writing, Joanna enjoys theater, baseball, and bookmarking recipes she will never make. A child of the 80's, she regrets that she no longer receives pizza coupons in exchange for reading books.

You can find Joanna at www.joannamonahan.com where she blogs about books, writing, and life, and on Instagram @joanna-monahanauthor where she regularly torments her characters by participating in writing challenges.

Printed in the USA
CPSIA information can be obtained
at www.ICGtesting.com
LVHW091200070324
773798LV00002B/237